Critical acclaim for *New York Times* bestseller,

TRICKSTER'S POINT

"Although there's plenty of excitement in this plot, Krueger is moving deeper into psychological territory with each book in this series."

—*St. Paul Pioneer Press*

"While the murder mystery is an essential element of the novel, more important is the look at the relationships of the various characters, to each other and to the locale."

—*Midwest Book Review*

"Krueger has crafted a strong and memorable series that never fails to surpass itself with each installment. *Trickster's Point* continues that tradition, containing some of Krueger's best prose to date in what is perhaps his strongest, most intriguing novel yet."

—*Book Reporter*

"Unlike many series, Cork and company age and evolve with each book. Time does not stand still and we share in the triumphs and tragedies of Cork. We watch his children grow up and, in some cases, move away. That constant change makes these novels all the more compelling."

—*Crimespree Magazine*

"Mystery fans can count on William Kent Krueger for an absorbing book with lots of twists and turns. He's an author who isn't afraid to take chances with his characters."

—*Denver Post*

"An absorbing plot and a rewarding read."

—*Minneapolis Star Tribune*

Critical acclaim for

THUNDER BAY,

winner of Lovey Award for Best PI/Police Procedural Novel •
Dilys Award • Northeastern Minnesota Book Award • Minnesota Book
Award . . . and nominated for the 2008 Anthony Award for Best Novel

"The deftly plotted seventh Cork O'Connor novel represents a return to top form for Anthony-winner Krueger. . . . The action builds to a violent and satisfying denouement."

—*Publishers Weekly* (starred review)

"Krueger keeps up the pace and the suspense. . . . Crisp writing and original plots make this a series to watch."

—*Library Journal*

"The cast of characters is vivid, the plotting is strong, and O'Connor's retirement gets off to the kind of start that usually marks the launching of a career. It's great fun."

—*Washington Times*

"Krueger's insightful portrayal of small-town life and his deepening exploration of Cork's character . . . propel the story."

—*Booklist*

"Krueger weaves together multiple stories of love and loss, family and place in this strong and satisfying novel. I'm already looking forward to No. 8 in the series."

—*Journal and Courier* (Lafayette, IN)

"Perfect. . . . It may be the best mystery you read this year!"

—*The Capital Times* (Madison, WI)

"[Krueger] has a knack for taking us into the woods and losing us in a good story."

—*Argus Leader* (Sioux Falls, SD)

Also by William Kent Krueger

THUNDER
BAY

A NOVEL

WILLIAM
KENT KRUEGER

ATRIA PAPERBACK

NEW YORK LONDON TORONTO SYDNEY NEW DELHI

ATRIA
PAPERBACK

A Division of Simon & Schuster, Inc.
1230 Avenue of the Americas
New York, NY 10020

This Atria Paperback edition August 2009

ATRIA PAPERBACK and colophon are trademarks of Simon & Schuster, Inc.

For information about special discounts for bulk purchases, please contact Simon & Schuster Special Sales at 1-866-506-1949 or business@simonandschuster.com.

The Simon & Schuster Speakers Bureau can bring authors to your live event. For more information or to book an event contact the Simon & Schuster Speakers Bureau at 1-866-248-3049 or visit our website at www.simonspeakers.com.

Manufactured in the United States of America

17   19   20   18

ISBN 978-1-4391-5782-4
ISBN 978-1-4165-4649-8 (ebook)

To my coconspirators in the Minnesota Crime Wave,
Ellen Hart and Carl Brookins;
we've never traveled a road together that we didn't like.

ACKNOWLEDGMENTS

Of course, buckets of gratitude to all the members of my writers group, Crème de la Crime, for their suggestions, large and small, that make all the difference.

To Danielle Egan-Miller and the whole crew at Browne & Miller, thank you for your hard work on my behalf. We've come a long way together, and there's still plenty of road ahead.

I'm deeply indebted to my editor, Sarah Branham, whose insights keep me honest and whose enthusiasm keeps me hopeful; and a huge thank-you is due to David Brown, publicist extraordinaire, for all the gymnastics, verbal and otherwise, in his efforts to get the word out.

Finally, as always, here's to the St. Clair Broiler. During half a century, Jim Theros and his staff have created a haven, a comfortable place for folks to gather in order to connect and to gossip, to eat and to drink, to enjoy a little time away from the mad crush, and sometimes even to write. May its famous neon flame never be extinguished.

PART I
MANITOU ISLAND

ONE

The promise, as I remember it, happened this way.

A warm August morning, early. Wally Schanno's already waiting at the landing. His truck's parked in the lot, his boat's in the water. He's drinking coffee from a red thermos big as a fireplug.

Iron Lake is glass. East, it mirrors the peach-colored dawn. West, it still reflects the hard bruise of night. Tall pines, dark in the early morning light, make a black ragged frame around the water.

The dock's old, weathered, the wood gone fuzzy, flaking gray. The boards sag under my weight, groan a little.

"Coffee?" Schanno offers.

I shake my head, toss my gear into his boat. "Let's fish."

We're far north of Aurora, Minnesota. Among the trees on the shoreline, an occasional light glimmers from one of the cabins hidden there. Schanno motors slowly toward a spot off a rocky point where the bottom falls away quickly. Cuts the engine. Sorts through his tackle box. Pulls out a pearl white minnow flash, a decent clear-water lure for walleye. Clips it on his line. Casts.

Me, I choose a smoky Twister Tail and add a little fish scent. Half a minute after Schanno's, my lure hits the water.

August isn't the best time to fish. For one thing, the bugs are awful. Also, the water near the surface is often too warm. The big fish—walleye and bass—dive deep, seeking cooler currents. Unless you use sonar, they can be impossible to locate. There are shallows near a half-submerged log off to the north where something smaller—perch or crappies—might be feeding. But I've already guessed that fishing isn't what's on Schanno's mind.

The afternoon before, he'd come to Sam's Place, the burger joint I own on Iron Lake. He'd leaned in the window and asked for a chocolate shake. I couldn't remember the last time Schanno had actually ordered something from me. He stood with the big Sweetheart cup in his hand, not sipping from the straw, not saying anything, but not leaving either. His wife, Arletta, had died a few months before. A victim of Alzheimer's, she'd succumbed to a massive stroke. She'd been a fine woman, a teacher. Both my daughters, Jenny and Anne, had passed through her third-grade classroom years before. Loved her. Everybody did. Schanno's children had moved far away, to Bethesda, Maryland, and Seattle, Washington. Arletta's death left Wally alone in the house he'd shared with her for over forty years. He'd begun to hang around Johnny's Pinewood Broiler for hours, drinking coffee, talking with the regulars, other men who'd lost wives, jobs, direction. He walked the streets of town and stood staring a long time at window displays. He was well into his sixties, a big man—shoes specially made from the Red Wing factory—with a strong build, hands like an orangutan. A couple of years earlier, because of Arletta's illness, he'd retired as sheriff of Tamarack County, which was a job I'd held twice myself. Some men, idle time suits them. Others, it's a death sentence. Wally Schanno looked like a man condemned.

When he suggested we go fishing in the morning, I'd said sure.

Now we're alone on the lake—me, Schanno, and a couple of loons fifty yards to our right diving for breakfast. The sun creeps above the trees. Suddenly everything has color. We breathe in the scent of evergreen and clean water and the faint fish odor coming from the bottom of Schanno's boat. Half an hour and we haven't said a word. The only sounds are the sizzle of line as we cast, the plop of the lures hitting water, and the occasional cry of the loons.

I'm happy to be there on that August morning. Happy to be fishing, although I hold no hope of catching anything. Happy to be sharing the boat and the moment with a man like Schanno.

"Heard you got yourself a PI license," Schanno says.

I wind my reel smoothly, jerking the rod back occasionally to make the lure dart in the water like a little fish. There aren't any walleyes to fool, but it's what you do when you're fishing.

"Yep," I reply.

"Gonna hang out a shingle or something?"

The line as I draw it in leaves the smallest of wakes on the glassy surface, dark wrinkles crawling across the reflected sky. "I haven't decided."

"Figure there's enough business to support a PI here?"

He asks this without looking at me, pretending to watch his line.

"Guess I'll find out," I tell him.

"Not happy running Sam's Place?"

"I like it fine. But I'm closed all winter. Need something to keep me occupied and out of mischief."

"What's Jo think?" Talking about my wife.

"So long as I don't put on a badge again, she's happy."

Schanno says, "I feel like I'm dying, Cork."

"Are you sick?"

"No, no." He's quick to wave off my concern. "I'm bored. Bored to death. I'm too old for law enforcement, too young for a rocking chair."

"They're always hiring security at the casino."

Shakes his head. "Sit-on-your-ass kind of job. Not for me."

"What exactly are you asking, Wally?"

"Just that if something, you know, comes your way that you need help with, something you can't handle on your own, well, maybe you'll think about giving me a call."

"You don't have a license."

"I could get one. Or just make me a consultant. Hell, I'll do it for free."

The sun's shooting fire at us across the water. Another boat has appeared half a mile south. The loons take off, flapping north.

"Tell you what, Wally. Anything comes my way I think you could help me with, I promise I'll let you know."

He looks satisfied. In fact, he looks damn happy.

We both change lures and make a dozen more casts without a bite. Another boat appears.

"The lake's getting crowded," I say. "How 'bout we call it and have some breakfast at the Broiler."

"On me," Schanno offers, beaming.

We reel in our lines. Head back toward the landing. Feeling pretty good.

Nights when I cannot sleep and the demons of my past come to torment me, the promise I made to Wally Schanno that fine August morning is always among them.

TWO

Sam's Place is an old Quonset hut on the shore of Iron Lake just north of Aurora. It's divided by an interior wall. The back has a small living area—kitchen, bathroom, table, bunk. The front is set up for preparing food and serving it through a couple of windows to customers outside. I've got a griddle for burgers and hot dogs and such, a hot-oil well for deep fry, a shake machine, a carbonated-drink dispenser, a large freezer. Pretty simple fare. In season, I do a fine business.

It's called Sam's Place after the man who made it what it is—Sam Winter Moon. When my father died, Sam gave me a hand in a lot of unselfish ways. I grew up working summers at Sam's Place, advised and gently guided by Sam as I stumbled my way into manhood. When Sam died, he passed the place to me.

The Quonset hut houses my livelihood, but it also holds part of my heart. So many good memories from my adolescence involve the smell of a hot griddle coupled with the drumroll of Sam's easy laugh. Several years into my marriage, when my wife and I were having serious trouble and my life was at its darkest point, I lived at Sam's Place. It was a haven. In recent years, my children have worked beside me there, earning their spending money, learning lessons about business and people that I believe will serve them well.

I've been sheriff of Tamarack County twice. The first time was for seven years, at the end of which the constituency removed me in a recall election that resulted both from my own inadequacies and from things beyond my control. The second time it was for thirteen weeks, and I stepped down of my own accord. People who don't know me well wonder that I'd give up my badge for an apron, thinking that flipping burgers is a big step down. If they asked me, which they don't, I would tell them that when a man stumbles onto happiness, he'd be a fool to pass it by. It's as simple as that. Sam's Place makes me happy.

North of the Quonset hut is the Bearpaw Brewery. South there's nothing for a quarter mile except a copse of poplars that hides the ruins of an old ironworks. The road to Sam's Place is a couple hundred yards of gravel that starts just outside town, crosses a big vacant field, then humps over the Burlington Northern tracks. It isn't particularly easy to get to, but people seem to find it without any problem.

In season, from early May, when tourists begin to flock north, until the end of October, when the fall color is gone, I arrive for work at ten A.M. I spend an hour getting ready for business. Turn on the griddle, heat the fry oil, get the ice-milk machine churning, restock the rack of chips, double-check the serving supplies, put cash in the register drawer. A few minutes before eleven, help arrives. In the summer months, it's one of my daughters, either Jenny or Anne.

That morning after I fished with Schanno, as I was getting ready to slide open the serving windows, I saw Anne jogging up the road to Sam's Place. She was sixteen, very Irish with her wild red hair. She was an athlete hoping for a scholarship to Notre Dame.

"Where's Jenny?" I asked when she came in. "She's on the schedule this morning."

"She had kind of a hard night." She reached into the closet for a serving apron. "She wasn't feeling well. We traded shifts. She's coming in this afternoon."

The night before, Jenny had been out on a date with her boyfriend, Sean. I'd heard her come in. Sean had finished his first year at Macalester, a small, elite college in St. Paul, and was home for the summer, working in his father's drugstore. Jenny had graduated from high school in June. Most of the past year, their relationship had been long distance. Sean was a bright kid. Like Jenny, he wanted to be a writer. One of the places, Jenny often said, where their spirits connected. They'd been out a lot together that summer.

"A hard night?" I pressed her. "Something happen between her and Sean?"

She concentrated on tying her apron. "What do I know?"

"You're answering a question with a question. What's going on, Annie?"

She gave me the look of a runner caught in a squeeze between third base and home.

"Is it bad?" I asked.

"Define bad." She caught my scowl. "Not really bad. Worrisome, I'd say."

"Just tell me, Annie."

"Dad, I promised."

"I'm going to find out anyway. The minute Jenny walks in here I'm going to grill her."

"Talk to Mom first."

"Does *she* know?"

"You know Mom and Jenny. They talk about everything."

"So everybody knows what's going on except me?"

Behind Annie, the window opened onto the parking lot, the long gravel road to Sam's Place, and the distant town bright in the morning sun. She turned away and watched a car raising dust on the road to the Quonset hut. "We have customers," she said, sounding greatly relieved.

Just before the lunch rush, Kate Buker, one of Annie's friends who worked for me part-time, arrived. When the rush was over and the girls were handling things up front, I slipped away to call my wife, Jo. It was Saturday, so she was home. When she answered, I could tell by the shuffle of papers on her end that she was working in her office. She's an attorney.

"How's it going?" I asked.

"Quiet. Getting lots done."

I could see her, black reading glasses perched on her nose, ice blond hair probably roughed from running a hand through it, her blue eyes sharp and focused. On weekends, she usually works at home, overseeing the rights of her clients. She often represents the Iron Lake Ojibwe. Long before they had their own staff of attorneys, she was legal counsel for the reservation, and they still rely on her expertise in a number of areas.

"What's Stevie up to?" I said, asking about our young son.

"Playing with Dumbarton in the backyard."

Dumbarton was a big sheepdog that belonged to a couple on our block. Sometimes he'd wander down to our yard, much to Stevie's delight. At our house, the only pet was a turtle named Clyde.

"Jo, is Jenny there?"

"Upstairs getting ready for work," she said.

"Is there something I should know? Something about Sean and her?"

"What makes you think that?"

There it was again. I was being answered with a question.

"Just tell me, Jo."

"Look, Cork, it's not a good time to talk right now. Let's sit down tonight, okay?"

"How about I just talk to her this afternoon when she comes to work?"

"Don't do that. Let me talk to you first."

I hesitated before asking about the concern that came most readily to mind. "She's not pregnant, is she?"

Jo laughed. "Heavens no."

"Well, that's a relief."

"Look, we'll talk this evening. But promise me you won't say anything to Jenny."

"Annie says it's worrisome."

"Promise me, Cork."

"All right. I'll talk to you first."

I put the phone down just as Anne stepped into the back of Sam's Place.

"Dad," she said. "George LeDuc is outside. He says it's important."

George was waiting for me in the parking lot. A big gray bear of a man seventy years old, he was the Iron Lake Ojibwe tribal chairman. He was wearing a short-sleeved white shirt with a bolo tie, jeans, boots. He'd been staring intently at the lake, but when I came out he swung his gaze toward me.

"*Boozhoo*, George," I greeted him. "What's up?"

In the Ojibwe fashion, his face betrayed nothing, though the news he brought was deeply troubling. "It's Henry Meloux, Cork. He's dying."

THREE

Henry Meloux was the oldest man I knew. He'd had white hair ever since I could remember, which was well over four decades. His face was heavily lined. There were age spots like patches of rust on his skin. His eyes were brown and soft and deep, and you couldn't look into them without feeling Henry saw all the way down to some dark room in your soul where you kept your worst secrets locked away. And you understood that it was all right that he knew. He was a Mide, one of the Midewiwin, a member of the Grand Medicine Society. He'd spent his life following the path of Ojibwe healing.

When Sam Winter Moon died, Meloux filled the void in my life left by Sam's passing. I'm part Anishinaabe—what most people know as Ojibwe—on my mother's side. Not only had Meloux's good advice guided me during a lot of confusing times, but also, on several occasions, his intervention had actually saved my life.

Now he was dying.

And the Iron Lake Reservation had gathered to keep vigil.

LeDuc and I made our way through the crowd in the lobby of the Aurora Community Hospital, greeting everyone we knew as we went. On the way there, George had explained to me what happened.

LeDuc owned a general store in Allouette, the larger of the two communities on the rez. That morning Henry had walked into the store to buy a few groceries. Meloux lived on Crow Point, an isolated finger of land on Iron Lake far north on the reservation. There was no road to his cabin, and no matter the season, he hiked to town, a good five miles, mostly over forest trails. LeDuc and Meloux passed some time talking, then the old man paid, put his things in a knapsack he carried on his back, and went outside. A few minutes later, LeDuc heard a commotion in the street. He rushed out to find Meloux collapsed on the pavement and people crowding around. LeDuc called 911. The paramedics took Meloux to the hospital. The old man had been conscious when he arrived. He was weak, barely able to speak, but he'd asked for me.

Meloux was in intensive care. They weren't going to let me see him. Relatives only. But Ernie Champoux, Meloux's great-nephew, put up a stink, and the doctor in charge, a young resident named Wrigley, finally relented.

"Do you know what's wrong?" I asked.

"His heart," Wrigley said. "I suspect an occlusion, but we need to run tests to be sure. Only a few minutes, all right? He needs his strength."

Meloux lay on the bed, tubes and wires running from him every which way. It made me think of a butterfly in a spider's web. I'd never seen him looking so frail, so vulnerable. In his day, he'd been a great hunter. Because he'd saved my life, I also knew him as a warrior. It was hard seeing him this way.

His brown eyes tracked me as I came to the bedside.

"Corcoran O'Connor," he whispered. "I knew you would come."

I pulled up a chair and sat beside him. "I'm sorry, Henry."

"My heart."

"The doctor told me."

He shook his head faintly. "My heart is in pain."

"The doctor suspects an occlusion. A blockage, I think that means."

Again he shook his head. "It is sadness, Corcoran O'Connor. Too heavy for my heart."

"What sadness, Henry?"

"I will tell you, but you must promise to help me."

"I'll do what I can, Henry. What's the sadness?"

Meloux hesitated a moment, gathering strength. "My son."

Son? In the forty-some years I'd known him, I'd never heard Meloux speak of a son. As far as I knew, no one had.

"You have a son? Where?"

"I do not know. Help me find him, Corcoran O'Connor."

"What's his name, Henry?"

Meloux stared up at me. For the first time I could ever recall, he looked lost.

"You don't know his name?" I didn't hide my surprise. "Do you know anything about him?"

"His mother's name. Maria."

"Just Maria?"

"Lima."

"Maria Lima. How long ago, Henry?"

He closed his eyes and thought a moment. "A lifetime."

"Thirty years? Forty? Fifty?"

"Seventy-three winters."

Seventy-three years. My God.

"It's a big world, Henry. Can you tell me where to begin?"

"Canada," he whispered. "Ontario."

I could tell our conversation, spare though it was, was draining him. I had three pieces of information. A mother's name. An approximate year. And a place to start looking.

"Have you ever seen your son, Henry?"

"In visions," Meloux replied.

"What does he look like?"

"I have only seen his spirit, not his face." A faint smile touched his lips. "He will look like his father."

"He'll look like his mother, too, Henry. It would be nice to know what she looked like."

He motioned me nearer. "In my cabin. A box under my bed. A gold watch."

"All right."

"And Walleye. He will be alone and hungry."

"I'll take care of Walleye, Henry."

Meloux seemed comforted. "*Migwech*," he said. Thank you.

Outside the room, LeDuc was waiting.

"What did he want, Cork?"

"He's worried about Walleye," I said. "He wanted me to take care of the dog."

The rest had been told in confidence, and I couldn't repeat it. Nor could I say what I really thought. That what Meloux was asking was nothing short of a miracle.

FOUR

George LeDuc dropped me back at Sam's Place. Jenny was there, looking pale, but she seemed to be doing fine. Several customers stood lined up at the serving window. I pulled her aside for a moment and asked how she was feeling.

"Okay now." She offered me a brief smile. "Customers," she said and turned back to her window.

As they went about their work, I filled the girls in on Meloux, what I could tell them anyway, and asked if they'd hold down the fort while I took care of what the old man needed. Jenny said she'd call in Jodi Bollendorf, who wasn't on the schedule that day but would be glad to help.

I hopped in the Bronco and headed home.

My house is on Gooseberry Lane, a quiet street of old homes, mostly two-story wood frame. We don't have fences, though often lilac hedges or shrubbery serve that purpose. I grew up on Gooseberry Lane, a child in the house where I've raised my own children. Until his death—the result of a gun battle in the line of duty—my father was sheriff of Tamarack County. He'd come from Chicago, married my mother who was half Ojibwe, half Irish. Her mother, Grandma Dilsey to me, was a true-blood Iron Lake Ojibwe, though she preferred to call herself Anishinaabe—or Shinnob—as do many on the rez. That makes me one-quarter Ojibwe. Though the other three-quarters is Irish, Grandma Dilsey always swore it was the blood of The People that counted most.

Until I was elected sheriff, my heritage was never much of an issue. After I put on the badge, whenever conflicts arose between the two cultures, red and white, I found that I was never Ojibwe enough for the Ojibwe or white enough for the whites. That wasn't the reason I resigned my office. I turned in my badge when it became clear to me that my responsibility as a lawman was often at odds with my duty as a husband and father. I was lucky. I had Sam's Place to fall back on. At least during the warm months, between May and November. The long winters were always a concern. The PI license I'd recently acquired would, I hoped, give me something to do in all those dark months.

Stevie was playing by himself in the front yard. My son was eight, then, small for his age. With his straight black hair and hard almond eyes, he was, of all my children, the one who showed most clearly his Anishinaabe heritage. He'd recently discovered golf, and that afternoon he stood in the shade of our big elm, a driver in his hand, swinging at a big Wiffle ball that sailed twenty yards when he hit it. I spotted a number of divots in the grass. When he saw me pull into the driveway, he dropped the club and came running.

"What are you doing home, Dad?" He looked hopeful. He was the youngest kid on the block, and with Jenny and Anne often working at Sam's Place, I knew he was sometimes lonely.

I ruffled his hair. "Work to do, buddy."

"Mom's working, too," he said, disappointed.

"Where's Dumbarton?" I asked, speaking of the neighbor's dog.

"They called him in."

I nodded toward the driver lying in the grass. "How's that backswing coming?"

He shrugged.

"Maybe later we'll play a few holes together," I said.

"Really?"

"We'll see what we can do. Mom's inside?"

"In her office."

"Remember, head down and keep your eye on the ball."

I went in the house. He turned back to his game.

It was cool inside and quiet. I walked to the kitchen, ran some tap water into a glass, and took a long drink.

"Stevie?" Jo called from her office.

"No. Me."

A moment later she came in wearing her reading glasses, blue eyes big behind the lenses. She's a beautiful woman, Jo. A few years younger than me, but looks even more. One of the smartest women I've ever known. Also one of the most courageous. For years, she's represented the Ojibwe of the Iron Lake Reservation in litigation that has often put her on the unpopular side of a legal issue. She's never flinched. We've had our problems. Show me a couple married twenty years who hasn't. But we were in a good period that summer.

"What are you doing home?" she asked.

"Meloux's in the hospital."

"Henry? Why?"

"He collapsed this morning in Allouette. The doctor thinks it's his heart. Meloux thinks so, too, but in a different way."

"What way?"

"He has a son, Jo."

Surprise showed in her eyes. "He's never said a word."

"He has now. But only to me, so you can't say anything to anyone else." I'd told her because she's my wife and a lawyer and understands about client privilege. "He asked me to find this son of his."

"Did he tell you where to look?"

"Ontario, Canada."

"That's it?"

"That's it."

"Did he give you a name?"

"The mother's name."

"Anything else?"

"Yeah. He fathered the child over seventy years ago. And he's only seen him in visions."

"Then how can he be sure?"

"He's Meloux."

"What are you going to do?"

"First, head to his cabin. There's something I'm supposed to find."

"What?"

"A watch. Also, he asked me to take care of Walleye while he's in the hospital."

"Do you have any idea how you're going to do this?"

"I'm waiting for inspiration to strike. Okay if I take Stevie with me? He's looking a little bored."

"Thanks. I'm kind of overwhelmed with paperwork."

I filled my water glass again and took another drink. Jo pulled a cup from the cupboard and poured herself what was left in the coffeemaker on the counter.

"I saw Jenny at Sam's Place," I told her. "Whatever had her sick this morning, she seems better now. Sick from drinking, maybe? Is that what we need to talk about?"

"Tonight, Cork. We'll talk. You need to get out to Meloux's." She practically pushed me out the front door.

Outside, Stevie was using the driver as a rifle, kneeling behind the railing of the front porch, firing off imaginary rounds.

"Okay, Davy Crockett," I said. "Time to desert the Alamo. I'm going up to Henry Meloux's cabin. Want to come?"

He jumped at the prospect. "Is Henry there?"

Meloux and my son had a special bond. Stevie had gone through a traumatic experience a couple of years earlier, a kidnapping. The old Mide had spent a good deal of time with him afterward, helping him deal with his fears and return to wholeness.

"Henry's in the hospital, Stevie."

"Is he sick?"

"Yes. And we're going to help."

"Can we visit him?"

"We'll see. But Walleye's alone at the cabin. We need to take care of him."

Walleye and Stevie. Another special bond.

He dropped the golf club on the porch and ran to my Bronco.

FIVE

I pulled to the side of a dusty county road a few miles north of Aurora. Far behind me were the last of the resorts on Iron Lake, hidden in the deep cover of red pines and black spruce. All around me was national forest land. A few miles farther north lay the Boundary Waters Canoe Area Wilderness. I parked near a double-trunk birch that marked the beginning of the trail to Meloux's cabin on Crow Point.

Stevie leaped from the Bronco. He was already on the trail before I locked up, skipping far ahead. I followed more slowly. Age, yeah, but also because the trail to Meloux's cabin always had a sacred feel to me. It was a hot afternoon, typical of early August. We were in the middle of a grasshopper infestation, and the woods were full of their buzz, a sound like tiny saws cutting the air. Sunlight broke through the canopy of pine boughs overhead and lay in shattered pieces on the ground. Thirty yards in front of me, Stevie danced through caverns of shadow and into moments of radiant light. I loved him deeply, my son. Every day, I counted him—and my daughters—a blessing.

Meloux had never seen his own son. Never carried him on his shoulders or held him when he cried. Never felt the small boy's breath, warm and sweet smelling, break against his face. Never knew the pleasure of being for his son the slayer of monsters imagined in the night.

God, I thought, *the emptiness.*

Yet I'd never felt that from Meloux until, lying on that hospital bed in a web of modern medicine, he'd looked up at me, lost, and asked a favor, father to father.

I didn't doubt Meloux, didn't doubt that he had a son he'd seen only in visions. Over time, I'd experienced too many unexplainable moments with the old Mide to be skeptical about something like this. It did make me wonder deeply, though, about the circumstances.

The trail cut through national forest land for a while, then entered the rez. We crossed Wine Creek and a few minutes later broke from the trees. Fifty yards ahead stood Meloux's cabin, an ancient structure but sturdy, made of cedar logs with a shake roof covered by birch bark. Meloux had built the cabin himself, and as long as I'd known him, had lived there year-round. He had no running water, no indoor plumbing. He used an outhouse.

The door was open. As we approached, something in the dark inside the cabin moved. A long, yellow face appeared, big brown eyes patiently watching us come.

"Walleye," Stevie called and raced toward the dog.

The mutt padded out, tail wagging.

Many rural people in Tamarack County keep dogs. They have them for a variety of reasons. Companionship, of course. But also security. A dog will bark a warning. Not Walleye. Or at least, not when it was Stevie coming. The two had become good friends over the past couple of years. Stevie threw his arms around the big mutt and buried his face in Walleye's fur.

"Hey, boy, how you been?" he said. "Missed me?"

I gave the dog's head a good patting and stepped through the doorway into the cabin.

The structure was a single room. Meloux's bunk was against one wall. In the center near the potbelly stove stood a table with a few chairs around it. The four windows had curtains that had been a gift from one of the old man's nieces. On the walls hung a number of items that harked back to a different time: a deer-prong pipe, a birch-bark basket, a small toboggan, a Skelly gas station calendar nearly sixty years out of date.

Stevie came up beside me. "He didn't close his door."

"I'm sure he thought he'd be back soon and left it open so Walleye could come and go as he pleased."

"He never locks his door. Isn't he afraid someone's going to steal from him?"

"I think Henry believes that what's in here wouldn't interest anyone but him."

"I think it's cool stuff."

"So do I, Stevie."

Meloux had told me to look under the bunk for the watch. I crossed the floorboards, knelt, and peered into the dark beneath the bed frame. Shoved into a far corner against the wall was a wooden box. I lay down on my belly, stretched out my arm, snagged the box, and pulled it into the light. It was cedar, ten inches long, six inches wide and deep. Carved into the top was an image of *animikii*, the Thunderbird. Under the bed, undisturbed, it should have had some dust on it, a few cobwebs attached, but the box was clean. Meloux had handled it recently. I opened the lid. Inside, on top of a stack of folded papers, lay a gold pocket watch.

I picked up the watch and snapped it open. Opposite the watch face was a tiny photograph of a handsome young woman with long black hair.

Stevie looked over my shoulder. "What's that?"

"Not what, Stevie. Who. Her name is Maria Lima."

"That picture looks old."

"It is. More than seventy years old."

"What are you going to do with it?"

"Keep it, for now. I might need it."

"Why?"

"Henry asked me to do something for him. Two things actually. And one of them was to take care of Walleye."

I put the watch in my shirt pocket, closed the box, and slid it back into the corner where I'd found it.

"If Henry is in the hospital, maybe we should stay out here," Stevie suggested. "So Walleye won't get lonely."

"I have a better idea," I said. "Why don't we take him home?"

"Really?" A huge, eager smile bloomed on his face.

"Just until Henry's better." Though I didn't know if that was going to happen.

Walleye had padded into the cabin behind us and sat on his haunches, watching. Stevie turned to him and scratched the fur at the dog's neck.

"You want to come home with us, boy? I'll take good care of you."

Walleye's tail swept back and forth across the floor.

"Come on, boy. Come on, Walleye." Stevie slapped the side of his leg and headed out with the dog at his heels.

I closed the door behind us. There was no lock.

Walleye paused beside me, looked back at the closed door, then followed my son, who danced ahead of us down the trail as if he were the Pied Piper.

SIX

That night when I walked in from closing up Sam's Place, Jo was sitting on the living room sofa, reading a book. She looked up and smiled. "Good night at Sam's?"

"We made a buck or two." I kissed the top of her head and sat down beside her. "Where's Walleye?"

"Sleeping with Stevie."

I was surprised. That afternoon when she saw the dog follow Stevie through the front door, she hadn't been happy. I'd explained my dilemma, and she reluctantly relented. She wouldn't allow the dog in the house, however. Not only because Walleye had come from the woods and might have ticks or fleas but, more important, because Jenny was allergic to dogs. And cats, too. Our pets had always been turtles and fish, and once we had a canary that wouldn't shut up. Jenny named it The Artist Formerly Known As Tweety. We called it Art.

"We put up a tent in the backyard," Jo said. "They're both out there. Is Jenny with Sean?"

"Yeah. She promised to be home by midnight. So now do I finally get to hear what the big secret is?"

Jo closed her book and set it on the end table. She composed herself. I'd seen her do this sometimes before difficult summations in court. It didn't do a lot to reassure me.

"Sean's not going back to Macalester this fall," she began calmly. "He's taking the money in his bank account and using it to go to Paris to live for a year."

"Do his folks know that?"

"As I understand it, not yet."

"Can't imagine that's going to please Lane. He's been counting on

Sean to finish his degree and take over the pharmacy. What's this got to do with Jenny?"

"Sean wants her to go with him."

"That's it?" I laughed with relief. "Hell, Jenny's too sensible for that."

Jo didn't laugh.

"Isn't she?"

"She's thinking about it, Cork."

"Running off to Europe instead of college? And what? She and Sean'll live together?"

"She thinks Sean's going to ask her to marry him first."

"Oh, Christ."

I couldn't sit still. I got up and began pacing.

Jenny's the academic in the family, takes after her mother. That June, she'd graduated from high school, valedictorian. For a long time, she'd had her sights set on Northwestern University, in Evanston, Illinois. It was her mother's alma mater and had an excellent writing program. When she'd gone with Jo to look at the school, horrible things had happened—not to her but to Jo—and the result was that the idea of attending Northwestern had turned bitter. She'd chosen the University of Iowa instead, hoping eventually to be accepted into the writing workshop, which she said had a terrific reputation. Robert Frost had taught there, and Robert Penn Warren. We did the financial calculations, Jo and I, and told Jenny that we could foot the bill for out-of-state tuition for the first couple of years without help. Or she could do her best to get a scholarship and we might be able to give her a hand all four years. Like her mother, whenever she puts her mind to something, she makes it happen. She got a good scholarship. And a couple of grants, and a hefty student loan, and the promise of a job on campus. Jo and I still needed to kick in a lot. I was hoping the PI license might help toward that. All the pieces of the crazy jigsaw puzzle of her educational financing had fallen into place, and she was prepared to go.

Or was she?

She's gone through phases. Hasn't every kid? Her hair's been every color of the rainbow. For several months at the beginning of her junior year, she was into Goth. Thank God the only things she'd pierced were her earlobes. A week after she turned eighteen and no longer needed our consent, she got a tattoo. A small yellow butterfly on her shoulder. When I found out, I nearly went ballistic, but Jo pointed out that there were worse things than a small butterfly.

She was back to the color of hair God had given her—ice blond, like her mother's. Like Jo, too, she was willowy and had smart blue eyes. The truth is that it never mattered to me what she chose to look like on the outside. I saw her with a father's eyes, and she was lovely. And intelligent. I always knew she would leave Aurora, go out into the world to make her mark. I'd steeled myself for that separation long ago.

It had never occurred to me that she might decide to marry at eighteen.

"How long have you known?" I asked.

"A couple of weeks."

"Great. I just love being on the outside of things."

"She asked me not to say anything because she was afraid you'd get upset and overreact."

"Me? Why would I overreact? Just because they're kids and Jenny's got her whole future ahead of her and Sean can't see beyond some crazy dream of being Hemingway."

"He's a poet."

"What?"

"Sean writes poetry."

"Whatever."

"You see?"

"I have a right to be concerned. Hell, *we* have a right to be concerned. Why are you taking all this so calmly?"

"Because Sean hasn't proposed, and if he does, she'll talk to us before she decides anything. We need to give her room, Cork, and trust her. Jenny's nothing if not levelheaded."

I stopped pacing for a moment. "What if he doesn't propose, just asks her to go off and live with him in Paris?" That brought another thought to mind. "Jo, are they already sleeping together?"

"She's eighteen."

I stared at her. "What does that mean?"

"What she chooses to do with her body is her own right."

"Meaning she's sleeping with Sean."

"I don't know, Cork."

"So she could be pregnant."

"We've had multiple discussions about safe sex. Jenny isn't stupid or impulsive." She stood up and kissed my cheek. "We just have to be patient, Cork, and trust her, okay? She'll talk to us before she decides anything."

I rubbed my temples. "God, I don't know if I'm ready for this. It was so much easier when the question was whether or not she should have braces."

"Any word on Meloux?" Jo said, obviously changing the subject.

"No. I called George LeDuc from Sam's Place, but he couldn't tell me anything."

"What are you going to do about your promise to find his son?"

"What every self-respecting detective does these days. Get on the Internet. Mind if I use your computer?"

"Be my guest."

I left her to her reading and went into her office, which was down the hallway beyond the stairs.

It took me an hour of Googling before I had what I believed was a decent lead.

I found Maria Lima referenced on a site named Ontario Past. When I clicked on the site, I discovered there was a school in the town of Flame Lake called the Wellington School, which had been built in 1932 with funds donated by Maria Lima Wellington. The town had been constructed by Northern Mining and Manufacturing, a large company founded by Leonard Wellington, in order to house workers from the nearby gold mine he owned. Using Google again, I found that Maria Lima Wellington was the daughter of Carlos Lima and the first wife of Leonard Wellington. She'd died young, leaving a son. The son's name was Henry.

According to the Internet information, Henry Wellington was the man responsible for making Northern Mining and Manufacturing (NMM) a major corporation. He had an interesting history. After receiving his engineering degree from McMaster University in Hamilton, Ontario, he joined the Canadian Air Force. Although no Canadian fighter squadrons were involved in the Korean War, as part of an exchange program, Wellington served with a U.S. squadron of Sabre-equipped fighter interceptors. He was the only Canadian to achieve the coveted rating of Ace. After the war, he became a test pilot. When his father died, he took over NMM. As a result of what one of his contemporaries characterized as his "brilliant, restless, and iconoclastic" mind, he developed innovative techniques for refining minerals, and held a number of lucrative patents. Under his direction, NMM had expanded its mining operations across Canada, and into other parts of the world. He invested in diverse enterprises, among them the fledgling Canadian film industry. He became a popular escort (some reports said consort) of several stunningly beautiful starlets, one of whom he finally married. He was often referred to as the Howard Hughes of Canada. I searched until I found a date of birth, and after a calculation, realized Henry Wellington was seventy-two years old. Seventy-three winters, Meloux had said, dating his relationship with Maria Lima. Given the normal gestation period of nine months, Henry Wellington would be right on the money.

He was still alive, according to the Internet, and living in Thunder Bay, Canada, where NMM was headquartered. He was a widower with two grown children. And that, according to the Web information, was part of the problem. His wife had died six years earlier, and in the time since, Wellington had become a notorious recluse. Again, the comparisons with Howard Hughes. Speculation was that the industrialist had gone into a deep depression following his wife's death. Although he was still on the board of NMM, he no longer ran the company, nor did he appear in public. I couldn't find any recent photographs of him, but I did find several taken earlier in his life. His hair was black, his face angular and high cheeked, his eyes dark and penetrating. Did he look like Meloux? Or like the photograph in Meloux's gold watch? I honestly couldn't say.

Near the end, I found one odd, but compelling, piece of information that, as much as anything else, pointed toward a connection between Wellington and Meloux. As a child, one of Henry Wellington's favorite possessions had been a stuffed cormorant given to him by his mother. The cormorant is one of the clans of the Ojibwe. Henry Meloux was cormorant clan.

By the time I clicked off the computer, Annie had come home and both she and Jo had gone to bed. It was after midnight. Jenny was still out with Sean.

I went to the kitchen and fished a couple of chocolate chip cookies out of the cookie jar on the counter. The jar was shaped like Ernie from *Sesame Street*. We'd had it since the kids were small. I poured some milk and sat down at the table.

Moths crawled the screen on the window over the kitchen sink, seeking the light. Occasionally, I heard small thumps. The grasshoppers, who seemed never to sleep. Jenny hadn't left for Iowa City yet, but the house felt different already, emptier.

I could have gone to bed but didn't feel like sleeping. I was thinking about Meloux, who had a son out there—an old man himself now—who'd been even less than a stranger to his father. And I was thinking about my own children, Jenny especially. I thought I knew them pretty well, but Jenny's hesitation, if that's what it was, to step forward into the future she'd worked so hard to open for herself worried me. It wasn't like her. Sean was pressuring her, I figured. He was basically a good kid. I'd never been unhappy that he and Jenny had decided to date only each other. In my day, we'd called it going steady. Now it was "exclusive." Whatever. Sean came from a good family. His mother was a math teacher, his father a pharmacist. They were Methodist, not Catholic; no big deal. Good kid and good family notwithstanding, I wasn't going to stand by and let them make a mistake they'd both regret somewhere down the line. When you live in a town your whole life, you see the arc of those marriages that began with a high school romance. More often than not, when the teenage passion fades, and it always does, they're left with the realization of all they wouldn't know about themselves and others—lovers especially—and sooner or later one of them wonders and wanders and the marriage becomes history. Pathetically predictable.

The front door opened. A half minute later Jenny stood in the kitchen doorway.

"Still up, Dad?"

"Couldn't sleep. Have a good time with Sean?"

"Okay."

"You're still on target for Iowa, right?"

She looked at me warily. "Mom said something, didn't she?"

"We talked."

I hadn't touched one of the cookies. I offered it to her. She accepted and took a bite.

"Did he pop the question?" I asked.

"No."

"Would you go with him to Paris anyway?"

"Dad, I don't know." A strong note of irritation.

"And if he does pop the question?"

Her blue eyes bounced around the room, as if looking for a way to escape. "See, this is why I didn't want you to know. I knew you'd interrogate me."

"Interrogate? I just asked a question."

"It's the way you asked. And it's only the beginning."

"Jenny, I'm your father. I ought to be allowed to question your thinking and your actions. It's what I've done for eighteen years. And if you don't mind me saying so, it's served us both pretty well."

"It has." Her face was intense. Beautiful and serious. "It's helped make me who I am, a woman capable of making her own decisions." Each word had the feel of cold steel.

"I never suggested you weren't."

"I love him, Dad. He loves me."

Love? I wanted to say. *What do you know about love, Jenny? Do you know what it's like to hold on by your fingernails through doubt and deception and betrayal and despair? To go on hoping when you're so exhausted by the struggle of love that giving up would be easy? To believe in the face of all contradiction? To walk alone in the dark— because in all love there are times of heartbreaking darkness—until you find that small flame still burning somewhere? Oh, Jenny, I wanted to say, there's so much you don't know.*

What I said was, "Will you talk to us before you make a decision?"

"Yes, all right?" she snapped.

She turned away without saying good night and started upstairs, but she stopped. "Dad?"

"Yeah?"

"I'd like to go with Sean for a drive along the North Shore tomorrow. I asked Jodi to fill in for me. She said she would. Is it okay?"

"Go," I said.

I listened to her feet hammer up the stairs.

I turned out the kitchen light and trudged up to bed.

SEVEN

Early the next morning I went to the hospital to see Meloux. He was still in the ICU, still looking like he had a toehold in the next world. His eyes were closed. I thought he was sleeping and I turned to go.

"You have news?"

His eyelids lifted wearily. Behind them, his almond eyes were dull.

"Maybe," I said.

One of the monitors bleeped incessantly. A cart with a squeaky wheel warbled past his door. In another room someone moaned. This had to be hard on Henry. He was used to the song of birds in the morning all around his cabin. If he were to pass from this life, it shouldn't have been there in that sterile place but in the woods that had been his home for God knows how long.

"Tell me," he said.

I walked to his bedside.

"I found a woman, Henry. Maria Lima. Her father was a man named Carlos Lima."

Meloux's eyes were no longer dull.

"Carlos Lima," he said. The name meant something to him, and not in a good way.

"She passed away many years ago."

He didn't seem surprised. A man as old as Henry probably expected everyone from his youth to be dead by now.

"She was married, Henry. To a man named Wellington."

From the way his face went rigid, I might as well have hit him with my fist.

"Wellington," he repeated.

"Maria Lima Wellington had a son," I went on. "She named him Henry."

His eyes changed again, a spark there.

"And he was born seventy-two years ago."

"What month?"

"June."

He seemed to do the calculation in his head and was satisfied with the result.

"Is he . . . ?"

"Alive? Yeah, Henry, he is. He lives in Thunder Bay, Canada. Just across the border."

Meloux nodded, thinking it over.

"I want to see him," he said.

"Henry, you're not getting out of here until you're better."

"Bring him to me."

"It was a miracle just finding him. Bringing him here? I don't know, Henry."

"You did not believe you would find him."

This was true, though I hadn't said anything like that to Meloux. Somehow he'd known my thoughts. Typical of the old Mide.

"You will find a way," he said.

"Look, I might be able to talk to him, but I can't promise anything. Honestly, I'm not sure how I can make any of this sound believable."

"The watch, you found it?"

"Yes."

"Show him the watch."

"I'll see what I can do."

Meloux seemed comforted. He smiled, satisfied.

"I will see my son," he said. His eyes drifted closed.

I started out.

"Walleye?" the old man said.

I turned back. "We're taking good care of him, Henry."

He nodded and once again closed his eyes.

* * *

I spoke with Ernie Champoux, Meloux's great-nephew, who was in the waiting room. He told me the doctors were puzzled by the symptoms the old man was presenting and were still running tests. Things didn't look good, though.

I'd dressed for church, suit and tie, and when I was finished at the hospital I met Jo and the kids at St. Agnes for Mass. I didn't pay much attention to the service. I was thinking about Thunder Bay and how to go about keeping my second promise to Meloux. I thought about some guy approaching me with the kind of story I was going to toss at Wellington. It would sound exactly like a con. On the other hand, maybe the man was already aware of some of this. Who knew? The watch might have some effect on Henry Wellington. But how to get an audience with the notorious recluse in order to show him the item?

It would have been better to know the whole story: how a Shinnob had come to father—apparently illegitimately—the man who'd headed a major Canadian corporation. That had to be some tale. If the old Mide had been stronger, I might have pressed him.

"You seemed distracted," Jo said at home. "How did it go with Meloux?"

"The news did him good, I think. He asked me to bring his son to him."

We were in our bedroom, changing. Jo stepped out of her slip and threw me a questioning look.

"You promised?"

I pulled off my tie. "It felt that way."

"Good luck, cowboy. If I were Meloux's son and you told me this story, I'd have you locked up." She unbuttoned her cream-colored blouse and went to the closet to hang it up.

"Maybe the guy knows the story." I took off my shirt.

"What exactly is the whole story? How did Meloux come to father a son he's never seen?"

"He's not saying."

Jo stood at the closet door in her white bra and in panties that had little yellow flowers all over them. She'd been through hell in the year since the brutal events in Evanston. But the human spirit—with the help of counseling—is amazingly resilient, and looking at her as she stood ankle deep in a puddle of sunshine, I thought she'd never been more lovely.

I dropped my shirt on the chair next to our dresser and walked to her. I put my hand gently on her cheek.

"Part of your question I can answer," I said.

"Oh? And which part would that be?"

"How he fathered a son."

I kissed her.

"You have to open Sam's Place in half an hour," she reminded me.

"Old pros like us can accomplish a lot in half an hour."

She smiled seductively, took my hand, and together we went to the bed.

EIGHT

During the day, whenever I had a break from customers, I slipped into the back of Sam's Place and made telephone calls. I tried the headquarters of Northern Mining and Manufacturing in Thunder Bay. Because it was Sunday, all I got was a recording, pretty much what I'd expected. I'd been unable to find a listing on the Internet for Henry Wellington and had no better luck with directory assistance. Among the information I'd gathered the night before, however, was the name of Wellington's younger half brother, Rupert Wellington, president and CEO of NMM, and also a resident of Thunder Bay. I tried the number for Rupert I'd pulled off the Internet. The man who answered told me rather crossly that he was not *that* Rupert Wellington and he was sick and tired of getting the other guy's calls, thank you very much.

I'd also learned that Wellington had two children, a son and a daughter. The son worked for a conservation organization in Vancouver, British Columbia. His name was Alan. The daughter, Maria, was a physician in Montreal. I didn't have a phone number for either of them, but I did have one for the conservation organization, a group called Nature's Child. I dialed, thinking there was no way on a Sunday. Someone answered on the fourth ring.

"Nature's Child. This is Heidi."

"Heidi, my name is Corcoran O'Connor. I'm trying to reach Alan Wellington."

"He's not here."

"Would it be possible to reach him at home?"

"I suppose you could try."

"I would but I don't have his number."

"And I can't give it out."

"It's a bit of an emergency. It's about his family."

"His father?"

I wondered why it would occur to her automatically that it would be about Henry Wellington.

"His grandfather, actually. He's very sick."

"And you would be?"

"As I said, my name's Corcoran O'Connor. I'm acting on his grandfather's behalf."

"An attorney?"

"A friend. Look, I hate to be pressing, but the old man is dying."

There was a brief hesitation on the other end as she considered. Then: "Just a moment."

Within a minute, I had the number and was dialing Alan Wellington's home phone.

"Hello?" A woman's voice.

"I'd like to speak with Alan Wellington, please."

"May I say who's calling?"

I gave her my name.

A few seconds later, a man came on the line. Firm, deep voice, but not hard. "This is Alan."

"Mr. Wellington, my name is Cork O'Connor. I'm calling from Minnesota. I've come into possession of a watch that I believe belonged to your grandmother. There's a rather interesting story attached to it. I'd like to give the watch to your father and tell him the story, but he's a difficult man to contact."

"Not difficult, Mr. O'Connor. Impossible."

"That's why I'm contacting you. I was hoping you might help."

"You can certainly send me the watch and the story along with it. I'll make sure my father gets them."

"I'd rather deliver them to him in person."

"I'm afraid I can't help you with that."

"Just a telephone number?"

"Mr. O'Connor, I don't know the truth of what you're telling me, though it sounds a little suspect. You have no idea the number of people who've tried to get to my father through me. And my sister. My father wants simply to be left alone. As much as I'm able, I intend to help him with that. If you'd like to send me the watch, I'll see that he gets it. Otherwise, we have nothing further to discuss."

"Time is of the essence here, Mr. Wellington. A man who wants very much to contact your father is dying."

"A man. Not you?"

"Someone I represent."

"You're an attorney?"

"No."

"And who is this man?"

I didn't know how to explain it. I stumbled on. "He was a very good friend of your grandmother. He has important information about her that your father ought to know."

"If you tell me, I'll see that he gets it."

"I can't really do that."

"Then, as I said before—Mr. O'Connor, was it? We have nothing further to discuss."

The call ended on that abrupt and chilly note.

Jo stopped by in the late afternoon. She brought Stevie and Walleye and dropped them off.

"Mind if they hang out here for a while?" she asked. "I have shopping to do. The dog can't come into the store, and Stevie won't go anywhere without him."

"No problem," I said.

After she left, I watched them chase around outside. Stevie ran; Walleye bounded after him, barking joyously. It was hot and a little humid and Walleye was no spring chicken, so after a while, the dog crept into the shade under the picnic table out front and lay down, panting. Stevie crawled under and sat with him, talking to him quietly and gently stroking his fur.

I thought about my son. He had friends, kids in the neighborhood he played with, but he didn't have a best friend. He possessed a fine imagination and often played alone, games he invented or adventures he concocted in his mind's eye. I didn't worry about him. He seemed pretty comfortable with who he was. I knew he was lonely sometimes. Who wasn't? But watching him with Meloux's old dog, I wondered if maybe there wasn't an essential connection missing in his life, the kind of affection offered by a best friend. Or a lovable old hound.

After a while, they came out from under the picnic table. Walleye followed Stevie to the Quonset hut. A few moments later, my son poked his head into the serving area.

"Can I go fishing?"

"Don't think much'll be biting in this heat, buddy, but be my guest."

I kept fishing gear in the back room. Stevie knew where. In a bit, he walked through afternoon sunlight toward the lake with Walleye padding along patiently at his side. They sat at the end of the dock. Stevie took off his shoes, put his feet in the water, and tossed his line. Walleye lay down, his head on his paws, and they hung out together in the comfortable quiet of two good friends.

At home that night I told Jo, "I'm driving to Thunder Bay in the morning."

She was sitting up in bed, propped against the headboard, reading a file in a manila folder, something from work, I was sure. She often read in bed at night, her glasses perched on her nose, making small noises in response to the text.

"What about Sam's Place?" She took off her glasses and laid them at her side.

I slipped into a pair of gym shorts and a clean T-shirt, my usual sleep attire. I turned from the dresser. "Jenny and Annie can handle it. Is Jenny here?"

"She came in a while ago."

"Did she have a good time driving the North Shore with Sean?"

"She didn't talk much."

I sat down on the bed. "Is that good or bad?"

"It's neither, I'd say. She's just thinking, I imagine. Weighing everything."

"Weighing an offer of marriage?"

"I don't know that there's been one."

"If I were Sean and wanted to pop the question, I'd take her to someplace like the North Shore, sit her down with a gorgeous view of Lake Superior."

"I suppose you would. That's basically how you proposed to me. On Lake Michigan, a beautiful evening, a dinner cruise. That glorious question. Then you threw up."

"I hadn't planned on getting seasick. And you accepted anyway."

"Jenny's in a different place than I was, Cork. I think we should trust her."

"That doesn't mean we can't nudge her in the direction we'd like her to go."

"You think she doesn't know what we'd prefer?"

"I'd like her to think of it as what's best rather than just what we prefer."

"I'm sure you would. What do you hope to accomplish in Thunder Bay?"

"A face-to-face meeting with Henry Wellington."

"And how do you intend to go about that?"

"As nearly as I can tell, his brother—half brother—Rupert runs the company now, so he's probably accessible. I'm hoping to use him to get to Wellington."

"And you'll get an audience with the brother how?"

"The watch. I'm banking on it opening the door."

"Four-hour drive up, four-hour drive back. Could be all for nothing."

"Not for nothing. It's for Henry. And you have a better idea?"

She put the manila folder on the nightstand, leaned over, and kissed me. "You'll be leaving early. Get some sleep."

NINE

I stopped by the hospital on my way out of town. I spoke with Dr. Wrigley, who was pretty familiar by then with my association with Meloux, though he didn't know anything of what the old man had requested of me. There'd been little change in Meloux's condition. When I asked what exactly that condition was, Wrigley couldn't give me an answer.

"There doesn't seem to be any occlusion. We've run all the tests we can run here. I'm thinking of transferring him down to Saint Luke's, in Duluth. Their heart people might be able to figure this one out."

Meloux was awake. He smiled weakly when I entered his room.

"How you doing, Henry?"

"I don't sleep so good. I don't crap so good. Mostly my heart is heavy. Like a bear on my chest."

"I'm going up to Thunder Bay today, try to talk to the man who may be your son."

"The watch?"

"I have it."

I'd put it in a small white jewelry box Jo had given me. I opened the box, took out the watch, and handed it to Meloux. His fingers were brittle-looking things, thin sticks, but they handled that watch gently. He opened it and studied the photograph inside.

"She was beautiful," I said.

The old Mide looked up. "Her beauty was a knife, Corcoran O'Connor."

He handed the watch back.

"You will bring me my son," he said.

* * *

I followed Highway 1 southeast and reached the North Shore in an hour. I turned left at Ilgen City and took Highway 61 north along Lake Superior.

It was a beautiful August day. The lake looked hard as blue concrete. Sunlight shattered on its surface into glittering shards. Far to the east, where the pale wall of the sky hit the water, the horizon was a solid line, the meeting of two perfect geometric planes. To the west rose the Sawbill Mountains, covered with second- and third-growth timber. The road often cut along steep cliffs or ran beside a shoreline littered with great slabs of rock broken by the chisel of ice and time and the relentless hammering of waves. I drove through Schroeder, Tofte, Grand Marais, and finally Grand Portage, small towns full of tourists come north for the scenery and to escape the sweltering Midwest heat farther south.

I crossed the border at the Pigeon River, and less than an hour later, I entered the unimpressive outskirts of Thunder Bay.

Thunder Bay is really the modern merging of two rival municipalities, Fort William and Port Arthur. As I understand it, the French fur traders started things rolling with a settlement protected by a rustic fort near the mouth of the Kaministiquia River, which emptied into a bay on Lake Superior the French called Baie de Tonnaire. The British, when they took over the fur-trading business, built a more impressive outpost they named Fort William. A few years later, when the new Canadian government wanted to build a road through the wilderness, a site a few miles north of Fort William was chosen. It was christened Port Arthur, and the two towns began trading verbal potshots, something that went on for the next hundred years or so, until they shook hands, erased the borders, and took to calling the new union Thunder Bay. The truth is, it didn't end the rivalry. Ask anyone who lives in the city where they're from and no one says Thunder Bay. Either they're from Port Arthur or Fort William.

The city's an old port. Like a lot of towns on the western side of Lake Superior, it's long past its heyday. But it's trying.

The bay is created by a long, southerly sweeping peninsula dominated by an impressive geological formation called Sleeping Giant, so named because that's what the formation resembles. The Ojibwe story is that it's Nanabozho, the trickster spirit, turned to stone when white men learned the secret of the peninsula, which was that a rich silver mine was hidden there.

From what I'd gathered on the Internet, Henry Wellington lived on a remote island called Manitou, which was just off Thunder Cape, the tip of Sleeping Giant. Manitou is an Ojibwe word that means spirit. That's exactly what Wellington seemed to be. More spirit than flesh, more spoken about than seen.

I made my way to the Thunder Bay Marina, which was at the eastern edge of the downtown area, just off Water Street. The city's old railroad station had been remodeled into shops and a little restaurant/bar. There were three main docks. Most of the slips were filled with modest sailboats and large motor launches. I walked to the end of the first dock and stared out across the bay toward Sleeping Giant, dark gray in the distance.

"Interested in a tour?"

I glanced back. A woman stood on the deck of a sailboat docked not far away, a can of Labatt Blue in her hand. She wore white shorts, a yellow tank top, a red visor. She looked maybe sixty—a healthy, tanned, fit sixty. The kind of sixty I hoped to be when I got there.

"Nope. Just one island. Manitou."

"Hunting Henry Wellington," she said and took a drink from her beer. "Where's your camera?"

"I don't want a picture."

"Good. Because the chances of getting one are next to nothing."

"I just want to talk to the man."

She laughed. "Hell, that's harder than an audience with the pope. Everybody knows that."

"Where's Manitou Island?"

She pointed toward the enormous landform on the far side of the bay, miles away. "At the base of Sleeping Giant. Too far to see from here."

"I understand the only way to get there is by boat."

"There's a helipad."

"The man likes his privacy."

"The man's obsessed with it. You're not a reporter, eh?"

"Private investigator." I walked to her boat, reached across the gunwale, and gave her my card. It was the first one I'd given out since I had them printed. I got a thrill from it. "Hired by a family member to deliver a piece of information. You seem to know a lot about Wellington."

"Mostly what everyone in Thunder Bay knows. But with my slip right here, I pretty much see who comes and goes to the island."

"Could you get me out there?"

"Wouldn't do you any good. Wellington's got dogs, men with guns."

"Ever seen him?"

"Every once in a while if I'm passing near the island at sundown, I see a wisp of white moving among the trees. More like a ghost than a man, eh. I figure that's got to be Wellington."

"Thanks."

"No problem. You decide you want a tour, you know where to find me."

"What do you charge?"

"A six-pack and conversation, sweetheart." She winked and went back to her beer.

Northern Mining and Manufacturing headquarters were on a campus just north of the city. There was a tall central structure of modern design—a slanted box of polished girder and smoked glass—surrounded by several smaller buildings of similar but less striking construction. I parked in the visitors' lot, put on a tie and sport coat, and went inside the grand, central structure. At the reception desk in the lobby, I was directed to the fifteenth floor, the top.

The waiting area was large enough that if the floor had been ice, I could have played hockey. There was a plush sofa of nice chocolate brown leather and an easy chair of the same color and material. There was a large aquarium with darting fish in psychedelic colors and patterns. And there was a desk with a secretary who turned from her computer and watched me cross the room.

"I'd like to see Mr. Wellington," I told her.

She was young—twenty-seven, maybe thirty—nicely made up and wearing a dark blue suit over a cream-colored blouse. A thin gold chain looped her neck. The nameplate on the desk read MS. HELPRIN. She looked up at me, pleasant but professional.

"Do you have an appointment?"

"I don't. Could I make one?"

"What's the nature of your business?"

"It's personal and rather urgent."

"Mr. Wellington is extremely busy."

"Of course," I said, very understanding. "It concerns a family heirloom that's recently come into my possession. I believe he'd be interested."

"What is the heirloom?"

I took out the watch, opened it, and handed it to her. "That's a photograph of his father's first wife, Maria. My guess would be that there's significant sentimental value in it."

"And you simply want to give this to him?" She seemed to think it was a sweet idea.

"Not exactly."

"Do you wish to offer it for sale?" This seemed to strike her as not such a sweet idea.

"No. I'd like to tell him a story that goes along with it, and to ask him something."

"Ask him what?"

"That's between him and me, Ms. Helprin."

She looked at the watch, then at me, her face young and uncertain.

"If you could just show him the watch," I said, "I'm betting he'll see me."

Betting? That was a long shot.

"Mr. Wellington is currently in a meeting. If you'd care to wait, I'll see what I can do."

"Thank you."

It was a waiting room without reading material. I sat in the easy chair and stared at the exotic fish shooting through the water in the aquarium. For a long time, the only sound was the click of Ms. Helprin's keyboard as she typed and the burble of the aerator in the fish tank. I thought about what I might say to Wellington: *Your brother's history isn't what it seems.*

Or maybe it was. Maybe it was a well-known and well-kept family secret that Henry Wellington had been sired by a Shinnob. On the other hand, maybe it was all a horrible coincidence, and Henry Wellington had no connection whatsoever with Meloux.

Fifteen minutes passed slowly. Without any apparent indication that her boss was free, Ms. Helprin stood up and said, "I'll be right back." She disappeared through another door. A couple of minutes later, she returned. "Mr. Wellington will see you now."

The man at the big glass desk in the inner office stood up to shake my hand. From what I'd learned on the Internet, I knew he was sixty-two years old, though he looked a decade younger. He was small and fit, with a crown of silver hair around a balding center. He wore an expensive gray suit, white shirt, red tie. His eyes were earth brown and sharp in their appraisal. In our conversation, he was succinct without being rude.

"I appreciate your time, Mr. Wellington," I said.

"I can only spare a minute, Mr. O'Connor. Have a seat."

I sat in a chair with a curved, gray-metal back and a soft leather cushion that molded perfectly to my butt and spine. The office had a rich, spare feel to it. Not much furniture, all of it modern and well made. The wall behind Wellington was all glass, with a beautiful view of the bay and Sleeping Giant in the distance.

"The watch, of course, intrigued me. You have a story that goes with it, I understand." He folded his hands on his desk and leaned forward.

"The photograph is of Maria Wellington, yes?"

He nodded. "My father's first wife."

"She wasn't your mother, correct?"

"That's right. After her death, my father remarried. Do I get to hear the story?"

"Only if your brother chooses to tell it to you. The man who gave me that watch and its story asked me to share it only with Henry Wellington."

"Ah." He sat back and looked disappointed. "So it's really my brother you're trying to see." His eyes narrowed. "Mr. O'Connor, my brother wants to be left in peace. A simple request. Yet he's hounded mercilessly by people like you. I'm tired of all the schemes concocted to try to get to him. Exactly what tabloid do you work for?"

"I'm not a journalist. I'm a private investigator." I hauled out my wallet and handed him a business card. "I've been retained by the man who gave me that watch to deliver it and its history personally to Henry Wellington. This is important. My client is dying."

"The man's name?"

"That's for the ears of Henry Wellington." It was my turn to lean forward, not an easy thing in the curved chair. "Look, for a lot of years I was the sheriff of Tamarack County, down in Minnesota. If you need a character reference, I'd urge you to call the sheriff's office. I'm not trying to scam you. It's simply an unusual and pressing situation. Keep the watch for the time being. All I'm asking is fifteen minutes of your brother's time. I guarantee that what I have to tell him, he'll want to hear. It's important to him. And urgent as well."

A man in his position, I figured, had to be able to size up circumstances—and people—quickly. Wellington considered for all of ten seconds, staring at the watch in his hand.

"I can't guarantee anything, Mr. O'Connor. Henry has the final say as to whether he sees you or not. And I can tell you right now, he sees almost no one these days."

"I can't ask any more than that. Thank you."

"How can you be reached?"

"My cell phone. The number's on my card."

He stood up and offered his hand in parting. *A gracious gesture*, I thought. "Again," he cautioned, "I make no promises."

"I understand. And the watch?"

"It will be returned to you before you see my brother."

I was hoping he'd add something like "Scout's honor," but all he gave me was a steady stare as I walked to the door and left.

TEN

It was two thirty in the afternoon. I needed lunch. I went back to the marina, to the little restaurant/bar in the remodeled depot. I got a table on the deck overlooking the docks, ordered a Reuben and a beer, and stared out at the sailboats cutting across the bay. The wind off the lake was cool and pleasant.

I got the Moosehead first, and while I drank it, I thought about what I'd accomplished so far. In two days, I'd identified the man I suspected was Meloux's son, tracked him down, and had, I believed, a good shot at an interview. It seemed impressive. While I was more than willing to give myself credit for brilliant detecting, it felt too easy. Something was wrong with the picture, but I couldn't exactly say what.

The one solid fact was that the woman Meloux had called Maria Lima—not a common name in Canada, I was pretty sure—had become the first wife of Leonard Wellington. About her I felt certain. That she had a son named Henry who was born in the year and month when, according to Meloux, his own son would have been born had the distant possibility of coincidence. That I would be allowed to see this man who'd become Canada's most notorious recluse seemed the biggest stretch.

Yet that was exactly what Meloux had predicted. The watch would be my passport.

I ate the Reuben, a pretty good one, and was working on my second beer when my cell phone rang. No information on caller ID.

"O'Connor here."

"This is Henry Wellington."

"Mr. Wellington—" I began.

"Be at the Thunder Bay Marina at three thirty, the end of dock number one. You'll be met by a man named Edward Morrissey, my personal assistant. He'll bring you to Manitou Island."

"Thank you."

"Mr. O'Connor, should you be tempted to speak to the media before or after your visit, rest assured I'll see that you wish you hadn't."

"I understand."

"Good."

"What about the watch?"

"It will be in Mr. Morrissey's possession."

Without so much as a good-bye, he was gone.

I strolled down to the dock a few minutes early. Edward Morrissey was already there.

He wasn't an imposing man at first glance. Not tall—just under six feet. Dark curly hair. I put him in his midthirties. When I got closer, I saw that he was hard all over, well muscled, with a broad chest, narrow waist, thick arms, and a neck like a section of concrete pillar. He wore sunglasses and didn't remove them. I saw myself, small, approaching in their reflection.

"You O'Connor?"

He'd been leaning against the railing of the dock, but came off when I neared him. He wore jeans, tight over buffed-up thighs, white sneakers, a black windbreaker.

"That's me."

"Morrissey," he said. He didn't offer his hand. "Supposed to take you to the island."

"I'm ready."

He stepped close to me. "Lift your arms."

"What?"

"I need to pat you down."

"I'm not carrying."

"I need to be sure. Also, I'll be checking for any camera you might have hidden."

"This is ridiculous."

"You want to see Mr. Wellington?"

I lifted my arms. While Morrissey went over me with his big hands, I noticed the woman on her sailboat a few slips down who'd talked with me that morning. She was sitting on a canvas deck chair, drinking from a beer bottle, watching the proceedings with amusement. She lifted her beer in a toast to me.

"All right," Morrissey said when he was satisfied I was clean. "Let's go."

"You're supposed to give me something."

Morrissey reached into the pocket of his windbreaker and brought out the little box that contained the watch. "This?"

"Yes."

I held out my hand, but Morrissey slipped the box back into his pocket.

"Mr. Wellington instructed me to deliver it directly to him," Morrissey said.

"The other Mr. Wellington promised me—"

"I don't work for the other Mr. Wellington." He turned and walked toward the end of the pier, where a launch was waiting with a pilot at the wheel.

Morrissey was dead silent most of the way out. He sat directly opposite me on the small launch, his arms crossed, the wind batting his curly hair and pulling at the collar of his windbreaker. His eyes behind the impenetrable dark of his shades might have been closed and he might have been sleeping, but I guessed not. I figured he was taking my measure. My assessment of Edward Morrissey was that he was less a personal assistant than a bodyguard, and the bulge under his black windbreaker wasn't a whisk broom to dust lint from his employer's black suit.

We crossed the bay at a good clip. As we drew nearer Sleeping Giant, an island emerged, taking shape against the rugged backdrop of the peninsula. It lay, I guessed, a quarter mile off the mainland. It was relatively level and heavily covered with boreal forest, tall pines mostly. Finally I made out the white outline of a dock jutting into the lake. A few minutes later, the pilot at the wheel cut the engine and began to maneuver us in. We moved at a crawl, and when I looked over the gunwale of the launch, I understood why. Beneath the clear water of Lake Superior, I could see a series of wicked shoals through which the pilot was carefully navigating.

From a kiosk at the far end of the dock, a man emerged and walked out to meet us. He wore white shorts, a white shirt, boat shoes. As we came nearer, I saw that he also wore a gun belt with a filled holster.

The launch nosed up to the dock. Morrissey stood up and tossed a line to the man.

When we were tied off, Morrissey said, "After you, O'Connor."

I disembarked. Morrissey was right behind me.

The man on the dock returned to the kiosk. We met him there. He wrote something on a sheet attached to a clipboard, then said to me, "Lift your arms, please."

"Another pat down? I've already been through that routine with Morrissey here. Hey, I like a good tickle as well as the next guy, but come on."

The man had cold gray eyes. "Arms, please," he said in a voice that told me he wasn't amused.

I suffered another body check.

"You the one who gives out the hall passes?" I said when he'd finished.

He went back to his clipboard, made another brief notation. "Stick with him," he advised me, pointing toward Morrissey, "and there won't be any trouble."

"This way, O'Connor," Morrissey said.

He stepped off the dock onto a path of crushed limestone that disappeared into the trees cloaking the island.

ELEVEN

*This is the forest primeval. The towering pines and the hemlocks
bearded like druids of eld . . . something, something.*

Longfellow, I think. Jenny would have been able to quote the
whole damn thing. Me, I could barely remember the first couple of
lines. Primeval was right, though. The trees grew close together, tall
and, in this place, forbidding. They formed a dark roof over us and a
wall around us. Green-black moss crept over everything—the pines,
the rocks, the rotting, fallen tree trunks. It was cool but not so quiet. I
heard dogs barking somewhere in the trees. The only other sounds
were the crunch of limestone under our feet and the sizzle of Morrissey's windbreaker as he swung his heavy arms.

He kept me in front of him.

"Just stick with the path," he said.

Which didn't follow a straight line, but wound through the trees
so that periodically what was behind was as lost to me as what was
ahead. After a few minutes, we walked into a large clearing. At the
center stood a mansion built of stone. It was two stories with a couple
of wings off the large center section. There was a portico with Greek-
looking pillars, and on the second story each of the rooms had a bal-
cony. Half a dozen chimneys pushed through the roof. I could see that
gardens had brightened the grounds at one time, but now the plots
were a tangle of wild undergrowth.

I'd learned from my Internet research that Manitou Island had
been the family retreat. After his wife's death, Wellington had sold his
luxurious home in Thunder Bay and retired to the island permanently. In the past five years, he'd been seen publicly on only a handful of occasions, the last nearly two years before.

People were entitled to their privacy, but it also seemed that, like the banning of a book, the obsession with privacy increased the attraction of what could not be had.

The few relatively recent photos that I'd found on the Internet were of a robed figure, druidlike, among the trees of Manitou Island. The white wisp the woman at the marina had spoken of.

Morrissey's hand on my back urged me forward.

"I don't know what's in that box," he said as we mounted the steps to the lodge, "but it must be something. Mr. W. sees nobody, I mean nobody, from the outside anymore."

He stepped ahead and opened the door, beckoning me to enter.

The moment I was inside I caught the smell of disinfectant or bleach. It pervaded the place. Not overwhelming, but everywhere. It was also uncomfortably warm and stuffy.

The common area we entered was a maze of stacked newspapers hip high, with a couple of narrow corridors running through it. Sheets covered the furniture, which had been pushed to the walls. Morrissey had pulled off his shades. He pointed toward the stairs beyond the clutter, and we maneuvered our way there. Upstairs, he directed me down a dark hallway to a door near the end of one of the wings. We entered a kind of anteroom. Morrissey went to another door and knocked.

"Who is it?"

"Morrissey, Mr. Wellington. I've got your visitor."

"Show him in."

Before we entered, Morrissey reached to a table beside the door and pulled a surgical mask from a small box there. He handed it to me. "Put this on."

"You're kidding."

"You want to see Mr. W., you put on the mask."

I took it, and as I tied it around my face, Morrissey did the same with another. In addition, he took a pair of latex examination gloves from another box on the table.

"Should I put on gloves?" I asked.

"You planning on touching anything?"

"Not intentionally."

"See that you don't."

He opened the door and stepped in ahead of me.

The gloom of the hallway, of the whole place, hadn't prepared me for what lay beyond that door. The room was claustrophobic, tiny for such a great house. Jammed into it were a bed neatly made and covered with a snow white comforter, an easy chair of smooth white leather, an enormous television with a fifty-two-inch screen, a rolling garment hanger hung with nothing but white robes, and, lining the walls, stack upon stack of unopened Kleenex tissue boxes. The room was dark except for a tall standing lamp of highly polished steel that cast a small circle of cold light down around the easy chair. The chair faced the television, so all I could see was its smooth white back.

The television was on, tuned to a station broadcasting the intimate, unpleasant details of a heart operation. I watched the heart pump away inside the open chest cavity, while several hands in bloody surgical gloves worked around it with scissors and clamps. Everything in the gaping wound glistened, wet and raw.

"Did you close the door?"

The voice came from the chair, the same voice I'd heard from the hallway. It was thin and a little peevish, like a bad clarinet.

"It's closed," Morrissey said.

The bloody hands on the television gripped the heart, and I was afraid maybe they were going to pull it out of the body.

The screen went black. I didn't mind.

The chair swiveled slowly, bringing me face-to-face with Henry Wellington.

His hair was long and white, very much like Meloux's. Although he wore a white robe, it was clear the fabric hung on a slender frame. His face, like mine and Morrissey's, was half covered by a surgical mask. I tried to look into his eyes, to see if there was something of Meloux there, but his turning had put the lamp at his back and his face was deep in shadow.

"Bring me the box," he said to Morrissey.

Like a good lackey, Morrissey stepped forward, took the little jewelry box from the pocket of his windbreaker, and, with his latex-covered hands, delivered it to Wellington. Then he retreated to the place where he'd stood before, just at my back.

Wellington fumbled with the watch. For an engineer, he seemed oddly stumped by how to open such a simple mechanism. Finally he succeeded in freeing the catch. For a minute, he studied the photograph inside.

"You have some story about the item and my mother?"

"It's for your ears only," I said.

"Leave us, Mr. Morrissey."

"I'm not sure that's such a good idea, Mr. Wellington," Morrissey cautiously offered. "I think I should be here if you need me."

A reasonable argument from a bodyguard, I thought. Whatever else I felt about Morrissey, he was a man who took his job seriously.

"I believe, Mr. Wellington, that what I have to say you won't want anyone else to hear," I countered.

"I'll say it only once more, Mr. Morrissey. Leave us." The reedy voice suddenly had volume and power, and I could tell that somewhere in all that withered white was a man with the ability to command, the kind of man I'd talked to on my cell phone earlier.

"Yes, sir," Morrissey said.

I didn't turn, but I heard the door open and close at my back.

The air was close and warm. I was sweating.

"The story," Wellington said, holding up the watch so that it dangled at the end of its gold fob.

"That watch was given to me by an old man. He was given it by your mother. His name is Henry Meloux. He's dying."

I tried to pierce the shadow over his face, to see in that frail wizened face something of Meloux. The eyes were dark, but not Henry's, I finally decided. More like the woman in the photograph, perhaps.

"A rather short story," he said.

"He gave me that watch and asked me to give it to the man who may be his son."

The corners of his eyes crinkled. Was he amused?

"He believes I'm his son?"

"He didn't reveal the whole story to me, but it's clear he was involved with your mother in a way that could have produced a son. Apparently the timing of your birth is right. And you're named Henry, like him."

He considered this, but it was hard to say what he might have been thinking.

"What does he want?'

"To see you, that's all."

"You said he's dying. Where is he?"

"In a hospital in Minnesota."

"He wants me to go there?"

"Yes."

He picked up an atomizer that had been tucked beside him in the chair, and he sprayed the air between us.

"Tell me more about this Meloux," he said.

"He's Ojibwe. He's what we call a Mide, a member of the Grand Medicine Society. He heals."

He leaned forward, and his upper face became clear to me, something carved out of marble, white, hard, and cold.

"An Indian?"

"Yes."

He stood up, tall and brittle-looking, hollow featured. A ghost of a man.

"Do you realize what you're saying about my mother? What kind of woman would take up with an Indian buck?" He pointed a curling nail at me. "If I were ten years younger, I'd knock you down."

I tried again to speak reasonably. "Think about it, Mr. Wellington. You were born two months after your parents married. You were conceived out of wedlock. And I also know that as a child your favorite toy was a stuffed cormorant given to you by your mother. In the Ojibwe totemic system, Henry Meloux is cormorant clan."

I'd hoped, I suppose, that in the same mysterious way Meloux knew he had a son, the son would recognize Meloux as his father. Not exactly a brilliant strategy.

"Edward!" Wellington called angrily. "Edward!"

The door burst open. "Yes, Mr. Wellington?"

"Show this man out. I don't wish any further conversation with him."

"Sure thing, Mr. Wellington."

I could hear the pleasure in Morrissey's voice.

"The watch," I said.

"What?" Wellington squinted at me.

"I'd like the watch back."

"I'd say it belongs to my family."

"I'd say not."

"Edward," Wellington commanded.

"Come on, O'Connor."

I shook off his hand. "I'm not leaving without that watch."

Morrissey gripped my shoulder hard. I turned and swung, catching him full on his jaw. He went down, looking stunned. I spun back and sprang toward Wellington.

"Stay back," he cried. He cringed a moment, then threw the watch at me like a spoiled child and spat, "All right then, *here.*"

I heard Morrissey struggling up at my back. I turned to meet him.

"Enough, Edward," Wellington ordered. "Just get him out of here."

Morrissey was breathing hard, and I could see he wanted a piece of me. Hell, he wanted the whole enchilada. But Wellington once more said, "Enough."

Though Morrissey relaxed his body, his eyes were still tight. "Yes, sir." He nodded toward the door. "After you, O'Connor."

TWELVE

He jumped me on the limestone path.

We were out of sight of the mansion, winding our way through the pines toward the dock. Morrissey was behind me. He hadn't said a word since we left the room where Henry Wellington sat trapped in his antiseptic craziness, and I wondered where the bodyguard's head was at. He couldn't be happy with himself. He hadn't done his job particularly well. I was in possession of the watch, and if Wellington hadn't thrown it at me, I'd have actually laid my germ-infested hands on him. Plus, I'd clipped Morrissey's jaw pretty well.

So as he brooded behind me, I wondered.

Then he hit me.

In my left kidney.

A blow like a cannonball.

I arched against the impact and the pain. My knees buckled and I went down, kneeling in the crushed limestone.

Morrissey danced to the side and kicked me below the ribs. I toppled and went fetal, my knees to my chest, my arms wrapped around my head to protect myself.

But Morrissey had done all the damage he intended. Except to bend down and deliver this: "Shithead. You ever swing on me again, I'll kill your sorry ass."

I heard the crunch of limestone as he stepped back.

To be on the safe side, I waited several seconds then carefully uncurled. Morrissey stood a dozen feet away, arms crossed, shades in place, watching me get to my feet. No emotion on his face now. A volcano that had finished erupting. His right hand rested on his windbreaker, near the bulge that was not a whisk broom.

Some days you eat the bear, some days the bear eats you.

I turned and headed to the dock with Morrissey behind me at a safe distance.

He handed me over to the guy in the kiosk with the clipboard, who signed me out. Morrissey spoke quietly to the pilot of the launch, who eyed me and nodded. Morrissey cast us off and stayed on the island, while the pilot maneuvered through the shoals to open water, then hit the throttle, and we sped toward Thunder Bay.

My back ached, but I didn't think Morrissey had done any permanent damage. Maybe a bruise that would bug me for a while, and the knowledge that if I ever encountered him again, he was a man I would keep in front of me.

At the marina, I disembarked. The pilot immediately swung around to return to Manitou Island.

"Beer?"

I turned in the direction of the voice and saw the woman standing on the deck of her sailboat, a bottle lifted in offering.

"Thanks."

I walked to her sailboat and climbed aboard.

She handed me a Labatt Blue. "You actually got on the island?"

"Yeah." I unscrewed the cap and took a long drink. It was ice cold. Perfect.

"What was it like?"

"Not a place I'd choose for a vacation," I said.

"You actually talked with Wellington?"

"We conversed a bit."

"What's he like?"

"A man who wants his privacy. I think he's entitled to it."

"I saw them frisk you before you left. Careful people."

"I didn't catch your name," I said.

"Trinky Pollard. Royal Canadian Mounted Police. Retired."

"Cork O'Connor. Former sheriff of Tamarack County, Minnesota."

"You told me earlier that you're a PI now."

"Part-time. Mostly I'm up here as a guy trying to do a friend a favor."

We shook hands. Hers was impressively strong.

"You look too young to be a retired cop," she said.

"Not retired. I quit."

"What do you do when you're not investigating privately?"

"Mostly I make hamburgers."

She smiled at that, then glanced toward the island. "So you delivered a cheeseburger and fries to Wellington, eh." She laughed. "Accomplish whatever it was you were after?"

"I guess you could say I got my man."

I lifted my bottle, and we toasted.

I looked at my watch. "Thanks for the beer, Trinky. If I'm going to make it home tonight, I'd best be on my way."

She saw me off her boat, still sipping her beer. When I looked back, she was staring toward Sleeping Giant.

Before I left the marina, I used my cell to call Jo.

"Hello, sweetheart," she said. "Where are you?"

"Still in Thunder Bay. How are things there?"

She hesitated a moment, which worried me.

"How's Meloux?" I asked, expecting the worst.

"Ernie Champoux called. Meloux's left the hospital," she said.

"Left?"

"Walked out. Against all advice. According to Ernie, he just sat up, told the doctor he was well and ready to leave. Ernie convinced him to let them run a few tests. It was amazing, Cork. They couldn't find anything wrong. All the signs, everything, perfectly normal. The doctor can't explain it."

"Did Meloux say anything?"

"He told them the weight was off his heart, that he was at peace."

"He believes he's going to see his son. Damn."

"Damn? What does that mean?"

I told her about Meloux's son, a man I wasn't certain any father would want to claim as the fruit of his loins.

"What are you going to do?" she asked.

"What can I do? I've got to tell him the truth."

"When will you be home?"

"Well after dark. How're the kids?"

Once again, she was quiet. And I realized that what I'd picked up in her voice earlier had nothing to do with Meloux.

"What is it, Jo? Is it Jenny? Did Sean finally pop the question?"

"It's more complicated than that."

"Oh. How so?"

I heard her take a deep breath. "Cork, you were right to be worried. She's pregnant."

THIRTEEN

Long before I turned inland on the drive home to Aurora, the moon rose out of Lake Superior, full and yellow as a lemon. A long finger of light pushed across the surface of the dark water, pointing at me in what seemed an accusing way.

Jenny was pregnant. God, my little girl. If you'd tried to tell me at that moment that she was, in fact, a grown woman, I'd have grabbed you by the neck and wrung you like a mop. To me she wasn't much more than a child. And now she had a child of her own on the way. How screwed was that? There went the University of Iowa and that writer's workshop she was hot to get into. There went her future, everything she'd worked hard for over so many years down the drain, lost in a thoughtless moment, wiped away in a stupid spill of passion.

Though probably it wasn't a moment. Probably they'd been having sex for a while. They'd gone together since Jenny was a sophomore. That was a long time to remain celibate against an onslaught of hormones. I understood that. But Jo had been so certain of Jenny's sense of responsibility about sex. Why hadn't my daughter been responsible enough to be safe?

And Sean. He sure as hell wasn't innocent in all this. Him I wanted to use as a soccer ball.

With that finger of moonlight pointing at me, I wondered what I'd done or hadn't done that had helped bring this situation about. What kind of father was I? What kind had I been?

Then there was Meloux. His health had apparently taken a remarkable turn after I told him I would go to Thunder Bay. The old Mide believed he would finally see his son. As nearly as I could tell, that belief alone had been enough to work a miracle.

Now what was I going to tell him? What kind of son was I offering him? I was afraid of what the truth might do to the old man. But if I hedged in any way, Meloux would know.

It was nearly midnight when I pulled onto Gooseberry Lane and turned into my driveway. Jo was waiting up. The kids had gone to bed. She kissed me and settled on the sofa beside me.

"You look tired," she said.

"And sore." I told her about Morrissey, the kidney punch and the kick.

"Let me see."

I lifted my shirt, and she checked my back.

"Oh, Cork, there's an ugly bruise forming. Do you think you should have it checked?"

"A handful of ibuprofen before I go to bed and I'll be fine."

"These men, they sound perfectly awful."

"How do I tell Henry?"

"Be straight with him. Anything else and he'll know you're not being truthful."

"It might kill him."

"I don't think so. I think it was the not knowing that hurt him. But how a good man like Henry could have fathered a son like this Wellington, I don't know."

I looked around the living room. "Where's Walleye?"

"In the backyard, sleeping in the tent with Stevie."

"Stevie knows Walleye will be going home tomorrow?"

She nodded. "He took it pretty hard, poor little guy."

Everywhere I looked, nothing but disappointment.

"So," I said. "Jenny."

"She's confused, Cork."

"How long has she known?"

"A few days. Her period is usually regular as clockwork. When it was overdue, she did one of those home pregnancy tests."

"No chance the test was wrong?"

"She repeated it. Different brand, same result."

"Does Sean know?"

"Yes."

"What does Jenny want to do?"

"Go back in time and make different decisions would be my first guess."

"Don't we all. Really, what's she thinking?"

Jo hesitated. I knew I wasn't going to like what I heard.

"When she and Sean went for that drive to Lake Superior yesterday, it wasn't a pleasure trip. They went to a Planned Parenthood clinic in Duluth."

"An abortion?"

"She didn't do anything, Cork. She just wanted information."

"Oh, Jesus, Jo. This has got to be so hard for her."

"I'm glad you understand that."

"Why wouldn't I?" I looked at her, didn't hide that I was hurt. "She poured all this out to you because she's afraid of me, is that it?"

"She's not afraid of you, Cork. But she is afraid of what you'll think of her. You have no idea how much your respect means to her."

I felt exhausted and empty. I laid my head against Jo's shoulder. "I have to talk to her."

"She knows that."

"And we have to talk to Sean. His folks, too. Do they know?"

"He was going to tell them tonight. We'll probably be calling them tomorrow about the same time they call us."

"Guess this is the end of Paris."

"It doesn't mean their dreams will end, Cork."

"No, but it's one hell of a detour off the yellow brick road. What do we do?"

"What can we do? We tell her how we feel, we listen, we pray, we hope, and whatever she decides, we're there for her."

"Couldn't I just spank her and send her to her room?"

"You never spanked her."

"Maybe it's not too late."

She kissed the top of my head. "Ready for bed?"

"Let me check on Stevie and Walleye, then I'll be up."

I wandered out to the tent in the backyard. My son was in his sleeping bag, snoring softly. Walleye lay beside him. The old dog lifted his head when I peeked through the flap, and his tail brushed the tent floor.

A boy and his dog. Only, the dog belonged to someone else and would be going back when the sun came up.

I wasn't looking forward to morning. To wresting from my son his very good friend. To telling Meloux the truth about his own son. To listening while my daughter and the father of her baby tried to sort out what the hell their future might be.

I stood there in the dark of my backyard thinking that sometimes life sucks and that's all there is to it.

FOURTEEN

I was up early. Stevie walked into the kitchen from the backyard while I was making coffee. He rubbed his sleepy eyes.

"Hungry, guy?" I asked.

He nodded. "But I should feed Walleye first."

From the pantry, he took the bag of dried dog food we'd bought and went back outside. Through the kitchen window, I watched him fill the bowl—he'd insisted we buy a special dish for Walleye—then he sat in the grass and petted the dog while it ate. I saw his lips move, talking to his friend. When Walleye was finished, Stevie returned to the kitchen and put the dog food back in the pantry.

"After breakfast, you want to go with me when I take him to Henry?" I asked.

He looked dismal. "Okay."

We had raisin bran and orange juice I'd made in a pitcher from a can of frozen Minute Maid. I drank coffee. We were rinsing our dishes in the sink when Jo came in, wearing her white robe.

"We're off to see Meloux," I told her.

"We have to take Walleye back," Stevie explained, sounding brave.

Jo sat down and motioned Stevie to her. She hugged him. "I'm sure Henry misses him. He's all alone out there."

"Yeah."

You could tell he understood, but it didn't make him want to do cartwheels.

"How about you get Walleye into the Bronco," I said to him. "I'll be right there."

When he was gone, Jo looked up at me and said, "I didn't realize this would be so hard on him."

I poured her a cup of coffee. "He'll be fine."

"You know, a turtle's not much of a pet."

"Don't start, Jo." I handed her the coffee. "I thought I heard Jenny upstairs."

She took a sip. "She's throwing up in the bathroom. I think she'll go back to bed for a while after that. As soon as you get home, we should all talk."

I leaned down and kissed her cheek. "I'll come back in a gentle mood, promise."

Stevie was quiet in the Bronco. He kept his arm around Walleye, who sat between us, tongue hanging out, watching through the windshield. Walleye had always seemed to possess much of the same reasonable sensibility and patience as Meloux, but I'd never had much experience with dogs and didn't know whether it was common for pets to resemble the personalities of the people who kept them.

We drove north along Iron Lake past cabins and small resorts nestled among pines and spruce and stands of paper birch. At the north end of the lake, we turned off the paved highway onto the gravel county road that serviced the last of the resorts before the reservation began. It had been a dry summer, and the Bronco kicked up a thick tail of dust that hung a long time in the still morning air. A quarter mile along, I glanced into my rearview mirror and saw an SUV swing off the highway and plow into the cloud I'd raised. I felt a little bad throwing up all that dust, but there was nothing I could do about it.

Another mile and I pulled to the side of the road and parked near the double-trunk birch that marked the trail to Meloux's cabin. Stevie opened his door and Walleye leaped across him eagerly. The dog's tail was going crazy, and it was clear he was happy to be in his own territory again. Stevie saw it, too, and he sighed.

I opened my door just as the SUV behind us shot past. It was silver-gray, but coated everywhere with the red-brown dust of the county road, except for a couple of streaky arcs on the windshield where the wipers had tried to clean. I yanked the door shut, glad I'd pulled far off to the side. Whoever was driving the SUV couldn't have seen the Bronco in time to avoid hitting it. As it was, I almost lost the driver's door. The SUV sped past and kept heading northeast.

Stevie and Walleye trotted ahead. I trailed behind, noting my son's slumped little shoulders. I found myself agreeing with Jo. A turtle was no kind of pet for a boy.

We broke from the trees amid the buzz of the grasshoppers still infesting the woods. On Crow Point, smoke drifted up from the stovepipe on Meloux's cabin. Walleye loped ahead, barking. Meloux opened the door and stepped into view. He smiled at the sight of his old friend, bent down, and his ancient hands caressed the dog.

Looking up at us as we approached, he said in formal greeting, "*Anin*, Corcoran O'Connor. *Anin*, Stephen." He stood up. "*Migwech*," he finished, thanking us.

He had on a pair of worn khakis held up with new blue suspenders. The sleeves of his denim shirt were rolled above his elbows. He wore hiking boots, much scuffed about the toes. His long white hair fell over his shoulders. His eyes were clear and sharp. He looked healthy. He looked very much like the Meloux I'd known all my life.

"I have made coffee," he said, inviting us in.

We stepped out of the sunshine into the cool shade of his cabin. He closed the door, but not before a couple of grasshoppers slipped into the cabin with us.

There were three chairs around his table. Stevie and I sat down. Meloux went to his black potbelly stove where coffee sat perking in a dented aluminum pot. He poured dark brew into three cups already placed around the table, as if we'd been expected. Stevie looked at the coffee then at me. I nodded okay.

Walleye had padded quietly back and forth with Meloux. When the old man finally sat down, Walleye settled at his feet. Stevie watched the dog dolefully.

I sipped the coffee, which was hot and strong. "Henry, I was more than a little surprised to hear that you'd left the hospital."

The old man shook his head. "The surprise for me was finding myself there. I did not realize the weight I carried on my heart, it had been there so long. Tell me about my son."

Wisps of steam rose from our speckled blue cups. Stevie blew across the surface of his coffee and lifted his cup. He jerked back from the touch of the hot brew against his lips.

"He's a sick man, Henry."

I explained as simply as I could what I had observed. The old man listened without showing any emotion. As I talked, the two grasshoppers explored the cabin. When they took to the air, their wings made a sound like the rattle of tiny dry bones. They hit the wall a couple of times, small, dull thuds. Meloux didn't seem to notice.

When I finished, the old man said, "He would not come?"

"No, Henry."

Meloux nodded and stared for a little while out the small window at the sunlit meadow beside his cabin.

"It may be that the weight I felt on my heart was not mine alone. It may be that I felt his, too." He touched his chest. "*Miziweyaa*"—which meant wholeness—"is here. The way is always here. But sometimes a man needs help in understanding the way."

The coffee had cooled. Stevie took a polite sip and squeezed his eyes against the bitter taste.

"We will return to the island called Manitou," Meloux declared. "We will see my son together, and I will show him the way toward *miziweyaa*."

I started to object, but Meloux cut me off.

"If my son is ill in the way you say, we need to leave today, this afternoon."

Twice over I owed Meloux my life. And what was he asking for, really? In the decades I'd known him, I'd experienced things that had no rational explanation, and I felt the rightness of what he was pressing for now. Still, I was a man with obligations of my own.

"Tomorrow, Henry," I offered. "We'll go tomorrow. I have things to do first."

"What things?"

"I have a business to put in order. I have a wife to explain this to." I didn't mention Jenny. "Give me a day, Henry. One day. Please."

He seemed to realize what he'd asked. "I'm sorry, Corcoran O'Connor. I was being selfish."

But I was the one feeling selfish, knowing that if it were Stevie in trouble, sick in the way Meloux's son was sick, I'd want to leave immediately.

"First thing in the morning," I promised.

I reached into my shirt pocket and drew out the watch. I handed it to Henry. He opened it and spent a moment staring at the photograph inside.

"Come on, Stevie," I said, standing.

Stevie leaned over and patted Walleye. "Good-bye, boy."

Meloux got up, and the dog with him, and they saw us to the door. The meadow was full of grasshoppers. They jumped around in front of the cabin, climbed the log walls. A big grasshopper lit on Meloux's arm. He eyed the bug, and the bug eyed him.

"What do you make of all these insects?" I asked the old Mide.

He thought a moment. "The lakes and rivers are full of grasshoppers. The fish who eat them are fat. The bears who eat the fish are fat. If our people still ate the bear, we would all be fat." He grinned, plucked the bug off his arm, and put it on the ground, rather gently I thought. "Tomorrow, Corcoran O'Connor. When the sun comes up, I will be ready."

We crossed the meadow and entered the woods. Stevie kept in step beside me without a word. In that heavy silence, the walk back to the road felt long.

We found the Bronco covered with grasshoppers. They flew off the doors as we reached for the handles. The grill was full of the insects we'd plowed through on our way there.

When we were inside Stevie asked, "Are there grasshoppers everywhere?"

"I think so," I said. I put the key in the ignition.

"This many everywhere?" he said.

I was glad to see he was curious and had moved on to a subject other than Walleye.

"I don't think so, buddy," I said. "This is pretty unusual."

I turned the engine over.

"There were grasshoppers smashed all over the Canada car," Stevie said.

"What Canada car?"

I checked the road behind me, preparing to turn around and head toward town.

"The one that went by when we stopped."

"It was from Canada?" I looked over at my son. "How do you know?"

"The license plate in back. I saw it."

Even deep in his concern over giving Walleye back to Meloux, my son had caught details that escaped me. But then, I'd been more worried about the SUV taking off my door. It wasn't necessarily a significant thing. Canadians came across the border into Minnesota all the time. But it struck me as chillingly coincidental, especially in light of the fact that up the gravel road where the SUV had gone there was no real destination.

Instead of turning around, I drove straight ahead. Not far from the double-trunk birch, I came to one of the old logging trails, unused for so long it was mostly overgrown with weeds. Parked just far enough among the trees off the road so that it couldn't be too easily seen was the SUV.

I reached across to the glove box where I kept my cell phone, intending to call the sheriff's department, but I was too far north of town to get a signal. I swung the Bronco around so quickly Stevie fell against his door.

"What are you doing, Dad?"

"Henry's in trouble."

"Why?"

"I don't know, son. I just know he is."

I drove past the trail to Henry's cabin. A quarter mile farther I came to a lane that headed toward Iron Lake. A big wood-burned sign was posted at the entrance to the lane. NORTHERN LIGHTS RESORT. The resort cabins stood on the shoreline a couple of hundred yards through the trees. They were owned by Melissa and Joe Krick, both Aurora natives. I'd known them all my life.

I said to Stevie, "I want you to run as fast as you can down to the Kricks'. Tell them that Henry's in trouble, that someone's trying to hurt him. Tell them to call the sheriff's office and get deputies out to Henry's cabin right away."

"What are you going to do?"

"Try to help Henry."

"I want to be with you."

"Just do what I ask," I snapped at him. He looked surprised and hurt. "This is important, Stevie. For me and for Henry and for Wall-eye." I reached across him and popped his door open. "Go. As fast as you can. Go!"

He hesitated a moment more, then leaped out and his little legs pumped like crazy as he ran down the dirt lane.

FIFTEEN

I'd used precious minutes taking Stevie to the Kricks'. I didn't really think the sheriff's people would arrive in time to be of use, but I wanted to be certain Stevie was out of harm's way.

I pulled to the side of the road at the double-trunk birch. I jumped out, ran to the rear of the Bronco, and popped the tailgate. There was a locked toolbox welded to the frame in back, which I opened with one of the keys on my ring. Inside was a smaller lockbox. I opened that with another key. The lockbox held a basket-weave holster, a .38 police special wrapped in oilcloth, and six cartridges. As a result of incidences that had occurred when I was sheriff of Tamarack County, I'd taken to keeping the firearm in the Bronco, close at hand. I pulled it out once in a while to clean it, but since I'd given up my badge, I hadn't fired it except to practice.

I slipped the holster on my belt, filled the cylinder of the .38, and slapped it closed. I dropped the weapon into the holster and secured the snap. Then I hit the trail at a sprint, heading for Meloux's place.

I'd completed two marathons in my life, but during all the unpleasantness on Chicago's North Shore the year before, I'd taken a bullet in my leg and I still wasn't a hundred percent. I figured I could make it the half mile to the clearing in three or four minutes. I was breathing hard by the time I reached Wine Creek, halfway to the cabin. As I danced over the stones that formed a loose bridge across the stream, I heard Walleye begin barking fiercely in the distance ahead. A few moments later came a rifle shot and a pained yelp and Walleye stopped barking. A second shot followed immediately.

I reached the edge of the trees. Much as I wanted to bolt for the cabin to check on Meloux, I forced myself to stop. From the shadows

I surveyed the clearing, the cabin, the outhouse. Except for the grasshoppers springing up everywhere among the wildflowers and the long grass, nothing moved.

The door to Meloux's cabin stood open, but I couldn't see anything in the dark inside.

Two shots. Heavy weapon. A rifle.

I scanned the meadow, the lakeshore, and finally eyed the outcrop of rocks just beyond Meloux's cabin. A path led from the cabin through the rocks to a fire ring where Meloux often sat and burned cedar and sage to clear his spirit. It would provide good cover if someone wanted to take out the old man.

The meadow grass stood more than knee high. I lay on my belly and crawled from the trees into the grass, making my way slowly across the clearing. Every few yards I lifted my head to check the situation.

As I neared the cabin, I heard a low wail. It came from the rocks where the trail snaked through to the fire ring. I paused, listened, and finally understood. I got to my feet and cautiously took the trail from the cabin. Beyond the rocks, I found Meloux.

The old Mide sat cross-legged near the circle of stones, which was full of ash from many fires. At his back, the blue water of Iron Lake stretched away, a perfect mirror of a cloudless sky. Next to him lay Walleye, a graze of blood along his flank. The dog licked at the wound. In front of Meloux, facedown, was sprawled the body of a man. The back of his head had exploded in a gaping wound full of white skull fragments, raw pink brain matter, and blood.

Meloux's eyes were closed as he sang. I recognized the chant. He was singing the dead man along the Path of Souls.

I sat down and waited. When he finished, the old man looked at me.

"Are you all right, Henry?" I asked.

"I am confused." His dark eyes dropped to the dead man, where a grasshopper crawled across the thick, white neck. "He hunted me. What kind of game is an old man like me?"

"What happened?"

"You left and Walleye sensed something. He's old like me, but that nose of his is like a pup's. The scent he caught was not good, I could tell. I took my rifle from the wall and I put in a cartridge. We were downwind of the rocks, which would be a good place for a bad man to hide. I was not thinking it was a man, though, but a different animal—a wolf, maybe, or a mountain lion. So he surprised me. But a man does not get old like me without luck. Just before he fired, a grasshopper flew into his face. His shot went wide. Mine did not." Meloux reached out and gently patted Walleye. "His bullet nicked my good friend. My good companion." He shook his head. "What satisfaction is there in hunting an old man and an old dog?"

I got to my feet and walked to the body. Although I knew I shouldn't move it, I rolled the corpse just enough to see the face. Meloux's bullet had entered the right eye, but the features were still quite recognizable.

I'd never again have to worry about turning my back on Henry Wellington's bodyguard. Edward Morrissey was dead.

SIXTEEN

When I resigned as sheriff of Tamarack County, I gave as my reason the ill effect the position had on my family and personal life. In light of all that had happened in the weeks before my resignation, most people seemed to understand. For a couple of months, Captain Ed Larson, who headed up major crime investigations for the sheriff's department, performed the duties as acting sheriff. But Ed made it abundantly clear that he didn't want the job permanently. When the county commissioners finally got around to holding a special election, one of my best deputies ran for the position and won: Marsha Dross. I'd hired her as the first female law enforcement officer in the department. Eight years later, she became the county's first female sheriff.

She stood just inside the doorway of Meloux's cabin, leaning against the wall with her arms crossed, listening while Ed sat with me at the table, taking me through the questions. She was tall, with hair the color of an acorn and cut short. When I was sheriff, I wore the uniform. The guy before me had preferred three-piece suits and looked like a banker. Dross had her own look. She generally wore jeans, neatly creased, a tasteful sweater or flannel shirt from the likes of Lands' End, and a pair of chukka boots. The ensemble looked good at a town meeting, but wasn't at all out of place at a crime scene in the Northwoods.

The motorboat the department used for patrolling Iron Lake had come up from Aurora. Morrissey's body, zipped in a bag, had been loaded aboard and transported to the marina in town where it would be transferred to a hearse and taken to Nelson's Funeral Home, there to be kept in cold storage until a decision had been made about whether to perform an autopsy. Cause of death was pretty apparent, and Tamarack County's budget would be sorely affected by the cost of the autopsy, so my sense was that in this case, the postmortem examination would be relatively perfunctory.

I'd told Ed everything I'd observed that morning. I'd also told him about my trip to Thunder Bay. He was going over it all again to be certain of the details and to try to make sense of the attack on Meloux. He'd already interviewed the old Mide, who'd been taken into town to give a full, written statement. Jo was going to meet him there to make certain he had legal representation. Meloux had told Ed everything, so I didn't see any reason to hold back.

"Did Morrissey see the watch?" Dross asked. It was the first question she'd offered in the interview.

I nodded. "When Wellington tossed it to me."

"You're sure he hadn't seen it before that?"

"When I met him at the marina in Thunder Bay, he gave me the box and indicated he didn't know what was in it."

"Considering what he tried here, he doesn't strike me as a man whose word ought to be taken at face value," Dross said. "Where's the watch?"

"Meloux has it."

"Worth much, do you think?"

"You're asking the wrong guy, Marsha. To me, the prize in a box of Cracker Jacks is a big deal."

"What I'm getting at—"

"I know what you're getting at, and I don't know. I suppose Morrissey could have been after the watch, but I can't imagine it's worth a man's life."

In the cool corner of the cabin where he lay, Walleye moved and whimpered a little. Meloux and I had taken a good look at the wound. The bullet had grazed a path a few inches long across the dog's left haunch. It had stopped bleeding, but stitches would be a good idea. I told Meloux when he left for the sheriff's department not to worry, that as soon as we could, Stevie and I would get Walleye to a vet.

"It's possible the watch was more important to Wellington than you realized," Larson said. "Maybe he sent Morrissey after it."

"And killing the old man was the way?"

"That could have been Morrissey's idea," Dross said. "Where were you exactly when you handed the watch back to Meloux?"

"Sitting right here at this table."

Dross walked over and looked through the window toward the rocks where Meloux had been attacked.

"Morrissey had field glasses," she said. "He could easily have observed the exchange of the watch and known it was in Meloux's possession."

"Okay," Larson said, moving us along, "the watch is a possible motive. What else?"

"Have you got an idea, Ed?" I asked.

"As a matter of fact. How about rage?"

Ed Larson was the brightest officer in the department, always had been. When I was first elected sheriff many years ago, I'd sent Ed to Quantico to learn from the FBI. He'd gone back periodically for training in profiling and other areas related to law enforcement. He didn't just look at the known facts of a crime. More often than not, he had a pretty good speculation about the psychology behind the crime. This time, however, I wasn't so sure.

"Rage?" I said.

"Directed at the father who wasn't there his whole life, then suddenly shows up out of the blue. You said Wellington's mental state was precarious."

"I said he wasn't hitting on all cylinders, but I didn't say I thought he was capable of murder. Especially the murder of his father."

"You didn't say it," Dross threw in, "but what do you think?"

"I spoke with the man for ten minutes. I honestly couldn't say."

Dross nodded, returned to the wall, crossed her arms, and leaned back. "Clearly we need to interview him."

Larson stood up. "I'll call the provincial authorities as soon as I get back to the office, start setting things up."

Dross said, "It's incredible that an old man like Meloux got the drop on somebody like this Morrissey."

"Incredible?" I shook my head. "There's almost nothing about Henry Meloux that would surprise me anymore."

We were the last to leave the scene. Larson and Dross walked ahead of me on the trail through the meadow and into the trees, which was the only way to get from Meloux's back to the road. Those who came to see Meloux came on foot. I walked more slowly than the other two, keeping company with Walleye, who was limping. I considered carrying him, but it wouldn't have been comfortable for either of us. We just took our time.

When we reached my Bronco, the road was empty, though a cloud of yellow dust kicked up by the sheriff's vehicle still hung over it. Morrissey's SUV had been impounded, would be gone over for evidence. I helped Walleye up onto the seat, then set out for the Kricks' resort, where Stevie was waiting for me.

Melissa pointed me to the dock. I found Stevie sitting with his feet dangling in the water. From there, Crow Point, where Meloux's cabin stood, was a small sliver of dark land far in the distance. He was looking in that direction when I came up beside him.

"It's all over," I said quietly.

He jumped up and hugged me.

I bent and kissed the top of his head. "Melissa said she told you Henry was okay."

He turned his face up toward mine, and I saw the ghost of worry still there. "I was still kind of scared."

"She say anything else about what happened at Meloux's?"

"No."

"Why don't you come on home with me and I'll tell you everything. Walleye's waiting for us. He's hurting a little. He could use some good attention."

"Oh boy." He grabbed his sneakers and socks and ran ahead, toward the cabins.

First stop was Hakala's Animal Clinic. We were walk-ins and had to wait a bit. I dialed the number for Jo's cell phone. She told me that she and Meloux had finished at the sheriff's department and were at the house. She said the girls were at Sam's Place and had everything there under control.

Stevie went into the exam room with me when Leslie Hakala, who was in practice with her father, Einer, called us in. She took a look at the wound. Walleye patiently suffered the probing of her fingers around the area.

"Bullet, you say?" She looked up at me. "Careless hunter?"

"A bad guy," Stevie said. "He tried to kill Henry Meloux, but missed and got Walleye instead."

The vet's eyebrows lifted noticeably. "That so?" She glanced at me. "The old Indian who lives up north?"

"Yeah."

"Why would anyone want to kill him?"

"Long story," I said. "And the details are still sketchy. What about Walleye here?"

"Well, I think we'll deaden the area and clean it good, put a few stitches in, and that should be fine. You'll have to watch him closely for a while though, make sure no infection sets in."

"We will," Stevie assured her. He petted the dog earnestly.

She tried to get more information from me as she worked, but I held back on the harsher details. In a town like Aurora, she'd hear them soon enough.

We left the clinic and made a quick stop at Sam's Place. Just as Jo had said, Jenny and Annie had things well under control. They'd called in their friends and were busy with the lunch rush. They knew, more or less, what had happened and were full of questions, but I didn't want to talk about it between customers. I told them I'd be back later and we'd discuss it then.

Jenny avoided looking at me directly. That was fine. It wasn't the right time or place for us to deal with her situation. I thanked them all and returned to the Bronco, where Stevie and Walleye patiently waited.

It was going on two o'clock when I pulled into the drive on Gooseberry Lane. We'd been gone six hours, but it felt like days. A lot had happened since Stevie and I sat at the kitchen table munching our raisin bran. I realized, as we stepped into the cool of the house, that I was hungry. I smelled something cooking and, following my nose, I found Jo and Meloux in the kitchen eating fried bologna sandwiches—the Ojibwe often call bologna "Indian steak"—leftover Jell-O salad, and chips. They both were drinking a diet Pepsi.

"You guys okay?" I asked.

"Good," Meloux answered. "We are good. And Walleye?"

"He's with Stevie in the backyard. The vet stitched him up and gave me some antibiotic pills he'll need to take for a while to fight infection."

"Hungry?" Jo asked, and began to get up.

I waved her back down. "Relax. I'll fix it."

I started a flame under the skillet that still sat on a burner of the stove and took the bologna from the refrigerator.

"Henry and I have been trying to figure out why this Morrissey tried to kill him," Jo said.

"Marsha, Ed, and I have been doing the same. You guys come up with anything?"

Jo sipped her Pepsi. "I think it was the watch. Henry showed it to me. It's gold, quite original, and could be valuable."

"What do you think, Henry?"

"Just an old watch," Meloux replied with a shrug. "Important to me, but who am I?"

I slapped two slices of bologna in the skillet, one for me, one for Stevie.

"Henry, it may be that Morrissey was sent to get the watch."

Meloux fixed his dark, unwavering eyes on me. "I do not believe my son would ask that man to kill me."

"Maybe the killing wasn't part of his instructions. Morrissey may have come up with that on his own."

Stevie stepped into the kitchen.

I nodded toward the skillet. "I've got a fried bologna sandwich coming up in a minute, buddy. Hungry?"

"Can I eat outside?" he asked.

"Sure. Milk and chips with that?"

"Thanks."

Jo left the table and hugged Stevie. "That was very important, what you did this morning."

"What did I do?" Stevie said.

"Getting the Kricks to call the sheriff."

"That was easy." Stevie looked down. "I should have been with Dad and Henry and Walleye."

"Your mom's right, guy," I said. "What you did was exactly what you needed to do. We're very proud of you."

Stevie didn't look convinced. He squirmed out of Jo's arms and said to Meloux, "Walleye's okay, Henry."

"I have been told. Stephen, I would like to ask a big favor."

"Sure."

"I will be gone for a while. Will you take care of my friend for me?"

"Will I!" he said eagerly.

"Gone?" I turned from the stove.

"Tomorrow we will go to see my son."

I shook my head. "Things have changed, Henry. A man's dead. There's a police investigation in progress. Until they've had a chance to interview Henry Wellington, we need to keep out of this. Besides, I'd say it's doubtful at best that Wellington would agree to see you."

"I will offer the watch."

"Henry, I know how important this is to you, but you need to be patient. Let the police do their work first."

"I know about patience," the old man said testily. I couldn't remember Meloux ever getting upset with me, but it was clear he was headed in that direction. "This is something else, and it must be done quickly."

"Like the vet sewing up Walleye?" Stevie offered.

"Yes, Stephen," Meloux said. "My son is not well. He needs me to heal him."

Jo pointed toward the stove. "Cork, your bologna's burning."

The doorbell rang. Jo brought back Meloux's nephew, Ernie Champoux, who'd come for the old man. Until this business was concluded, Ernie intended to have his great-uncle stay with him. He'd taken a couple of days off from work for that reason.

"Sunrise tomorrow, I will be ready," Meloux said as he went out the front door.

"Henry, I won't be there," I called after him. I didn't like being brusque, but I wasn't going to back down. Seeing his son at this juncture was a bad idea on so many levels.

Meloux stopped, turned, and his eyes hit me like a couple of rocks.

"Give the authorities a little time, Henry," I tried, "then we'll see."

He didn't reply. I watched, feeling like a lousy son of a bitch, as he walked to Ernie's truck, which was parked at the curb. Ernie pulled away with Meloux beside him, sitting stiff as iron and staring straight ahead.

Jo took my arm. "Do you really think it would be so bad for Henry to see his son?"

"A man tried to kill him—we have no idea why—and that man's dead. Rushing ahead is a terrible idea. Hell, Meloux's waited seventy years to see his son. Will a couple more days make much difference?"

I went back to the kitchen. My burned fried bologna was cold. I looked out the window. Stevie was feeding his burned bologna to Walleye.

SEVENTEEN

Later that afternoon I returned to Sam's Place. The rush was over, and the girls were listening to the radio. Jenny wasn't there.

"Sean picked her up a little while ago," Anne said. "We're doing fine without her. So how's Henry?"

Kate Buker and Jodi Bollendorf, the two girls helping out that day, leaned against the serving counter and listened as eagerly as Anne.

"Confused," I said.

"We heard the dead guy's from Canada," Kate said.

"Yes."

"He, like, followed you back, right?" Anne said.

"That's how it looks."

She scrunched her freckled face in bewilderment. "Dad, why would anyone try to kill a nice old guy like Henry?"

The question of the day. I told them the police on both sides of the border were working on that one.

"What about you, Mr. O'Connor?" Jodi asked. "Anne said you've got a license to be a private investigator. Like that old *Rockford Files* show, right? This is your kind of thing."

"And Henry's your friend," Anne added.

"Customers," I said, pointing toward the people spilling from a blue van in the parking lot.

The rest of the afternoon turned out to be full of folks who were as interested in what happened out at Meloux's cabin as in ordering food. I deflected their questions as best I could, but it amazed me how much information was already abroad in Aurora.

Around five thirty, Wally Schanno pulled up in his red Ford pickup. He stepped out, holding a leash. A little black-and-white puppy leaped down from the seat after him and immediately peed on the truck's front tire. Schanno waited patiently. The little dog finished and began sniffing its way across the lot toward the Quonset hut. It caught the scent of the Dumpster and tried to pull Schanno that way, but Wally held back. Eventually they both made it to the serving window.

Annie leaned out and cooed, "What a cute puppy. Is it yours, Mr. Schanno?"

"Yeah," Schanno said. He didn't sound ecstatic. "Her name's Trixie."

"What is she?"

"A mutt. Part border collie, part greyhound, part God knows what. I got her from Sally Fellows. She's a handful, all right. Say, Cork," he called past Anne. "Talk to you a minute?"

"Meet you round back," I said.

When I stepped outside, Trixie was all over me. She barely reached my knees, but she kept trying to jump higher.

"She's got a lot of energy, Wally." I knelt down to pet her. Her face was a black mask on a white background, with a couple of soft brown eyes staring out. "Did you get her for security or companionship?"

"Security I can take care of on my own. I figured I was spending too much time by myself in the house. I thought maybe a dog'd help. Hey, Cork, I heard about what went down at Henry Meloux's place. Is he doing okay?"

"He's fine, Wally."

We stood in the sun. Trixie nosed at the gravel in the lot. Schanno scratched his neck with his huge hand and squinted. He was getting around to something, taking his time.

"Sounds like trouble followed you down from Thunder Bay. Going back?" he asked.

"Meloux's pushing me to. He wants to go with me."

"True he's got a son up there?"

"Where'd you hear that?"

He shrugged. He was wearing a short-sleeved khaki shirt, pressed jeans, a belt with a big silver buckle, looking almost natty. It was good to see him taking an interest in his appearance again. And in having company around. I watched Trixie tug at the leash, eager to get at the Dumpster.

"So, are you going back?" he asked.

"If Meloux had his way, we'd already be on the road."

"But?"

I looked up at him and said impatiently, "There's an international investigation under way. Do you think I want to step into the middle of that?"

"Come on, Cork. Across borders, nothing moves fast."

"Including me. Look, I'm guessing you're here thinking that there's something major in the works and maybe you can help with it. Well, I'm telling you that's not the case. I've done what I promised for Henry Meloux, and I'm finished. The police will take it from here, and that's fine with me. All right?"

He eyed me, surprised. "You're not even curious?"

"Of course I'm curious. Hell, I feel responsible. That guy followed me out to Meloux's. Damn, I should have spotted him."

"Give yourself a break," Schanno suggested. "You had a lot on your mind."

"I'm not about to make matters worse by wading in any deeper. I've got a business to run. I've got a family to think about. We're not cops anymore, you and me. Let's let the people who're wearing the badges do their jobs, okay?"

A grasshopper banged against the side of the Quonset hut and fell into the gravel at our feet. Trixie tried to attack it and yanked Schanno hard. The grasshopper took an enormous hop. Trixie leaped at it, hit the end of the leash, and fell back with a pained yelp.

"All right, then," Schanno said curtly. He turned away and walked Trixie back to his truck.

I watched him go, feeling not at all good about how I'd treated him, but wondering, too, resentfully, why it was that everyone else seemed to have such a clear idea of what I ought to do.

Sheriff Marsha Dross drove into the parking lot of Sam's Place in the brittle blue light well after sunset. In town, the streetlamps and the shop lights had come on. I don't have a big lighted sign for the Quonset hut, just a tall pole with a halogen lamp on top that brightens the area in front of the serving windows. Dross got out of her cruiser, came up to the windows, and asked to see me outside. That's never a good sign.

We walked to the picnic table under the big red pine near the shoreline. We were out of the light there. A warm wind blew across Iron Lake and small waves slapped near our feet. The moon wasn't up yet, and the other side of the lake was sliding into restless black.

Dross got right to the point.

"Cork, you said Morrissey worked for Henry Wellington."

"That's right."

"According to the Canadian authorities Ed Larson spoke with, Morrissey runs a guide service, takes hunters and fishermen up into the wilderness of northern Ontario."

"The only place he guided me was out to Manitou Island."

"Where, according to the Ontario police, Henry Wellington is not currently in residence. They say they're trying to talk to Rupert Wellington, but he's been unavailable."

"Unavailable?"

"Whatever that means."

"He was in Thunder Bay yesterday and quite available. And Henry Wellington was definitely on Manitou Island. Are you getting good information?"

Even in the dark, I could see the consternation on her face. "It's all being done by fax and phone. They're sending an investigator down to talk to us, maybe tomorrow or the next day."

"Why doesn't Ed pay them a visit?"

"They haven't exactly invited us. Ed thinks we're being stonewalled."

"What do you think?"

"Why would they stonewall us?" she asked.

"Pressure from powerful people, maybe. The Wellingtons are powerful. Or maybe a little territorial posturing. They're not always happy with their neighbors to the south. Maybe they're just busy and doing things as they're able. The shooting didn't occur in their jurisdiction." I stood up and stretched my back. The place where Morrissey had sucker-punched me was feeling pretty sore. "Did Morrissey have family?"

"Not that we've been able to identify so far. The Ontario police are still checking."

"So maybe in the end he's the kind of man nobody cared much about alive or dead."

"And maybe the kind of guy who'd kill an old man over an antique watch? I don't know."

"Neither do I. Care to speculate?"

"I don't know enough."

"So what are you going to do?" I asked.

She stood up and stared out at the lake that was almost fully black now. "Just be patient, I guess. I'll see what the Ontario investigator has to say and go from there." She turned to me. "But, Cork, if Morrissey wasn't acting on his own, the people who sent him still don't have what they want, whether it's the watch or Henry Meloux dead."

"He's with his nephew, Ernie Champoux, out on the rez. Strangers come looking for him, word'll get out fast, and nobody's going to give them directions."

"All right," she said. She headed back to her cruiser.

After the sheriff left, I went inside. "Let's close up early," I told the girls. "You guys have had a hard day."

"Like you haven't," Anne said.

I called Jo and told her I was going out to the rez to check on Meloux.

"Cork, Jenny's here. She wants to talk."

"Can it wait until after I see Meloux?"

"Will you be long?"

"I don't think so."

"We'll wait up," Jo said.

EIGHTEEN

It wasn't hard dark yet as I headed up the eastern shoreline of Iron Lake toward the reservation. In the west, the sky still held a whisper of pale blue daylight. Far across the water, the lights of isolated cabins and resorts had emerged, like the eyes of night animals awakening. The road was empty, but I took it slow anyway. Twilight's when the deer and moose haunt the edges of highways.

Ernie Champoux had been twice married, both times to smart, pretty women. Neither of the marriages took, but the divorces sure took Ernie. Because he was Iron Lake Ojibwe, he received a nice distribution from the casino profits, but much of that money went right out in alimony. Ernie also liked vehicles. He had snowmobiles, ATVs, a personal watercraft, motorcycles—two dirt bikes and a slick red Suzuki—a couple of pickups, an SUV, a station wagon, and an old yellow VW bug he'd spent a good deal of time restoring. What money didn't go for supporting the lifestyles of his ex-wives went to maintaining his fleet. As a result, Ernie held down a job. He'd been employed at the Chippewa Grand Casino since it had opened several years earlier. These days he worked swing shift, heading up a maintenance crew.

So I was surprised when I approached his cabin, which was situated in a stand of poplars on the lakeshore just south of Allouette, and the old VW pulled out of his drive and swung wide, directly into the path of my Bronco. I swerved. The VW jerked back toward the proper lane and rolled on down the road. I watched the taillights in my rearview mirror. The brake lights flashed a good deal. Whoever was driving was riding the brake pedal. I was concerned they were drunk, but I wasn't a cop anymore, and chasing down a DUI wasn't my responsibility.

Champoux's vehicles were parked in a neat row next to the garage where he did all his own maintenance and mechanic work. I saw that there were a couple of gaps, like missing teeth, in the row. Gone were one of Ernie's pickups and the VW. I thought about the Bug I'd narrowly missed and figured a relative of Ernie's had taken it. On the rez, property was loaned and borrowed freely. Lights were on in the cabin, and I hoped Meloux was still up, though it was late for an old man, especially an old man who lit his own place with a kerosene lamp. I wore my knuckles out on the door. Finally I tried the knob.

"Henry!" I called and poked my head inside. "Ernie! It's Cork O'Connor."

Ernie Champoux kept his vehicles in better shape than he did his home. There was clutter everywhere and the sour smell of a dishcloth gone too long without washing. I checked the place briefly. No one was home.

Then I thought about the VW driven by someone who'd been drinking. Not a drunk, I realized, but an old man who never drove.

I caught up with him near the south end of the lake. He'd stopped dead in the road and was standing in front of the VW, staring toward the woods. I pulled up behind the Bug, got out.

"I hit a deer," he said sadly. "It ran off into the woods, but it is hurt."

"We can't follow it in this dark."

The old man nodded.

"Where were you going, Henry?"

Meloux turned his gaze toward the road ahead, lit for fifty yards by headlights. His own shadow created a long, dark emptiness there. His voice held no trace of apology. "Canada."

What I'd figured.

"You don't have a driver's license, do you, Henry?"

"No."

"How did you intend to get across the border?"

"I was going to think about that on the way. For a man who knows what he wants, there is always a way."

"Let's park the VW and pick it up tomorrow. Then we can go back to your nephew's place and talk. I'd like to know the whole story, Henry, how you came to have a son you've never seen."

He drew himself up. In the glare of the headlights, his eyes were like fire. "These things I will tell you, but secrets come at a price."

"What price, Henry?"

"You will take me to Manitou Island. You will take me to my son."

"I can't promise."

"Then, Corcoran O'Connor, we cannot talk."

"Wait here."

I slid into the VW, which was still running, and parked it on the gravel shoulder.

"Let's go back to Ernie's," I said, walking to the Bronco. "I'll think about your offer."

I drove slowly, watching carefully for deer and rolling around in my mind the deal the old Mide had laid out. It was clear he was determined, one way or another, to see his son. The truth was that I wanted to be there when he did. Based on my own recent experience, I knew he'd need someone to watch his back. Also, the story Meloux had kept to himself for more than seven decades was one I wanted very much to hear.

The old man had me. That was all there was to it.

I parked at the cabin, and we went inside.

"Where's Ernie?" I asked. "He told me he'd taken a couple of days off."

"A man is sick. They called. My nephew went."

Considering the attack on Meloux that morning, the choice Ernie had made didn't seem a good one. On the other hand, in all this, I'd miscalculated a lot myself, so who was I to criticize?

"All right, Henry. You've got a deal," I said. "Tell me your story, and we'll go to Thunder Bay together."

He looked around at the clutter in the cabin. "Not here. We will sit by the lake. We will smoke. Then I will talk, and you will listen."

I took a pack of Marlboros from a carton Ernie kept on top of his refrigerator, and I found a box of wooden matches in a kitchen drawer. We left the cabin and walked across the backyard, through the poplars to the lake. The moon had just risen, and its reflection cut a path across the black water solid enough to walk on. We sat on a bench Ernie had fashioned from a split log set on a couple of stumps. I handed Meloux the pack of cigarettes. He took one out, tore the paper, crumbled the tobacco into his hand, and made an offering. Then he tapped out a cigarette for each of us. We smoked a few minutes in silence. For Henry, as for many Shinnobs, tobacco is a sacred element, and smoking has nothing to do with habit.

"You have always thought of me as old, Corcoran O'Connor."

"You are old, Henry. God only knows how old."

"When you were born, I was in my forty-third year."

"That's pretty old to a kid. Besides, as long as I've known you, your hair's been white as a bleached sheet."

"It was not always that color. In my nineteenth year, it turned white overnight."

"What happened?"

"It was something I saw, Corcoran O'Connor. And something I did."

Meloux studied the moon, and I waited.

PART II
MELOUX'S STORY

NINETEEN

He didn't keep track of years by numbers, but it was the same year President Harding died and Calvin Coolidge took his place in the White House. Sometime in the early '20s, probably. He remembered Coolidge because in a certain way the man was like the Ojibwe. He didn't speak much, but when he did he was worth listening to.

That day Henry watched the farmer's son coming across the field of low corn. Under the brim of a straw hat, the kid's face was dark with shadow. He was taller than Henry and, at seventeen, older by two years. He looked like the farmer, right down to the mean little eyes.

It was late June, hot in South Dakota, and Henry worked in overalls without a shirt. His shoes, supplied by the government boarding school in Flandreau, were falling apart. Although he'd tried to line the shoes with straw to block the holes, dirt and pebbles still found their way inside. Periodically, he stopped his work to remove the shoes and dump them clean. He was sitting at the edge of a dry irrigation ditch with his left shoe off when he spotted the farmer's son approaching.

"My old man don't pay you to sit on your ass," the kid said when he got to Henry.

"Your old man doesn't pay me at all," Henry pointed out. He put on his left shoe and began to remove the other.

"You eat his food, sleep under his roof," the kid threw back.

Henry could have pointed out that this choice was not his. The Flandreau school had a policy called "outing" that placed the Indian students in jobs during the summer months. The girls typically became domestics, the boys farmhands. The school superintendent spoke of the program proudly, claiming it taught skills that the students would use to better themselves, that would help them assimilate. But Henry Meloux had no use for farmwork. In the Northwoods of Minnesota, where his people lived, there was little farmland. He knew the truth of the outing program; usually a placement simply provided cheap labor for a local family.

Henry took his time with his second shoe while the other kid stood above him, arms crossed over his chest, watching with that disdain common to the whites in the communities around the Flandreau school.

"Ain't you one ungrateful son of a bitch," the farmer's son said.

Henry finished with his shoes and stood up. "You walked a long way out here just to tell me that."

"How come you never look at me?" the kid said.

"I look."

"You never look me in the eye."

"I have work to do," Henry told him. He picked up the shovel that he'd laid in the dirt, ready to return to the irrigation ditch he'd been cleaning.

"Look me in the eye," the kid demanded.

Henry paused, half turned away.

"You heard what I said. Look me in the eye."

The prairie sun pressed on Henry like a hot iron. He felt the crawl of sweat down his chest and back and sides, the sting of it dripping into his eyes. He gripped the handle of the shovel with his strong, calloused hands and gauged the heft, the easy swing.

"You deaf all of a sudden?"

Henry turned slowly. He lifted his dark eyes and stared at the other boy.

The farmer's son grinned with stupid satisfaction. "You got a letter up to the house. My old man says to come get it."

Henry pulled his shirt—long sleeved and white, made of thin cotton—from the branch of the bush next to the ditch where he'd hung it when he'd begun his work. He carried it with him as he followed the long rows between the knee-high corn plants, dirt sifting into his shoes at every step. At the farmhouse, he let the kid go inside first while he took a few minutes to dump his shoes clean again and to wash himself off at the water pump in the yard. He put on his shirt, buttoned it carefully all the way up to his throat, and went into the house through the back door.

The kitchen still smelled of dinner, the noon meal, which was two hours gone. It had been generous portions of boiled ham, baked chicken, fried potatoes, corn casserole, waxed beans, heavy brown bread, and rhubarb pie. The farmer's wife was a fine cook and a decent woman. When Henry had first come to the place, three weeks earlier, she'd stood firm that he should eat as well as any of the family because he worked his share. Mealtime, she put his plate together and brought it to the barn where he ate in his small quarters, which was an old tack room, no longer used for that purpose because the farmer, a prosperous man, had a Ford tractor now.

The farmer sat at the kitchen table drinking from a glass full of cloudy liquid. He was a tense, willowy man with a German name and a head as bald as a rock. Over his glass, his small, mean eyes took in Henry.

"Lemonade, Henry?" said the wife. She stood at the gaping oven door, her face red from the heat. She was small and plump. Her eyes were a sad blue.

"Thank you." Henry stood politely, just inside the door.

She filled the glass and took it to him, looking as if she were about to speak something comforting, but her husband cut in.

"A letter come for you. From the boarding school. Took the liberty of reading it since I wasn't sure you could."

"I can read," Henry said.

"The upshot of it is that your father's dead, boy. Logging accident. I understand it's dangerous work."

"Karl," the woman said. "Give the boy the letter and the decency of reading it on his own."

"You snap at me like that again, Emma, I'll take the strap to you. Don't think I won't."

"Yah, you lay me up and who's going to feed you, huh? Give the boy the letter."

The farmer reached into the shirt beneath his overalls and pulled out a folded sheet of paper. "Come on," he said holding it out. "Take it, boy."

"For heaven's sake." The woman plucked the letter from her husband's hand and brought it to Henry. "I'm so sorry. You take that lemonade and letter and you find you some shade. Take all the time you need, Henry."

He sat under a crab-apple tree near the vegetable garden he helped the woman hoe. The writing was neat, the letters precisely made.

> Dear Nephew,
>   It is sad news I tell you your father my brother die in that logging camp he works a white man drive here to tell me your father killed by log rolling over him he bring the body for me to bury and I have done beside your mother's grave this news is heavy on me and I know will be for you great sorrow.
>
>   Woodrow Meloux

There was no date on the letter, no way of knowing when the death had occurred. It didn't matter; it was done. His mother had died of tuberculosis three years before. His father worked as a logger and was away most of the time and could not care for his children. Henry had been sent to the Indian boarding school in Flandreau, South Dakota. His two younger sisters had gone to a boarding school in Wisconsin.

Henry read the letter again, folded it, and put it in his pocket.

Even in the shade the air felt thick, hot, heavy. He sat for a long time without drinking from the glass of lemonade the farmer's wife had given him. He listened to the bawling of cattle in the pen beyond the barn. He stared across the cultivated fields and his dark eyes followed the flat line of the horizon that circled and imprisoned him.

TWENTY

Long after dark, Henry rose from his cot in the old tack room. He put on his white shirt, overalls, and shoddy boarding-school shoes. He left the barn and walked out to the yard. Stars lay across the sky like a dusting of pollen, and the moon, nearly full, made everything around Henry silver. The farm dog, a German shepherd they called Joey, barked a couple of times, then recognized him and settled back onto the grass near the back door of the house. Henry started toward the dirt road that ran in front of the farmhouse, but stopped when he heard the hinges of the screen door creak.

She came toward him, a small, pale figure that seemed to float in her nightgown. Her feet were bare, but her hands were full. She held out a potato sack.

"You'll be hungry, I expect. It's not much. Couple of sandwiches, a jar of pickles, some cookies. And here." She put coins in his hand. "Fifty cents. It's all I can spare without him knowing. And take a blanket with you, the one on your bunk. You'll be sleeping out some, I expect."

He looked at the coins burning in the silver light. *"Migwech."*

She eyed him with puzzlement.

"It means thank you," he said.

"God be with you, Henry."

She floated back to the house.

He rolled the blanket and tied it with a length of scrap rope he found in the barn. He slung the bedroll and the potato sack over his shoulder and left.

He followed roads that headed toward the east, toward Minnesota. Near dawn he lay down in a haystack in a field far from any house. When he woke, the sun was not yet directly overhead. He ate one of the sandwiches, a pickle, and a cookie and took to the road again. Whenever he spotted dust rising ahead of or behind him, he lay in the tall grass at the side of the road until the vehicle had passed. When he was thirsty, he drank from the creeks along the way. Near sunset, on the outskirts of a small town, he came across a train paused on a siding, loading from a grain elevator. The engine was pointed east. Henry climbed onto a coupling between cars and waited. Just as the sun hit the horizon, the train pulled out.

Near sunset of the third day, he reached the mission on the Iron Lake Reservation. It was a small, white clapboard building in the middle of a forest clearing between the tiny communities of Allouette and Brandywine. Behind it lay the cemetery, enclosed by a low wrought-iron fence. The clearing was empty and quiet. The sun threw a soft blanket of yellow light across the meadow, and the mission walls were the color of buttered bread. Henry stood at the cemetery gate looking at the assortment of headstones and memorials and grave houses and at the long shadows they cast. He'd been here many times in the past. Under the white man's authority, Henry's people died too easily. Diseases, especially tuberculosis, took them in great numbers.

He eased the gate open. The hinges cried like a hurt dog. He knew the place where his mother was buried. Beside her marker was another: a smooth, varnished wood plank with his father's name burned across the face, and below that the figure of a cormorant, his father's clan, upside down to indicate death. He sat down cross-legged, weary to the bone. He'd determined along the way that when this moment came, he would not cry. At the boarding school, he'd never cried, though many nights he'd listened to the sobbing of other lonely, homesick boys. He understood that crying did no good. It could not change what had passed. It could not change what was, nor what was coming. Even so, he felt like spilling tears, felt more empty and alone than he ever had.

He lay down in the uncut cemetery grass, more tired than hungry, and went to sleep.

That night he had his first vision. It was like a dream, but it was not a dream. He stood outside himself, watching the part he played, feeling everything that occurred but at the same time remaining a separate observer. This was the vision: A huge white snake slithered among the stones and markers and grave houses of the cemetery. It swallowed Henry. Then it sprouted wings and took him on a long journey deep into the wilderness, far beyond Noopiming, the great woods of his home. It disgorged him on the shore of a lake he did not know. The lake glowed, as if a fire burned at the bottom. Fire under the water? How could this be? When he turned back, the snake had vanished.

He woke on the ground, curled and cramped, his blanket covered with dew. Dawn was just breaking, and he was hungry. It was mid-summer, blueberry season, and he knew where the patches grew. He feasted on ripe berries as the sun rose above the pines and he continued his way north, toward the cabin his father had built. He figured the boarding school had probably alerted the local authorities that he'd run away, and he kept off the main roads, following instead the forest trails he'd known since childhood. He saw not a soul that morning, a good sign, he decided.

It was nearly noon when he reached the small cabin where he'd been born—and his sisters, too—where he'd spent the first twelve years of his life collecting fine memories that would remain strong even when he was an old man. The cabin stood at the edge of a pond. The water was still and blue and full of reeds along the edges. Wild grass had grown up around the cabin, and honeysuckle vines crept up the log walls. Henry came toward it slowly, with the knowledge that what awaited him there was little different from what the cemetery had offered. But he had nowhere else to go. He pushed the door open and stepped inside.

It was one room, mostly bare now, with a plank floor. The table where his family had eaten was overturned. One chair remained. The black stove that had heated the cabin and on which his mother had cooked was there, the stovepipe still thrust through the roof. The frame of the bed his father had made for himself and his wife stood against the far wall beneath a small window that had once been covered by oilcloth. The oilcloth was gone. The bedding and the straw mattress were gone, too. He checked the cupboards. Empty except for a few cans with flour and salt and baking soda and one dented pot. He also found a can of kerosene that had been used to fill the lamps that

were no longer in the cabin. Henry knew it was possible that Shinnobs on the rez had stripped the place, come and cleared out what was
usable, but it was more likely white people looking for things they
could take for themselves or sell as Indian souvenirs.

The floor was covered with dust, the corners hung with cobwebs.
This day he did not feel like weeping. He wanted to bring life back to
his home. He left the door open to let in the sunlight and the
evergreen-scented air. Outside he used his pocketknife and cut pine
branches with thick needles and bundled them together to use as a
broom. He swept the floor and every surface. He cleared the cobwebs.
From the cupboard he took the one remaining pot and filled it with
water from the pond. His shirt became a washrag, and he scrubbed
the place clean. He cut more pine boughs and laid them on the bed
frame as a temporary mattress.

In the late afternoon he gathered wood for the stove and built a
fire. He made biscuits with what he'd found in the cans. He ate the
biscuits with the last of the blueberries he'd picked. Afterward, he sat
outside and watched the night come on and tried to think what he
should do. He was fifteen years old. His parents were dead and buried.
His sisters were far to the east. In the letters they'd sent him, his sisters told him they liked the school in Wisconsin. The people were decent to them there. Henry didn't want to go back to the boarding
school in Flandreau, ever. He knew the white authorities would be
looking for him. Maybe even some Shinnobs who thought it best to
do what the white men wanted. If he went to anyone on the rez for
help, it might mean trouble for them. The last thing a Shinnob needed
was trouble with white men.

In the long dark before the rise of the moon, Henry listened to
the woods, which were alive all around him. Tree frogs and crickets.
The hoot of an owl. The wind dancing in the tops of the pine trees.

Even if they found him tomorrow and dragged him back to Flandreau, he was glad he'd made the journey. He was glad to be home.

TWENTY-ONE

W<sub>ake up."

Henry felt a shove and opened his eyes. The words had been spoken in the language of his people, the first he'd heard in that tongue in a great while. Henry lay on the blanket he'd spread over the pine boughs on his parents' bed. He rolled over to see who'd rudely awakened him.

It was not yet dawn. Barely any light came through the cabin windows. The door was open.

"You sleep like a deaf old dog, Nephew."

Woodrow Meloux, whose Ojibwe name was Miskwanowe, which meant "red cheeks," was not tall. Several inches less than six feet, he was broad across the chest, and strong. He wore his black hair in a long braid. His eyes were deep brown. He resembled Henry's father in many ways, but harder. He had never taken a wife, never fathered children.

"Uncle." Henry sat up on the bed and rubbed his eyes. "How did you know I was here?"

A leather pouch hung from Woodrow's belt. He undid the pouch, reached inside, and took out a strip of deer jerky, which he handed to Henry. He sat on the bed beside the young man.

"Everyone on the rez knows you're here. The smoke from the stove."

Henry chewed on the jerky. He loved the texture and flavor, which he hadn't tasted in three years.

His uncle said, "The whites were in Allouette yesterday. They warned there will be trouble if we do not send you back."

"I won't go back," Henry said.

Woodrow took a piece of jerky for himself and gave another to Henry. They ate in silence while the sky turned red, filling the cabin with an angry hue.

Woodrow looked around the room and shook his head. "White people came here after your father died. They took what they wanted. They are like fat, greedy squirrels. They pile nuts they will never eat." He stood up and retied his pouch. "We have a long walk."

"I'm not leaving the cabin."

"They will look for you here, and they will take you back to that school."

"I'm leaving. But I'm not leaving the cabin my father built. I don't want the whites or anyone else in here again."

Henry got off the bed. He put on his government shoes and walked to the corner where the can of kerosene sat, useless without the lamps it was meant to fill. He removed the cap and began to spread fuel across the cabin floor.

"You have things?" his uncle asked.

"Only what I'm wearing," Henry replied.

Henry took the box of matches from near the stove. He stood at the door with his uncle. He struck a flame and threw it into the wet line that lay across the floor. Fire crawled through the cabin like a yellow snake. Henry waited until he was sure the logs were burning well, then he turned away with his uncle and never looked back.

They walked for several hours, keeping to the trails, skirting Allouette and the cabins and shanties that spotted the woods. Henry knew where they were headed. His uncle had a parcel of land in the northwest corner of the reservation, a small, rocky finger that jutted into Iron Lake. It was far from Allouette, far from any other dwelling. Woodrow had named it *aandeg*, or crow, because the trees were a favorite rookery for the crafty black birds. His uncle had built a *wiigiwam*, a traditional Ojibwe dwelling, a simple framework of ironwood poles covered by bulrush mats and roofed with rolls of birch bark. There, in the summer of his fifteenth year, Henry Meloux began to live in the old way.

* * *

His uncle didn't work at the jobs the whites offered most Ojibwe—logging, mining, serving the tourists who came north in greater numbers every year. Woodrow trapped and fished and hunted in the vast forest to the north, which the whites called the Quetico-Superior wilderness. Through an outfitter named Aini Luukkonen, who operated on Iron Lake near the town of Aurora, he sometimes agreed to hire on as a guide to take white people into the wilderness and see that they came out safely. Because he knew the northern forest and the lakes better than any other man, he was always in demand.

Through that summer, through the season of the wild-rice harvest that followed, through the long winter when Grandmother Earth slept and the time for storytelling came and passed, through *iskigamizige-giizis*, the time of collecting maple sap and boiling it into syrup, Henry Meloux watched his uncle and listened and learned. Woodrow could track an animal over stony ground. With his rifle, he could bring down a deer at over a hundred yards with a single chest shot, even in thick cover. From the shoreline, he could read the depth of ice across a frozen lake and see where to cross safely. He could take a canoe through white water and knew portages no white man had ever walked. He knew how to start a fire with tinder, flint, and steel. He knew the old way of making a bear trap. All this knowledge he passed to Henry.

Woodrow didn't spend money on food. Food came from the forest, and if you could not get food, you did without. Sometimes, especially in the deep winter, Henry learned that to fast was a useful discipline. Woodrow traded for most of what he needed that he could not shoot, trap, gather, or manufacture. He traded furs or wild rice or syrup for an ax or knife or gun oil. That first year, he traded for many cartridges and patiently taught Henry how to shoot the rifle. Woodrow possessed little—a conscious choice—and his rifle he prized above all else. By summer, Henry could put a kill shot in a moving buck at nearly a quarter mile.

One morning in early May, Woodrow said, "You will go with me to see Aini Luukkonen."

Occasionally Henry had accompanied his uncle to Allouette. Although there were Shinnobs on the rez who wouldn't hesitate to report his presence to the white authorities, his uncle didn't worry.

"White men are too lazy to come all the way to Crow Point for a runaway Indian," he said.

As nearly as Henry had been able to tell, Woodrow was right. He'd seen no white people anywhere near his uncle's *wiigiwam*. But he knew that Luukkonen's place was not far from Aurora, a town full of whites, and Henry had no desire to be snatched by a cop and sent back to the Flandreau boarding school.

"You have grown," Woodrow told him. "Your hair is long now. You are not the boy you were. Do not look at the whites or speak to them. They will not even see you."

They took Woodrow's canoe, a twelve-foot canvas Old Town, one of the few possessions Henry's uncle had paid cash for, cash he'd earned as a guide. They paddled steadily the five miles to Luukkonen's. Wraiths of white mist crept over the surface of the dark water. As the sun topped the pine and spruce trees, the mist turned to fire and burned away. Among the trees along the shore, Henry could see that cabins were appearing in greater number. The whites were spreading farther and farther north. He feared for the woods and the animals in it. And he feared for his people. The whites went wherever they wanted and took what they fancied, and the laws that the grandfathers of the Anishinaabeg had agreed to were ignored.

They drew the canoe onto the shore near the dock behind Luukkonen's and tipped it onto the grass. The old Finn operated out of a big log structure built thirty yards off the lake. A Ford pickup stood parked in the yard. Attached was a trailer with a rack that cradled half a dozen canoes. On the wall of a shed to the left, someone had stretched a black bearskin. As they approached the porch, Henry spotted snowshoes hung near the front door. When they stepped inside, a bell over the threshold jingled. The place smelled of coffee and frying bacon.

"Yah," called a voice from someone out of sight. "Be dere in a minute. Hold your horses."

The outpost was full of goods a man might need in the woods. Axes and hatchets, knives in a display behind the counter, wool blankets, rope coils, fishing gear, lanterns, small stoves, hats, gloves. Henry hadn't been in a store in a good long while, and he stood silent, feeling weighted by the wealth of goods around him.

A man came through a door near the rear. He was stout, bald, but with a big walrus mustache that nearly hid his mouth. The mustache was salted with gray and, at the moment, stained with crusted egg yolk.

"Woodrow," he said in hearty greeting. "Been expecting you." He came close and eyed Henry in a friendly way. "Dis da boy, den?"

They'd talked about him, Henry understood. That made him nervous.

Luukkonen put out a hand, which was missing the index finger. Reluctantly, Henry took it. He didn't like shaking hands. It was a thing white people did.

"Does he know?" Luukkonen asked Henry's uncle.

Woodrow shook his head.

Know what? Henry wondered.

"Well, let's do it, den."

The Finn disappeared through the rear door. Henry and Woodrow waited in silence. When Luukkonen returned, he carried a rifle in his hands.

"Came in yesterday, just like I told you," he said to Woodrow. "Been dealing with dese folks a long time now."

He handed the rifle to Henry's uncle, who inspected it and nodded his approval. Woodrow held it out toward Henry.

"Yours," he said.

For a moment, Henry couldn't move. The gift stunned him. It was what he'd dreamed of but never expected. A rifle of his own.

"Well, go on dere. Take da blasted ting." Luukkonen smiled big under his walrus mustache.

The moment his fingers touched it, Henry felt the magic. It fit in his hands like something he'd been holding since he was born. It felt alive, intimate. It felt like a brother.

"A good piece dat. Your uncle, he knows." Luukkonen winked.

Henry lifted his eyes briefly. "*Migwech.*"

Woodrow nodded, accepting the thanks.

"Say, I got a job for you, you want it."

"What job?" Woodrow asked.

"Two men itching to go up near the Quetico. Need a guide. Say they'll pay premium for someone good. I mentioned your name."

"Hunters?"

"No. Ain't fishermen neither. Prospectors, I'd guess."

"Gold," Woodrow said.

"Gold?" The first white word Henry had spoken that morning.

Luukkonen tugged at the corner of his mustache and said to Henry, "We get 'em sometimes. People been talking a long time about da possibility. Dey say da geology's right, but nobody's found gold yet. Tank God. Imagine what'd happen if dey ever found anyting. Be de end of dis beautiful place, you betcha. So, Woodrow, what you tink?"

"Henry comes, too."

"I don't know if dey'd pay for two guides."

"He will not be paid."

"A free hand? Hell, what dey got to lose? Be here sunup day after tomorrow. Enjoy da rifle, Henry. She's a beauty, dat one. You'll need cartridges. Here." He handed over two boxes of shells. "On da house."

They were quiet paddling back to Crow Point. Henry thought about the rifle his uncle had given him. He'd never been given a gift so extravagant, and it confused him. He'd grown up on the rez with so little. Everyone on the rez had little. Having more than others, having too much, this was not Ojibwe.

As if divining his nephew's thoughts, Woodrow said from the stern, "The rifle you will need. Use it to eat, and what you don't eat give to The People."

Which made the gift different. It wasn't just for Henry. It served a greater purpose. With it he could provide for the elders and widows and others who could not hunt and did not work.

"These men," Henry said, speaking of the other concern that had settled on him that day. "What will they be like?"

"Some are good, some are not. The good ones will respect your skill and respect the land you take them into. The others will not. The worst are the ones with much money. Often they believe that the money makes them better than you. They might try to hide this, but it's what they believe. Many do not bother to hide it at all."

"Do you get angry?"

"Why would I be angry? Because they believe a thing does not make it so. There is no dignity in anger. But I am also not a kicked dog."

"If they treat you that way, what do you do?"

"I leave them."

"Alone? Up north?"

"It is a good lesson."

"How do they get back?"

"Who says they do?"

Henry twisted around, expecting to see a grin on his uncle's face. Woodrow didn't smile. He dipped his paddle and pushed hard toward Crow Point.

TWENTY-TWO

Two days later, in the dark before sunup, Henry set out with his uncle once again for Luukkonen's outpost.

The men were waiting, the outfitter with them. They were quiet white men but with eyes that said much. Eyes that said, *Business.* That said, *No questions.* That said, *We will watch you, boy.*

Like all white men, they shook hands.

"Leonard Wellington," the tall one said. He had a big nose, deep-set eyes, light brown hair. He was older than Henry by a decade, maybe two. It was hard for Henry to judge.

The other looked to be Woodrow's age, nearing fifty. He was smaller and heavier than Wellington, with a mustache like a thin black scar across his upper lip. Carlos Lima, he said his name was. He spoke in a way Henry had not heard before, a strange accent that rolled melodically off his tongue. He smiled often, baring teeth white as bleached bone.

The men's gear and the packed supplies were already in the back of Luukkonen's pickup. Henry and Woodrow threw in their own belongings and climbed into the open bed. The two white men sat up front with Luukkonen. It was a cool morning in late August, *manoominike-giizis,* the month of ricing, and the ride into the woods chilled Henry. They followed old logging roads for an hour through territory Henry barely knew, though Woodrow knew it well.

The outfitter finally pulled to a stop at the edge of a long, narrow lake backed by steep hills crowned with aspen. They unloaded two canoes from the trailer and stowed the gear. In the white men's canoe was equipment whose purpose Henry didn't know, although he suspected from what his uncle and Luukkonen had said that it was for finding gold.

"Two weeks from today," Luukkonen said to Woodrow. "Noon. I'll be waiting."

"I will have them here," Woodrow promised.

They paddled all day—six lakes, four portages, one rough passage along a swift rocky stream. The two white men spoke mostly to each other but at every portage conferred with Woodrow. They asked about rocks and hills and ridges, and Woodrow listened and nodded and pointed this way or that.

To Henry, Woodrow spoke the Anishinaabe name for each lake—Bear, Cedar, Face In A Cloud—and Henry committed them and the landscape to memory.

They camped that night beside a lake Woodrow called Opwagun, which meant a pipe bowl. It made sense considering the hills that ringed the water. Henry caught bass, which his uncle cleaned and pan-fried and served to the white men with wild rice and mushrooms. The men sat apart afterward, smoking cigars. They drank from a silver flask.

"Where are we going?" Henry asked in Ojibwemowin so the white men, if they heard, would not understand.

"North," Woodrow replied. "Three more lakes. Tomorrow by noon."

"Is there gold?"

Woodrow's eyes hung heavily on the white men sitting near the lake at the edge of the firelight, then he stared up at the sky. The stars were like frost on the dark windowpane of night.

"If there is, and the white men find it, I will kill them."

"Why?"

"When I was a boy, I traveled with my uncle to a place called the Black Hills. You have heard of it?"

Henry had read about it at the school in Flandreau. In his dormitory there was a Lakota, Sunning Turtle, who'd come from the Black Hills. Sunning Turtle was one of the boys who cried at night.

"It belonged to the Lakota by treaty, but white men found gold there. They stole the land, ripped the earth, turned the clear streams to mud, and built towns filled with the worst kind of people. Now, since the end of the Great War, I have heard that gold is even more valuable to white men. I believe, Henry, that if the hearts of their grandmothers were made of gold, they would cut them out." His eyes went back to the men drinking by the fire. "If there is gold here, I would die to keep it a secret. And I would kill for that, too."

Henry lay awake a long time that night thinking about killing the two men. He did not hate them and knew that Woodrow didn't either. The killing, if it came to that, was not about hate. It was, in a way, about love, and even more about respect, emotions he felt strongly for Grandmother Earth. Killing was never a good thing, Henry decided, but perhaps sometimes it was the only thing.

They set up camp the next day at noon on the lake called Ishkode. The word meant fire, and Henry had been thinking about the vision he'd had of a lake with fire at the bottom. Was this what it had meant? The two men eagerly eyed the gray ridges along the far shore and spoke to each other in low, excited voices. They set off immediately with equipment, crossing the lake alone in their canoe. Henry took his new rifle into the woods and shot a wild turkey, which Woodrow prepared and roasted on a spit. The men returned near sunset looking tired and grumbling in reply whenever Woodrow spoke to them.

Good, thought Henry. *They have been disappointed.*

For three days it went this way. On the fourth, the men returned in a different mood. They didn't say anything about what they'd found to Woodrow or Henry, but it was in their faces and in the bounce of the words they spoke to each other.

That night, lying beside his uncle after the men slept, Henry asked, "Did they find the gold?"

Woodrow said, "Not the gold, I think. They would be drunk. But something that makes them believe they might find gold."

Soon after dawn the next day, the men left. This time Woodrow followed.

Henry fished and caught several walleye that would easily fill all their bellies that evening. He cleaned his rifle and waited, scanning the lake with uneasiness in the direction all the men had gone.

The two whites came first. Their boots and the legs of their pants were caked with mud. Woodrow was not with them.

"Where's your uncle?" the man named Wellington asked. He

didn't seem as excited as he'd been the day before, but neither was he surly. Henry wasn't sure what that meant.

Henry didn't want to speak to them. He answered, "I do not know."

"I hope you have a meal ready, boy," the man named Lima said. "A *big* meal." With his accent the word came out *beeg*. "I could eat a moose."

Henry fed them the walleye, which he rolled in cornmeal and fried. He made drop biscuits and gave them blueberries he'd gathered and the men were happy.

Dark came, but not Woodrow.

"Should we worry, boy?" Lima asked. Then he grinned. A joke.

Henry remembered what his uncle had said about leaving people who treated him badly. These men were not so bad as many other whites, but maybe they'd said something to Woodrow.

The men sat at the fire. They'd put their pants near the flames to dry the mud. They drank coffee Henry had made and into which they poured some of whatever was in the silver flask. Their faces were flushed. The color was from spending the day under the sun and maybe from the work they did while they were gone across the lake, and from the paddling necessary to get there and back, and even a little from the heat of the fire. But it was also from what they drank.

Wellington wrote in a book bound in leather. Every night they'd camped, he'd spent time after supper writing by the firelight. He looked up from his book and caught Henry staring.

"Writing my memoirs," Wellington said with a laugh. "I figure I'll publish them someday, get famous."

"You read, boy?" Lima asked.

Henry was tired of being called boy, but he held his tongue. He stirred the fire with a long, sturdy maple stick. "I read," he said.

"Mission school or something?" Wellington asked.

"A school in South Dakota."

"South Dakota?" Wellington laughed. "A world traveler, eh? Ever been to Canada?"

"No," Henry said.

"I'm from Port Arthur. Know where that is?"

"No," Henry said.

"You're not alone." Wellington gave a snort. "Me, I'm going to put that burg on the map, eh."

Lima pulled a cigar from the vest pocket of his jacket. "You smoke, boy?"

"No," Henry said.

Lima ran the cigar along the line of his mustache under his nose and inhaled deeply. "These are my own cigars. It's what I do. Manufacture good smokes. You know the island Cuba?"

He'd heard of it, but had no clear idea of its location in relation to anything he knew.

"The best cigars, they come from Cuba, from my factory. Have one, boy. On me."

Lima held it out, long and brown like the dropping of a big animal. Henry didn't want the cigar, but he didn't want to offend the man. He took it.

Lima pulled out a cigar for himself. "Now, you clip the tip like this." He pulled out his knife and deftly sliced off a small nub at the end of the cigar.

Henry took his own knife and did the same. He was aware that Wellington watched him with gleaming eyes.

Lima struck a match on one of the rocks Henry had used to ring the fire. "Before you light your cigar, make sure the sulfur is burned out of the match head, okay? Sulfur can kill the taste of a good cigar. Don't put the cigar in your mouth yet. Hold it in your hand and rotate it near the flame, like this." He rolled the cigar between his index finger and thumb, near the match flame, until the entire tip on all sides glowed with ember. "Now you put it in your mouth and take a gentle puff or two to blow out the taste of anything not tobacco that may have come from lighting it. Only then are you ready to enjoy the pleasure of this truly fine product." He looked at Henry expectantly. "Well, go on, boy."

Henry imitated Lima's actions and soon the cigar smoke crawled down his throat like a thick snake.

"Good, good," Lima said with a big grin. "Enjoy."

Henry didn't. He got sick. After he'd puffed for a while, he became dizzy and had to lie down. The men guffawed. A little later, he stood up, stumbled out of the firelight, and puked. The men roared with laughter.

"Don't worry, boy," Lima called. "We'll make a man of you yet."

Later, as Henry lay in his bedroll, he thought to himself that if his uncle didn't kill these men, he would do it himself.

He woke to the rustle of the tent flap. Woodrow entered and lay down on his bedroll.

"You fed them?" he asked.

"Yes," Henry answered.

He wanted to ask where his uncle had been, but he knew if Woodrow meant for him to know, he would say. In a few minutes, he could hear the soft susurrus of deep breathing that told him Woodrow had gone to sleep.

Next morning he watched his uncle leave to follow the two white men again. Henry stayed back, dealt with the aftermath of breakfast, then took his rifle and a handful of cartridges and began to circle the lake on foot. Although he told himself he was going hunting, he didn't look for signs of game. An hour later he came to the place along the far shoreline where the white men had drawn up their canoe. He didn't see any sign of his uncle's canoe, but he hadn't expected to. Woodrow would have hidden it.

Henry easily found a trail broken through the undergrowth. It led toward the base of the ridge that ran the length of the lake and beyond. Henry paused, listened carefully, but heard nothing except the complaining of jays in the branches of a nearby poplar. He was curious about the men. He felt on the outside of whatever it was his uncle was thinking. He wondered at Woodrow's silence, wondered if his uncle was merely watching or actively stalking. Truthfully, if Woodrow intended to kill the men to keep any gold they found a secret, Henry believed he should be a part of that. It wasn't something he anticipated with pleasure, but it felt to him like a responsibility he should shoulder. Though Woodrow had not asked for his help, Henry believed it was the kind of thing a man—a true-blood Ojibwe— should be prepared to do.

The ridge was steep gray rock two hundred feet high. The top was capped with a mix of lithe aspen and sturdy spruce that shivered in a wind Henry couldn't feel. The trail followed the base and was easy to read despite the rocky ground. From the far side of the lake, the ridge had looked solid. After half a mile, however, Henry came to a place where a second ridge folded against the first with a narrow break between them through which a tiny creek ran. The trail left by the men led beside the creek, and Henry followed.

On the other side of the ridges, he found a great expanse of marsh and understood immediately the mud that had caked the men's boots and pants. He lost the trail in the soup of black water and yellow marsh grass. He climbed the ridge to high ground and scanned the tamarack trees that grew in profusion along the edges of the wetland. He saw no sign of the men or Woodrow.

It was midmorning. The sun had climbed halfway to its zenith. The day was turning hot. Henry found a place in the shade of a cedar and waited. Although he'd seen no evidence of Woodrow during his tracking, he was certain his uncle wasn't far behind the white men. He wasn't sure what waiting might accomplish, but he knew that the men would have to come back this way eventually—unless Woodrow did something to stop them.

He sat for two hours as the sun mounted directly overhead and the cedar shade shrank to nothing and the heat increased. His rifle lay across his legs. He'd chambered a cartridge, mostly to be able to say, if he was spotted, that he'd been hunting. He didn't know if the men would believe him.

The screams came to him first. They were distant sounds that might have been animals, though he'd never heard animals like that. Then he saw the two white men burst from the tamaracks at the northern edge of the marsh and flail their way into the black muck at a desperate run. Wellington was in the lead, Lima a few yards back. They made it halfway to the break in the ridges before an enormous bull moose crashed out of the trees behind them, head lowered, his rack aimed at the men. Henry had no idea what the white men had done to enrage the animal, but in the North Country even an idiot knew enough to stay clear of a moose. Not even the biggest black bear was a match for a raging bull.

The legs of the moose lifted it high above the swamp water. It closed on the men quickly. Henry had no time to think. He knelt and brought his rifle into position. The Winchester was meant for smaller game, deer at most. As he sighted, Henry tried to think how with a single shot of a too-small-caliber bullet he could stop the moose. The round would never penetrate deep enough to reach the heart.

Out of the corner of his open eye, he saw Lima stumble and go down. Henry led the moose, held his breath, then let it out slowly and squeezed the trigger. He lost the animal for a moment in the jar of the recoil. When he found it again, he saw the moose pitch forward, coming to rest only a few feet from where Lima cowered in the muck.

Henry sat back. He began to shake. Numbly, he watched Wellington return and kneel beside his fallen companion. A moment later the man looked up and spotted Henry on the ridge.

Henry stood, worked his way down, and waded into the swamp grass and black water. Even at a distance, he could hear Lima's moans.

Henry went first to the moose. The animal's right eye socket was nothing but a deep, bleeding hole. In the wake of the adrenaline flood he'd felt on the ridge, Henry experienced an overwhelming sadness at the death of this great and beautiful creature.

"You?" Wellington asked with disbelief. "It was you? That was one hell of a shot, boy."

Henry turned. "I'm not a boy."

"Son of a bitch," Lima moaned.

Wellington carefully lifted the other man's leg clear of the black soup. Lima shouted something in Spanish that Henry didn't understand but guessed was a curse. Wellington paid no heed as he worked his fingers along the muddy pants leg.

"Broken," he pronounced. "Pretty bad, I'd say. We've got to get him to a doctor."

Henry didn't know what to say. The nearest doctor was a lot of miles, a lot of paddling, a lot of portages away. How did he explain that to a man looking to him for help?

Wellington's eyes moved past Henry. Woodrow was slogging toward them across the marsh, rifle in hand. His eyes dropped to the moose as he passed.

"Can you walk?" he asked Lima.

"Fucking Christ no," the man replied, as if Woodrow had asked the world's stupidest question.

"We can carry him," Wellington suggested.

Woodrow shook his head. "Too far. We would only hurt him more. There is another way." He motioned to Henry. "Come with me."

"Where are you going?" Wellington grabbed Woodrow's arm.

Woodrow shot him a hard, dark look, and Wellington let go.

"We will be back," Woodrow said. He turned away and made for the break in the ridges.

Henry followed to the place where Woodrow had hidden his canoe. They paddled back to camp.

"Take the ax," Woodrow instructed. "Cut three saplings seven feet long. Strip the branches, then cut one of the saplings in half. Bring them back here."

Henry did as he'd been told. When he returned, he found Woodrow waiting with rope cut into many sections of varying lengths. His uncle lashed the saplings together in a rectangle seven feet long and half that wide. He tied the sections of rope across the frame in a kind of mesh hammock.

A travois, Henry realized. They were going to lay the white man on it and haul him out of the woods.

They placed Woodrow's construction across the gunwales of the canoe. Before they shoved off, Woodrow fixed Henry with a cold stare.

"I have never seen a better shot from a hunter."

Henry looked down. "Kitchimanidoo must have guided me," he said, giving credit to the Great Spirit.

"Me," Woodrow replied, "I would have left them to the moose."

Henry's moment of pride in the beauty of his kill shot was shattered.

"It is done," Woodrow said, and he spoke of it no more.

At the marsh, they lifted Lima onto the travois. The man cried out, but once he was settled in the rope hammock, he grew quiet. Woodrow had fashioned a harness, which he shouldered himself.

To Henry he said, "Cut meat from the moose and bring it." Then he began the labor of hauling the injured man to the canoes.

They broke camp immediately. The rest of that day they retraced the route they'd followed coming in. Woodrow paddled the canoe in which Lima lay. Henry took the stern of the other with Wellington in the bow. At every portage, they lifted Lima onto the travois, and

Woodrow pulled him to the next lake. Henry and Wellington each shouldered a canoe and double packs that were slung across both chest and back. It was exhausting work, and they went much slower than when they'd entered the wilderness.

They took three days to reach the place where Luukkonen had dropped them.

"What now?" Wellington asked after they'd pulled the canoes onto shore. "That outfitter won't be here for a week."

"You and me, we will walk the logging road," Woodrow replied. "If we are lucky, a truck will pick us up."

"Why both of us?"

"Because a logging truck will not stop for an Indian."

"We leave Carlos alone with the boy?"

"He is not a boy. And he will care for your friend."

Wellington seemed to understand that there was no choice. He knelt beside Lima. "I'll be back, Carlos. I'll bring a doctor. We'll get you fixed up, eh."

Lima's eyes were bloodshot and shaded yellow. He squeezed Wellington's hand in parting.

Henry made camp. He constructed a lean-to that would shelter Carlos Lima from the sun and would keep the water off him if it rained. He gathered firewood. He made stew from the last of the moose meat and wild rice and dried mushrooms, which he fed to Lima in small spoonfuls.

That night he heard the howl of a wolf pack nearby. Had they caught the scent of Lima, he wondered, an animal injured and vulnerable to attack? Henry kept watch with a cartridge in the chamber of his rifle.

Midmorning the next day, the men returned in Luukkonen's pickup. They brought a doctor. While the physician examined Lima's leg, the outfitter hovered over his shoulder and shook his head.

"You're lucky it was Woodrow with you," he told Wellington.

Wellington scowled at Henry and his uncle. "I've been thinking. It strikes me as odd that you two just happened to be around when that moose charged. I'm thinking you were following us."

Henry didn't know what to say, but Woodrow spoke immediately.

"Your safety was our responsibility. We could not keep you safe if we could not see you."

"Forget it, Leonard," Lima said, grimacing. "There's nothing for us here. I hate this place. I will never come back."

The doctor stood. "We need to get him to my office right away if we're going to save that leg."

They put Lima in the bed of the pickup.

Luukkonen spoke quietly to Woodrow. "I'll come back for you and Henry directly. And I'll see to it these men pay the full two weeks. You've earned it."

Henry stood beside his uncle and watched the pickup disappear along the trail into the trees to the south. For a long time he could hear the growl of the engine and the clatter of the suspension. When he could hear it no more, he turned to Woodrow.

His uncle stared at the place where the truck and the men had gone. "Lima said they would not be back." His eyes slid to Henry. "The hand of Kitchimanidoo." He nodded once in sober agreement and, Henry thought, acceptance, because Woodrow had believed they were better dead.

"What now, Uncle?"

Woodrow drew a tobacco pouch from his shirt pocket. "First we give thanks." He turned in a circle, sprinkling a bit to the north, west, south, and east, and finally dropping a little in the center of the circle. "Now I'm going into the lake and wash away the smell of the white men." He leaned toward Henry and sniffed. "And you, Nephew, you could outstink a skunk."

Woodrow walked to the lake. Henry stood a little longer looking in the direction the truck had gone. Kitchimanidoo had saved the white men. Why, Henry couldn't say. It didn't matter. He was rid of them. He would never have to see them again.

Or so he believed.

TWENTY-THREE

For the next two years Henry continued to live with his uncle on Crow Point, growing well into his manhood, strong in body and spirit, and strong in his resolve to live the old ways. He saw unhappy changes continue to creep onto the reservation. Some Shinnobs managed to purchase automobiles, and the dust they raised could be seen above the trees, like smoke from a spreading fire. In Allouette there was electricity and plans for a telephone line. There were radios and, in Aurora, access to movies. He sometimes ran into young Shinnobs who'd graduated from the boarding schools and they told him about jazz and Charlie Chaplin and dances like the Charleston and the shimmy. He heard that the Ojibwe on the Red Lake Reservation had created a lucrative commercial-fishing industry and were selling tons of netted walleye to retailers in Minneapolis and St. Paul and Chicago. White people had always believed that what they had was what the Ojibwe should aspire to. That seemed to be the growing sentiment among Shinnobs on the rez as well. As more and more whites crowded the forests, the Ojibwe, in the things they wanted and in the dreams they had, came more and more to resemble them.

There was another change, this one more personal. In the summer he turned eighteen, Henry fell in love. It was Woodrow's fault.

"There's a girl," his uncle said one day when he'd returned from town. "She lost her folks years ago and went to a government school in Wisconsin. She knows your sisters there. Her name is Broken Wing."

"Dilsey," Henry said. He remembered her from long ago. She'd already gone to the boarding school at Hayward, Wisconsin, before he was sent to Flandreau. She was younger than he, and Henry remembered her as scrawny and silly.

"She has come back to teach on the rez," Woodrow said. "She is staying with her mother's uncle."

Henry was concentrating on cutting strips of birch bark to use in making a torch for spearfishing that night. Without looking up he said, "So?"

"Go to Allouette, Nephew. See her."

Henry couldn't imagine why he'd want to see the girl, but he did as his uncle suggested.

He didn't find her in town; he was directed to the mission. It was late afternoon when he arrived. The shadows of the trees at the western edge of the clearing were growing long, turning the meadow grass a brooding blue. Henry approached the clapboard building. He heard her voice first, high and beautiful, singing words to a song he didn't know.

" 'Yes, we have no bananas, we have no bananas today . . .' "

He stepped through the open door into the one-room building. He was startled to find not the scrawny, silly girl he remembered, but a woman with long coal black hair and smart brown eyes. She was arranging books on a shelf along one wall of the mission. His shadow slid into the room ahead of him, and seeing it, she stopped singing and turned.

"Yes?" she asked.

"Dilsey?"

"Who are you?"

What Henry wanted to say was, *The man you're going to marry.* What came off his tongue was, "Uh . . . uh . . ."

The rest of his efforts at courting weren't much better. For all his skill in the forest, his knowledge of the plants and the animals, his legendary prowess with his rifle, he was an awkward suitor. Dilsey seemed amused by him, but not moved in the same way as he. When, in the spring of the following year, a white teacher from Chicago named Liam O'Connor came to Allouette to open a real school on the reservation, Dilsey's true affections quickly and obviously settled on the newcomer, whom she soon married. This left Henry cold and bitter.

"You sit and scowl like an old badger," Woodrow declared not long after. "Get up, Nephew. It is time to build."

For the rest of that summer and into the early fall, Henry labored with his uncle to cut and lay the logs for a one-room cabin on Crow Point. The logs were cedar, and the roof was cedar covered with birch bark. Woodrow arranged for floor planks to be cut at the mill in Brandywine, which was owned and operated by Shinnobs.

When the first snow fell in early November, the cabin was finished. It was a blessing because, in the depth of the winter that followed, Woodrow fell ill. There were no doctors on the reservation. Henry turned to Dollie Bellanger, who was a Mide, a healer, to do what she could for Woodrow. The winter was long and harsh, and life slipped further and further from his body, until all that was left one overcast day in April were a few ragged breaths and his final words to Henry:

"My life with you has been good, Nephew. Do not be alone now."

Henry buried Woodrow in the cemetery behind the mission. Despite his uncle's advice, he remained alone in the cabin on Crow Point. There were relatives across the rez, uncles and aunts and cousins, but Henry kept away from them all. He tried to disappear into the forest, but it seemed an empty place without Woodrow. Finally he simply settled into the cabin and did not leave.

In the early fall, more than four months after Woodrow died, as Henry fished from the rocks along the shore of Iron Lake, he spotted a canoe gliding toward him from the south. In a few minutes, he could make out that it was Luukkonen, the outfitter. Although he'd had offers to guide after his uncle passed away, Henry had turned them all down. He had no need of money, and going into the wilderness without Woodrow was still too hard.

Luukkonen pulled up to shore. "*Anin*," he greeted Henry, formally and cordially.

"What do you want?" Henry replied.

The outfitter stepped from his canoe and, though he hadn't been invited, sat down near Henry. He smoothed his walrus mustache and watched Henry's fishing line in the water.

"A man come looking for your uncle dis morning," he finally

began. "I told him Woodrow had gone to his reward and he asked about you. Wants to hire you."

"I don't guide anymore."

"I told him dat. He's pretty stubborn, dis one."

"I don't care."

"I know it's hard for you in dese woods. I imagine everywhere you go reminds you of Woodrow. But dis is different, Henry. He wants to go way up nort. Canada."

Henry began to reel in his line. He was tired of talking to the man.

"I don't want to go to Canada."

"You ever been in a airplane, Henry? Dis man, he's going to fly you up dere. Sounds pretty good."

"I'm not interested."

Luukkonen leaned nearer. "Henry, I'm tinking it would be good for you. I'm tinking you need to get away for a while."

Away.

Away hadn't occurred to Henry. Away meant the boarding school in Flandreau. Or for Dilsey and his sisters, the school in Wisconsin. Or for his parents and Woodrow and so many others on the rez, away simply meant death.

"Dere's nutting for you here right now, Henry. Go away for a while. Maybe when you come back, tings will be different."

The outfitter was right. What was there for him here? What he loved had passed or was passing. Go away, Luukkonen advised. The Finn was offering him a different kind of away than he'd thought of before, one that suddenly and powerfully appealed to Henry.

"All right," he agreed.

"One ting I didn't tell you," Luukkonen said. "Dis man who wants you. You know him. His name is Wellington. Leonard Wellington."

TWENTY-FOUR

Wellington had changed little. He didn't seem as tall to Henry, who'd grown several inches since their last meeting. His hair was thinner. But he still had a hatchet blade for a nose and a too proud look in his eyes.

Wellington stared at Henry with astonishment.

"Christ, you've filled out," he said. "Left that boy you were a good distance back, eh." He offered his hand. It was tanned and rough. "I was sorry to hear about your uncle, but awfully glad to have you on the expedition. Luukkonen told me you understood the terms."

They had been simple. Henry agreed to sign on for as long as necessary at five dollars a week. He was to maintain camp, provide fresh meat and other native food to supplement the supplies, and see to the safety of the expedition members, meaning Wellington and his partner, Carlos Lima. "As long as necessary" was vague, but Henry wasn't concerned. He didn't care how long he was gone. And he could already feel fall in the air and knew that it wouldn't be long before winter closed the door to any expedition far to the north.

"Well then." Wellington rubbed his hands together eagerly. "Let's get started."

Henry had canoed past a floatplane tethered to the dock behind the outpost. He'd seen a few such planes. Sometimes men used them to reach lakes deep in the Northwoods without having to paddle and portage their way in. It struck Henry as not only lazy but disrespectful to the spirits of the deep forest.

Yet here he was throwing the propeller to help Wellington start the plane and then climbing afterward into the belly of the beast with the same purpose in mind. Wellington had observed that the boy

Henry had been was far behind him. As he felt the plane glide across the surface of Iron Lake and lift free of Grandmother Earth, it seemed to Henry that he'd never been so far from who he'd thought he would become.

To see the earth as an eagle would, what magic. The lakes like puddles of rainwater in deep grass. The high, formidable ridges no more than wrinkles. The great woods a green sea stretching away as far as he could see. Once inside the plane, Wellington didn't speak to Henry. He sat at the controls and seemed deep in thought. The plane had only two seats and Henry wondered where he would sit once Lima was aboard. There was an empty area in the rear that Henry suspected was waiting to be filled with supplies. He also suspected he'd end up there, too. He didn't care.

Near noon, a great shining water appeared ahead of them. The plane began its descent.

Wellington finally spoke to Henry. "Lake Superior."

Kitchigami, Henry thought. He'd never seen the big water, though it was well known to him.

As they flew over the squat buildings of a town below, Wellington spoke again. "Fort William. And up there across the river, that's Port Arthur."

Canada, Henry understood.

The plane landed smoothly and motored to a dock where Henry saw two people waiting. One he recognized. Carlos Lima. The other was a woman about Henry's age.

"Damn," Wellington swore under his breath then cut the engine.

Lima tied the plane to the dock. Wellington opened his door and stepped down. Henry followed him. Lima had changed, grown visibly older. He'd put on weight and his mustache was thicker, with a dullness to it that made Henry think of a little gray mouse. Lima looked on him with the same disdain he'd had in the summer Henry saved his life.

"Where's the other one?" Lima said to Wellington.

"Henry's uncle died last winter. Henry has agreed to work for us."

Lima's dark, distrustful eyes did a long assessment of Henry. "You've grown," he finally said and gave a nod as if he grudgingly approved.

Wellington said, "What's Maria doing here? I thought we agreed."

Lima shrugged. "You know her."

"This isn't a trip for a girl, Carlos."

"She's strong, Leonard. And pigheaded."

"You're her father."

"You've never been a father. You don't know."

The girl was near enough to hear the talk about her, but she seemed not to notice. Or maybe she simply didn't care. What she did was to look frankly at Henry, who burned under the gaze of her dark eyes.

"All right," Wellington said, finally giving in. "Let's get loaded. We have a long way to go."

Lima called to a man in a truck parked at the end of the dock. The man hopped from the driver's seat and dropped the gate on the bed that was covered with a canvas tarp. He threw back the tarp, lifted a box, and headed toward the plane. Wellington went about refueling from metal barrels on the dock while Lima and Henry helped load supplies. Maria also stepped up to lend a hand, and at the back of the truck her shoulder brushed against Henry. He felt it as deeply as if she'd burned him with a hot coal.

They organized the cargo area in such a way that there was a small space for Maria and Henry, who sat facing each other, seated on rolled tents. The plane was heavily loaded and seemed to struggle to rise off the lake. Once it did, it headed directly into the afternoon sun for a few minutes, then curled toward the vast green wilderness waiting to the northwest.

They'd been introduced on the dock in a perfunctory way by Wellington. Maria Lima. She'd smiled, but not like her father, whose smile was a snake's grin. Hers was genuine, though there was something hidden in it that Henry couldn't decipher. To her chipper "How do you do?" he'd mumbled a reply.

Now they sat facing each other in the belly of the plane, legs drawn up like two babies in the same womb. The machine bounced and shook and noisily rode the currents. Up front, Lima pulled a rolled map from a tube, spread it out before him, and he and Wellington talked. Henry caught snatches of their conversation, but not enough to follow the thread.

To keep from staring at the young woman, Henry pretended to

sleep, but he kept his eyes open a slit. He watched her take a notebook bound in leather from her canvas bag and spend a long time writing with a fountain pen.

The plane dropped suddenly. The supplies in back shifted with a bump. Henry's eyes flew open.

"Air pocket," Wellington said over his shoulder, shouting to be heard above the noise of the engine and rattle of the fuselage. "Happens sometimes, eh."

Maria put the notebook and pen back into her bag and took out a book. Henry couldn't see the title. She opened it, then looked at Henry. She said something Henry couldn't quite hear. He held up his hands in question.

"Do . . . you . . . read?" she said, louder this time and speaking slowly.

"I can read," he answered.

She laughed. It was odd that he could hear it amid all the other noises. It was a sound both beautiful and disconcerting. "I figured that. I asked *do* you read."

Henry hadn't looked at a book since boarding school. With Woodrow, there'd been no need.

"Listen to this," she said. "It's about bullfighting, about a matador named Pedro Romero, who is fighting a bull to impress a woman." She spent a moment finding the right page, then read aloud, enunciating carefully.

" 'Never once did he look up. He made it stronger that way, and did it for himself, too, as well as for her. Because he did not look up to ask if it pleased he did it all for himself inside, and it strengthened him, and yet he did it for her, too. But he did not do it for her at any loss to himself. He gained by it all through the afternoon.' "

She finished and looked hard at Meloux, in a way that made him uncomfortable. "He is killing the bull for her. For himself, too, yes, but it is also for her. Does that make sense?"

Henry tried to think about it, but his brain was too full. Full of the young woman—her smell that was clean and flowerlike, her eyes that were like black bullets, the bones that fiercely shaped her face, the notes that made her voice sing. Her nearness, too, their knees almost touching.

"It's by a man named Ernest Hemingway," she went on. "Have you heard of him?"

Henry hadn't. But he wished he had.

"What I wonder is, do men really believe that that kind of brutality is impressive to a woman?"

Henry stared at her, feeling dumb as a cow.

"It takes place in Spain and in Paris, a city in France. I was there last summer. It's a fine place, but . . ." She stopped and her eyes went to the window at the front of the plane. "I like it here much better. I think what people build can be very beautiful, but what God builds goes beyond beauty. You stand outside Notre Dame, say, and you marvel at the accomplishment, but you can't really connect. It's artificial, do you see? It's only a representation of something. Spirit, holiness, maybe even God. But it's not the thing itself. Out here, it's all there before you, around you. You're steeped in it, the real thing. Spirit. Holiness. God."

She was Lima's daughter. Henry could see traces of the father in her—the slight shadow of the skin, the black hair, the slender nose—but Henry thought her mother must have been terribly beautiful. She didn't speak like Lima. There wasn't the odd roll to her language. She sounded little different from the whites Henry had known all his life. He wondered about that.

"I'm sorry," she said suddenly. "Sometimes I go on and on. You're tired, I'm sure. You probably want to sleep."

Henry wasn't tired, and he liked hearing her talk. But he felt tense and awkward and had a pressing need to escape for a while.

"Yes, I am tired," he said. He closed his eyes.

He did, in fact, sleep. He woke as he heard the engine throttled back and felt the plane descending. They landed on a lake surrounded by forest, and Wellington guided the plane to shore, where a small cabin and dock had been built. The men got out, then Maria and Henry. A scruffy man who looked Indian in his features greeted Wellington, and they talked briefly, then set about refueling the plane from a metal barrel. Maria spoke to her father, who pointed toward an outhouse near the cabin. Henry walked into the woods and relieved himself. In a few minutes, they were in the air again.

It was late afternoon by the time they finally glided to rest on the shore of an immense lake contained on three sides by steep ridges. They unloaded the equipment and set up their tents. There was one for each of them. Lima and Wellington set up their own tents, located next to each other. Henry put up Maria's. She asked for it to be as far from her father as possible because she said he snored terribly. Henry erected his own tent a bit away from the others. By the time he'd finished, the treetops had punctured the sun, and it was sinking fast. Henry canvassed the area for wood and quickly built a fire. Wellington opened a big tin of soup from the supplies that Lima had brought and heated it directly on the coals. Shortly after dark they all crawled into their tents.

Henry lay awake that night, and though he was in the middle of a vast Canadian wilderness, the sounds he heard were as familiar to him as his own breathing. The chirr of crickets and tree frogs. The creak of branches stirred by the wind. The lap of the lake against the shoreline. The smell was like home, evergreen pitch and clean water. But he was as far from home as he'd ever been, and he felt it. This was not like the government boarding school where the trees were spare and the land was flat and cultivated and smelled of manure. This was a different distance. He had the sense that he'd embarked on a long journey, without any idea of his destination.

TWENTY-FIVE

At first there was routine to the days.

After breakfast, Wellington and Lima took off with their packs full of instruments. Sometimes they used the collapsible boat they'd brought in the plane, which they called a Folbot; sometimes they struck out on foot. Always they headed toward the ridges. Usually they were gone until late afternoon, often until almost dark.

Henry's principal job was to feed the expedition and see to the safety of the camp—and Maria. Henry didn't wonder that Lima trusted him to be alone with his daughter. He understood clearly that Lima thought of him as little better than a stock animal—a horse or an ox, say—something to be worked hard, put up for the night, and forgotten. That his daughter might look at Henry in a different way probably never occurred to Lima. That was fine with Henry. On the plane he'd been intrigued by the young woman. When he discovered that she was his responsibility, he was no happier with the arrangement than she. Lima forbade her leaving camp unless Henry accompanied her. And Henry was forbidden to leave her alone. He was eager to explore the area and to hunt game, but when she walked in the forest, Maria made more racket than a wounded moose. Henry hated taking her with him. For several days he confined himself to camp. He dug three pit toilets—one for the white men, one for Maria, and one for himself—and constructed rudimentary seating for each using a sturdy section of limb lashed to supporting Y branches. He built a shelter suitable to eat under when it rained. Much of the rest of his time was passed fishing for walleye and trout from the lake. Maria spent the bulk of her time reading or writing in her journal and looking bored or unhappy.

"I'm sick of fish," she declared on the fourth day, after her father and Wellington had left. "And I'm sick of sitting." She squatted on a flat rock, half hidden by leatherleaf, at the edge of the water, and she looked across the lake at the tallest ridge. "I'm hiking up there today."

"There are wolves," Henry said.

It was true. He'd heard the howl of a pack at night. Mostly, though, he said it to scare her.

"Wolves don't hunt in the day. And they won't attack unless they believe you're sick or infirm."

"You read that in one of your books?"

"As a matter of fact."

Henry had his hands in a bucket full of leeches he'd collected for fishing. "If they're hungry, wolves will attack a bull moose in broad daylight. They'll tear it apart."

"I don't believe you."

Henry shrugged.

"I'm going." She put down the book she'd been reading and stood up.

"I'm not ready to go," he said.

"I don't care." She stomped off, following the shoreline.

Henry sighed and waited. When she was out of sight, he took up his rifle and followed, keeping himself hidden.

Henry expected her to tire quickly, but he was surprised by her endurance. The lake snaked for more than two miles to the west and Maria followed the shoreline at a steady pace. She stopped several times to drink from small streams and once to relieve herself. Henry looked away. By noon she'd reached the base of the ridge. She paused for a while, taking the measure of the height and looking, Henry supposed, for the best route up. Finally she began her ascent.

Henry gave her a little head start, then slung his rifle over his shoulder and started up himself. He stayed a couple of hundred yards west of her and downslope, keeping to the scrub jack pines and black spruce whose roots dug tenaciously into the cracks in the rock. The bare stone often had a thin skin of slippery green-gold lichen, making the climb more treacherous. The crest of the ridge was a good three hundred feet above the lake. Maria clambered up quickly and steadily. Between his own climbing and his tracking of Maria, Henry had his hands full.

In twenty minutes, Henry neared the top. Maria wasn't far below and he pushed hard to be there ahead of her. He positioned himself in a copse of aspen whose leaves in that early autumn were gold as new doubloons. Maria stood on a jut of gray rock, smiling in the sunshine, looking at the scene below her. The ridges that cupped the lake lay at the meeting of two topographies. South, the land was folded in a series of rugged hills; north, the forest ran flat all the way to the horizon. The deep ravines of the hills were lined with ragged outcrops that erupted from the earth like fractured bone through flesh. It reminded Henry of Noopiming, the woods that Woodrow had taught him to love.

Maybe it was the beauty of the scene and the way it lightened his heart, or maybe it was because he saw that Maria had been moved by it, too; whatever the reason, he found himself walking toward her, purposely making just enough noise that she would hear. She turned and did not look happy.

"What are you doing here?" she asked.

"What I'm paid to do."

"You followed me. I should have known."

He wanted to say something to her, something soothing, but the words wouldn't come. "I'm sorry," he finally said. "I'll wait below." He turned away.

"No," she said to his back. Then more gently, "Stay."

They stood together, for a long time silent, drinking in the magnificence of what lay before them.

"Why don't you want me with you when you go into the woods?" Maria asked.

"You make too much noise. You scare the game."

"I don't mean to. You could teach me how to be quiet. I learn quickly."

He liked the sound of her voice. It reminded him of water pushed by wind.

"Why did you come?" he asked.

Instead of answering she said, "Do you have family?"

"My parents are gone. Two sisters are in school in Wisconsin."

"I've heard my father and Leonard talk about someone named Woodrow."

"My uncle. He is gone, too."

She nodded, and her eyes rested on the deep green that reached to the horizon. "My mother died when I was a little girl. Since then I've lived in boarding schools, mostly in the States."

"I know about boarding schools," Henry said.

"Nuns." Maria made a sour face, and Henry laughed. "You don't do that much," she told him.

"What?"

"Laugh."

He thought about it. Woodrow could make him laugh. Since his uncle had passed away, Henry hadn't felt like laughing.

She sat down on the rock and hugged her knees. Henry sat down and laid his rifle on the ground.

She said, "They're hunting gold, you know."

"I know."

"Leonard is a geologist. He knows where to look, but he doesn't have the money to prospect. My father foots the bill. They met in a casino in Havana. My father was probably throwing away money, as usual. He loves to gamble. I'm sure that's part of the attraction of looking for gold. They've found it twice already. First in Australia, but it turned out not to be a very rich strike. Then again in South America, but they lost that claim somehow. They won't talk about it. Anyway, I thought maybe if I came with him this time, it might be a chance to get to know him."

Henry didn't like her father and couldn't imagine why anyone would want to know him better. Family made a difference, he supposed.

"I should be in college, a place called Bennington. It's in Vermont. My second year there. But I have no interest in it. Not right now."

"What now?" Henry heard himself asking.

She smiled and it made him burn with happiness. She opened her arms. "This. Something that's not Paris or New York or Havana. Something . . . transcendent."

Henry didn't know what the word meant, but her voice told him and he understood.

Her face glistened with a sheen of sweat from the hike and the climb. Henry's body was damp, too. The wind pushed over the ridge and fanned him cool. Maria's hair rippled like black water, and she closed her eyes.

"Would you like to hunt with me?" Henry asked.

"Yes."

"Have you ever seen an animal killed?"

"In Cuba once. I watched a pig slaughtered for roast."

"To your eyes it might not be pretty."

"I can take it. What will you hunt?"

"We passed through a meadow on our way here. I saw rabbit droppings."

She stood eagerly. "Hasenpfeffer for dinner?"

Henry looked up at her dumbly.

"Fancy roast rabbit," she said.

"I don't know about fancy." He smiled and rose beside her.

They returned to camp in the early afternoon with a fat, dead snowshoe rabbit in hand. Its coat was dark brown. Henry had explained to Maria that in winter, the fur would turn soft white to match the snow. He set about the skinning and cleaning and quartering, and Maria did not turn away. When he'd finished, he made a fire, settled a pot of water at the edge, and put the cut-up rabbit in to stew.

Maria said, "I'm going for a swim. Come with me?"

Henry laughed, thinking she was joking. The nights were cold and the lake would be like ice.

"All right then." She disappeared into her tent and came out a few minutes later dressed in shorts and a man's white undershirt. Her feet were bare, and Henry saw that her toes were painted red. "Last chance," she said.

Henry shook his head. "You'll be out fast enough."

"Think so?"

She dashed toward the lake and dove in. She disappeared for a long time. Henry left the fire and ran to the rocky shore. He was about to go in after her when she burst through the surface and began stroking evenly away. He watched her, admiring how smoothly she moved through the water, leaving a wake like a comet's tail.

Henry went back to the fire and cut onions and carrots and potatoes to add to the stew. All the while he kept an eye on Maria. She stayed a long time in water Henry knew would make his own muscles cramp.

Finally she returned to shore and climbed from the lake. Strands of her black hair clung to her cheeks. Beneath the thin wet cotton of her undershirt her skin was visible and pink. The dark areolas of her breasts were like eyes behind a veil.

Henry looked away, but not before she caught him looking and not before she smiled.

TWENTY-SIX

Henry couldn't sleep. He lay in his tent staring up at canvas that was drenched in silver moonlight. It wasn't the canvas he was seeing. It was Maria, stepping soft and pink from the lake. He didn't understand what was happening to him or the way he felt. Strong, but also very weak. Full of fire and at the same time ice. Hard in every muscle but yielding deep inside. He'd never felt anything like this, not even during his brief courtship of Dilsey.

He threw back his blanket and stepped into the night. The ground was cool against his bare soles. The four tents had been arranged in a semicircle around the campfire. He crossed to Maria's tent, his shadow crawling up the canvas. He longed to see her, even a glimpse, and he considered pulling her tent flap aside just for a moment.

But he was afraid.

Instead, he walked to the lake. The water was silver fire. The ridges on the far side stood gray and ghostly against the black southern sky. Henry glanced back at the camp, then quietly undressed. He stepped into the lake. The cold hammered his legs, but he pushed on, farther and deeper. He wanted the icy water to kill the fire that wouldn't stop burning in him. He let out his breath and sank toward a place where the moonlight didn't reach.

He felt a disturbance of the water and came up quickly. He looked toward shore and saw her slender figure slipping into the lake. He wasn't certain, but he thought she was naked. She swam toward him, her face a pale, beautiful bubble. Henry stared at her, too amazed to speak. He felt the loop of her arms around him and the press of her warm body. She kissed him, her lips the softest touch he'd ever known.

"You're freezing," she said. "Come with me."

Out of the water and in the moonlight, her naked skin was jeweled with shining droplets that rolled down the line of her spine, along the curve of her buttocks, and fell from her like pearls off a broken string. She stooped and gathered her clothing and his and led him to her tent. She drew aside the flap and slipped inside. Henry hesitated. Her hand appeared, beckoning him in. He followed.

Her sleeping bag was open. She lay on it in the silver-green light of the moonlit canvas. She reached out and took his hand and drew him down to her.

"Let me warm you," she murmured.

She rolled on top of him, blanketing him with her own body, her breasts against his chest, her thighs cupping his. She kissed him again, and he grew hard and kissed her back. Her lips broke away and drifted across his cheek, his neck, his chest.

"Maria," he whispered, desperate and grateful.

She put her finger to his mouth. "Shhhh. No noise."

She pushed herself up to straddle him and looked deeply into his eyes. Her own eyes were full of silver-green fire. She moved ever so slightly, and he was surprised and amazed to find himself inside her, a place warmer and more welcoming than he'd ever imagined. He grasped her hips and tried to push deeper, but she laid a hand on his chest and shook her head.

She leaned to his ear and whispered, "Let me." She kissed him for a long time.

The first time was over quickly, and Henry wasn't sure if he'd done things right. He'd been divided, worrying about what he was doing with Maria and worrying about whether the white men would hear. But Maria smiled and snuggled into his arms and whispered he was wonderful, and like magic he was ready again. This time he did not worry about the white men.

Since he was sixteen Henry had had dreams full of animal desire from which he woke breathless and emptied. The first night with Maria was like nothing he'd ever dreamed, nothing he could ever have imagined. Their desire was a well without bottom. Henry had never been as happy as he was with Maria in his arms.

Long before dawn, long before the white men would be stirring, he rose and returned to his own tent, but he couldn't sleep. He was too full of Maria.

She didn't appear at breakfast. Wellington and Lima ate the biscuits and the oatmeal Henry had prepared. As sunlight began to climb the distant ridges, they set off across the lake. When they were out of sight, Henry went to Maria's tent. He reached out, but held back from opening the flap, suddenly unsure.

"I'm awake," she said from inside.

He found her still in her sleeping bag, looking at him with a tired smile on her face. He lay down beside her.

"You smell like smoke," she said. "Take your clothes off and sleep with me."

He dreamed of a snowfall that covered the forest, so deep he could barely move. Among the trees, wolves circled and he knew he could not escape them.

"You're shivering," she said, and that woke him.

They made love again. The tent was warm in the sunlight, and, afterward, they lay together, wet with their own sweat.

Henry heard the sound of music, a muffled chime.

"What's that?" he said.

Maria reached into her canvas bag and pulled out a small box. Inside was a gold watch.

"It's a present for my father," she said.

She snapped it open and handed it to Henry. Opposite the face of the watch was Maria's face, a small photograph behind glass.

"His birthday is next week. On the front, see the writing? It's Spanish. It says, 'To my beloved papa.' I wish it said 'To my beloved Henry.' I wish I had something to give you. A present."

"You already gave me a present, the best I ever had."

He handed the watch back and she put it away.

That afternoon she swam again while Henry plucked the feathers from a grouse he'd killed. He could barely take his eyes off her. She swam naked now. She told him women had more fat on their bodies than men and could stand the cold, but Henry could see no fat on her.

Out of the corner of his eye, he caught a flash of reflected sunlight among the trees on a point a quarter mile to the west. It was a prolonged and brilliant glinting, the kind that came from glass or polished metal or some other thing that didn't occur naturally in the forest. Henry laid the half-plucked grouse on the ground. He grabbed his rifle, slipped into the woods, and worked his way soundlessly toward the point. Fifty yards away, he slowed and moved like a big cat hunting—creep and pause, creep and pause—while his eyes dissected every nuance of light and shadow.

He arrived at the place along the shoreline where he'd spotted the reflection. There was nothing to be seen. Henry studied the ground carefully. It was rocky terrain. The stones that poked through the soil were covered with lichen. On several stones, patches of the lichen had been scraped away by the careless placement of a foot. Henry widened his search. Twenty yards away he found a trail of broken ground cover leading west. In soft earth a hundred yards farther on, he found the imprint of a moccasin.

Henry stood up, certain now that he hadn't been the only one enjoying the sight of Maria swimming.

His inclination was to begin tracking immediately, but he had no idea how far that would take him or how long he would be gone, and there was still the evening meal to prepare. He held to the patience Woodrow had taught him. When he returned to camp, Maria had finished swimming and was dressed.

"Where did you go?" she asked and kissed him.

"I saw something."

She looked at his rifle. "What?"

He told her. She didn't seem frightened.

"What should we do?" she asked.

"We will find him," Henry said.

"Him?"

He didn't think a woman would be alone in this deep wilderness, but Maria was right. He had no idea.

"When will we find him?" she asked.

"Tomorrow."

"What about tonight? What if he—or she—comes back tonight while we're sleeping?"

"I won't sleep."

She smiled. "I'll help you stay awake."

Wellington and Lima came back arguing. Henry could hear their angry voices across the water. When their canoe touched shore, they stepped out and continued throwing words at each other.

"The geology's right," Wellington insisted. "And don't forget, Carlos, you heard the same story I did."

"I am not an impatient man, but I am also not a man without limits, Leonard. That goes for my money, too. And remember what happened in Ecuador."

"Ecuador was a lesson for both of us."

"An expensive lesson," Lima said.

"Education doesn't come cheap, eh?"

Lima moved close to the other white man. "You think that was funny? A joke?"

"The hell with you, Carlos. I need a drink." Wellington brushed past him and stomped to his tent.

That night after the meal, Lima went to bed. Wellington continued the drinking he'd begun on his return. Like Maria, he spent time every evening by the fire, filling the blank pages of a leather-bound notebook with writing. In the shifting light of the fire, Henry watched the man's eyes, which that night stayed dark and brooding as they lifted from his writing and held for long moments on Maria.

"The good daughter," Wellington finally said.

Maria looked up from her notebook. "I try to be."

"That's why you're here? To be the good daughter? You're only making him nervous, you know that?"

"Nervous?"

"He wants to get you back to civilization as soon as he can." He drank from the tin cup into which he'd poured his liquor. "A girl doesn't belong on something like this."

"I'm not a girl," she replied coolly and went back to her writing.

Wellington made a sound that might have been a laugh but came out more like a grunt. "I've noticed." His glare shifted to Henry. "What about you, Henry? Bet you've noticed, eh."

Henry burned. Wellington's tone spoke disrespect. Henry had lived with that tone much of his life and had learned to ignore it, but when Maria was included, that was too much. He'd been sitting near the fire, stirring the embers with a long, thick spruce stick to keep the flames alive for Maria's writing. Now he stood with the stick in his hand, the tip glowing, an angry red eye at the end of his arm.

Wellington didn't see. He stared at the fire and drank his liquor. Maria saw, however. She shook her head at Henry, her eyes afraid of what he might be about to do.

Wellington took a final long swallow. "Fuck it," he said and stumbled to his tent.

Soon afterward, they heard his snores join those of Lima. Henry let the fire die. Maria went to her tent. Henry gathered dried leaves and sticks from the woods and spread them around Maria's tent. Then he picked up his rifle and joined her.

That night clouds blocked the moon, but Henry knew Maria's beauty without light. The down of her cheeks, the wet oval of her lips, the curve of her breasts, all of it soft as dreaming. He fit himself to her until he couldn't feel a separation, couldn't feel the place where his own body ended and hers began. They were one skin, one breath, one heart.

Her lips brushed his neck. "I wish . . ."

"What?"

"I wish you'd been my first."

"It doesn't matter."

Later he said, "What were they like?"

"Rich. Sophisticated. Spoiled. Weak in ways you're not." She laughed quietly. "I guess I'm like that, too. Everything I have I've been given. I've never had to make my own way. All my friends are like that." She nestled deep into his arms. "You're different from anyone I've ever known, Henry. I felt safe with you from the beginning. Here we are a thousand miles from everything and I've never felt so safe."

He felt the same. She was like nothing he'd ever known. That they shared their bodies so quickly, so easily, so completely didn't surprise him. He had the deep sense that being together this way had always been meant for them.

Maria fell asleep with her head against his chest. He was tired, too, but he lay awake, listening. With the dry leaves and the sticks surrounding the tent, even a careful man could not approach without Henry hearing.

TWENTY-SEVEN

Henry rose with the sound of the first birds. The clouds that obscured the moon had passed, leaving the sky clear and full of stars. A faint glow along the eastern horizon suggested dawn.

He built a fire, filled the pot with lake water, and began coffee brewing. He made oatmeal and flapjacks. A few minutes after the sun came up, Wellington emerged from his tent. He went immediately toward the woods to do his morning business. When he returned, he poured himself coffee and stood staring at the lake. Henry had seen men hungover, and Wellington looked hungover.

"What do you do all day?" Wellington said.

"Cut wood for the fire," Henry replied. "Fish. Hunt. Gather things to eat from the woods."

Wellington was silent and sipped his coffee. He blinked against the morning sun. "What about Maria?"

Henry stirred the oatmeal. "She reads her books."

"All day?"

"I can't leave her. She comes with me when I go after food."

"She doesn't scare away the game?"

"She takes well to the forest."

"She swims," Wellington said. "I've seen her hair wet. But I haven't seen wet clothes."

"She dries her things over the fire."

The flap of Lima's tent swung open and the man stepped out. He coughed and spit. He went into the woods, and the noise of his business was loud and unpleasant. He came back and took the coffee Henry held out to him.

"Let's go over the maps," he said to Wellington.

They sat together looking at their charts, drinking their coffee, eventually eating the food Henry had prepared. After passing an hour in this way, they climbed into their Folbot and headed southeast across the lake.

When they were out of sight, Henry slipped into Maria's tent. He kissed her forehead. "Wake up."

Her eyes, brown like acorns, fluttered open. "What is it?"

"Time to go hunting."

She dressed. They ate and started off. The morning was crisp, and at first their breath popped out in gray-white puffs. The sunlight sharpened the edge of everything, gave fine definition to color and shape. Henry had shown her how to walk in the forest on the outside of her feet to reduce the noise of her passage. He'd instructed her to keep silent, explaining how sounds in the woods carried far. They made their way to the place where Henry had found the moccasin tracks.

He eyed the western ridge that curved around the end of the lake. He pointed, indicating to Maria that that was the way.

The trail was a day old now, but Henry had little trouble following it. Whoever had left it wasn't concerned about being tracked. Henry wasn't sure how to interpret that, but hoped it meant the watcher didn't think he'd been seen and was careless. The trail led them along the bank of a creek that edged the base of the ridge and curled into the folds of the land to the south. After an hour, the tracks joined a deer trail that angled up another ridge. When they reached the far side of that ridge, Henry paused and pointed toward a white patch of haze in a hollow below.

Maria whispered, "Smoke?"

Henry put his finger to her mouth to silence her. He nodded.

The next mile they moved at a crawl. With Maria behind him, he took no chances. He paused frequently to listen. Eventually he heard the chunk of an ax biting into wood. They came to a path through the undergrowth along a small, fast-running brook. The path led in the direction of the chopping. Henry debated following it. A path that well used was a danger. On the other hand, it would reveal to them quickly who held the ax, and with Maria, who still did not move with Henry's stealth, it would mean a quieter approach. He chambered a cartridge and moved ahead.

He glimpsed the cabin fifty yards through the trees. He signaled

Maria to drop into a crouch. They crept forward this way, low to the ground. The chopping stopped. Henry stopped. He listened. Suddenly the sound of whistling came from ahead. Henry spotted movement, then saw a figure carrying a load of split wood in his arms. The figure was dressed in buckskin britches. Long gray hair flowed over a buckskin tunic. Henry also saw moccasins on the feet. The figure stepped through the cabin door and disappeared. Henry signaled Maria, and they moved forward again and slipped into brush that edged the small clearing where the cabin stood. Henry lay on his belly. Maria did the same beside him.

The brook flowed behind the structure, which was a log construction similar to the cabin Henry and Woodrow had built on Crow Point, but looked much older than theirs. A winter supply of wood lay cut and stacked against the west wall. The cut wood occupied almost as much space in the little clearing as the cabin did. Fifteen yards away was another, smaller structure that Henry recognized as a smokehouse. A cleaned deer hide was stretched across the smokehouse wall. A chopping block stood a dozen yards from the cabin door, an ax blade sunk into the scarred, flat top. Split wood and wood chips lay strewn about the base like bone fragments. Whistling came from the cabin, but it was too dark inside for Henry to see anything.

They waited patiently. In ten minutes, the figure emerged and headed back to the block. This time Henry could see the face clearly, and he was surprised. The skin was very dark, mud brown. He glanced at Maria, who gave him a look of puzzlement. The man gathered an armload of wood to add to the stack against the wall. Henry made his move.

He strode forward before the man could unburden his arms and said, "Stop."

The man dropped the wood, spun toward Henry, saw the rifle, and looked poised to run.

"Don't move," Henry said.

The man held himself tense, ready, but he didn't move.

"Maria," Henry called.

She came from the underbrush and stood beside him. The man's eyes shifted from Henry to Maria. Something changed in them, but Henry couldn't tell what that meant.

"Who are you?" Henry demanded.

The man didn't respond.

"Maybe he doesn't understand English," Maria suggested. "*Bonjour*," she said.

The man waited, then nodded tentatively to her. "*Bonjour*."

"*Votre nom?*" she asked.

"Maurice," he replied.

"*Je m'appelle* Maria Lima," she said. She touched Henry. "Henry Meloux."

For the next couple of minutes, while Henry held the rifle and the man did not move, Maria carried on a conversation with him. At the end, she said to Henry, "He didn't mean any disrespect by watching me. He was just curious about who'd come to his land."

"His land?"

"That's what he called it."

"What did you tell him?"

"I told him I came with my father and my father's friend."

"What about me?"

"I told him you were my husband."

Henry looked at her.

"He saw me swimming naked and you watching. I thought it was best. He's apologized. I think you can put the rifle down, Henry."

Henry studied the man's face. It was old in a way that couldn't be pinned down in years. A face worn by the wilderness and what the wilderness required. Henry had seen the same weathering in Woodrow's face.

"He's a Negro," Henry said.

Maria laughed. "That's very observant, husband, but it's no reason to keep holding a gun on him."

Henry and the man locked gazes. Henry indicated that he was going to lower the rifle. The man nodded. Henry pointed the rifle barrel toward the ground and shifted the weapon to his left hand. If the man attacked, it would be difficult—probably impossible—to swing the rifle up in time to be of any use. Both men understood that.

Maurice spoke to Maria, who translated for Henry. "He's asked if we would eat with him."

Henry said, "We should accept."

She smiled. "I already have."

Inside, the cabin was spare but neat. It was a single room, like Henry's cabin on Crow Point, with a floor of hewn pine. Maurice had built a hearth and fireplace of stone. There was a bunk in one corner with a wool-blanket covering. In the center was a small table with two chairs. The man, Henry thought, had not always been alone.

They shared a meal of venison stew and, while they ate, Maria and Maurice talked.

"He has been here twenty winters," Maria told Henry. "He came with his wife whose name was Hummingbird."

"Hummingbird?"

"She was Odawa, he says."

"Odawa?"

Kin. Long ago the Odawa, like the Ojibwe and other Algonquin people, had migrated west to the Great Lakes after their enemy the Iroquois drove them from their land near the eastern sea.

Henry addressed Maurice. "*Anin,*" he said, in formal greeting.

"*Anin,*" Maurice replied. In the language of the Odawa, which was very nearly the language of Henry's people, Maurice and Henry talked.

"I am of the Iron Lake Anishinaabeg," Henry told him.

"I am from Quebec," Maurice replied. "I married an Odawa woman and lived with her happily for twenty years here."

"Where is she?"

"She died five winters ago."

"Your children?"

"We had none. Only each other."

"What is he saying?" Maria asked.

"He is a widower. A man, I think, who still misses his wife."

Maria spoke to Maurice, who smiled and said, "*Merci.*"

"Why did you come here?" Henry asked.

"Because I was a black man in a white world. Here the color of my skin doesn't matter."

That was something Henry understood well.

"We need to go back," Henry finally said.

"You will come again?" Maurice asked eagerly.

"He would like us to return," Henry told Maria.

She smiled at Maurice and said, "*Mais oui.*"

TWENTY-EIGHT

The days passed quickly. Henry and Maria often visited Maurice, who proved to be a wonderful and grateful host. Over time, they learned his story.

His father came from Haiti, where he'd been a carpenter, working on a sugar plantation. One night he got into a fight with the plantation owner's son over a woman and he beat the white man badly. He was forced to run. He took the woman with him and she became his wife. They fled to Canada, to Quebec, where a small colony of black Haitians was already established. Maurice was their first child.

His mother was white, and Maurice grew up with the names *half-breed*, *mule*, and *mongrel* thrown at him like stones. All his life he dreamed of rising to a place where he could look down on those who'd taunted him. Money, he'd believed, would be the way. He'd grown up with stories of wealth waiting to be discovered in the great, unexplored wilderness to the northwest. As soon as he was able—when he was seventeen—he left home and set out to find that wealth.

For the next fifteen years, he spent summers exploring rivers and streams he suspected no man had ever followed. Winters, he worked as a hand in a mill in Fort William owned by a French-speaking Quebecois.

One summer day he came across a village of Odawa where a young woman named Hummingbird lived. Love, he told Henry and Maria, struck him with the force of a bullet in his heart. All his loneliness leaked out and what filled its place was happiness. Hummingbird left her village and they traveled far into the wilderness, to the place beside the stream, where they'd built the cabin and lived together for twenty years. There was an Odawa village three days to the south where they traded for things they could not hunt or trap or gather—coffee, molasses, flour—which the villagers got from the government.

"It has been lonely since Hummingbird died?"

"Yes," Maurice admitted.

"Why did you stay?"

"I came here looking for gold. I found something better. These hills, this forest, the lakes and streams, the memories of Hummingbird, all these are worth more to me than gold."

"It must be a hard life here," Henry said.

"It is hard." Maurice nodded. "But I decided long ago that life among white people would be harder."

Lima and Wellington continued to return at day's end tired and discouraged. In the evening, they drank by the fire and discussed the next day's plan. One evening, Maria asked why they'd even bothered to come to this place anyway.

Wellington, whose tongue was loosened by drink, said, "We heard a story."

"Leonard," Lima cautioned and gave him a dark, warning look.

Wellington ignored him. "We heard a story from a man named Goodkin who canoed up here on the Pipestone River two years ago. He spent a night in an Ottawa village. While he was there, he heard a story about a Negro who dressed in buckskin and came a couple of times a year to trade for goods. The Indians said the Negro always traded gold. Goodkin didn't believe them, but they showed him a deerskin pouch covered with the residue of what looked like it could be gold dust. Goodkin bought the pouch and brought it back with him to have it tested. Sure enough, gold dust.

"A few months ago, Carlos and I flew up to the village. The Ottawa people didn't know exactly where the Negro lived. He was always clever in his coming and going and they couldn't follow his trail. But they told us it was generally up this way. We flew over the region and I liked the look of this lake. I did a brief preliminary survey and took samples of the sediment on the lake bottom. The results were extremely promising and we decided to return and spend more time before the snows came."

"Promising? Hell, you said you were certain," Lima snarled at Wellington. "So far we have found nothing."

"It's here, Carlos."

"How can you be so sure?" Maria asked.

Wellington stood up and paced restlessly as he spoke. The firelight ran the length of his body, so that he seemed to be a man in flames. "Gold is found in the oldest rock on earth, Maria. Usually that rock is too deep beneath the surface to get at the gold, eh. But where the rock has been pushed up through the surface—by volcanic action, for example—that's a good place to look. Also in a place scraped clean by glaciers in the Ice Age. Like the Quetico-Superior wilderness area north of where Henry lives. Or here. Those ridges across the lake are volcanic in origin. And the rock that underlies all this area is some of the oldest exposed rock on earth, the Canadian Shield. When I heard the story of the Negro's gold and saw this place, I knew it had to be true."

Maria spoke up. "But it is, as you said, the Negro's gold."

"Not if he hasn't filed a claim," Wellington said.

"And if he has?"

"Then we'll strike a deal. It's just a question of figuring out what a man like this Negro would want."

"What if there's nothing he wants?"

Wellington looked at her as if she were hopelessly naive. "There's always something, Maria."

That night, Henry lay with Maria in his arms. They no longer made love at night; it was too difficult to be quiet, and Henry was afraid of what would happen if the white men knew. With Maria's head on his chest, her hair soft against his cheek, her breath rolling warm across his skin, Henry had never been so happy.

"They know about Maurice," Maria whispered.

"They've found nothing. Maybe they will give up."

"Maybe," Maria said. "What are we going to do about us?"

"What do you mean?"

"I don't ever want to leave you, but when my father's finished here . . ."

Henry hadn't thought beyond the moment, beyond the happiness beside that wilderness lake. Which was unusual for him, in a way. His life depended on looking forward, reading the signs in autumn that would tell him about the winter to come, watching the skies in spring for the return of the birds, whose timing and number revealed much about the summer ahead.

"We could live here," Maria said. "Like Maurice and Hummingbird. They were happy."

Henry understood how hard that life would be. For the woman who'd loved Maurice, it was different. She'd been of this country and knew the hardship. Maria had lived another life.

There was something else to consider: Henry didn't know about love. He didn't know if love would always be enough for Maria.

He kissed her hair. "Sleep," he told her. "Just sleep."

He woke in the morning later than he'd intended. The tent canvas already glowed faintly with dawn. He slid away from Maria, who was still deep in sleep, her face relaxed and so beautiful he risked a kiss, a touch of his lips to her eyebrow. She stirred but didn't wake. He crouched at the tent entrance and reached out to open the flap. From outside came the cough and spit with which Carlos Lima greeted most mornings. Henry heard the crackle of fallen leaves as Lima made his way to his toilet. Henry waited a minute before leaving the tent, to be certain Lima had settled into his business. He eased the flap aside just a slit and peeked out to check the campsite. It looked clear. Quickly, he slipped from Maria's tent. As he stood and turned toward his own tent, he spied Leonard Wellington standing ten yards away, urinating into the underbrush. Wellington spotted Henry at the same time. The white man's eyes held on him, slid to Maria's tent, then crawled back to Henry.

"Appears that wolves aren't the only nocturnal predators up here. Carlos!" he called.

"I'm busy!"

Wellington buttoned his trousers. "Finish up, compadre. You have family business to attend to." He circled, watching, as if Henry were an animal about to bolt. "Carlos, get your Cuban ass over here."

Though there was menace in the white man's voice, Henry wasn't afraid of him. He was afraid for Maria because he didn't know what

Wellington and Lima might do to her because of this sin. He kept his position blocking the opening to her tent.

Lima appeared, hiking up his trousers as he came. "There you are, Henry. Where's the fire, damn it? And hell, boy, where's the coffee?"

"Henry's been busy with other things, Carlos. I just caught him sneaking from your daughter's tent."

Lima, as he walked, had been concentrating on the buttons of his pants. When he heard Wellington's words, he stopped. His eyes rolled up and he took in Henry and the tent where his only daughter slept. Rage flared on his face.

"You savage son of a bitch," he spat. "I will kill you."

He ran at Henry. Lima wasn't a big man, but he was powerfully built, especially in his upper body. He raised his arms and lowered his head. He reminded Henry of a charging moose.

Henry dropped low, caught Lima in the gut with his shoulder, and used the man's momentum to lift him off his feet. Lima tumbled over Henry and landed flat on his back. He tried to rise, but clearly the wind had been knocked out of him.

Wellington started toward Henry, but not with commitment.

At the government school in Flandreau, Henry had learned to box. Now he braced himself, brought his fists to the ready, and dropped into an easy fighter's crouch. It was enough to make Wellington pause.

"Henry?" The canvas flap rustled at his back. Maria touched his shoulder. "Oh, no." She rushed past him and knelt at her father's side. "Papa?" She looked at Henry. "Did you hit him?"

Before Henry could reply, Wellington said, "Your father was just trying to defend your honor. Henry nearly killed him."

"Maria?" Lima's breath had returned. He reached out and took his daughter's hand. "Tell me it's not the way it looks."

"Papa, I love Henry."

"Love?" He snatched back his hand. He rolled to his side and pushed onto his knees. "Love?" he bellowed. He brought himself up fully and leaned threateningly toward his daughter. "This is not love. This is rutting. This is what wild animals do. I did not raise you to rut like an animal."

"I'm not an animal. And Henry's not an animal."

"He's not a man." Lima turned to Henry. "A man would not take advantage of a girl this way."

Maria grasped her father's arm. "I'm not a girl."

He pulled away. "Clearly not anymore."

"I'm a woman, Papa."

"Maybe." He glared at her. "But you will never be a lady. Not after *him*. What man would want you now? I gave you the best of everything, and this is how you thank me? You are no better than a street whore."

He slapped her hard and she spun away. He raised his hand to hit her again. Henry lunged and grabbed Lima's arm. The man turned angrily. Henry hit him full in the face and felt the shatter of bone. The man went down. His head hit one of the rocks that ringed the fire, and he lay still, blood leaking from the left side of his head.

"Jesus," Wellington said. "You've killed him."

"Papa!" Maria sprang up and ran to her father's side. She knelt and put her hand to his cheek. "Papa?" She bent near his lips. "He's breathing. Henry, get me some water."

Henry grabbed a tin cup and sprinted to the lake. He dipped the cup full and brought it to Maria. She tore a strip from the bottom of the undershirt she wore, soaked it in the water, and dabbed at her father's blood.

"Papa?" she tried again.

Lima didn't respond.

Wellington threw a menacing look at Henry. "Let's get him into his tent."

They carried him in and laid him on his sleeping bag. Maria sat beside him.

"I'm sorry," Henry told her.

"He'll be all right." She gave him a brief smile, but Henry heard the lie in her voice.

Outside the tent, Wellington stormed about the campsite. "Damn you, Meloux. If he dies, I'll see you rot in prison. God as my witness, I'll see you hang."

Henry made a fire and coffee and biscuits because it was something to do while they waited. He poured a cup of coffee for Maria and put two biscuits on a plate with a puddle of honey. Wellington barred his way into the tent. Henry handed the food to the white man, who took it inside. Wellington and Maria spoke in voices too soft for Henry to hear the words. Wellington emerged, drilled Henry with a killing glare, and headed toward the lake. He waded to the floatplane anchored just offshore, disappeared inside, and came out with a small satchel that he took into the tent.

Henry, in his life, had seen a good deal of death. Usually it came at the end of a long, hopeless vigil. This was different. In truth, he cared little about Carlos Lima, and he thought if the man recovered and ever struck Maria again, he would kill him for sure the next time. But if Lima died, could Maria ever forgive the murder? Or would her love for Henry die as surely as her father had? That was a possibility Henry couldn't bear. He stood at the edge of the lake and he prayed— to Kitchimanidoo, to God, to all the spirits of the woods—to keep Lima alive.

Near noon, Wellington threw aside the flap on Lima's tent and stepped into the sunlight. He walked to where Henry stood on the lakeshore.

"He's not getting better. He needs a doctor. Maria and I are going to fly him out of here. Give me a hand getting the plane ready."

They laid bedding in the small cargo area, then returned for Lima. Inside the tent, Maria sat beside her father. She looked so tired and worn that Henry wanted to hold her and weep. He took his place on one side of Lima, with Wellington on the other. They lifted the unconscious man, carried him to the lake, waded to the airplane, and eased him inside. Maria had gathered a few of her things in a knapsack, and after her father was inside, she got into the plane. Henry saw the edge of her journal jutting out from under the flap of the knapsack. Even in desperate circumstances, she couldn't bear to leave it behind.

Wellington said to Henry, "Help me get some things from camp."

"Maria—" Henry tried to step up to the door, but Wellington grabbed his arm.

"Now!" Wellington ordered.

"Hurry, Henry," Maria called to him.

When they neared the tents, Wellington stopped and turned on Henry. "You're staying here, you redskin son of a bitch. You make sure this equipment is safe until I come back. And you better hope to God that Carlos doesn't die. Because if he does, I'm coming back with police, and you can kiss your red ass good-bye."

Henry glanced toward the plane. "Maria."

"I hear her name from your lips one more time and I'll kill you where you stand."

Henry wasn't afraid of the threat. He'd been threatened by white men all his life. Mostly, they were nothing but words. But he'd made enough trouble already.

He said, "I'll wait here."

"Damn right you will. Give me a hand with the propeller."

Wellington spun on his heel and hurried back to the plane. He pulled up the anchor, scrambled inside, and shut the door. Henry stood on the pontoon, and when Wellington gave him the signal, he threw the propeller. The engine coughed; the propeller made a couple of lethargic turns on its own, then caught. Henry stepped back onto the shoreline, and the plane maneuvered slowly toward the middle of the lake. Henry saw Maria's face at the window. Her lips moved, but he couldn't hear the words. He watched the wings square for a run across the water.

"Maria!" The word flew desperately from his lips.

He ran toward the plane and splashed into the water. The lake ate his body, swallowed him to the waist.

The floatplane began its run, leaving a silver crack in the water behind it.

"Maria!" Henry threw himself forward, swimming wildly toward the floatplane as it picked up speed and lifted into the air. "Maria!" he screamed.

He watched the plane grow small as a dragonfly and disappear beyond the ridges to the south. Then he let himself sink into the ice blue grip of the lake, which squeezed him until he was numb all the way down to his heart.

TWENTY-NINE

Henry sat all afternoon feeding the fire, watching the southern sky, though he knew it was useless to hope. He beat himself with the unknowns. Would Maria ever come back? Would he spend the rest of his life in prison? Should he run now instead of waiting for Wellington to bring the police? If he did that, how would he ever find her?

No matter how he looked at the situation, Maria was gone. Gone forever.

He'd lost much in his life, but losing Maria left him wanting nothing but to die.

A familiar voice at his back startled him out of his reverie. "I thought you had left." Maurice came from the trees and sat by the fire near Henry. "I heard the airplane," he said. "You look terrible, my friend. What happened?"

Henry explained the events. "They know about you, Maurice. They will be back. I don't know what to do," he confessed.

Maurice thought awhile. "Come with me."

"But if they come back—"

"They won't be back today. Come with me. There's something I want to show you, something that might help."

Henry followed in dismal silence. Never had the woods felt so empty. Never had he seemed so far from home.

They reached Maurice's cabin on the swift little stream. Maurice led him inside and blew into the embers of the fire and stoked the flame. He put water on to boil.

"Some tea will help. Hummingbird's recipe. Burdock root, sheep sorrel, slippery elm, and red clover."

Henry sat in the cabin, but his mind was still on the airplane he'd watched lift off the lake that morning, spray streaming from the floats, Maria vanishing.

The hot cup was suddenly in his hands.

"Drink," Maurice said gently. "And listen to me." He settled into a chair facing Henry and leaned close. A shaft of afternoon light came through the open window and struck his face. The sharp cheekbones above his beard were like dark, polished cherry wood. "In all my time among white people, the one thing I understood best was that for them, money forgives everything. In their courts, money can undo any wrong, even murder."

"Not murder," Henry said hopelessly.

Maurice shook his head. "Money will buy a good lawyer, and a good lawyer with enough money behind him can sell a lie to anyone."

"What lie? I didn't mean to kill him."

"You kill a white man, it doesn't matter why. They won't listen. Money will make them listen."

"I don't have money," Henry said miserably.

"What I want to show you."

Maurice rose from his chair, went to the bunk, and pulled it away from the wall. Henry saw the outline of a trapdoor beneath, cut into the floorboards. A knotted rope served as a handle. Maurice grasped the rope and lifted. He beckoned Henry to look. Beneath the floor lay a dozen deer-hide pouches, each larger than a man's fist.

"Take one," Maurice said. "Open it."

Henry lifted one of the pouches, surprised by its weight. He undid the leather cord and looked at the heaping of yellow grains inside.

"Do you know what that is?" Maurice asked.

Henry said, "Gold."

"It's yours. As much as you want."

"Why?"

Maurice smiled kindly. "I came looking for this. Once I had it, I realized I'd found something better here with Hummingbird. Happiness. We had each other. We had food and shelter. We had this land whose spirit is generous and beautiful. Children would have been good, but . . ." He shrugged that thought away. "So we stayed. When Hummingbird died, I thought about leaving. Except all my memories are here. Her spirit is here, too. I feel her with me all the time." He put a hand on Henry's shoulder. "What need do I have for gold?"

Henry closed up the pouch and carefully tied the cord. "If I take the gold, they will know where it came from. They will be back."

"They will be back anyway. It is only a matter of time."

"I will think about it," Henry said.

He stayed awhile with Maurice, but his mind was drawn to the campsite and the empty sky above the lake.

"I should go back and wait," he finally said.

"I'll wait with you," Maurice offered.

Henry didn't want to risk the white men seeing Maurice. "I will wait alone."

Maurice nodded. "If that's what you want. Remember, the gold is here for you. It will always be here."

They left the cabin. Maurice looked at the sky and sniffed the air.

"Your people don't come back soon, it won't matter much," he said to Henry. "Snow is on the way. I can smell it. I've got food if you need to spend the winter."

Henry thanked him and left. He made his way to camp and sat down to wait.

That night, Henry slept in Maria's tent. The smell of her on the sleeping bag was next to heaven. In the night, he heard music, the little chime of the gold watch. He found it among the things she'd left behind. He went outside and stirred the embers and stoked the fire until he had a flame bright enough to see by. He spent the rest of the night dividing his time between staring at the stars and staring at Maria's tiny image. Near dawn, he put the watch in his pocket, where it would stay. He didn't care if it was stealing.

They didn't come the next day or the next. That night Henry dreamed: The lake had turned to ice. The ridges were white with snow. He stood at the shoreline staring at Wellington's plane, which sat on frozen water. Flakes began to drift from the cloudy sky, and soon a curtain of falling snow descended, so that all Henry could see was the dim outline of the floatplane. He wanted to rush to it, to find out if it had brought Maria back to him, but his feet wouldn't move.

The door opened. A figure clambered out. Henry thought it was Wellington, but he couldn't be sure. The figure walked toward him.

As it came, it grew, taking on huge dimensions. The head became a ragged growth of shaggy hair. The fingers grew into long claws. Through the white gauze of snow, the eyes glowed red as hot coals. Henry realized that what was coming for him was not a man but a windigo, the mythic beast out of the horror stories of his childhood, a cannibal giant with a heart of ice. He turned and tried to run, but he could not move his legs. He looked back. The beast was almost upon him. Henry tried to cry out. His jaw locked in place, and only a terrified moan escaped. The foul smell of the windigo—the stench of rotted meat—was all around him. He saw the great mouth open, revealing teeth like a row of bloody knives. The beast reached for him. Henry tensed and cringed, prepared to be torn apart.

He jerked awake in the cold gray of early morning. Outside the tent, the sky was overcast. In the air, he could smell the approach of snow.

The airplane came at noon. Henry was napping. He heard the low thrum in the sky from the eastern end of the lake. He grabbed his jacket and ran out of the tent. The plane dropped toward the water like a swan descending. The floats touched, shattering the glassy lake surface, and the wings squared toward the shoreline where Henry stood. He couldn't see into the cockpit. The engine cut out, the blur of the propeller ceased, the blades froze. The plane nosed up to solid ground. The door opened.

Leonard Wellington climbed out. He walked along the pontoon with a rope in his hand. Leaping ashore, he tethered the floatplane to one of the large, heavy rocks that littered the shore. He went back to the cabin door and spoke to someone inside. Finally he looked at Henry.

"Wasn't sure you'd still be here," he said, stepping off the pontoon. "If I was you, I'd have taken to the woods. Vamoosed."

Henry only half heard. He was staring at the open cabin door. His heart was a wild horse galloping in his chest. He could barely breathe.

Another man climbed from the belly of the plane. He carried a rifle. Henry's hope cracked into a thousand pieces.

Wellington saw his face. "Expecting Maria? You'll never see her again, Henry. That's the way she wants it. You killed her father. That's right, he's dead. Yesterday."

Henry stared at the man who'd come with Wellington. He didn't look like a policeman. He looked Indian, and familiar.

"Maria told me about the Negro, Henry," Wellington went on. "We have a deal to offer you. Take me to him and the police will never know it was you who killed Carlos Lima. You have my word, eh."

Henry didn't answer. He felt dull, thick-witted. Nothing made sense.

"She hates you," Wellington said. "She wanted to come with me and tell you that herself, but I persuaded her to let me handle this, man to man."

Henry opened his mouth. He had no idea what he was going to say. What came out was, "I don't believe you." He eyed the Indian, who now stood behind Wellington, the rifle cradled across his chest.

Wellington smiled sadly. "I understand, Henry. You love her. Love makes you blind. But if I was lying, how would I know about the Negro? She told me everything. Except she couldn't tell me how to get to his cabin."

Henry studied the Indian. He was as tall as Wellington, over six feet, lanky but powerful-looking. His black hair was cut short in the way of a white man, with flecks of silver throughout. Henry remembered where he'd seen the man before, on the dock at the lake where the floatplane had landed to refuel on the flight north.

"*Boozhoo*," Henry said to him.

The man showed no sign of understanding the familiar Ojibwe greeting.

"I want to make a deal with this Negro fellow," Wellington went on.

Henry focused on Wellington's eyes, dark and small, like rabbit droppings. "I don't know what you're talking about."

Wellington lost his smile. "I'm talking about the gold, Henry."

"I don't know about any gold. I don't know about this Negro."

Wellington reached behind him, under his leather jacket, to the small of his back. When his hand reappeared, it held a revolver with a blued barrel, which he pointed at Henry. "I'd just as soon kill you, but I need what's in your head. You've got five seconds to start telling me how to find the Negro's cabin."

Henry eyed the Indian, who watched impassively.

"One. Two. Three. Spill it, Henry. Four. Five."

The revolver popped. Wellington's hand jerked. The bullet struck Henry's right leg, high above the knee. It felt as if he'd been hit with a baseball bat. He went down, sprawled on the ground. He grabbed his thigh. Worms of blood crawled between his fingers.

"Tell me where it is, Henry, or the other leg is next."

Henry bit down hard and held to his silence.

"Another five count. One. Two. Three." Wellington thumbed the hammer back. "Four. Five."

The gun barked again. This time the bullet burrowed into the dirt next to Henry's left leg.

Wellington grinned. "I thought you might be reluctant. That's why I brought Pierre with me. Claims to be the best tracker in northern Ontario. Guess we'll have to see. With all that traipsing back and forth you and Maria did to the Negro's cabin, I figure you must've left a decent trail, eh." He spoke over his shoulder to the Indian. "There's some rope in that far tent. Get it."

The Indian did as he was instructed and returned with a coil of hemp rope.

"Get him over to that tree. I don't imagine he'll be able to travel on that leg, but let's make sure he's not tempted."

The Indian tossed Wellington the rope and slung his rifle over his shoulder. He grasped Henry under the arms and dragged him across the campsite to the pine tree Wellington had indicated. He lifted Henry to his feet, shoved him against the trunk, and held him there. Wellington stuffed the revolver in his belt and uncoiled the rope.

Henry tried to keep his weight off the wounded leg and his mind off the pain. As Wellington bound him to the tree, he tried also to flex all his muscles and expand his chest. Wellington cinched the rope tight from neck to ankle and stepped away.

"I'll be back for you, Henry. Unless the wolves get you first." Wellington turned to Pierre. "Find the trail."

The Indian began in a slow arc at the edge of the camp, following one lead after another. Half an hour later, at the western edge of the campsite, he signaled with a whistle.

Wellington rose from where he'd been sitting near the black pine. "The hunt is on."

The two men disappeared into the woods, following, Henry knew, the trail that would lead them to Maurice's cabin. He was angry with himself for not having been more careful, but he hadn't worried about leaving a trail. The white men couldn't have followed the signs to save their lives. The surprise was the Indian.

His thigh was on fire. The leg of his jeans was soaked with red, but Henry thought the wound had stopped bleeding. He knew he was lucky. The revolver hadn't been a big caliber, and the bullet hadn't hit bone or an artery. He was also lucky in a way he didn't understand. Why hadn't Wellington killed him? The only thing that made sense was that if the Indian couldn't follow the trail, Henry was the fallback.

But Henry was determined not to wait for Wellington's return.

As soon as the two men were out of sight, he began to work on his bonds. He couldn't move his head. The rope about his throat gave him so little slack he could barely swallow. Wellington hadn't been as careful with the other loops, and Henry found that much of the advantage he'd hoped for in tensing his muscles he'd actually achieved. His hands and arms could move ever so slightly. First he worked his right hand back and forth, up and down. The rough pine bark scraped away the skin of his wrist, but he kept at it. Over the next half hour, by fractions of an inch, Henry gradually eased his hand free. Next was his left, easier because the release of his right hand created more slack in the rope. Gradually, he slipped both arms free, and when that was done, the loops fairly fell away. When he was free, he collapsed and lay at the base of the tree.

Wellington and his tracker had an hour's head start, and they each had two good legs. Henry dragged himself up and limped to his tent. He cut two strips of the soft canvas flap. The first strip he folded and placed over the wound in his thigh. The second he wrapped around his leg and tied to hold the compress in place. From inside the tent, he took his rifle and stuffed the pockets of his jacket with cartridges. He grabbed a tent pole to lean on as he walked. With his rifle slung over his shoulder, he followed where the two men had gone.

THIRTY

Henry knew the way to the cabin. In this he had an advantage over Wellington, who had to wait for the tracker to read the trail. He desperately hoped this would work in his favor, allowing him to catch up with the men before they reached Maurice. His leg was the problem. Even with the tent pole to lean on, walking was agony. When he came to those places that required him to climb—over a fallen tree, up a low rock face, along the whole of a ridge—the struggle ate his strength. Normally it took him an hour to reach Maurice's cabin. At the rate he was moving, it would take two or three times that. He was often forced to rest. There was nothing he could do about that. He had to gather his strength before he could go on, yet every second stretched into forever.

He reached the final ridge, the most difficult to climb. Looking up the long rocky slope, he wasn't sure he had the strength. His breaths came in deep heaves. Salty streams of sweat stung his eyes and soaked his shirt. The canvas over his thigh was wet with blood. He sat on a boulder, tired beyond measure.

He reckoned more than two hours had passed since he'd left camp. He'd hoped Pierre's prowess as a tracker might prove to be nothing but talk. It wasn't. The whole way he'd seen evidence of the passage of the two men, an X cut into the bark of trees, deep enough to show the white wood beneath. He wondered at that. Why mark a trail the Indian could obviously read? He was certain they were already at the cabin. His hope was that Maurice had not been there when they arrived, and that he would become aware of them before it was too late.

There was, perhaps, another hope: Wellington would strike a deal that left Maurice unharmed. But that would be like a wolf trying to eat a rabbit without damaging the fur. He pushed to his feet, forced himself beyond the pain, and began the long climb up. He felt a cold tingle on his face and glanced at the sky. Small snowflakes had begun to drift down from the clouds.

When he topped the ridge, Henry could see a thread of gray wood smoke rising from the cabin, still half a mile distant. He worked his way down the ridge and followed the little stream. The wind shifted in his direction, and he could smell the burning wood. As he neared the clearing where the cabin and outbuildings stood, he slid several rounds into his rifle. He hid in the underbrush and studied the cabin. The door was closed. He saw no sign of Maurice or Wellington or Pierre. Had they taken Maurice away, forced him to show them the gold deposit? Which way was that?

He wanted to make a dash for the cabin, slip along the wall, and listen for anything inside. His leg would never give him that speed. He settled on a different strategy. Between Henry's position and the cabin on the far side of the clearing, stood the outhouse. He decided to go for that first and from there to the cabin. He limped his way painfully across ten yards of open ground and fell against the back of the little structure. He paused there to catch his breath.

That's when he heard the men coming. They approached from upstream, from the west. Henry eased himself along the wall and peered around the corner of the outhouse.

"You go on. Don't worry about me." Wellington's voice boomed like the bellow of a moose.

A moment later, they stepped into the clearing, Pierre first, with Wellington not far behind. No Maurice.

"You're sure you remember the way?" Wellington said to the Indian's back.

"I remember."

"More's the pity," Wellington said.

He reached to the small of his back and produced his revolver. He pointed the barrel at the tracker. From three paces back, he couldn't miss. The revolver popped. The Indian's head jerked forward, as if hit with a club, and he dropped. Wellington stood over him. He slipped the pistol into his belt, grabbed the man's legs, and dragged him into the cabin.

Henry understood now the reason for the Xs carved into the trees. They were Wellington's assurance of finding his way back without the guide. He looked down at the rifle in his hands. Why hadn't he used it? He should have shot Wellington when the man was in the open. But the scene—the execution of the Indian—had surprised him.

Snow drifted out of the sky and coldly kissed Henry's face. He lifted his rifle, sighted on the door, and waited. He steeled himself for what he was about to do. He'd killed often, killed well and without regret. But this was different. This was no bear or moose or deer. This was a man like himself.

Not *like me,* Henry thought.

He was weak from his wound and from the long, difficult walk. His arms trembled as he tried to hold the rifle steady.

Wellington had been in the cabin for a long time when the wisp of smoke from the chimney turned into a billow, black against the gray clouds and the white snowflakes. In another minute, dark smoke began to roll out the cabin door and windows. Henry lifted his head away from the rifle stock. Where was Wellington? Where was Maurice? Why was the cabin burning?

Wellington stumbled from the cabin door, smoke clinging to his back. Henry quickly sighted. The wind hit the smoke from the cabin and, for a moment, a black curtain was drawn between Henry and his target. Henry pulled off the round anyway, keeping his aim at the spot where Wellington had been.

The smoke cleared a moment later. Wellington had vanished.

"Henry?" Wellington called. "Is that you, Henry?"

The voice came from the protection of the far side of the cabin. Henry's arms and shoulders ached from the long ordeal of trying to hold his stance.

"Your friend the Negro, he's inside, Henry. He's still alive, but he's going to burn to death pretty soon. You going to let that happen?"

Maurice alive? Was Wellington lying?

Yellow hands of flame thrust through the black smoke and felt their way along the top of the door and windows.

"Know what it's like to burn alive, Henry? Another couple of minutes and you'll be hearing his screams. It'll be too late by then."

Henry tried to think. There was nothing between him and the cabin, no cover of any kind. If he tried to save Maurice, he would be a clear target for Wellington. Henry considered Wellington's revolver. He didn't know much about handguns, but he thought the weapon's cylinder carried only six bullets. Wellington had fired two at the campsite and one into the Indian. Three left, if he hadn't reloaded. What was the effective range of a pistol? Not far, Henry hoped.

He had no choice. He stepped into the open.

Through the ragged veil of smoke that drifted across the clearing, Henry saw Wellington's head and shoulder appear around the corner of the cabin. His arm snaked around next, the revolver in his hand. The first shot hit the outhouse wall far to the left of Henry. Wellington fired again, this time hitting nothing. Henry kept coming. The next time the pistol popped, Henry was no more than fifteen yards away. The bullet creased his left arm, but by now Henry was like the cabin, full of fire. He barely took note of the bullet, and he felt no pain. He saw Wellington pull the trigger again and again. Nothing happened. The man's eyes grew large and afraid and he vanished behind the cabin. Henry hobbled as quickly as he could to the corner, his rifle raised and read to fire, but Wellington was gone.

Henry limped along the back wall to the far corner. No sign of the man. He completed a circle of the cabin. It was clear to him that Wellington had fled into the forest. Henry would gladly have hunted him down, but Maurice was still inside the burning cabin.

Through the doorway all Henry could see was the murk of the smoke and the yellow-orange dance of flame. He slung his rifle over his shoulder and dropped to the ground. On all fours, he crawled inside. He came to the Indian first. The man lay on his back. The side of his head was missing a chunk, and the raw pink of his brain hung in pieces along the ragged hole in his skull. To Henry's great astonishment, however, the Indian wasn't dead. His eyes followed Henry and his mouth moved, speaking words Henry couldn't hear above the rage of the fire. Henry hesitated only a moment before moving on to find Maurice.

His friend was slumped in a chair to which he'd been bound with rope. His chin lay on his chest. His eyes were closed. Henry pulled out his pocket knife, snapped open the blade, and cut the ropes. Maurice fell into his arms. Henry scooted across the floor to the door, dragging his friend with him. He inched past Pierre, whose terrified eyes tracked him and whose mouth kept working in soundless desperation. Henry tugged Maurice across the threshold and outside. Twenty yards from the cabin, his strength gave out and he collapsed and lay on the ground coughing out soot and smoke.

He wanted to lie there, to do nothing more, but he couldn't let the Indian burn to death. He scanned the clearing to make sure there was still no sign of Wellington, then he gathered his strength and crawled back to the cabin. The smoke had thickened, and Henry's eyes watered, so that he couldn't see. He felt his way along until he touched the Indian. He hooked his hands under the man's arms and hauled as he inched himself back out. Exhausted, coughing up black junk, a beast of pain chewing on his leg, he lay between Maurice and Pierre while the cabin burned.

"Henry." Maurice's voice was a low, choking rattle.

Henry propped himself on his arm. Next to him, Maurice's face was a mass of drying blood and swelling. His right eye was completely closed. He wore no shirt, and across his chest and stomach Henry saw lakes of discoloration darker than his skin. Maurice coughed and his face squeezed against the pain. Bright red blood leaked from his mouth.

"South," he whispered to Henry. "Go south. The river. Village."

"I'll take you with me."

Maurice gave his head a faint shake. "Legs. They broke them both." He coughed again, hard, and groaned painfully.

Henry studied the bruises on his friend's body. He didn't know what Wellington and the Indian had used—their fists or clubs of some kind—but they'd made a mess of Maurice. He was probably bleeding badly inside.

"They did this for the gold?" Henry asked.

"I tried not to tell them. I knew what they would do to this place once they found it."

Henry understood. The beauty of the land Maurice loved would not survive what Wellington would do to get at the gold it held.

Henry rolled toward the Indian, who lay on the other side. The man's face was slack, but his dark eyes said a great deal. Said *fear*, *pain, please help.* His mouth worked at words that never reached his lips. All that came from him was an unintelligible moaning.

There was nothing Henry could do for him. He turned back to Maurice. He shrugged off his coat, slipped it under his friend's bare back, and wrapped it around him for warmth.

Maurice shook his head again, faint but insistent. "South," he whispered urgently. *"Now."*

The west wall of the cabin collapsed in an explosion of spark and cinder. The south wall followed a few minutes later. The heat from the fire kept him warm, but the temperature was dropping. When the cabin was reduced to a smoldering ruin, he gathered logs from the winter store and built a fire in the clearing near where the two men lay. In the smokehouse, he found a wooden bowl that he cleaned in the stream and filled with clear water. He brought it to Maurice, who sipped a little, then Henry tried to get the Indian to drink. The man wasn't able to swallow, and Henry finally gave up. He took some deer meat from the smokehouse and tried to feed Maurice, who shook his head at the offering. He'd stopped insisting that Henry leave and lay on the ground staring up at the snowflakes that made his eyes flicker when they lit on his lashes.

Henry kept his rifle with him at all times. He figured Wellington was long gone, had made his way back to camp and the floatplane and had lifted off before the snow could prevent him. He considered going back to the camp himself, but decided that Wellington, if he was smart, had taken anything useful, and what he hadn't taken he would have destroyed. Wellington's best hope in all this was that the long winter would claim the wounded left behind. Henry had to admit it was a pretty good plan.

The snow fell fitfully into the night. Henry fed the fire and huddled near it. He heard the howl of a wolf pack on the ridge and, a while later, saw the glow of many eyes at the edges of the firelight. He fired a round into the air. The eyes vanished.

It was a long night as Henry kept his vigil, waiting for his good friend to die.

THIRTY-ONE

In the gray of the next morning, Henry did the hardest thing he'd ever done or would ever do.

Maurice had lasted the night. His breathing came, weak and labored. He hurt terribly from the damage of the beating he'd taken. He could barely drink the water Henry offered, and he would not eat. He drifted in and out of consciousness, never asleep, but falling instead into a fevered and incoherent kind of raving. Several times he called out to Hummingbird.

Dawn was hard to distinguish when it came. The snowfall had become steady. Wind blew along the ridge, and the snow, as it piled up, twirled into wraiths that danced across the clearing. Henry knew that if he didn't start soon, he'd never make it south to the river and the village Maurice said was there.

In his moments of clarity, Maurice knew it, too. The snow dusted his face and turned his beard white. Despite the fire and the coat Henry had put around him, he'd begun to shiver uncontrollably. He rolled his eyes toward Henry and whispered hoarsely, "Hummingbird told me about the Path of Souls. She told me she would be waiting for me at the end."

Henry knew of the Path of Souls. It led west, and those who died followed it to a beautiful place.

"Henry, I want to be on the Path of Souls. I want to be with Hummingbird."

"Don't ask me for this," Henry said.

"I hurt, Henry. And I'm going to die anyway, we both know it. I don't mind. It has been a good place to live. It is a good place to die, too. Henry, you would do as much for a wounded bear."

"You're not a bear."

"It has been good to have you with me these many days. It was like having a son." He reached out slowly, feebly, and laid his hand over Henry's. "It is hard for you, I understand. It is harder for me to think that you would die, too. I want you to live, Henry. I want you to have a good, long life. Do this for me."

Henry fought the tears, fought the rage that it should come to this, fought his great resistance to do what he understood was best.

He stood and stepped to the Indian, who'd also survived the night. He reached down and took the big hunting knife that was sheathed on the Indian's belt. The Indian's eyes followed him. He turned back to Maurice and knelt beside his friend.

"*Migwech*," Maurice said. He smiled at Henry, and he turned his head and closed his eyes.

Henry did not hesitate. He'd killed animals in this same way. He drew the blade quickly and expertly across Maurice's neck, severing the artery. The blood pulsed out and stained the snow around him. Maurice showed no sign of pain. He breathed raggedly several more times, then his body relaxed. He never opened his eyes again.

On his knees, Henry lifted his face to the sky that seemed to fall on him in shattered pieces. He let out a terrible cry and plunged the knife uselessly into the ground again and again, as if the earth itself were the enemy. He bent over his friend, and he wept bitterly.

When he was finished, he stood again. The wind had blown a small drift of snow against Maurice. Henry knew he couldn't bury him. He had nothing to dig with and neither the time nor the strength to gather stones and cover his body to protect it against the scavengers. Instead, he dragged Maurice into the smokehouse. He removed the coat he'd put on Maurice and shrugged it back on his own body. He couldn't remember the proper words for burial, neither the Ojibwe songs nor the prayers he'd heard at the mission on the rez and at the school in Flandreau. In the dark of the smokehouse that smelled of the meats Maurice had prepared to see him through the winter, Henry said, "He is on his way to you, Hummingbird. Receive him kindly."

Henry had a long and difficult journey ahead. Three days to the village on the river, Maurice had told him. Three days for a man with two good legs. He would need food. There was plenty in the smoke-house, but Henry had no pack or knapsack to carry it in.

Then he remembered the pouches of gold under the cabin floor.

He made his way among the smoking ruins, stepping carefully around fallen beams still alive with glowing embers. The east and north walls remained intact, and most of the floorboards, though black with char, were still sound. He cleared the debris, scraped away black ash, and found the trapdoor. The rope had burned away, leaving a small hole into which Henry stuck his finger and lifted. Below, the deer-hide pouches were undamaged. Henry emptied two, pouring the gold dust over the remaining pouches. He carefully closed the trap-door and covered it again with debris and ash so that it was invisible to the eye.

In the smokehouse, he filled the pouches with jerky and hung them from his belt. He also found a cigar box that held the flint and steel and tinder that Maurice used for the smokehouse fires. He re-moved them from the box and stuffed them in the pocket of his coat. He took one final look at his friend, silently wished him speed on his journey along the Path of Souls, and left. He closed the door behind him.

Snow lay several inches deep across the clearing. The storm showed no signs of letting up. He knew it could go on this way for days, the drifts growing deeper and deeper by the hour, until a man could not move through the woods without snowshoes. He walked to the Indian. The man stared up at him.

He was tough, Henry had to grant him that. With his head blown open and a cold night behind him, he still clung to life. Henry bent, undid the man's belt, and took his sheath. He put it on his own belt and sheathed the hunting knife there. He spoke, though he wasn't sure what the Indian understood.

"I'm leaving. Wolves came last night. They'll come again. They have the scent of blood."

The man's mouth no longer worked in its wordless way, but his eyes blinked.

"I could leave you to the wolves. Serve you right to be torn apart while you're still alive. I'm not going to do that."

Henry slipped the rifle off his shoulder. He chambered a round and pointed the barrel at the man's heart.

"You understand."

The man blinked, but his eyes stayed open, staring up at Henry.

Henry pulled the trigger. The shot shattered both the stillness in the clearing and the Indian's chest. Henry waited a moment to be certain of what he'd done. When he was satisfied, he turned and began to limp his way south.

THIRTY-TWO

Snow fell throughout the day. Henry struggled to keep his heading. There was no sun, nothing to navigate by, so he used a trick Woodrow had taught him early on. He picked a distant tree in the line he was traveling and made straight for it. Tree by tree, he limped his way toward the river and the village Maurice had promised.

The first night he camped at the edge of a small lake. In the lee of a fallen spruce, he built a fire. He cut pine boughs and laid them on the snow near the flames and sat down to eat. The jerky tasted good, and the warmth of the fire was comforting. Then he undid the canvas wrapping on his leg, eased his pants down, and took a look at his wound. It no longer bled, but it hurt like hell, an ache and burn that never subsided. There was only one hole, the entry wound. He felt a lump at the back of his thigh, under the skin where the bullet had lodged. When Henry was a child on the rez, an older cousin named Edgar Fineday had cut his foot with an ax. He'd neglected the wound, and the skin had turned green and dark green lines had run up his leg. His cousin died. Henry didn't want that to happen to him. He knew the bullet in him was poison. He knew the wound was prone to infection. He didn't have much choice but to get the bullet out and do what he could to seal the wounds.

He held the blade of the hunting knife in the fire to sterilize it, then laid it on the snow to cool before he cut. He didn't have to go deep to find the bullet, which he pulled out with his fingers. That was the easy part. He put the knife in the fire again. When the blade glowed red, he grasped the handle and laid the searing steel against the cut on the back of his thigh. He cried out and fell back onto the pine boughs, gasping. For several minutes, he lay still, feeling the burn gradually subside.

Slowly he sat up and looked at the bullet hole above his knee. He picked up his knife and once again shoved the blade into the glowing coals.

Wellington, he thought bitterly. He wrapped his resolve around the hatred he felt for the man. Henry had never hated before, not like this. This was a feeling like the hot knife blade. It seared and at the same time sealed, so the hate would be in him forever.

He drew the knife from the fire. He squeezed the bullet wound until the skin came together, then he laid the blade along the small fold. This time he did not cry out. He ate the pain. He fed the hate.

Snow piled on the ledge of his shoulders as he hunched toward the fire. He slept fitfully, sitting up. When he wasn't steeling himself against the pain or chewing on the bare, bitter bone of his hatred, he stared at the tiny photograph inside the gold watch and thought about Maria. Why had she told Wellington about Maurice? Blaming Henry for her father's death, even hating him for it, Henry could understand. Giving away Maurice, who'd done nothing but offer his friendship, and striking a deal for gold, this confused him. How could gold balance the murder of her father? For a man like Wellington, such a trade made sense. But Henry thought he knew Maria, and throwing in with Wellington was something he couldn't imagine of her.

Did he really know her? He began to worry feverishly in the cold dark as the flames died. He'd never loved a woman before. Did love blind people? Had what he'd felt in her arms made him stupid? The fear that he'd been wrong about her, about everything with her, hurt him worse than the bullet or the burning knife blade.

"Maria!" he cried to the empty woods.

He fell back on the pine boughs and curled into a ball around his pain.

He woke stiff and feverish. The fire was all ash. The snow was over a foot deep. The sun was still hiding. He rose and shook off the snow. His leg felt hot and tender to his touch. He put weight on it. It held. He ate jerky, drank lake water, slipped his rifle over his shoulder, and suddenly realized he wasn't sure of south.

How had he reached the lake? He scanned for tracks, but the snow had obliterated every trace of his coming there. He looked up at the sky, a gray slate that spit white flakes and revealed nothing. The fever, he thought. He was not thinking clearly because of the fever. He grabbed a handful of snow and rubbed it over his face. It cooled his skin, but did nothing to clear his head.

Pick a tree and a direction, he decided, and leave it to God and Kitchimanidoo where it took him.

For two more days, he limped and stumbled on. The third day the sun finally appeared, and Henry realized his heading was off. He'd been traveling southwest. He was exhausted. His leg hurt constantly. His fever raged. He'd begun to see things among the trees, movement out of the corner of his eye, but when he looked, nothing was there. He heard things, too, sounds in the wind and the creaking of branches that seemed like voices. He'd never been afraid of the woods; now he eyed the forest anxiously. He carried his rifle with a chambered round. He dreaded the night. His fires seemed too small against the overwhelming dark around him. He woke often in the black hours, certain he was being watched by something beyond the weak, flickering light.

In the deepest part of him, however, deeper than the fear, so clear that it was never blunted by the confusion in his mind, was the burning hate he held for the white man Leonard Wellington.

On the fourth day—or maybe it was the fifth, he'd lost track—he saw Wellington. The man stood on a hill directly ahead of him. The blinding sun was at Wellington's back. Now Henry understood why he felt he was being stalked. Wellington hadn't left in his airplane. He'd followed, waiting for his chance to attack. Henry ripped the rifle off his shoulder, shoved his cheek against the stock, and fired. Wellington disappeared in a sparkling spray of powdery snow. When Henry reached the spot, he found signs of flight, tracks that looked like deer but Henry was sure were not.

"Wellington!" he screamed. "I will eat your heart!"

He didn't sleep that night, knowing the white man was hoping for just such a chance. Nor did he build a fire that would give him away. By moonlight, he kept watch, his rifle on his lap.

Wellington didn't come that night. In the morning, clouds swept in again, bringing more snow. All day as he struggled ahead, Henry could feel Wellington in the storm, a looming presence just beyond the limits of his eyes and ears.

He lost interest in the river, in the village there. He only wanted Wellington dead. He wanted to feed on Wellington's heart.

The storm brought an early night. Henry didn't look for a sheltered place. He simply stopped walking and sat down in the snow. Dark settled over him, dark so thick he could hold it in his hands. Time passed.

His eyes snapped open. He realized he'd fallen asleep. The storm had ended. The clouds had moved on. The wind had ceased. A half-moon had risen. The forest around him was bone white snow and tar black shadow, and the silence was stone solid.

He knew Wellington was near. He knew it in the way he understood what weather the wind would bring or the direction in which a deer would run. It wasn't something he had to think about. The rifle lay across his knees. His finger rested inside the trigger guard.

A cracking of branches came from his left. His eyes swung toward a gap in the pines where the half-moon floated like a silver leaf on black water.

Henry was surprised. The silhouette that appeared was much larger than a man. It didn't worry him. He stood to meet his enemy. He reached to his belt for the knife he'd used to kill his friend, but touched only matted hair. He looked down at himself, surprised to find that his belt was gone; in fact, all his clothing was gone. His body no longer looked pale and human. He'd become a hairy beast, massive as a bear. He felt empty inside, except for an icy ball where his heart should have been. He was ravenous, hungrier than he ever remembered, and he could not wait to rip out Wellington's heart and feast on it.

He could smell his enemy, smell the odor of carnage, the stink of rotting flesh. Far from repulsing him, it made him hungrier.

He opened his mouth to spit out a taunt. What came instead was an inhuman roar. It was answered in kind by Wellington, who was no longer Wellington but a windigo. In the moonlight, they charged at each other, kicking up an explosion of powdered snow as they attacked.

They met like mountains colliding. Henry sank his teeth into the neck of the other and tasted icy blood. The bellow of the windigo shook the snow from the trees.

They battled savagely, filling their mouths with blood, tearing out chunks of hair-covered flesh. Hunger drove Henry to a frenzy, and at last he plunged his hand into the other's chest, grasped its heart in his claws, and ripped it out. The windigo let fly a death cry that was as appetizing to Henry as the heart on which he began to feed. He gobbled up the organ while it still beat.

He stood over the lifeless form of the windigo that had once been Wellington. He lifted his bloody face to the black sky and gave an angry howl. He'd thought that eating the man's heart would fill him, but it didn't. He was hungrier than ever.

THIRTY-THREE

Henry woke to the smell of sage and cedar burning. He opened his eyes and found himself in a *wiigiwam*, wrapped in a bearskin. A few feet away a woman sat tending a small fire. She had long gray hair woven into a single thick braid that hung over the shoulder of the plaid wool shirt she wore. When Henry stirred, she looked up.

"Where am I?" Without thinking, he'd spoken in the language of his people.

"Some men from the village found you. They brought you here."

Henry understood her words, but she said them in a way he'd never heard before.

"Are you Ojibwe?" he asked.

She shook her head and added a cedar sprig to the fire. "Odawa."

The deerskin flap that hung across the doorway was drawn aside, and an old man entered. Bright sunlight slipped into the *wiigiwam* with him.

"Finally awake." He sat next to Henry. His knee joints popped like walnuts cracking. "Who are you?"

Henry said, "Niibaa-waabii." His Ojibwe name. It meant Sees At Night.

"I am Ziibi-aawi. This is my daughter, Maanaajii-ngamo. You have been sick a long time."

"How long?"

"Seven days ago you were brought here."

"Fever?"

"That and other things. You are not Odawa," the old man said.

"Ojibwe."

"A lost Ojibwe."

"Not lost. I was looking for the village."

"Where you were headed, you would not have found it. You were lucky the men stumbled onto you. They thought at first you were an old man gone out into the woods to die alone."

"Old man?" Henry said.

Ziibi-aawi waved an age-spotted hand toward Henry's head. "Your hair."

Henry reached up and grasped a handful of the fine black hair, which he'd let grow long since he left the boarding school. When he looked at what he held, he didn't understand. His hand was full of strands white as spider's silk.

"My hair," he said. "What happened to my hair?"

"You are young for hair so old."

"It was black," Henry said. "Black as crow feathers."

Ziibi-aawi gazed at him with deep interest. "What a thing it must have been."

"My hair?"

The old man shook his head. "Whatever turned it white. It is a story I would like to hear."

Henry told him about his battle with the windigo. The old man listened, and his daughter, too.

"Look at yourself." Ziibi-aawi pulled away the bearskin.

Except for the wounds on his leg, which were healing, Henry saw no marks on his naked body.

"It was a vision," the old man explained. "The windigo is a beast of the spirit. It feeds on hate, and it is never full. There is only one way to kill a windigo. You must become a windigo, too. But when the beast is dead, there is a great danger that you will stay a windigo forever. You must be fed something warm to melt the ice inside you, to melt you down to the size of other men."

Henry looked toward Maanaajii-ngamo, who fed cleansing sage and cedar to the fire.

"I am Mide," Ziibi-aawi said. "Maanaajii-ngamo is also Mide. You know the Grand Medicine Society?"

Henry knew of it. Healers of the body and spirit. Since the coming of the white men, those among the Ojibwe who understood the healing secrets had become few.

"This is an important vision. You have had visions before?"

Henry thought about the dream in which he was flown north by a snake with wings to a lake where a golden fire burned under the water. He thought about the kind of man Wellington was and the gold that had brought him far north, to the lake.

"Yes," he said.

"Kitchimanidoo has guided you here. You understand?"

Henry said, "What if the windigo had eaten my heart instead?"

"You would be a different man with a different destiny."

"Or you would be dead," Maanaajii-ngamo said.

"You have been marked. You have been given the gift of visions," the old man said. "You are welcome to stay with us as long as you need in order to understand this gift."

Henry felt as if he'd already traveled to the end of the earth, but he realized he still had a very long way to go before his journey was finished.

"*Migwech,*" he said, and closed his eyes to rest.

PART III
THE LAKE OF FIRE

THIRTY-FOUR

By the time Meloux finished his story, it was well after midnight. We sat beside the lake, and I could see Henry clearly in the bright moon glow. He was an old man; it had been a long, hard day; he was tired. Hell, I was tired, but there were still questions left unanswered, things I needed to know.

"How long did you stay with the Mides?" I asked.

"In the spring, Ziibi-aawi traveled the Path of Souls. That summer, Maanaajii-ngamo took me down the river. We stayed with another of the Midewiwin, a good man named Waagosh. For seven years I learned from him. When I left, I was Mide, too."

"You came back to Iron Lake?"

"Two more summers, I journeyed."

"You were gone for almost ten years?"

Meloux looked up at the moon. The light washed over his face and made me think of a man gazing up through silver water. "When I came back, people on the rez did not recognize me. When they learned I was one of the Midewiwin, they were suspicious of me. They looked at my hair and thought of me in the way white men think of witches. Some Shinnobs still do."

"You never talked to the police about what Wellington had done?"

"I was a man who had killed three times. I have never told anyone these things until now."

"And you never tried to find Maria?"

"For half a moon I knew Maria. I loved her. I have never loved another woman. My life, Corcoran O'Connor, has been about something different from that kind of love. For many years, I did not think about her."

"But you knew you had a son. How?"

"From visions. They began soon after Maria left me."

"You weren't curious about your son?"

"I am fortunate. I have often felt guided. If I was not meant to see my son, that was the way of it."

"Then why this sudden heaviness of heart over him? Why the rush to find him?"

Something splashed in the water a dozen yards out. A fish jumping, maybe, or a muskrat diving. In the moonlight, the place was marked with a circle of black ripples edged with silver.

"I have had visions," Meloux said. "They have told me my son needs me."

"Henry, I don't mean any disrespect, but from the way he looked the last time I saw him, he could have used your help a long time ago. I think it's too late now."

"There is a reason for the visions."

"Well, I'll be goddamned if I know what that is, Henry."

"They are not your visions, Corcoran O'Connor. They are not for you to understand. I will talk to him, then I will know."

"Henry, there's no way this man is going to talk to you. Christ, he tried to have you killed."

"I do not believe my son would do that."

"There's sure a lot of evidence to the contrary."

"I will see my son. I will see him with or without your help."

"You can be exasperating, you know that, Henry?"

"Which is stronger," the old man said, "the rock or the water? In the end, the rock always washes away."

"Stow it, Henry. You've won. I'll take you, okay?"

"*Migwech*," the old man said.

"We both need rest, Henry. We'll leave in the morning."

I heard a car turn off the road, and headlights swept the trees around us.

"Your nephew's home from the casino," I said. "Let's break the news to him."

Ernie Champoux wasn't happy, but what could he do? He was just another rock, and Meloux, as always, was the damn water.

* * *

When I pulled onto Gooseberry Lane I could see lights on inside my house. I parked in the driveway and went in through the side door. A couple of plates full of crumbs sat on the kitchen table. On the counter were two glasses filmed with white residue. Cookies and milk. Jo and Jenny had probably enjoyed a little comfort food while they waited for me. The house was quiet. I walked to the living room and found Jo asleep on the sofa. Jenny wasn't there.

"Jo." I spoke softly.

Her eyes fluttered open. "Cork?" She sat up. "What time is it?"

"A little after one. Jenny gone to bed?"

She nodded and yawned. Her hair was wild on the side where her head had rested, and there was a red line, from her nose almost to her ear, where her cheek had pressed against the seam of the sofa pillow. It looked like a battle scar. The look she gave me was a little warlike as well.

"Sorry I'm so late," I said.

"You said you'd be home so we could all talk."

"Henry had a lot to tell me."

Despite her irritation, it was clear she was curious about Meloux's story. "What exactly did he say?"

I told her a briefer version of the story Meloux had told me. Even though the hour was late and she was tired, she listened closely.

"So all this might be about keeping an old crime from coming to light?" she said.

"It could be much larger than that. I've been thinking about the mining claim. From what I gathered on the Internet, the wealth of Northern Mining and Manufacturing is based on what came out of that first mine in northwestern Ontario. Could be that a lot of the wealth rightfully belongs to someone else."

"Any living relatives of the man named Maurice?"

"It's a possibility. It would sure be a reason to keep Henry from telling his story."

"What are you going to do?"

I wasn't looking forward to this part. With all that was going on with Jenny, I knew I needed to be home.

I said, "In the morning, I'm taking Meloux to Thunder Bay to see his son."

I thought maybe it was because she was tired that Jo didn't hit me. She weighed the information and nodded. "Before you go, though, we need to sit down and talk with Jenny."

"How's she doing?"

"Struggling. Trying to figure this thing out. It's huge."

"Jesus, I don't want it to crush her."

"She's strong, Cork."

"What if she decides to have an abortion?"

"I don't think she will."

"And if she decides to keep the baby and raise it alone?"

"She won't have to do it alone."

"Oh God, Jo, what if they decide to get married?"

"Then they'll march down the aisle with all our love behind them."

"You make it sound easy."

"None of her choices is easy, but there's not one of them that's impossible."

"Have I told you lately that you're amazing?"

"Not lately."

"Good. I wouldn't want it to go to your head. Should we talk to her now or wait until morning?"

"Morning. She's pregnant. She needs her sleep."

"And I'm old," I said, "and need mine."

I got up and began to turn out the lights. Another uncomfortable thought occurred to me.

"Have you talked to Sean's folks?"

"To Virginia. Sean told her everything. Lane doesn't know yet."

I could understand. Lane wasn't an ogre, but I had the feeling he could be unpleasant in a confrontation. Still, he was the father of the young man whose destiny was supposed to have been transforming Pflugleman's Rexall Drugs into Pflugleman and Son, and it seemed to me he had a right to know what was happening.

When I'd switched off the last of the lights, I put my arm around Jo, and we started up the stairs to bed.

"Cork, I don't think you and Henry should go to Thunder Bay alone."

"Don't worry. I plan on taking backup."

She didn't ask who. It may have been because she was too tired. It was more likely that she already knew.

THIRTY-FIVE

Except for Sundays, Johnny Papp opens the door of his Pinewood Broiler in the morning at six sharp.

At five fifty A.M., I found Wally Schanno waiting out front in the cool blue of that summer morning. Those days he was always at the Broiler first thing, waiting for the doors to swing wide and offer him the company of the regulars. His back was to me. He was staring down Oak Street past the dark, locked shops as if he was waiting for something to arrive along that empty pavement.

For better or worse, I was it.

I startled him with a tap on his shoulder.

He spun around. "Jesus."

Schanno was a devout Lutheran, Missouri Synod. I'd never heard him say Jesus in quite that way. Arletta's death continued to work changes in him.

"Sorry, Wally. I didn't mean to sneak up on you. You looked deep in thought."

"I was just thinking it's a pretty town. I'll miss it."

"Miss it? You're leaving?"

He was wearing a white-knit golf shirt. He had several more at home in various pastel shades. In their last years together, Arletta had been after him to take up the game as a way of relaxing. The shirts had been just the beginning. She gave him clubs and a bag. He was an atrocious golfer, and he hated the game, but he went out on the links once a week or so anyway because Arletta had done these things for him and he wanted her to know he was grateful. He never told me this. It's just my interpretation of events.

His big shoulders hunched together, and his huge right hand went to rubbing the back of his neck above the collar of the golf shirt. "I tossed and turned most of last night. My daughter's been trying to convince me to move to Maryland to be closer to my grandkids. 'Bout three A.M. I decided she was right. Nothing for me here."

Inside the Broiler the lights went on. I saw Johnny Papp chalking the breakfast special on the blackboard behind the register.

"Not leaving right away, are you?" I asked.

Schanno picked up on something in my voice and squinted at me. His eyebrows were nearly white as milkweed fluff.

"What's up?"

"I'm taking Henry Meloux to Thunder Bay today. I could use your help, if you're willing."

"So it's true. He's got a son up there."

Johnny Papp unlocked the door and poked his head outside. "Get in here," he ordered, "before you scare the good customers away."

I said to Schanno, "Let me buy you a cup of coffee. I've got a story to tell."

The moment I walked into the house I smelled coffee brewing, and I saw that the dining room table was set. Jo came from the kitchen with a small pitcher of half-and-half in her hand.

"Lane and Virginia are on their way over with Sean," she said. "We're going to talk."

"At seven thirty in the morning?"

"Lane found out about everything late last night. He'd have come over then but Virginia convinced him to wait."

"Jenny?"

"Upstairs being sick."

"This can't wait?"

Jo had headed toward the kitchen, but she stopped and turned back to me sharply. "Until when? You're leaving with Meloux today."

"What's with the table settings?"

"Virginia's bringing coffee cake. I've got juice and coffee."

"Very civilized," I said. "Should I shave?"

"Just sit quietly and listen."

Jenny came downstairs, her face drained of color. She'd brushed her hair and put on a little makeup. She wore jeans and a powder blue top.

"How're you doing, kiddo?" I asked.

"Okay, Dad." She stood away from me a bit and stuffed her hands in the back pockets of her Levi's. "How's Henry Meloux?"

"I'm still working on that. Right now let's focus on you." I went to her and took her in my arms. I laid my cheek against her hair.

"I'm sorry about all this," she said.

"Me, too. But we'll figure it out, okay?"

"You're not mad?"

"I'm not exactly ecstatic."

"Complicates things, huh?"

"Sit down." I pulled a chair from the table. "Tell me what you're thinking."

Jo had come back from the kitchen, and she sat down, too.

Jenny began in a calm, rational voice, but before long she was crying, and it was clear she didn't know at all what she was going to do.

When I was a cop, people cried in front of me all the time. Because they were scared or grieving or trying to manipulate. It almost never bothered me. Jenny's tears were like drops of acid on my heart. She slid into her mother's arms and sobbed.

The doorbell rang. Oh, joy.

I opened the door. Lane Pflugleman was there, with Virginia and Sean at his back.

I'm not tall—just under six feet—and Lane Pflugleman is a head shorter. He's slender, congenial, though generally quiet, and he wears a mustache, mouse brown going gray, that always puts me in mind of a moth with spread wings resting on his upper lip. I've known him all my life. He'd been a couple of grades behind me in school, and I wouldn't have taken much notice of him except for his wrestling. In his junior year and again in his senior, he took state in his weight class. In Aurora, wrestling wasn't like football or basketball. It didn't have the same mystique. There weren't cheerleaders. There weren't fast breaks or Hail Mary passes or that sudden momentum that can sweep spectators up in a frenzy of hometown pride. The gym was never packed for meets. In fact, the team as a whole did poorly. Lane was the only bright spot, and he did his glory work in relative obscurity.

I watched him wrestle only once, the year after I'd graduated. I was home on a break from college. My mother was a friend of Lane's mother, who'd invited her to a meet. She asked me to accompany her, thinking that because I was a guy I'd understand the sport and could explain.

There wasn't much to Lane Pflugleman. He wrestled at 119 pounds. I'd been a football player. On the football field, Pflugleman would quickly have been reduced to a red smear on the green grass between a couple of white chalk lines. On the mat in the high school gymnasium, where less than two dozen people watched, Lane Pflugleman performed physical magic. You didn't need to know anything about the sport to admire how he moved, worked his opponent, understood his own body and what he could ask of it. I admired, too, his behavior after he easily won his match. A decent winner.

"Come in," I said and stood aside.

Sean walked behind his father. He was a tall kid, taller than his father, lean and strong, with thick black hair and a handsome, studious face. He wore wire-rims and had the haunting look of, I imagined, a poet. It was easy to understand why Jenny had been drawn to him. As he passed, he avoided looking at me directly.

"I brought coffee cake," Virginia said and handed Jo a platter covered with aluminum foil.

Virginia taught math at Aurora Middle School. Jenny had been one of her students. I remembered conferences with her, how pleasant she'd been and how complimentary of Jenny's work. She was a pretty woman, and it was from her that Sean had gotten his height.

Jenny had dried her tears, but it was obvious she'd been crying. She sat between Jo and me. Sean and his folks took places along the other side of the table.

"Coffee?" Jo asked. "I have orange juice, too."

Lane said, "Coffee, thank you."

"Yes," Virginia said.

"Sean?"

"Juice, thanks." He spoke toward his lap.

"I apologize for the hour," Lane said. "I know it's early."

"We were all up anyway," I said.

Things went quiet while Jo brought coffee and juice from the kitchen. She cut and served the coffee cake. In that awful stillness, the kind that often precedes uncomfortable discussions, I could hear cardinals singing in the maple out back. I stared through the window at the grass wet with dew, sparkling, as if my backyard was full of diamonds. I wanted not to be at the table, not to be a part of this torture that would test the love we had for our children and for one another. I knew Jenny and Sean were miserable. Lane and Virginia looked as if they hadn't slept at all. I was dreaming about being somewhere else, anywhere else. Only Jo seemed calm, but I'd seen her in court take ridiculously bad verdicts without batting an eye, then cry in the privacy of her office.

"I'm glad we're together this morning," Jo began. "Sean and Jenny have some difficult decisions ahead of them. The truth is, it's a tough situation for us all." She looked at her daughter with great compassion. "You know that Jenny had planned to leave for the University of Iowa in a couple of weeks."

"Sean was supposed to go back to Macalester," Virginia said.

"I'm not going." Sean's voice was quiet but definite.

"What do you intend to do instead?" his father asked. "Go to Paris? That's ridiculous, especially now."

"Is it? People in Paris have babies, too."

"Is that what you want, Jenny?" Jo said. "To have this baby and take it to Paris?"

"I don't know," she said.

Lane cleared his throat. "What I don't understand is why you weren't more careful. I'm a pharmacist, for god's sake. I have a store full of contraceptives."

"I told you, Dad. We were using condoms, all right?"

"Pregnancy rates with condoms can be as high as fifteen percent. And that's when they're used correctly." Lane eyed Jenny. "Why not the pill?"

"That, she's way too Catholic for," Sean said, as if it ought to be glaringly obvious. There also seemed to be blame in his voice, and I wanted to reach across the table and take a handful of his shirt and shake him until his teeth rattled.

"It seems to me the obvious choice here is marriage," Lane said.

That was answered with silence all around the table.

"You can go back to Macalester as a married student," Lane continued, "finish up there, and come back here to a partnership in the pharmacy."

"I don't want to be a pharmacist. I never wanted to be a fucking pharmacist."

"Sean!" Virginia's face went red. From shock maybe or embarrassment. Her eyes, full of sympathy, shot toward her husband in a way probably meant to signal, *He doesn't mean it.*

"It's what makes the most sense, Sean," Lane pushed on with admirable evenness in the face of his son's hostility. "From what I understand, you were thinking of asking Jenny to marry you anyhow."

"That was for Paris," Sean snapped. Then he seemed to realize how that sounded. "I mean . . ." He looked cornered. "I don't want to be a pharmacist, okay? I want to be a writer. I want to see the world. I don't want—"

"A baby holding you back," Jenny finished for him.

"I didn't say that."

"It's what you haven't been saying since I found out I was pregnant." There wasn't any accusation in her words, just a kind of dull, sad truth.

He faced her across the table, his soulful eyes full of the pain that was supposed to produce great poetry. "I love you, Jenny. I love you so much. But . . ." For a young man who wanted his life to revolve around words, he was suddenly at a loss for them.

"But a baby wasn't part of the bargain," she finished for him.

"Look, if you want to have this baby, I'll be there for you."

"You're a liar, Sean." She said it quietly, as tears rolled down her cheeks. "For you, this baby will always be something that trapped you and killed your dreams."

She got up and rushed from the table to the kitchen.

"Jenny!" he called hopelessly after her.

The hinges on the screen door squealed, and the door slapped shut as Jenny left the house.

Sean jumped up to follow her, but his father reached out to restrain him.

"Let her go. She doesn't want to talk to you right now."

"What do you know?" Sean eyed us all. "What do any of you know?"

He turned and stomped his way out the front door.

I saw Stevie sitting on the stairs in his pajamas, his dark eyes wide with interest.

"I'd hoped that would go better," Jo said.

Virginia laid a comforting hand on her husband's arm. "He doesn't mean all that, Lane. He's just upset."

Lane stared down at the coffee cake, untouched, on his plate. When he lifted his face, I thought I saw something of the wrestler in him that I'd admired a long time ago. Only now he wasn't dealing with an easy victory.

"I'm sorry," he said to us.

Stevie left the stairs and tentatively approached the table, his eyes locked on the coffee cake. "Is that just for adults, or can a kid get lucky?"

It wasn't funny, really, but it made us laugh.

Jo had a pretty good idea of where Jenny might have gone.

St. Agnes is an easy walk from our house. Father Ned Green, the young priest, opened the doors early every morning and encouraged his parishioners to drop in and start each day with quiet, personal prayer. Jo occasionally did that. Lately Jenny had taken to going with her, for reasons I now understood better.

She was in a pew near the back of the sanctuary. She wasn't using the kneeler, just sitting and staring up at the stained glass above the cross on the altar. It was a sunny morning, and the glass was brilliant.

"Mind?" Jo said as she sat down beside Jenny.

Our daughter shrugged.

I sat behind them, leaned forward, and kissed the back of Jenny's head. That morning we had the church to ourselves.

We sat together for a while without speaking.

"Sean doesn't want the baby," Jenny said.

"What about you?" Jo replied.

"I want to keep my baby."

"Then that's what you'll do."

She looked at Jo, then back at me. I saw so much child in her still, the little girl who loved to pet goats at the children's zoo in Duluth, who cried when she read *Little Women*, who fell in love with a mating pair of Canada geese who'd wintered on Iron Lake and who she'd named Romeo and Juliet. But I saw, too, the woman she had become and the one she was still becoming.

"What about college?" she said. "All your dreams for me."

Jo said, "We hope they were your dreams, too. Now you'll have different dreams. They'll include someone else, someone I guarantee you'll love amazingly well. And it doesn't mean college is out of the question."

"I don't want to get married."

"Then you won't."

"People will talk."

"Hell," I threw in from behind, "you're an O'Connor. They already do."

"What about Sean?"

Jo put her arm around Jenny, two blond heads touching. "He'll always be the father even if he isn't a husband."

"He doesn't want to be a father."

I thought about the story I'd heard from Meloux the night before. I wished Sean had loved Jenny as fiercely as Henry Meloux had loved Maria Lima. Different people, different times. Still, for Meloux, being a father mattered, even across decades of absence. Maybe someday the same would be true for Sean.

"Give him time," I advised. "When he sees this baby, he may change his mind."

"Or not," Jo said. "In any case, you won't raise this child alone, we promise."

Up front, the priest came into the sanctuary from the door that led to the church office and classrooms. He saw us, nodded, but made no move in our direction.

Jenny said, "You guys mind if I talk to Father Ned?"

"Go ahead, sweetheart," Jo said. "You want us with you?"

"No." Then she managed a smile. "You always are."

She stood up and left us.

I walked home with Jo. The morning was warm already, pointing toward a hot day. "We made it sound easier than it's going to be," I said.

"There'll be plenty of time for her to come to terms with the hard stuff."

I took her hand as we walked. "Know what the hardest part for me is?"

"What?"

"Lord in heaven, I'll be married to a grandma."

THIRTY-SIX

I picked Meloux up first. He had an old gym bag full of clothes and a few things for overnight. I didn't know if Ernie had gone back to the old man's cabin or simply loaned Henry what he might need. Walleye padded along beside him. Meloux sat up front. Walleye hopped in back and lay down on the seat.

"Get some sleep, Henry?"

"I rested," the old man said.

"Stevie's looking forward to taking care of Walleye again."

"The boy needs a dog."

"Don't go there, Henry. I've already been through this with Jo."

"Sometimes trying to talk sense to you, Corcoran O'Connor, is as useful as trying to talk a fart out of smelling."

"Is this a subject we're going to be stuck on the whole trip, Henry?"

"Stephen's dog? Or farts?"

We left Ernie Champoux's place, and Meloux stared out the window as we drove down the shoreline of Iron Lake. The road was thickly lined with trees, pines and poplars mostly. Pieces of broken sunlight slid off the windshield.

"We all need friends," the old man finished. "I will say no more."

"Stevie has friends."

The old man looked at me, tired despite what he said about resting. "Are we going to be stuck on this subject the whole trip?" He settled back and closed his eyes.

Schanno was waiting for us on his front porch. He had a black nylon carry-on that appeared fully stuffed. He also had a zippered vinyl rifle bag.

"I brought my Marlin and scope," he said as I opened the tailgate. He put the rifle inside, next to mine. "I didn't know what we'd need."

"I'm hoping we can do this smart enough not to need any firepower."

"Are you carrying?"

"Brought my rifle, that's all. You can't take a handgun into Canada. To get the rifles across the border, we'll have to convince them we're coming up to hunt." I watched him toss in his black bag. "You're not carrying, are you?"

"Of course not."

"Good. Getting to Wellington is going to be all the trouble we need."

Schanno opened the back door. "Well, hey there, fella." He ruffled Walleye's fur and slid in beside the dog. "Morning, Henry."

Schanno was damn near chipper, the most animated I'd seen him since Arletta's death.

"Walleye going with us?" he asked, as if the idea of taking an old dog along was perfectly okay with him.

"We're dropping him off at my place. Stevie's going to take care of him for Henry."

"Good. A boy needs a dog, Cork."

Out of the corner of my eye, I caught Meloux's smile.

"Where's that dog of yours? Trixie?" I asked.

"Boarding her with Sally Fellows until I get back."

Stevie was sitting on the sidewalk in front of the house. When he saw me coming down Gooseberry Lane, he jumped up. I pulled into the drive, and he ran to greet us. He opened the door in back. Walleye popped out. Stevie hugged him and buried his face in the old dog's soft fur. Meloux and Schanno both gave me pointed looks.

Jo came out the front door. She walked to the Bronco and leaned through the driver's door, which I'd left open when I got out.

"*Anin*, Henry," she said.

"*Anin*," he replied.

"Good morning, Wally."

"Jo." He gave her a big, rather dopey grin.

"Thank you," she said to him.

"My pleasure."

"You'll be careful?"

"Old pros," Wally said.

She turned to me. "Call."

"I will."

She hugged me. Stevie and Walleye trotted off together toward the backyard. I got into the Bronco, backed out of the drive, and returned the final wave Jo gave me.

Then I took us north toward Canada.

THIRTY-SEVEN

Canadians are sensible about firearms. They don't like them. They don't like the idea of their fellow citizens owning them. They've passed laws that give good, sharp teeth to gun control. The United States has a homicide rate three times that of Canada; two-thirds of those homicides are committed with firearms. A child in the United States is twelve times more likely to die of a firearm injury than a child in Canada. I could go on. The evidence in support of Canada's attitude and legislative action is so convincing only an idiot wouldn't get it.

For much of my life I've been a cop. I own a handgun. It was my father's before it was mine. He wore it on his hip when he was sheriff of Tamarack County. I did the same. I have hunted all my life. I feel comfortable handling a firearm. Too many people don't really get that a gun is made to kill. You can use it for target practice, sure, but it's like a lion on a leash, a bad gamble that it won't turn and draw innocent blood. An enormous percentage of people who are injured or killed by gunshot wounds are hit by a bullet that wasn't meant for them or even meant to be fired in the first place. They're accident victims. I'm not a gun-control freak, but even as a law officer I was all for getting firearms out of the hands of the ignorant and out of the reach of the criminally minded.

So I understood, in theory, the paperwork and the scrutiny the Canadian customs people put us through in order to get our rifles across their border.

It was black bear season in Ontario, and customs officials at the entry point north of the Pigeon River were used to hunters. Our problem was that none of us had a hunting license. I was able to give the woman who reviewed our firearms declarations the name of a lodge well north of Thunder Bay that, as a kid, I'd visited with my father, and I told her the outfitter had promised to obtain licenses for us. Although I knew that kind of arrangement wasn't unusual, I wasn't sure if she was going to buy the story.

Finally she addressed Meloux, who'd sat quietly while Schanno and I were being grilled.

"Are you hunting, too, Grandfather?"

Her hair was red-brown, her eyes moss green. She didn't look Shinnob. But neither do I.

"I am going to visit my son," Meloux said.

"Where does he live?"

"In Thunder Bay."

"These men are taking you?"

"Yes. It is kind of them."

"How long will you stay?"

"I do not know. He may not want to see me."

She looked concerned. "He should see you out of respect."

"We'll make sure it happens," I put in.

She approved our declarations and sent us on our way with a final word to Meloux. "Enjoy your visit, Grandfather."

"I will, Granddaughter."

As we drove away from the border entry, Schanno let out a low whistle. "Lucky she was Ojibwe."

"Lucky?" Meloux laughed quietly.

With the change to eastern standard time, we hit the outskirts of Thunder Bay at half-past three. It was hot and humid, and a mean-looking bank of black clouds was bullying its way into the western sky. I drove to the marina off Water Street, where I'd met Morrissey and the motor launch that had taken me to Manitou Island. I parked in the lot near the renovated train depot. We walked to the end of the first dock, where there was a small observation area overlooking the bay.

"Where's the island?" Schanno asked.

I pointed beyond the breakwater toward the great ridge on the peninsula in the distance. "It's nestled up against Sleeping Giant."

"I don't see anything."

"It's hard to distinguish from the mainland behind it. Here." I handed him the Leitz binoculars I'd pulled from the back of my Bronco.

Schanno put them to his eyes and held steady for a minute. "Nope. Still don't see anything."

"Believe me, it's there."

"*He's* there," Meloux said. His old eyes were intense, as if he could actually see his son on the far side of all that blue water.

"You're close, Henry," I told him.

Schanno handed back the binoculars. "How do we get across the bay?"

"In a boat."

"And what boat would that be?"

"One we rent, probably."

"Big bay, lot of water to cross." Schanno didn't sound excited. "Any way to come at it from the Sleeping Giant side?"

"As nearly as I can tell from the map, there's no harbor there. This is pretty much it."

"Where do we rent the boat?"

"This is a marina. They've got to rent boats somewhere."

"Any idea where?"

"No, but I know someone who could probably tell us."

I led them to the slip where Trinky Pollard docked her sailboat. The boat was tied up, but I didn't see Pollard on deck.

"Ahoy, Trinky!" I called.

"Ahoy?" Schanno said.

"I saw it in a movie. Trinky!" I tried again.

"What now?" Schanno said.

"Find an office and ask, I guess."

"Well-thought-out plan of action," Schanno noted.

"Remember, you volunteered."

We headed back toward the depot and the shops. As we approached, I heard a voice call out, "O'Connor?"

Trinky Pollard stood in the doorway of the Waterfront Restaurant, the little bar and grill at the end of the complex.

"Trinky, it's a pleasure to see you again," I said as we approached. She shook my hand and eyed my companions.

"This is Wally Schanno and Henry Meloux, friends from back home. Guys, this is Trinky Pollard."

"I was just having a beer inside," she said. "Care to join me?"

"We'll take a rain check on that, Trinky. Right now we're in the market to rent a boat."

She raised an eyebrow. "Another visit to Manitou Island?"

"Yeah."

"In a rented boat?" She looked at me knowingly. "No official invitation this time, I take it."

"Not exactly."

She was wearing a white billed cap over her silver hair, a T-shirt that said HARD ROCK CAFE LAS VEGAS, dungarees, and boat shoes. She stood in the doorway considering things.

"I think I know a boat with a captain who'd take you—if she had a better idea of what's going on," she said.

I glanced at Schanno and Meloux. I figured Henry didn't care one way or the other, but I wanted to be sure about Wally.

He shrugged. "If I'm going to be out on that lake, I'd just as soon be on a boat with someone who knows what she's doing."

I turned back to Pollard. "If you've got the boat, Captain, I've got the crew."

We sat on the deck of her sailboat drinking cold Labatts from a cooler. I told her what had happened on my last visit to the island and what had happened since. Then I gave her the salient details of Meloux's connection to the recluse across the bay.

"And your part in this?" she asked Schanno.

"I'm here as a consultant."

She laughed, an agreeable sound. "Now there's a word that tells people absolutely nothing."

"Wally was a cop, too," I explained. "County sheriff for a while before he retired."

"Really? You look too young to be retired," she said, which clearly pleased Schanno. "You're here to watch Cork's back, I'll bet."

"That I am."

She glanced at me and tilted her head slightly to let me know she approved of my choice in backup.

"Your wives, they're okay with this?"

"Jo understands."

Schanno said, "I'm a widower. My wife passed six months ago."

"I'm sorry."

While we sat, the wind had risen, and the bay had filled with whitecaps. Thunderheads tumbled out of the west like a stampede of black bulls.

"And you think that despite what the Canadian police have said, Wellington's on his island and at the bottom of all this?"

"That's about the size of it."

Trinky Pollard appraised the sky. "If we're going to make it today, we need to cast off soon."

I put my beer down. "I wasn't thinking we'd sail over in daylight."

She nodded at the clouds pouring in from the west. "Unless you want to wait until tomorrow night, we need to beat this storm. We'll anchor on the lee side of the island. It's not unusual for a sailboat to use Manitou as a windbreak. Come dark, we'll be very close to our objective."

"Our?"

"Take it or leave it," she said.

"I don't know how much help we'll be in a storm. We're not exactly old salts."

"A good captain can sail with a crew of kangaroos." She stood up. "Look lively, mates. We've got work to do."

THIRTY-EIGHT

As soon as we were clear of the breakwater, Pollard turned off the boat's engine, and we hoisted sails. With Pollard at the wheel and the wind hard at our backs, we shot toward Manitou Island just ahead of the storm. Meloux sat on deck looking so calmly at the rough water that you'd have thought he was on a pleasure cruise in the Caribbean. I didn't know a jib from a spinnaker, but Trinky Pollard was clear when she issued her orders, and the bow of the sailboat cut through the whitecaps with exhilarating grace.

"Ever lost a boat?" I called above the wind and the slosh of the waves breaking against the hull.

She kept her eyes on the island ahead. "No. But then I've never sailed in water this rough before."

I figured it had to be a joke. The look on Schanno's face said he wasn't so sure.

"Don't worry," she called out. "Do exactly as I say and we have a better than even chance of making it."

Behind us, the storm hit the city. I watched a curtain of rain close over the buildings of the central district of old Port Arthur, then it overtook the huge, abandoned industrial works along the shoreline. A tongue of lightning shot from the black clouds and licked the water half a mile back. Seconds later came the boom of thunder, and I couldn't tell if the quiver that ran through the deck was the shock wave or just another jolt from the hull as the bow split the whitecaps.

"I ought to warn you," Schanno yelled to Pollard, "I don't swim well."

"Doesn't matter," she hollered back. "You go down out here, even if you can swim, the water's so cold it'll kill you anyway."

Schanno looked green—from the roll and pitch of the sailboat or from what Pollard had said, I couldn't tell.

The yellow life vest Meloux wore nearly dwarfed him. He gazed without apparent emotion at the turbulent lake, at water that had turned black around us, as if it had been poisoned. Some of that was the Indian in him, but I thought it was also how Meloux had faced all the storms of his long life.

Trinky Pollard was clearly having fun at our expense. Even so, her face drew taut as she concentrated on studying the snap of sail and the surge of water. I knew only too well that even if you were good at what you did, sometimes things turned on you in unexpected and tragic ways.

We swung around Manitou Island from the south. Pollard ordered us to pull in the sails, and she kicked in the engine. She maneuvered us to a place fifty yards offshore, in the lee of the island, headed us into the wind, and dropped anchor just as the heavy rain engulfed Manitou and then us.

"Nothing to do now but wait," she said, tying off the wheel. "Might as well go below."

The cabin was small, with padded benches. We shed our life vests in order to fit inside. We sat down, except for Pollard, who threw open the ice chest and hauled out several Labatts. She tossed one to Schanno, one to me, and held out one to Meloux, who declined with a wave of his hand.

"I've got Pepsi," she offered.

The old man shook his head.

Schanno wasn't looking any too good.

"You okay with that beer, Wally?" I said.

"I'm fine," Schanno replied.

"You feel like getting sick, use the head over there." She pointed toward a narrow door.

"I told you, I'm fine." Schanno popped the top on his beer and took a conspicuously long draw.

"Any idea how long this storm will last?" I asked.

"The worst'll blow over pretty quick," Pollard said. "Once the leading edge is past, the wind should die down, and then it'll be just rain for a while. Last radio report I heard said it's supposed to go on till near midnight. Seems to me rain would provide decent cover for someone wanting to get onto Manitou without an invitation."

"They have security on the landing," I pointed out.

She took another long draw of beer. "The official landing, the one where invited guests arrive. I've anchored us near an inlet on the other side of the island. You can't really tell much about it because it's blocked by a wooded peninsula. But on occasion I've observed motor launches coming and going, so I assume there's another landing back there somewhere."

"You seem to have more than a passing interest in this place," Schanno said.

"Retired RCMP investigator," she replied. "These days, I take my mysteries where I can find them. And there's a lot about Manitou that's never added up."

"You're a retired Mountie?"

She scowled at Schanno. "I was never fond of that term. For a woman in a profession dominated by men, it was too easy to make a demeaning joke of it."

"Sure," Schanno said.

"You sail around Manitou a lot?" I asked.

"I sail a lot, period, but I do have an investigator's fascination with this place."

The boat bucked like a restless pony. I was anxious for the storm to move on and for things to settle down.

"What do you know about Wellington?" I asked.

"A creative and charismatic guy before . . ." She glanced at Henry. "Before he became so odd. He was a very public figure in Thunder Bay and in Canada in general. He took the money from his father's mining interests and created an industrial manufacturing empire with interests all over the world. Very popular, very public spirited and environmentally minded. Created the Wellington Foundation, a huge charitable organization. Then half a dozen years ago his wife died, and he withdrew from public view. Tabloids have always been after him. If you believe what you read in them, he's become a bizarre eccentric who's barricaded himself in his mansion."

"From what I saw, they weren't off the mark," I said. "Sorry, Henry."

Pollard got up and walked to the cabin door, not an easy maneuver with the pitching of the boat. She opened the door and eyed the sky. "Dark'll come early because of the rain. Another hour maybe."

"How do we get to the inlet?" Schanno asked.

"When the wind dies and the lake calms a bit, I'll see about taking the boat in." Pollard closed the door and returned to her seat.

"Dogs patrol the island," I said.

"You saw them?" She seemed surprised.

"I heard them. Didn't sound like animals I'd want to run into."

"People who visit the island sometimes comment on the dogs they hear, and the tabloids talk at length about how vicious they are."

"Guard dogs," I said with a shrug. "For a man so crazy about his privacy, it makes sense."

Pollard said, "I've never heard them except when I can tell from a docked boat that someone is visiting the island."

"What's so strange about that?" Schanno asked.

"Dogs are dogs. They like to bark, guests or no. Nature of the beast. They also like to run. I've sailed around this island dozens of times, and I've never seen the dogs being exercised. So far as I know, nobody has."

"You're saying what? That they're virtual guard dogs?"

"Cheap security."

"I ran into the expensive kind," I told her. "Guys with guns."

"How many?"

"There was Morrissey." I thought about it. "Then there was the guy who piloted the launch and the security guy at the dock."

"Benning and Dougherty," she said.

"You know them?"

"Everybody at the marina knows them. They bring the launch in two, three times a week. They go to dinner, take in a movie, buy groceries, go back to the island. Nice enough couple."

"Couple?"

"That's the speculation among the sailors at the marina."

"I didn't pick up on that."

"Why would you? You weren't looking for it. Bob Calhoun, guy who docks at the slip two down from mine, is gay. He claims his 'gaydar' tells him it's true. Did you see anybody else out there?"

"No."

"Nor have I. Benning, Dougherty, once in a while this guy you say was Morrissey, that's it."

"No house staff, no groundskeepers?"

"Not that I've ever seen."

"But you've seen Wellington, right?" Schanno said.

"Every so often around twilight, I catch a glimpse of him walking alone along the shoreline. Never in full daylight. He's like a ghost, all in white."

"He seems to prefer the dark," I said.

"Like a bat or a vampire," Pollard said. Then she glanced at Henry and said no more.

Although the lake hadn't settled down any, I could tell from the distance of the thunder that the electrical part of the storm had moved east. We still had time to kill until it was dark enough to approach the island, and Trinky Pollard hauled out three more beers.

Schanno said, "So, what do you do besides sail?"

"I read a lot. And drink more beer than is probably good for me."

"No men in your life?"

She tipped her can to her lips and drank before she answered. "I was married for a dozen years. My husband finally left me because he claimed my job was more important to me than he was. He was right. In my experience, when men start being serious in a relationship, that translates into something like ownership. My boat and my books are pretty good company. When I want anything more, I pop into the Waterfront at the marina. I know all the regulars there."

Schanno turned his beer can in his hands and seemed to study the label. "It takes a special person to understand the demands the job makes on a cop."

"Your wife, she understood?"

"Not always."

"But she didn't leave you."

"She did eventually. Not her choice."

"Sounds like you were a lucky man."

"Blessed is what I was."

She lifted her beer in a toast. "To blessings."

Schanno tapped her beer can with his own, and they drank.

THIRTY-NINE

Shortly before eight P.M., Pollard declared, "Time to get ready."

The heavy rain persisted and, along with it, a stiff wind that kept the lake churning. The leading edge of the storm had passed long ago, but what followed proved not much better. We stood up and struggled to steady ourselves.

Schanno fell into Pollard. Though she was much smaller, she caught him.

"I thought you said the wind was going to die down," he complained.

"Quoting the radio," she replied. "Obviously they were wrong. You want to cancel the landing party?"

Schanno looked at me.

"We're going," I said.

Pollard lifted one of the seats and, from the storage compartment beneath, hauled out a large canvas duffle bag with STEARNS printed on the side.

"What's that?" Schanno said.

"An inflatable dinghy."

"I thought you said you were going to take the sailboat in."

"If the wind and the lake calmed. They haven't. I don't want to take a chance on running aground. The dinghy will be safer."

"In these waves?" Schanno said.

"We're less than a hundred yards from shore. Once you're in the shelter of the inlet, it should be easy."

"Once *we're* in the inlet. What happened to you being part of this?"

"The dinghy's designed for two adults, or six hundred and fifty pounds. I think you three can probably fit. Four would be impossible. Besides, in this weather, I need to stay with the boat."

She waited, as if anticipating further argument from Schanno.

"You don't have to come, Wally," I said. "I'll take Meloux to the island."

"I'm coming."

"Cork, there's an electric air pump in that compartment over there," Trinky said. "Would you bring it topside?"

On deck the wind pushed the rain into our faces. I could see the island, charcoal colored in the false twilight of the storm. The shoreline was a rage of foaming waves, but the opening to the inlet was clear and the water beyond looked calm. Pollard unzipped the canvas bag and hauled out the rolled dinghy. She spread it on the deck and attached the hose from the electric air pump to one of the valves. As soon as she started the pump, the flat PVC material began to quiver like an animal coming to life. While Schanno and Pollard inflated the dinghy, I went belowdeck and retrieved the knapsack I'd filled with items from my Bronco before leaving the marina—a small pry bar, glass cutter, screwdriver, hammer, sheathed hunting knife, a couple of flashlights, and binoculars. I'd thought about bringing one of the rifles, but decided against it. I didn't want things to get out of hand that way. I slipped the hunting knife onto my belt and slung the pack on my back. By the time I got up on deck, the dinghy was ready to go. We eased it over the side, where the waves did their best to snatch it from us. We tossed in the oars, then Pollard and I held to ropes tied to the inflatable's bow and stern while Schanno climbed in. He grasped the railing and held on to the sailboat as we helped Meloux into the dinghy. Finally, I slid over the side and settled in the bow. Pollard released her rope, and we shoved into a wind that was doing its best to drive us into the open lake. Schanno and I got the oars into the locks and began to row for all we were worth toward Manitou Island.

I played football in high school. I thought I knew what a hundred yards was. That night a hundred yards seemed to stretch into forever. We pulled hard against waves that came at us foaming like mad dogs. In the wind, our bodies acted as sails, and the dinghy resisted fiercely as we fought to go forward. For a long time, we seemed suspended between the sailboat and the shore while the water of Lake Superior broke over the bow, soaking us with its bitter cold. I was tiring, and I figured Schanno, who had a dozen years on me, had to be exhausted. But the big man dug his oars into the lake and put his back into the effort, and together we inched the small boat toward Manitou.

We finally made the inlet. As soon as we rounded the tip of the peninsula, we escaped the waves and the worst of the wind. We found ourselves in a narrow passage twenty yards wide and four times as long. The shoreline was all rock, but as I looked over my shoulder I could see dark pilings and a platform at the far end of the inlet.

"There's a dock," I said.

"I see it," Schanno said.

"How're you doing, Henry?" I asked.

He looked at me over his shoulder and smiled enormously. "Corcoran O'Connor," he replied, "I have never been better."

Unlike the more public landing on the other side of the island, the dock in the inlet had no security kiosk and no lighting. We tied up and climbed out of the dinghy. The lake water had been freezing cold, but the rain and the summer air felt warm against my skin. There was a trail of crushed rock leading into the trees. We could see the lights of the great house glimmering through the sway of branches.

"Lead on, Macduff," Schanno said.

Deep in the cover of the pine trees, everything was dark enough that a flashlight would have helped, but it would also have given us away. We walked carefully, and as we approached the clearing, we slowed to a creep. We stopped before we broke from the woods. I took the binoculars from my knapsack.

The mansion stood at the center of the clearing. Lights were on inside, on both the first and second floors, but in different wings. Curtains blocked any view of the interior. On the far side of the clearing was what looked like a guesthouse. Lights were on there, too, but the shades were up and the curtains open. Through the windows of the guesthouse, I saw movement, shapes crossing through the light inside. I could see framed pictures on a wall and the polished edge of a baby grand piano. To someone it was home. I studied the big windows of the mansion. They gave away nothing. As I watched, the light went out in one of the second-floor rooms and, a few moments later, the curtain of another flared as the light behind it came on. It didn't stay on long. A minute later, a light flipped on in another room farther down the hall. Upstairs in the great house, someone was pacing restlessly.

"The police were wrong," I said. "He's home."

"What now?" Schanno asked.

I lowered the binoculars. "You hear any dogs?"

"Just the wind."

"I want to get around to the other side, see who's in the guesthouse. You stay here with Henry, okay?"

"What if they spot you?"

"I'll do what I can to distract and delay them while you see if you can get Henry into Wellington's house."

Schanno shook his head. "Better if I do the reconnaissance and you stay with Henry."

"Why?"

"You've been inside Wellington's place. If you have to move quickly, you have a better idea of the layout. And if I get caught by these guys, what are they going to do? Call the cops? Big deal. You, they could pull that brand-new license of yours."

What could I say? He made sense.

"I'll work around the perimeter, keeping to the trees in case they've got cameras," he said. "Be patient. This could take a while."

I handed him the binoculars. "Morrissey was a killer. I don't know about these guys, but you be careful, understand?"

"If it's Benning and Dougherty, Pollard claims they're a nice couple. They catch me, we'll talk drapes."

"I mean it."

"I know you do."

He hung the binoculars around his neck and turned to start away.

"Thanks, Wally."

He grinned at me. "You kidding? I'm having the time of my life."

Henry and I stood in the steady rain watching Schanno vanish among the shifting pines. Water dripped from my eyebrows and the end of my nose. My clothes were soaked. The trees blunted the wind, which was helpful. If the night hadn't been so warm, we'd have been in trouble.

"You okay, Henry?"

"I have been wet before, Corcoran O'Connor."

His eyes were on the house. Only fifty yards and the stone wall of the mansion separated him from his son. I wondered how he felt watching the lights go on and off, knowing his son was walking those empty corridors alone. I tried to imagine Wellington, the kind of loneliness that went along with the kind of life he'd made for himself. It left me feeling suffocated.

Schanno returned in less than fifteen minutes.

"Two men," he said. "One tall, thin, blond. The other stocky, dark. Both midthirties."

"Benning and Dougherty," I said. "What were they doing?"

"Watching television, eating popcorn. Very domestic."

"See any surveillance monitors?"

"Nothing."

I wiped rainwater from my eyes. "For a man fanatical about his privacy, Wellington's awfully slack with security."

"He's been hiding out here for six years," Schanno said. "Maybe at some point, rigorous security no longer became necessary. He's established a reputation. Substitutes virtual dogs for real dogs. Pares down his security force to a gay couple who don't mind the isolation. Saves a lot of money that way."

"And with a greeting committee like Morrissey, not many people want to take the chance of coming here unannounced. It fits, but . . ." I shook my head.

"You don't like the feel of it?"

"Do you?"

"Why don't we get inside and ask the man himself. Got a plan for how to do that?"

As a matter fact, I did.

FORTY

Several red maples had been planted in the clearing long ago, probably to provide shade for the mansion. They were magnificent things that in the fall would be on fire. Now they were thick with dark green summer leaves, and their wet branches flailed in the wind.

Schanno and Meloux followed me to the nearest tree.

"I need to cut a limb," I said, pointing up at the wealth of branches above us. "Give me a boost, Wally."

"Give you a boost?"

"You know." I intertwined my fingers and made a stirrup.

"How about you do the boosting for me?" he suggested.

Meloux said, "You could both lift me. A sparrow weighs more."

"You sure you'd be okay climbing this tree, Henry?"

He looked at me as if I was a hopeless idiot. "I am old, not feeble. You treat me like thin ice that will break. I will not break, Corcoran O'Connor."

"All right, Henry."

I took the sheathed knife from the knapsack and handed it to him.

"We need a branch strong enough to break a window. And it can't look as if it's been cut from the tree. It needs to look like the wind tore it loose."

"I understand," the old man said.

We stirruped our hands, Schanno and I, and lifted Meloux so that he could grasp the lower branches and pull himself into the maple. He spent a few minutes lost in the foliage, then a good stout branch, thick as my wrist, dropped to the ground.

"Will that do?" he called.

"Great, Henry. Come on down."

We helped him from the tree. He handed me the knife. I put it in the knapsack and gave the little pack to Schanno.

"You two get back to the cover of the pines," I told them. "I'll join you in a minute."

They slipped out of the clearing and I turned to the house. I knew the window I wanted: ground floor, above the patio in back, out of sight of the guesthouse. It was odd that the security on the estate was so lax, but I couldn't believe that there wouldn't be some sort of security system for the house itself. We'd see.

The patio was large and edged with a knee-high stone wall. There were stone benches and a couple of flower beds of irregular shape. The beds had been long in need of tending. I stepped over the wall and came at the window quickly with the "broken" end of the branch aimed at the center of the frame. The glass shattered and an alarm sounded inside. I left the branch stuck in the window among the shards of glass that jutted out from the frame and I leaped over the wall. As I hightailed it toward the pines, floodlights kicked on, illuminating the outside of the house in a blaze of white. Inside the mansion, all the lights seemed to come on, too, as if the whole household had been roused by the intrusion. From the direction of the guesthouse came the vicious barking of a pack of dogs.

I stood in the trees with Meloux and Schanno. I hoped Schanno's speculation about the virtual nature of the guard dogs was right, and we weren't simply waiting for them to attack and tear us apart.

In a couple of minutes, Benning and Dougherty appeared, nosing around the house. Each held a handgun and a flashlight whose feeble beams were consumed by the blaze of the floodlights. They were alone. No dogs. They found the offending branch and stood a few minutes in discussion. Benning looked around. His gaze settled on the nearest maple. He pointed toward it and said something to his partner. They studied the window some more. Finally Dougherty reached up and pulled the branch out of the window frame. Some of the remaining glass must have come with it because they both danced back. Dougherty stayed while Benning went back to the guesthouse.

After his partner had gone, Dougherty began examining the branch. He took a close look at the white wood where the "break" had occurred. He studied the patio under the window, crossed the wall, and walked to the maple tree, which was outside the glare of the lights. He shined his flashlight up among the branches, then dropped the beam and scanned the wet ground. Finally he shot the light toward the woods. Schanno, Meloux, and I each cozied up to the nearest tree trunk.

"Hey!"

I held my breath and wondered if Dougherty would actually use his firearm, and if he did, whether he would be any good.

"Hey, get back here, give me a hand with this window. I'm getting soaked, damn it."

The light swung away. A few moments later I risked a peek. Dougherty was walking back to the patio where Benning waited with a roll of opaque sheet plastic, a red toolbox, and an aluminum stepladder. The men spent a few minutes cutting a piece of the plastic and fitting it over the window. They used a staple gun to affix it to the frame. When they were finished, they gathered up their tools and materials and hurried back toward the guesthouse.

Schanno, Meloux, and I joined forces and waited a bit before approaching the house again.

"You notice anything strange?" I said.

Schanno kept his eyes on the corner of the mansion where Benning and Dougherty had disappeared. "Like what?"

"Wellington didn't come down to check the damage."

"That's what he has security for. Besides, he's an odd one. Rabid about germs. Probably doesn't want all that dirty fresh air and rain getting on him. Could be he's hiding in a safe room somewhere."

A safe room. I hadn't thought about that. Terrific. Just terrific.

The floodlights died. The dogs fell silent. The dark and the quiet that followed were a great relief. Inside the house, the lights that had blazed on with the alarm shut off all at the same time, but the rooms upstairs and down that had been lit before stayed lit. On the second floor, the slow progression of lights resumed.

Wellington was out and about again, restless as ever. So much for a safe room.

"Once more, dear friends, into the breach," Schanno said.

"You do that just to impress us?" I asked.

Schanno smiled sheepishly. "It's what happens when you live your whole life with a smart schoolteacher."

"Ready, Henry?" I said.

The old man nodded and we left the woods. On the patio, I took the knife from my knapsack and handed it to Henry.

"We're going to boost you up again and I want you to cut the plastic over the window so we can get inside. When that's done, if you can, clear the glass that's still in the frame so we don't cut ourselves climbing in."

"What if they have motion sensors inside?" Schanno said.

"With Wellington wandering around like that? I'm betting they don't. We've been lucky so far."

Luck. There was that word again. My first visit to the island had been plagued by its opposite. I'd been stonewalled by Wellington, sucker-punched by Morrissey, and had come away without accomplishing anything worthwhile. Meloux's presence made a difference. This expedition had been marked by good fortune. The sympathetic customs official. Trinky Pollard's offer of help. The storm that had covered our approach. Relaxed security on the island. I'd known Meloux all my life, and one of the things I'd observed about the old Mide was that circumstance seemed to favor him. Luck? When I'd used that word before, he'd laughed at me. Not many candles shy of a hundred years, yet he was still powerful in ways beyond my understanding.

We lifted him and he cut through the plastic, which began to flap in the wind. I looked up from where I provided one of the stirrups for his feet and saw him set the knife on the windowsill and begin carefully to remove the fragments of glass remaining in the frame.

"It is done," he said.

"Crawl inside, Henry. We'll join you," I told him.

Schanno went next, with a little help from me. Once inside, he reached down and gave me a hand up.

We found ourselves in a small, dark study that smelled musty even with the air drafting through from outside. I went to the door and opened it. The hallway beyond was dimly lit at the far end. I signaled and the others followed me. We crept toward the light, which turned out to be from the chandelier in the dining room. We turned left and went through a large room with a beautiful stone fireplace, a grand piano, stuffed leather chairs, and a long leather sofa. In one corner a standing lamp gave off a dim, cheerless light. Everything was neat and tidy. The top of the piano was propped open, as if ready to be played. The place had an airless, stuffy feel to it, however. Though sheets hadn't been draped over the furniture here, the room felt more than just empty. It seemed abandoned. It made me think of a church deserted not only by its congregation but by its god. Given what I knew of Wellington, I suspected the man seldom haunted this part of his mansion.

We entered the stacks of newspapers and followed the maze of corridors that ran through them until we reached the staircase, where we paused. Upstairs, a light blinked out in the hallway. We waited. Another came on, dimmer, farther away.

I started up. Schanno and Meloux came after me. I looked for security cameras, but didn't see any. I listened for some sound—a cough, a grumble, the squeak of a floorboard as he paced—but the man was like a ghost. All I heard was the hollow hammer of rain driven against the windowpanes.

Upstairs I stepped carefully into the hallway and looked in the direction the hall lights had indicated Wellington was moving. The hallway was empty. He'd probably gone into one of the many rooms, but which one? Had he finally retired for the night?

"He's been wandering around upstairs all evening," Schanno whispered. "He'll be out again in a minute. Do we surprise him?"

"We don't want to give him a heart attack," I said. "But we also don't want him locking himself away somewhere."

"Why don't we just slip into a room, crack the door, and wait for him to pass. Then we corner him before he can slip away."

That sounded as good as anything. We went to the nearest door— it was unlocked—and we slipped inside. In the moment while light came in from the hallway with us, I saw that it was a large bedroom with a canopy four-poster. We closed the door, leaving it open just a crack, and waited.

A long two minutes passed. I thought about Henry, finally on the verge of meeting his son, and I wished I were happier for him, wished that the man he was about to meet would make him happy and proud. But Henry knew he was not here for that reason. He was here to heal his son.

The light at the end of the hallway went out. I hadn't heard a door open or close. I leaned to the crack. The hallway was dark now. I listened for the sound of shuffling on carpet, breathing, anything that would tell me where Wellington was.

The light directly outside the room where we hid came on suddenly. I opened the door. The hallway was deserted. Wellington, it seemed, was truly a ghost after all.

Meloux said, "I do not understand."

"A timer, Henry," Schanno guessed. "The lights go on and off automatically. It's a way of making it appear someone is here when they really aren't."

"My son is not here?" Meloux looked confused and disappointed.

Schanno said, "When you saw him before, where was he, Cork?"

I led them to the other end of the hallway, to the anteroom where I'd been given my mask, then I opened the door to Wellington's sanitized inner sanctum. The bedroom was still glaring white, but Wellington wasn't there. I opened one of the doors leading off the bedroom. A bathroom with a sunken tub, a shower, and a pedestal sink, all tastefully done in white and sea green marble tile with modern stainless-steel fixtures. There was a vanity as well, the mirror outlined with bright bulbs, the sort of thing I associated with wealthy women who spent a lot of time on their makeup.

Behind me, Schanno said, "Take a look at this."

He came into the bathroom holding a white robe, the kind Wellington had been wearing when I saw him.

"Where'd you get that?"

"In the closet. Along with this." He held up a pair of black silk pajamas on a wooden hanger. "About as night and day as you can get." He looked around the bathroom. "Very nice. Anything interesting?"

"Check out the vanity."

"Whoa," Schanno said.

He was probably responding to the wig of long white hair draped over a wooden head-shaped stand on the vanity. I checked the drawers. Makeup, but not the kind most women wore. Theatrical stuff. Gum spirit, liquid latex, foundation, a crème color wheel, a contact lens case with brown-tinted lenses inside.

"Wellington's, you think?" Schanno asked.

"If it is, he's even stranger than I figured."

Meloux stood in the bathroom doorway, looking lost. "What does it mean?"

"I'm not entirely sure, Henry. Let's check the bedroom carefully."

In the closet hung several of the white robes, but also dress shirts, a couple of Hawaiian numbers, and slacks. In a shoe rack were casual shoes, deck shoes, and three pairs of New Balance athletic shoes. The dresser held briefs, undershirts, socks, sweaters, sweat suits. In the drawer of the nightstand were a couple of paperback mystery novels and a wire-bound notebook. The notebook contained dialogue sketches, exchanges like those between characters in a play.

Edwina: You can't mean that.
Gladstone: If you'd been paying attention, you'd have seen this
            coming.
(*Edwina crumples in a faint.*)
Gladstone: Your dramatics will do you no good, my dear.

I read a couple of pages; it didn't get any better. Behind the last page of the notebook was a flyer, folded in half. I opened it and discovered an advertisement for a production at the Loghouse Theatre, a melodrama titled *The Nightcap*, written and directed by Preston Ellsworth and starring the same. The production ran from June 1 until August 31, at eight P.M. every night except Monday.

Henry breathed deeply, almost a sigh of relief, I thought. "It was not my son you saw here."

"That's a good guess, Henry."

"But why this pretending?"

"The question of the day."

"What now?" Schanno asked.

I looked at my watch. A few minutes before nine.

"How long does a play last?" I asked. "Couple of hours?"

"About that."

"Takes the actors a while to change, get their makeup off?"

"I'd guess."

"So if we hurry, we might have a shot at catching Ellsworth before he leaves the Loghouse Theatre."

"A shot," Schanno agreed. "A long one." He glanced at Meloux. "Unless we get lucky."

FORTY-ONE

By the time we piled into the dinghy and began to row back to Trinky Pollard's sailboat, the wind and rain had let up a bit. While Schanno and I pulled on the oars, Meloux used the flashlight to signal. Pollard was waiting for us as we drew alongside. When we were aboard, she tied the dinghy to a stanchion at the stern.

"So?" She turned to us expectantly.

"How quickly can you get us back to Thunder Bay?"

"Is someone after you?"

"Other way around, Trinky. There's a man we need to get to. We know where he might be, but unless we get there fast, we could lose him."

"Then let's pull that anchor up and get under way."

She used the engine to take us back. It was faster, she explained, than lifting the sails and tacking against the wind. The dinghy trailed behind at the end of its line. As we rode the black swells of the bay, I filled her in on what we'd discovered on Manitou Island.

"A stand-in? Why? And why so eccentric?"

"If Ellsworth really is our man and we can get to him, maybe we'll have the answers."

"In the meantime," Pollard said, "why don't you three go below and get out of the rain. I don't have dry clothes to offer, but I've got a bottle of Glenlivet in the cupboard. It'll brace you some, warm your innards anyway. I'll let you know when we're inside the marina breakwater. You can give me a hand docking."

Schanno shook his big, wet head. "It doesn't sit right with me, you up here alone."

"I'm alone at this wheel most of the time," she told him. "There's nothing for you to do."

"Keep you company at least."

She seemed pleased. "If that's what you want. But you two"—she nodded at Meloux and me—"no reason both of you need to stay out in the weather."

I went below with the old Mide. I found the Scotch and offered it to Meloux, who declined. I decided against it, too. The water was rough, and although I hadn't experienced any seasickness on the way over, I didn't want to take any chances. We still had a lot ahead of us on the far side of the bay.

The swells knocked us about. Outside I couldn't see anything but the black night and black rain and the white spray that hit the window. Meloux seemed oblivious to the pounding the sailboat was taking. Silent and as near to brooding as I'd ever seen him, he stared at his hands, folded in his lap.

Even though Wellington's absence from Manitou Island was not my fault, I still felt as if I'd let Henry down. I'd given him false hope, led him to believe we'd find his son there. What we found were simply more questions. There might have been something hopeful in the fact that the madman I'd seen earlier probably wasn't Henry Wellington but someone pretending to be him. But what did that say about the real Wellington, that he was willing to allow such an unattractive portrayal? He probably was nuts, though not necessarily in the way people believed.

Schanno opened the cabin door and stepped in. "We're rounding the breakwater."

"You were good company for Trinky?" I asked.

"Remarkable woman," he said. "She's thinking of sailing down the Saint Lawrence and the East Coast to the Caribbean next year."

"Alone?"

"That's what's been holding her back. She'd like a mate."

"Speaking nautically?"

Schanno gave me a sour look. "Topside now," he said.

The breakwater had done its job, and the lake surface was relatively smooth as we entered the marina and docked. We tied up and hauled in the dinghy.

"I'll deflate it later," Pollard said. "Let's get you to the Loghouse Theatre."

"You know where it is?"

"In Thunder Bay, I know where everything is."

"Lucky for us," Schanno said and gave her a goofy, big-toothed grin.

We took my Bronco. Pollard sat up front with me and navigated. The Loghouse Theatre was in the old Fort William section of town. It took us fifteen minutes to get there. When we arrived, the parking lot was almost empty.

"Too late?" Schanno said.

"Lights are still on in the lobby. Let's give it a try."

The doors were locked, but we could see two kids inside, early twenties. The young man wore an old-fashioned white shirt with a black string tie, and his hair was slicked down and parted in the middle. The young woman wore a calico dress and had long gold curls with bangs. They were straightening up the lobby. I knocked on the glass of the front door.

The woman turned toward us and I saw her mouth the word *closed.*

"Please," I called. "It's important."

Her chest heaved with a theatrically tired sigh, but she came to the door. The young man went on with his work.

"I'm sorry, folks," she said as soon as she unlocked and opened up. "The performance is finished. We're done for the night."

She was pretty and heavily made up. Her golden Shirley Temple curls were a wig, I could see. One of the actors, I guessed.

"We've come a long way," I told her. "We'd like to see Preston Ellsworth. Please. Even just for a minute."

"You're fans?" She sounded surprised.

"Yes. Fans. His biggest," I said. "Even if we're too late for the performance, could we at least get an autograph?"

"You want Preston Ellsworth's autograph?" She glanced at the young man, who studiously avoided looking at her. "Well, okay, I'll tell him," she said. "Wait here."

The kid with the slicked-down hair grabbed a Bissell sweeper and began to push it back and forth over the carpet with a crisp zip of the brushes inside. I turned away from the door where the young woman had gone. I wanted my back to Ellsworth when he walked in so I could surprise him and see the look on his face when he recognized me.

"Here we are," said a cheery voice a minute later. "I understand you've come a long way."

It didn't sound like the same man who'd spoken to me at the mansion, but I supposed a good actor ought to be able to disguise his voice. I turned to him.

He was fiftyish, with a thin handsome face and pleasant gray eyes. He'd thrown on a tan sport coat over his white T-shirt and he wore jeans. His face was still heavily made up for performance. He appeared fit, not at all like the sickly madman in the white robe who'd screamed bloody murder when I'd approached him in the mansion. I'd thought the similarities would be obvious, but he looked so different. If he recognized me, he hid it well.

"Yes," I said. "From the States."

"Is that so?" He took in our wet clothes. "Did you swim here?" He smiled at his joke, showing beautiful, capped teeth. The teeth of the man on Manitou Island had been like moldy cheese. "Where in the States?"

"Minnesota," I said. "But then, you already knew that."

He looked puzzled, but still pleasant. "I did?" He shrugged it off. "Gloria said you were fans. Is that right?"

"Of one performance in particular," I said. "I think you know which one."

The puzzlement morphed into confusion laced with just a hint of annoyance. "I'm afraid I'm not following you at all."

"This isn't a bad performance either, Mr. Wellington."

"Look," he said, with a note of exasperation. "Is this a joke or something?"

"No joke. Although it might be a little funny if murder weren't involved."

Hands on his hips. Perturbation now. "Who are you and what's this all about?"

The kid with the Bissell sweeper kept at his work, but he wasn't missing a word.

"Me, you've already met," I said. "We almost did battle over a pocket watch, on Manitou Island. These are my colleagues. Wallace Schanno, former sheriff of Tamarack County, Minnesota. Trinky Pollard, formerly with the Royal Canadian Mounted Police. And this is Henry Meloux, the real father of the real Henry Wellington. As for what this is about, Mr. Ellsworth, it's about the attempt made on Henry's life the day after I spoke with you in the Wellington mansion on Manitou Island."

His brow furrowed. He eyed me in a threatening way. "I haven't the slightest idea what you're talking about."

Trinky Pollard said, "You can talk to us, or you can talk to one of my friends in the RCMP."

He hesitated. "You're talking about that crazy recluse on the island out there in the bay, right?"

We stared at him.

"I have no relationship whatsoever with Henry Wellington. All I know about the man is what I read in the papers. If you want to call your RCMP friend, fine. When he gets here, I'll ask him to charge you with harassment. Good night."

He turned away.

"Does this mean we don't get an autograph?" I said.

He slammed the door behind him.

"Is it him?" Schanno asked.

"I don't know, Wally. I thought if it was, I could bluff it out of him."

"He had me convinced," Schanno said.

"Either he's telling the truth or he's a very good actor."

The kid with the Bissell snorted.

Pollard turned his way. "You know him?"

The kid looked up at us and feigned surprise. "What?"

Pollard walked toward him. "Do you know Preston Ellsworth?"

The kid watched her approach and thought about it. "Oh yeah, I know him," he said with a smirk.

"Was he lying?"

"Hey, I don't—"

Pollard was very close to him now. "Was he lying?"

The kid leaned on the handle of his Bissell. "What you just witnessed was a performance."

"Thank you," she said.

"Here's something else for you. He drives a Ferrari. He does seasonal melodrama for a living, but he drives a Ferrari. How do you figure that?"

"Yes," Pollard agreed. "How do you figure that? I think we'll go back and talk to Mr. Ellsworth further."

The kid shrugged—no big deal to him—and went back to cleaning the lobby. "Through that doorway and down the hall. His dressing room's on the right. His name's on the door," he said without looking at us again.

The door was unlocked, and we went in without knocking. Ellsworth was at his dressing table. He'd removed his sport coat and was in his T-shirt. He was in the process of wiping cold cream off his face when he saw us in the mirror. He was clearly startled, then angry.

He swung toward us. "What the hell do you think you're doing here?"

"We came to congratulate you on a pretty good performance," I said. "And to get the truth from you."

"If you don't get out of here, I'm calling the police."

"Fine," Pollard said. "And when you do, maybe you can explain to them how an actor in local theater gets the kind of money it takes to buy a Ferrari. And if the police aren't interested, I have friends with the CRA who'd love to follow up on that."

"I pay my taxes."

By that time, I'd had enough. I was on him in two long strides. I grabbed a handful of his T-shirt, bunched it at his throat, and shoved him against the back of his chair. I put my face an inch from his. I could smell the greasepaint, the cold cream, the ghost of whiskey on his breath. His eyes bloomed with surprise and fear.

"I'm tired of being fucked around," I said. "That goon Morrissey followed me back to Minnesota and tried to kill my friend Henry. Morrissey's dead, but I want to know if there are going to be any others trying to make sure the killing gets done. I swear to God, what I'm about to do to you isn't a performance you'll soon forget. You want that face to be in shape for the stage tomorrow night, you'll answer my questions now. Who hired you?"

Ellsworth gave me no answer. I lifted him out of the chair and slammed him against the wall. The drywall behind him crunched.

"I can't tell you," he squawked.

"Can't?"

"Breach of contract. If I tell you, I lose everything."

"Everything's already lost, pal. The gig is over. We're busting Wellington wide open, and I've got no problem busting you open first. Who hired you?"

"Wellington," he said.

"Henry Wellington?"

"Yes."

I eased up a bit, let him off the wall. "Tell me about it."

"Six years ago. He called me to the island and laid out what he wanted."

"Which was?"

"Somebody to be him."

"Why?"

"I don't know. He offered me a deal I'd have been a fool to turn down. But there was a stipulation. I could never reveal the agreement, never tell anyone about my role."

"His idea to be so eccentric?"

"More or less. He said he'd been compared to Howard Hughes all his life. No reason to stop now. He thought it would be a good way to keep people at a distance. So I studied Hughes."

"He's okay with this character?"

"I assume. Once I signed the agreement, I never saw him again."

Meloux walked forward. Ellsworth shifted his eyes toward the old man.

"What was he like?" Henry said.

Ellsworth thought a moment. "Rather cold. Unhappy."

Meloux nodded.

"Who pays you?" I asked.

"I get a monthly amount deposited into my bank account. A retainer. And for each performance, I get something additional."

"How often do you perform?"

"A couple of times a month, usually. I make an appearance at twilight for the benefit of the gawkers. Every once in a while, like when you showed up, I'm called to make a special appearance. I use the darkened room and the mask bit to keep people from looking too closely."

"Wellington's never on the island?"

"As far as I know, he hasn't set foot there in six years."

"Where is he?"

"I haven't the foggiest."

"You know his brother, Rupert?"

"I know who he is. I've never met him."

"The money that's deposited in your account, where does it come from?"

"On my bank statement, the notation reads Entertaintec, Inc."

"You don't know anything about the company?"

"No."

"Who contacted you for my performance?"

"I have a cell phone dedicated to gigs on Manitou. Whenever they want me, they call me on it."

"Who's they?"

"I don't know. A voice I don't recognize."

"Has it always been just a voice?"

"At first it was Wellington himself. That lasted a couple of years. Then it was a different voice."

"No name?"

"No."

"And so no face to go with it, right?"

"That's right."

"What if you decided to contact your contact? Can you call him?"

"Yes. There's a number."

"He answers?"

"No. I leave a message. I don't do it often. They don't like it."

"If I had the number, I could have it traced," Pollard said to me.

"Give it to her," I told Ellsworth.

He went to his sport coat and took a pen from the inside pocket. He wrote the number on the back of a program lying on the dressing table and handed the program to Pollard.

"What can you tell me about Morrissey?" I said.

"Nothing. He sometimes rides out with me in the launch and sticks around until I go back. If there's anything special about the gig, he explains what Mr. Wellington wants. He told me you were coming and what he wanted me to do."

"Which was?"

"Listen to what you had to say and hold on to the watch."

"Did he tell you the importance of the watch?"

"No."

"And after I left, you told him everything I told you?"

"Yes."

"He passed the information along to Wellington?"

"I don't know. I'd done my part. Benning took us back to Thunder Bay. That's all there was to it."

"You said Morrissey comes out sometimes but not always. Who usually takes care of the details of your appearances on the island?"

"Benning and Dougherty."

"Why not that time?"

He shrugged.

I thought to myself, *Because that time, Meloux had to die.*

"Look, I've told you everything I know. I've probably screwed myself good."

"I think you can count on an end to the engagement," Pollard said. "When the police understand the nature of your involvement with the dead man, they'll want to talk to you, and as soon as they do, you're headline news. You're finished impersonating Henry Wellington, Mr. Ellsworth."

I thought it would hit him hard, facing the end of the luxurious ride he'd managed to get out of Wellington. But he brightened.

"Hey, I could get great publicity out of this. 'The man who was Wellington.' The media will love it."

"I'll contact the police," Pollard told him. "Where can you be reached?"

He gave her his home address and phone number.

"Stay available," she cautioned him.

"I'm all theirs," he said and opened his arms magnanimously.

In the lobby, the kid had finished sweeping the carpet. He watched us as we trooped past.

"How'd it go?" he asked.

"He brought down the house."

"That's a first. Was he really playing Henry Wellington?"

"He was."

"And he got a Ferrari out of it?"

"It appears he did."

As we walked out, the kid shook his head and grumbled, "No fucking justice."

FORTY-TWO

We headed back to the marina to take Pollard to her boat.

"What are you going to do now?" she asked along the way.

"Get rooms for the night," I said. "These wet jeans are starting to chafe."

"You're welcome to stay at my place," she offered.

"Don't think we'd all fit in the cabin of your sailboat, Trinky."

"I have a house. I'm not there much during sailing season, but it's a perfectly fine place. I've got a guest room, a sofa, a cot."

"We've already imposed enough," I said.

"Nonsense. This is the most fun I've had since I retired."

"Guys?" I said.

"I'm game," Schanno replied.

Meloux said, "*Migwech*."

Pollard said, "Eh?"

"Ojibwe," I told her. "Means thank you."

Instead of returning to the marina, we went directly to her little bungalow on a tree-shaded street northwest of the downtown district. I parked in the drive, we grabbed our bags, and headed toward the front door along a walk lined with flowers. We climbed four steps up to a small, covered porch with a swing. When we stepped inside the house, everything looked simple, neat, and clean.

"Nice woodwork," Schanno noted.

"That's what sold me on the place," she said. "I'd be happy to make coffee. Decaf, I suppose, at this time of night. And I've probably got frozen pizza I can throw in the oven. I don't know about you guys, but I'm starved."

She gave Meloux the guest room. From the hallway closet, she pulled a cot, which I set up in the living room. She brought in linen for it and for the sofa. Schanno offered to take the cot, but I could see that big as he was, his feet would hang over the end, and I argued him out of it.

By the time we'd changed into dry clothing, Pollard had the coffee ready. She pulled the pizza from the oven, and we sat around her dining room table, feeding our faces and talking about plans for the next day.

"We still haven't located Henry Wellington," I said. "I think we should talk to his brother, Rupert."

"Think he knows what's been going on?" Schanno said. "Sounds like it was Henry who set up the whole charade."

"Rupert can't be clueless. He probably knows where his brother is. Or at the very least, how to contact him."

Pollard said, "The contact number Ellsworth gave me, I'll have that checked, see if it leads us anywhere."

"Thanks, Trinky."

Meloux looked tired.

Pollard saw it, too. "We should all get some sleep," she suggested, rising from her chair. "Tomorrow'll be another busy day."

I woke in the night. I wasn't sure if I'd heard something or dreamed it. I lifted my head from the pillow and saw that the front door stood ajar. Through the open window overlooking the front porch, I heard the gentle *scree* of the chains as the swing went slowly back and forth.

I was about to check it out, just to be safe, when Schanno got up and shifted himself so that he could look through the porch window, which was directly behind the sofa. He stared awhile as the swing kept up its quiet rhythm. He glanced my way, and I pretended sleep. He slipped from the sofa and padded to the front door. After a minute of hesitation, he pushed the screen door open and stepped outside.

The regular beat of the porch swing ceased. I heard their voices, hushed. I heard rain dripping from the eaves. I heard a car drive past, its tires sighing on wet pavement.

Then the swing began again.

Wally Schanno did not return to the sofa that night.

In the morning, I found Schanno and Pollard in the kitchen. Crisp bacon lay on a plate on the table, eggs were frying in a pan on the stove, coffee was fresh and hot in the brew pot, and bread was ready to be dropped into the toaster. The rain had long ago ended, and the sun was rising in the sky like a bubble in a champagne glass. Pollard wore a white terry-cloth robe. Her feet were bare, her hair brushed, her eyes happy. Schanno had on a T-shirt, plaid sleep bottoms, and a big grin.

"Morning, sleepyhead," Pollard said. "Coffee?"

"Thanks."

"Sit down." Schanno wielded a spatula, which he aimed at the small kitchen table.

I sat. Pollard poured coffee while Schanno tended the eggs.

"Hungry?" she asked.

"Give me a minute. But probably."

"Hope you like your eggs over easy," Schanno said. "Only way I know how to cook 'em."

"Over easy's fine, Wally."

"How's that toast coming, Trinky?"

"Going down," she said.

Then she laughed, as if it was the funniest thing she'd heard in forever. Schanno laughed, too.

"You guys sleep okay?" I asked.

"Marvelously well," Pollard said.

Marvelously was drawn out and affected, the way Tallulah Bankhead might have said it. They both laughed some more.

"Henry up yet?" I asked.

"Gone for a walk," Schanno replied. "He said he'd be back for breakfast."

I heard the front door open, and at the same time, the toast popped up.

"On cue," Pollard sang. "What timing."

Meloux came in looking refreshed. He was beaming just as brightly as the other two. Everyone seemed to have had a better night than me.

"It is a good day," Henry pronounced. "On this day, I will see my son."

Schanno lifted the coffee cup that sat near him on the counter. "To this day," he toasted.

Trinky Pollard did the same.

Despite the sunny morning and dispositions, I'd awakened with a sense that we were all swimming upstream against a current of doom. Why, I didn't know. But I didn't want my concern to infect the others. Who was I, anyway, to blunt their optimism?

I raised my cup. "To this day, Henry," I said and hoped it was true.

Over breakfast, we talked specifics. I proposed that Meloux and I go together to see Rupert Wellington.

"I've spoken with him before, so he knows me. Henry will tell his story, and we'll see what Wellington does."

"What if he refuses to see you?" Schanno's elbows were on the table, and his coffee cup was lost in the grip of his big hands.

"When I trot out Preston Ellsworth's name, I'm betting he'll want to talk," I said.

Pollard said, "In the meantime, I'll see what I can run down on that contact number Ellsworth gave us. And also the company that's been paying for his performances."

"Don't say anything about this to the police yet, Trinky," I suggested. "I'd rather we get what we can from Rupert Wellington first."

"Understood."

"What about me?" Wally asked.

Over her cup, Pollard smiled at him, impish and beautiful. "You, Mr. Schanno, can do the dishes."

FORTY-THREE

Rupert Wellington saw us immediately. I didn't know what that meant beyond the probability that when his secretary passed Preston Ellsworth's name to him along with my own, I hit pay dirt.

He was standing in front of his glass-topped desk, which seemed like a postcard compared to the size of the window behind it that overlooked the bay, which dwarfed them both. He'd crossed his arms, not the most cordial body language for greeting visitors. Nor was the scowl on his face. He didn't ask us to sit in either of the plush visitors' chairs.

He got down to business the moment his secretary closed the door behind us. "What do you want?"

"First to introduce my friend here, Henry Meloux. Henry, Rupert Wellington."

Wellington refused to offer his hand—a tradition Henry had never been particularly fond of anyway—and we skipped the formality.

"Preston Ellsworth's name opened the door to us pretty fast. It's clear you know about Ellsworth."

"What are you here for? Money?"

"No."

"Then what exactly are you going to do with what you know?"

"At the moment, nothing."

"At the moment?"

"Eventually the police will have it, but I'd like to talk to your brother first."

"The whole point of hiring Preston Ellsworth was to keep people from bothering my brother. Look, Hank's a man who can have anything in this world, and all he wants is privacy, Mr. O'Connor. I'm not going to disappoint him in that."

"Would it matter why I want to see him?"

"It has to do with that watch, I presume."

"It's gone far beyond the watch, Mr. Wellington. Or didn't Morrissey tell you that before he died?"

"The police interviewed me yesterday afternoon. I'll tell you what I told them about Morrissey. I didn't know the man. I have no knowledge of the relationship that might exist between him and my brother. End of story."

"Who arranged for Morrissey to escort me to the island?"

"I don't know. My part in that was simply to pass along your request to Hank. What goes on with Manitou Island is completely in his hands. That's the way it's always been."

"Hank?" Meloux said, as if testing the word on his tongue.

Wellington glanced at him and seemed both puzzled and annoyed by his presence.

"You have nothing to do with the island?" I went on.

"My brother bought out my interest in the island when he decided to step back from the world. Whatever goes on there is in Hank's hands."

"And you have no idea why your brother might want Henry Meloux dead?"

Wellington paused a moment and understanding entered his blue eyes. "Henry Meloux. You're the one who shot this Morrissey fellow."

"He was going to shoot me," Henry said simply.

I tried again. "Do you know why your brother might want Henry dead?"

Wellington looked at me. The steel returned to his eyes. "That question presupposes that he does."

"Aren't you curious?"

Wellington finally uncrossed his arms. He turned away and wandered to the window where he stood looking at the bay that lay shining in the morning sun. From there, he could see Sleeping Giant and, in its shadow, Manitou Island.

"Since my brother stepped down as head of Northern Mining, I've tried very hard not to be curious about his activities. It's pointless, for one thing. Hank behaves as he behaves. That's all there is to it."

"For one thing?"

He faced us and looked resigned. "He's brilliant, Mr. O'Connor. But when Roslyn died—that was his wife—when she died, he had a bit of a crack-up. It was a rough time for him. He wanted to step back from everything. The company, the public, even from his own family. I tried to talk him out of it. We all did. His children, me, his friends. But with Hank, once he's made up his mind, that's pretty much all she wrote.

"He concocted this scheme, having an actor step in for him, to divert the eye of the media, and he slipped away to the solitude he desired. I believe that at first he thought it would be a short-term situation, just until he felt able to deal with life again. But he found the isolation to his liking. So far as I know, he's not planning to come back into the world anytime soon."

"What's your part in the charade?"

"I have no part except to keep Hank's behavior as separate from the name of Northern Mining as possible."

"You have nothing to do with the men who live on the island?"

"Benning and Dougherty? No, Hank hired them when he hired the Ellsworth fellow. I have no part in any of it. Except that sometimes, as when you showed up the other day, I pass requests along to him, but that's all. Hank takes it from there."

"I'm still having trouble with Morrissey."

"I really don't know anything about him. From what I understand, Hank knew Morrissey from the guide work the man sometimes did. It's rough country where my brother is, Mr. O'Connor. There are a lot of people who are capable of the kind of behavior this Morrissey displayed."

"Where is he?"

"I won't tell you that. It's Hank's decision."

"You'll let him know I want to see him?"

"I'll do that."

"You don't have much time before I go to the police and everything comes out."

"From what you've told me, it's all going to come out anyway. What does it matter about the time?"

"One attempt was already made on Henry Meloux's life. I want answers before anybody else gets hurt. You still have my cell phone number?"

He didn't answer. He looked pained, as if his stomach had knotted suddenly. Finally he said, "You talk about people being hurt. I care very much about my brother. What he's gone through, what he continues to struggle with, isn't easy. I'd prefer that his solitude be respected, but that's a choice he'll have to make. If it were up to me, I'd have you tossed out of Canada."

"You have my cell phone number?" I said again.

"Yes."

"Then I'll expect to hear from your brother."

He looked at me, unhappy and probably angry, and he looked at Meloux. We turned away and left his office.

In the elevator, Meloux said, "That is a man at war."

"With us?"

"It spills out at us, but it is something else, I think."

"He's going to have his hands full when the truth of all this comes out. Northern Mining and Manufacturing will have to perform some pretty amazing magic to give any of it a good spin."

Pollard and Schanno were drinking coffee in the front-porch swing when I pulled into the driveway. They looked comfortable together.

As we mounted the steps, Schanno asked, "How'd it go?"

"We'll have to see. Wellington promised to talk to his brother, but he couldn't guarantee anything. Hank Wellington makes his own decisions."

"Hank?"

"What his brother called him."

"I need a drink of water," Meloux said and went inside.

"How's he doing?" Trinky asked, her voice low and full of concern.

"Okay, I guess. We learned a little more about his son." I explained what Rupert had told me about his brother and the Manitou Island setup. "What did you find out about the number Ellsworth gave you?"

"An answering service," Trinky Pollard said. "Ellsworth leaves a message, the service notifies the account owner, who accesses the message. I'd need a court order to go any deeper. But I did find out that Entertaintec, which pays for Ellsworth's services, is a subsidiary of Larchmont Productions, which is owned by Henry Wellington."

"All roads continue to lead to Rome," I said.

"Wherever that is in Canada." Schanno shook his head.

"Any coffee left?" I asked.

"Half a pot," Pollard said. "Help yourself."

I'd turned toward the front door when my cell phone rang. I pulled it from my pocket. It was Jo.

"Hi, sweetheart," I answered.

"You're alive."

"And kicking."

"I'd hoped to hear from you."

"Sorry. It's been busy up here."

"How's it going?"

"Closing in, I hope. I'm waiting for a call from Henry Wellington, so as much as I love talking to you, I need to keep the line open. How're things on the home front?"

"You mean Jenny?"

"She's at the top of my list of concerns."

"She's doing remarkably well. She's strong, Cork."

"She'll need to be. How's everyone else?"

"Annie's working her rear end off at Sam's Place. And Stevie's in seventh heaven with Walleye around. Cork, we really need to consider getting him a dog."

"We'll talk when I'm home," I said, aware that I was putting it off again. "I need to keep this line open."

"Sure. You take care of yourself. And Meloux."

"I'm on it."

I poured myself some coffee. Meloux was at the kitchen sink, drinking water from a plastic tumbler. We headed back outside together.

"What now?" Schanno asked.

"Nothing to do but wait," I said.

We didn't have to wait long. In twenty minutes, my cell phone chirped. I answered and recognized the voice, the same one that, on my first visit to Thunder Bay, had given me the instructions that got me to Manitou Island.

"I'll see you, Mr. O'Connor," Henry Wellington said.

"When?"

"As soon as you can get here."

"Where's here?"

"Go to the marina, the south end of the parking lot. Mr. Benning will be waiting for you. He'll bring you to me."

"I'm not coming alone."

"The old man, the one called Meloux? You'll bring him?"

"Yes. And a colleague."

"Walter Schanno?"

Wellington was informed.

"Yes. Schanno."

"All right. Leave immediately. It's a long trip."

He hung up without the cordiality of a good-bye.

The others looked at me.

"The great and powerful Oz will see us," I said.

FORTY-FOUR

We took Trinky Pollard to the marina and let her off near the dock, where her boat was moored and where, she'd told us, her car was still parked.

She stood in the sunlight, blinking at us, clearly disappointed. "Sure you won't let me go?" The whole way she'd argued for the wisdom of taking her along to see Wellington.

I leaned out my window. "He only agreed to Henry and Wally. I don't want to blow this chance."

"He also tried to have Henry killed. He doesn't strike me as the most gracious host. You might need all the backup you can get."

"We'll be fine, Trinky," I said.

She came around to Schanno's side. "You'll be careful?"

"Always have been," he said.

She kissed him on the cheek. "When you get back, give me a call, promise?"

"Promise."

She stepped away. We headed toward the south end of the marina. In the rearview mirror, I watched her watching us. Then she turned toward her boat.

Benning was standing beside a black Ford Explorer, leaning against the driver's-side front door. The Explorer looked new and reflected sunlight shot from the polished finish in long bright arrows. Benning wore a T-shirt with the sleeves rolled up over impressive biceps. He had on a ball cap that shaded his face and sunglasses that hid his eyes. As we drove up, he looked our way. When I stopped, he pushed from his vehicle and walked to my side of the Bronco.

"I have instructions to take you to Mr. Wellington." He kept his shades on when he spoke to me.

"Lead the way."

"How's your gas?" he asked.

"I filled up on the way here."

He nodded and turned back to the Explorer.

"What if we get separated?" I said.

"We won't."

We followed him northwest out of Thunder Bay, keeping to Highway 17, part of the Trans-Canada Highway system. The sun had just passed its zenith when we finally put civilization behind us. For a long time after that, the highway cut through flat country with a lot of timber and not many towns.

A little over two hours later, we came to Ignace and turned north. We stopped at a gas station with a small restaurant. Benning pulled up to a pump and signaled us to do the same.

"Last chance for gas for quite a while," he said.

Meloux used the men's room while I filled the tank. Schanno went inside to get us some bottled water. He came back with three microwaved burritos as well. Within ten minutes, we were off again, following a hundred yards behind the Explorer. The burritos were hard beans and tasteless sauce wrapped in tortillas the texture of white leather, but we were all hungry and gobbled them down.

In a while, Meloux was napping in the backseat. Schanno and I talked.

"You and Trinky seemed to hit it off," I said.

Schanno thought about that and then nodded. "She's a good, sensible woman. Easy to talk to." He studied the pine trees that walled the highway. "It's been lonely."

"Sure," I said.

"Know what I miss most, Cork? Arletta used to sing around the house. It didn't matter what she was doing, she was always singing. I could tell from the nature of the tune just how she was feeling. A snappy song and she was happy. Something blue and she was down. But always her voice there, filling the house. Place seems so damned empty now, I almost hate being there."

"I can imagine," I said.

"It's been hard saying good-bye."

I didn't think that needed a response, so I studied my side-view mirror.

"Trinky's thinking of sailing up the Saint Lawrence to the Atlantic in a few weeks, then heading south along the East Coast to the Caribbean. Needs a good deckhand, she says."

"You told me. You interested in the job?"

"It'd be something to do."

"And you like the company."

He swung his gaze my way. "Is it too soon, you think?"

"Wally, I don't know that there's any blueprint for the affairs of the human heart. You try to do your best to listen to what it tells you, and do your best, when possible, to follow. That's how it seems to me."

He nodded. "Funny, you know, that I've got a dog named Trixie. Almost like Trinky. I called her Trixie last night."

"She hit you?"

"When I explained, she thought it was cute. Say, what's so interesting in that mirror of yours?"

"We're being followed."

He craned his neck to look back. It took a minute before the vehicle behind us came into view as it rounded a curve.

"How do you know it's following us? This is probably the only good road in a hundred miles."

"In the absence of evidence to the contrary, it's safest to assume the worst."

"The worst being?"

"Benning's ahead of us. If Wellington wanted to put us in a pinch, he'd have someone behind us as well."

Schanno unbuckled his seat belt and crawled into the back. Meloux was so deeply asleep he didn't notice the jostling. Schanno dug in his bag, then came back up front. He was holding a handgun and a box of cartridges.

"What the hell is that?" I said.

"A Colt Python."

"Jesus, you brought that over the border? We could have been arrested."

"You're forgetting Henry's luck."

"If you think he's so lucky, what do you need that for?"

"My dad always told me to hedge my bets." He began feeding cartridges into the Colt. "You think Rupert Wellington is involved in any of this?"

"I don't think a man in charge of a corporation like Northern Mining is as ignorant of what's going on as he'd like us to believe. What exactly his part is, I can't say."

The vehicle trailing us—a dark green SUV—kept its distance.

"If Benning slows down and that SUV behind us speeds up, I'll probably be glad you have that Colt," I said.

In the back, Meloux snorted in his deep slumber.

"I don't understand Henry," Schanno said. He snapped the cylinder closed. "Why worry about his son after seventy years? What good could it do him?"

"This isn't about his own good. Henry's worried about his son."

"He oughta be. We all know Morrissey wasn't after any pocket watch. Just between you and me, I think Henry's setting himself up for a big fall. What kind of son would behave like this Wellington?"

"A sick one. That's what Henry believes anyway. He also believes he can help."

"There are some people—and you understand I'm not one of them—who are going to say Henry's just out to get something, maybe a piece of Wellington's fortune."

"Anybody says that, they don't know Henry. Hell, he's never taken a cent of the distribution he's due from the rez's casino profits. He had Jo set up a fund. The money goes directly into it. After he's gone, it'll be used for college scholarships for Shinnobs."

"A guy like Henry, you've got to admit, Cork, seems too good to be true."

A horrible smell invaded the Bronco. I looked at Schanno and he looked at me. We both looked back at Meloux, who smiled in his sleep.

"I should have warned you about Henry and beans," I said. "Jesus, roll your window down."

Schanno took a deep breath of the fresh air that rushed in. "What I just said about Henry? You can forget it."

* * *

After five hours on the road and nearly three hundred additional miles on my old Bronco's odometer, we came to the outskirts of a small town called Flame Lake. It was the first sign of civilization we'd seen in a long time. Mostly, there'd been the gray pavement down the middle of an endless green corridor, with the occasional blue relief of a lake to break the monotony. Benning pulled off into a roadside park along a little river, and we followed him. He stopped, got out, and came to my side of the Bronco.

I was watching for the SUV in the mirror. So was Schanno. He had his loaded Colt in the glove box.

"Wait here," Benning said.

"What for?"

"I have to make a call. I've got to use a phone in town. Cells don't work up here. I'll be back in ten minutes."

"No choice, I guess."

"That's right."

Benning headed off in his Explorer. I got out, walked to the road, and looked back the way we'd come. I hadn't seen the SUV pass by us, and I wondered where it was. I had to look hard, but I could see it, pulled way off to the side. If we tried to head back to Thunder Bay at this point, it could easily cut us off. I thought about swinging the Bronco around and going back, just to see who it was. My guess was Dougherty. But Wellington was a man with unlimited resources, so, hell, it could have been anybody or, more likely, a platoon of anybodies.

Schanno came up beside me. "What do you think?"

"If they've got something up their sleeves, I doubt it'll happen here. We'll just have to be careful."

Schanno grunted, and I took that for agreement.

Meloux had climbed out, too. We were in an area of rugged hills covered with boreal growth, mostly jack pine and black spruce. Meloux stood near a picnic table and studied the hills. There was a little map posted near the parking area. It showed a lake—Flame Lake—curling in a long, lazy, ten-mile arc to the west of the town. It also showed the Flame Lake Mine, a few miles west of where we stood.

I walked to Meloux, who'd climbed onto the picnic table. Like an extra couple of feet would improve his view.

"What do you think, Henry? Familiar?" I asked.

"Seventy years, Corcoran O'Connor. A long time to remember anything. And these old eyes . . ." He shook his head and slowly climbed down.

The Explorer came back. Benning poked his head out the window. He still had on his shades. "Through town," he instructed. "At the intersection, keep straight on. Stay well back from me, though. Understand?"

"Not exactly, but I get your drift," I replied.

The town, what there was to it, was laid out at the eastern end of the lake. It reminded me of a lot of small towns on the Iron Range of Minnesota, places that had exploded with a burly energy when the iron mines were operating, but had had the wind knocked out of them once the operations shut down. Along the one-block business district, several storefronts were vacant. Among those still open were a grocery store, a couple of bars, and a little Mexican restaurant with a sign in the window hyping the blue margaritas. The variety store, a place called the Outpost that sold clothing, sporting goods, hardware, hunting and fishing licenses, and Minnetonka moccasins, seemed to be doing okay. We passed it all quickly and followed Benning north, out of town.

A couple of miles farther on we came to a turnoff onto another road that curved along the shoreline of Flame Lake. A large sign was posted at the intersection: PRIVATE ROAD. NO TRESPASSING. We took the turnoff and headed west on the private road. I tried to stay far enough back from the Explorer that we weren't eating the dust it kicked up. The cloud my Bronco left behind us kept me from seeing if the green SUV was still following.

After eight miles of this, the road ended. Benning pulled up before an expansive, two-story log house built on the lakeshore. It wasn't a new structure, but it had been well cared for. The logs were pine the color of dark honey. There were green shutters on the windows. A small apron of grass separated the house from the surrounding trees. Beds of flowers lined the foundation. We parked behind Benning, who got out and walked to the Bronco.

"Wait here. I'll let Mr. Wellington know you've arrived." He left us, jogged up the steps to the front porch, and went in the door.

Meloux slid from the Bronco and headed around the side of the house, toward the lake.

"Henry?" I called.

He didn't pay any attention. Schanno and I followed him. Meloux crossed the backyard, which was maybe a hundred feet of coarse grass, and stood at the edge of the lake, staring across the water toward the ridges on the far side.

We stayed back, giving him the space and time he seemed to need.

With his back to us, he said, "I stood here and watched Maria swim."

"Here? You're sure?"

"She was like an otter, sleek and beautiful."

For the first time since I'd brought him north across the border, he sounded deeply satisfied. I felt happy for him.

"Hey!"

We turned toward the house. Benning had come out onto the large rear deck.

"Inside," he called. He jammed his thumb toward the sliding glass door that stood open at his back. "Mr. Wellington is waiting."

FORTY-FIVE

We mounted the steps of the back deck and trailed Benning into the house. It was furnished sparely, but what was there was beautifully made. The whole place was strongly scented with the good smell of wood smoke, a scent comforting and welcoming, the essence, it had always seemed to me, of where the human experience and the wilderness met.

Benning led us to a room at the southwest end of the house. It was full of books and sunlight and Henry Wellington.

He was less imposing than the legends about him suggested. He stood six feet at most, taut, slender. His hair was white and thick. For a man of seventy, he had skin that was remarkably smooth and unblemished. His dark eyes regarded us calmly. He was dressed in white drawstring pants and a loose shirt of white cotton. He wore sandals. He didn't offer to shake hands, but he did invite us to sit, and he offered us something to drink. We declined.

He said simply, "You've come a long way to talk to me. I'm listening."

"When I was a young man," Meloux told him, "I loved your mother, and she loved me."

"My mother has been dead for sixty-five years."

"You are wrong," Meloux said. "In you, I can see that she lives still."

Wellington studied the old Mide carefully but not with a cold eye. "Tell me how you knew my mother."

Meloux told his story, much as he'd told it to me. As he talked, the box of sunlight on the polished floorboards changed. At one point, the wind rose slightly outside, and the sound of it through the pines was a steady, distant sigh. I heard heavy thuds from a far part of the house, but Wellington gave no sign that they were important. I wondered if there was someone else in the house besides Benning.

Wellington listened patiently and with an intensity that made me believe every word Meloux spoke was being processed and filed away and could be accessed a decade later, verbatim.

When Meloux finished, Wellington said, "I'm to believe that Leonard Wellington was not only not my father but was a killer as well?"

"No," Meloux replied. "The killing is on my shoulders."

"But he was a man with murder in his heart, yes?"

"That was one thing in his heart."

"Do you have the watch?"

Meloux brought it out from his shirt pocket. Wellington crossed the room, and took it from him. He walked to a window that looked south across the lake. The late-afternoon sun struck him and seemed to ignite the white he wore. He looked at the photograph in the pocket watch for a long time.

"This is the only proof you have?" he asked.

"She gave me her love and I stole the watch," Meloux said. "In their ways, they were gifts I did not ask for, but I took them gratefully."

Wellington turned. I couldn't read his face.

"I require more," he said.

He and Meloux locked eyes. For the next half minute, it was as if Schanno and I didn't exist.

"I will take you to Maurice's cabin," Meloux said.

"Now?"

"Now."

Wellington studied the sky outside the window. "In four hours, it will be too dark to see."

Meloux stood up. "Then you had better keep up with me."

Wellington smiled. "Very well."

He took a few minutes to change his clothes. Under Benning's watchful eye, Meloux, Schanno, and I went out to my Bronco, where I put a few things into my day pack: a flashlight, three bottled waters, bug repellent, and my Swiss Army knife. For good measure, I took

Schanno's loaded Colt from the glove box and slipped it in the pack. I didn't know Wellington, and I hadn't been able to read him. I didn't know what his true agenda might be. It was possible he was simply as intrigued as he appeared to be. It was also possible that he planned to have us all whacked in the isolation of the woods. Whoever it was that had trailed us in the green SUV was probably lurking somewhere near. The weight of the Colt in the day pack gave me a measure of comfort.

"What do you think?" Schanno asked, coming around the Bronco as I shut the door.

"About Wellington?"

"Him, yeah, but I also meant about Meloux hiking to the ruins of this burned-down cabin."

"Meloux hikes from Crow Point into Allouette all the time. A good ten miles round-trip."

Meloux was standing not far away, but his attention was focused on the lake and the distant ridges. He didn't seem to hear our conversation.

"Three days ago he was in the hospital, and word was that he wasn't coming out," Schanno said.

"Tell him your concern, if you want to."

"*My* concern? You think I'm not talking sense?"

"Try talking sense to Meloux. After everything he's been through to get here, if he told me he was going to fly to this cabin, I'd say happy landing."

"All right, how about this? It's been seventy years since he was here, Cork. Hell, I can't even remember what clothes I wore yesterday. You really think Meloux's going to be able to find his way?"

"I guess we'll see. By the way, your Colt Python is in the pack."

"Good. I've been thinking about the guys in that SUV. Should we take the rifles?"

"How good are you with the Colt?"

"Pretty good," Schanno said.

"Unless Wellington comes out with a bazooka, let's stick with that." I walked over to Meloux and risked intruding on his thoughts. "You doing okay, Henry?"

"I'm near the end of the journey, Corcoran O'Connor."

"Can you tell he's your son?" I thought about the faint copper color of Wellington's skin and his dark eyes. They could have been from Shinnob blood, or just as easily from the Cuban blood of his mother.

Meloux didn't answer immediately. The wrinkles around his eyes, already deep, went deeper as he stared at the log house. "My heart is out there waiting for his to come and meet it. We will see."

That didn't strike me as a resounding yes. Meloux had risked much to be here: his health, his life, and, because he'd admitted to murder, his freedom. I wanted the answer he gave me to be absolute and affirmative. I wanted him to say that the moment he set eyes on the man, he'd known Wellington was his son. All the evidence was there, yet I felt the old man holding back. To be a son, to be a father, these things were more than just a blood tie. Maybe that's what the hesitation was about. Did the relationship matter if, in the end, Wellington didn't give a damn?

Wellington came from the house and spoke to Benning on the front porch, a conversation too quiet to be overheard, then he joined us. He'd dressed rugged: L.L. Bean boots, Levi's, a brown, long-sleeved Henley, and a camouflage jungle hat. He also carried a small pack. I wondered how much our loads might resemble each other.

"After you, sir," he said to Meloux with what seemed to be genuine respect.

Meloux crossed the yard, heading west, parallel to the lake. Where the grass met the pines, he spent a few minutes studying the ground, then he was off, leading the way.

He didn't burn up the woods with his speed, but he did keep a remarkably steady pace for a man who'd seemed ancient to me my whole life, and who, as Schanno noted, was lying in a hospital bed only days before. It helped that he was following a trail. It wasn't well worn, but to an eye familiar with hunting or tracking, it was clear we were walking where others had walked before. This was August. The bugs swarmed: biting deerflies, blackflies, gnats, and mosquitoes. Schanno was slapping himself silly behind me, so we stopped and put on the DEET I'd brought. Wellington declined my offer to share the ointment, as did Henry. We crossed slender threads of creek water running silver between white rocks. In the middle of a small meadow,

Meloux stopped, not from weariness, I realized, but to take in the beauty of the lavender wild bergamot that grew in profusion and whose leaves filled the air with a refreshing mint scent. Smells are the time machines of human perception. A scent can take you instantly back to a particular place and time. Watching Meloux stand, transfixed, with his eyes gently shut, I wondered if, in that moment, he was a young man again, in love, walking through the meadow with Maria.

"Are you tired?" Wellington asked. "We can rest."

Meloux opened his eyes. The moment was gone. He shook his head and we moved on.

We came to the gray, rocky slope of a long ridge, where the trail disappeared. Meloux studied the incline. We'd been hiking for nearly an hour without a significant rest. Despite the DEET, bugs kept landing on my neck, trying to lap at the sweat there. I was aware that Schanno had been keeping a wary eye on the woods at our backs, and he was doing that now. Wellington watched the old Mide with intense interest.

Meloux put his hand on the stone of the slope. "Over seventy winters, things change. Trees die, others grow, and the way becomes clouded. But rocks do not change so easy. The rocks, I remember. There," he said and pointed upward toward a small, dark gray spire around which nothing grew. "I used to think of it as a *manidoo*, a spirit showing the way."

With that, he began to climb.

There's no adequate measure of the human spirit, no scale to weigh the courage of the human heart. Just when you think you've plumbed the depth, dredged the last bucketful from the well, you discover how wrong you are. Once, when I was a cop in Chicago, I was the first to respond to the report of a shooting in an apartment building on Hyde Street. I arrived at the scene, the third-floor hallway, to find a wounded man propped against a hissing radiator. He had a bullet in his heart. Two more had shattered bone in his chest and lodged somewhere deep in his internal organs. The bare floor under him was slick with his blood. A dead man lay at his feet, a .38 Ruger near his outstretched hand. The dead man's windpipe had been crushed. A small boy peeked from the doorway of the nearest apartment.

"Daddy?" he whispered toward the wounded man.

Somehow, from somewhere unimaginable, that father found the strength to smile. " 'S okay, Boo," he said. "He won't hurt you."

And if that weren't miracle enough, he managed to reach out and hug his son, who ran to him before I could prevent it.

It had been about drugs, about threatening the boy, and finally about what a father would do to protect his son. The wounded man died. The truth was that he was dead even as he crushed his killer's windpipe to keep his son safe, but he'd tapped the deep reservoir of strength that lay behind his love for his child, and he'd done what, as a father, he needed to do.

I watched Meloux haul his ninety-year-old body up the ridge, and I knew that at that moment there was more to his strength than could be accounted for by those long walks from Crow Point to Allouette. It was possible, I supposed, that he might kill himself in this effort, but I understood there was no way any of us could stop him.

We climbed out of the shadow of the ridge and into the sunlight of early evening. It was seven thirty P.M. So far north, the sun would still be around for quite a while. Meloux led us down the other side, into shade again, and onto a trail that ran along a rushing stream.

Ten minutes later, we entered a clearing grown over with fire-weed and lupine. On the far side stood an old log structure, five feet wide and twice as long. The roof had collapsed decades before, but the four walls were still solid. *The smokehouse*, I thought.

We were in a deep trough between two hills. Sunlight hit the higher slopes and the pine trees there burned yellow and I heard crows arguing in the branches. Where we stood, everything was shadow and silence.

Meloux walked ahead slowly, parting the deep weed cover, peering carefully. Finally he stopped and turned back to us. "Here," he said, indicating the ground at his feet. "Here, I cut the throat of the man who was my friend. And here, I put a bullet in the heart of a man who was not." He turned to his right and went a couple of dozen paces, then walked in a slow circle. Finally he signaled for us to come.

As I neared him, I saw, deep in the tangle of undergrowth, the long black bones of burned timbers half buried in the earth.

"Dig here," he instructed. "It should not be deep."

Schanno and I pulled the weeds, then got on our knees and began to dig with our hands. Three or four inches down, we hit solid wood. We scraped the dirt away, revealing rotted floorboards. Because I knew his story, I knew what Meloux expected to find, and we kept scraping at the dirt until we uncovered the thing.

"Here it is, Henry," I said. I took the knife from my day pack and ran the blade along the slits that outlined the trapdoor. I poked until I located the hole where a strand of rope had once served as a handle, and I cleaned it out. I glanced up at Meloux.

"Open it," he said.

I jabbed my index finger into the hole and lifted. The door resisted at first, then gave. The cool, earthy smell of trapped air escaped. The light in the clearing was waning, and the pit below the trapdoor was too dark to see into clearly.

"In the pack," I said to Schanno. "My flashlight."

He dug it out and handed it over. I flicked it on and shot the beam through the opening of the trapdoor. The pit appeared to be a cube three feet wide and deep. It was filled with deer-hide bags gone brittle with time, each as large as a softball. A quick count gave me a dozen.

I stood back. "Care to take a look, Mr. Wellington?"

I held the flashlight while he knelt and reached into the pit. The bag he grasped fell apart as he lifted it and dull yellow sand spilled out.

"I've never seen gold dust," I said, "but I imagine it looks pretty much like that, doesn't it?"

Wellington stood up. "Put the trapdoor back." He studied the sky. "We should start home. It'll be dark soon."

He didn't look at Meloux, just turned and headed toward the trail along the stream.

I lowered the door back into place. Quiet as a congregation leaving a church, we abandoned the clearing.

FORTY-SIX

We moved more slowly on the return and didn't make it back to the log home before nightfall. Wellington pulled a powerful light out of his pack and led the way. I brought up the rear with mine. Wellington had no trouble following the trail, faint as it was, and I figured this wasn't the first time he'd been to the burned ruins in the little clearing. We stopped often for Meloux to rest. He'd proved his point, and now he was feeling the physical cost of the journey. I shared the bottles of water in my pack. Wellington had brought his own. He also had trail mix, which he offered around. We didn't speak except for the necessity of safety: "Careful of that log," or "Watch your step." When I finally saw the lights of Wellington's place ahead of us, I felt a deep relief.

We crossed the yard, mounted the front porch, and went inside. I smelled food cooking and realized I was starved.

Wellington said, "It's too late for you to return tonight. You're welcome to stay here. There are plenty of rooms upstairs. I asked Benning to prepare dinner for us. As soon as you're settled, we can eat."

We brought our bags in from the Bronco, and Wellington himself showed us to our rooms.

"I'm going to wash up, and I'll see you downstairs in the dining room in a few minutes," he said. He went to his own room, which was at the far end of the hallway.

I shed my shirt. As I stood at the sink in my bathroom, washing off the dirt and sweat and DEET, Schanno knocked and came in. He stood in the bathroom doorway, trying to scrape the dirt from under his fingernails while I finished cleaning up.

"This guy Wellington is one cold fish," he said. "Meloux delivers all the evidence to back up his claims, and Wellington doesn't say a word to him. He might not be the kook Ellsworth played, but he's hard to figure."

"I imagine it's a lot to absorb."

"Sure, but most people are going to react somehow. Him, it's like he'd just watched you peel an orange."

"Henry Wellington's not much like other people."

"He was my son, I'd give him a kick in the ass."

I grabbed a towel from the rack and began to dry myself. "I have it on good authority, Wally, that you never raised a hand—or foot—to your kids."

"I'll take my Python back. There's still a lot we don't know, like why Morrissey went after Henry in the first place."

I hung the towel, pushed past Schanno, and grabbed the clean shirt I'd laid out on the bed. "Wellington's hard to read, I admit, but I didn't get a dangerous feel from him."

"All the same, I'm going to sleep with the Python under my pillow tonight."

"Suit yourself." I took the weapon from the pack and handed it over.

"How much you figure there is in gold up there?" he said.

I buttoned my shirt. "Enough to set you and me and Meloux for a lifetime. Drop in the bucket to Wellington."

We left my room, and I knocked on Meloux's door but got no answer.

"Maybe he's already downstairs," Schanno suggested.

I poked my head in the room. The old Mide lay on his bed, fully clothed, not dead—I could tell from the slow rise and fall of his chest and his soft snoring—but dead tired and dead to the world. I closed the door softly.

We found Wellington in the dining room, pouring mineral water into the glasses on the table. He'd changed back into his loose-fitting white clothing and sandals. A meat loaf sat on a platter in the middle of the table. An hour earlier, it had probably been perfect. Now it looked overcooked and dry. There was a big bowl of fresh green beans mixed with crisp bacon bits, roasted red potatoes, a tossed salad, and a good-looking dark bread.

"I don't have beer," Wellington said. "I can offer you wine, however. I still keep some good vintages on hand for when my family visits."

Schanno and I both settled for the water.

"And Mr. Meloux?" Wellington asked.

"He's sleeping," I said. "It's been a long, hard day."

We sat down to the meal. Once you got past the crust from the additional cooking time, the meat loaf was delicious, quite savory, as were the beans and the roasted potatoes. The salad contained pears and had a refreshing lime dressing. The bread was homemade, substantial and tasty.

"Benning usually does your cooking?" I asked.

"I live here alone most of the time, so generally I do my own."

I figured that was enough small talk. "You employed Edward Morrissey, Mr. Wellington, and Morrissey tried to murder Henry Meloux."

Wellington carefully dabbed his lips with his napkin. "So I understand."

"Why?"

"I really have no idea. Ed Morrissey worked for me on occasion, but he was what you might call a freelance security consultant. When Rupert telephoned and told me about the watch and your request for an interview, I contacted Morrissey to arrange for him to oversee your visit to Manitou Island. I wanted to know what you were up to, and I didn't want Ellsworth handling you alone. After your visit, Morrissey phoned in his report. He indicated you were simply working a con, trying to squeeze some money out of me. He told me he'd taken care of the situation discreetly, as he had on other occasions in the past. I was surprised when Rupert called to tell me the police were investigating the incident in Minnesota."

"Surprised but not troubled?"

"I didn't know Henry Meloux or his story."

"Morrissey never reported that part to you?"

"No."

"Doesn't that seem odd to you?"

"Of course it does, now."

"Why wouldn't he tell you everything?"

"That's a question for which I have no answer."

"What about Rupert?"

He shook his head. "Rupert's only part has been to pass along requests that seem to have some merit. Those have been blessedly few. He made it clear from the beginning that he wanted no part in my charade, and he's done his best to keep Northern Mining distanced."

"You don't care about Northern Mining?"

"I gave the company the best I could for most of my adult life. When I stepped away and secluded myself here, I severed myself from any worries about Northern Mining. It was an amicable divorce. I have no desire to renew the relationship."

"And you don't mind that Preston Ellsworth has played you as pretty much a lunatic?"

"My family knows the truth, Mr. O'Connor. What the rest of the world thinks of me is a concern I left behind a long time ago."

Benning came from the kitchen. "Would you care for dessert or coffee?"

"Gentlemen?" Wellington asked. "I have fresh strawberries and sweet cream."

My stomach was full, and I was tired, so I said no. Schanno did the same.

"We're fine, Sandy," Wellington said to Benning. "Why don't you call it a night? I'll clean up."

"You're sure, sir? It's no trouble."

"It was a good meal. I'll see you in the morning."

"Very good, sir." Benning vanished the way he'd come.

"I'd be glad to help," I said.

Wellington set his napkin on the table and waved off my offer. "I won't hear of it. You're my guests. I'm just going to fill the dishwasher anyway."

It felt as if the evening had been drawn to a close, but there were still many questions unanswered. Most of them didn't involve me. They were between Wellington and the man I was certain was his real father. I couldn't imagine Wellington not wanting to talk with Meloux, but I saw no sign of eagerness on his part.

I went upstairs to my room still at a loss to understand what kind of man he was and what kind of son.

FORTY-SEVEN

I was tired, but I tossed and turned in a restless sleep. I didn't think Wellington would have us all murdered in the night; still, there were a lot of unanswered questions flapping around in my brain. Why had Morrissey followed me to Meloux's and tried to kill the old man? Was he acting on his own or under orders? Orders from whom? The Wellingtons had something to lose, maybe, if the truth of Meloux's story was ever made public, but I figured a lot of fortunes had been built on the graves of innocent people. It wasn't that startling, and Leonard Wellington's treachery had happened a long time ago. Both sons—Rupert and Henry—seemed civilized, if a little on the chilly side. On the other hand, a lot of civilized people have convinced themselves that in the right cause it's acceptable—noble, even—to bloody your hands. If neither of the Wellingtons was responsible, then who? If it was all Morrissey's idea, then why?

I wasn't thinking only about Meloux, however. Jenny was heavy on my mind.

Sure, we would help her make a life for herself and her baby, but it wouldn't be the life we'd dreamed of for her or that she'd dreamed of for herself. That made me sad. I had no doubt she would love her child fiercely and be a great mother, but I knew that there would always be the demon of *if only* harping away in the back of her mind. Every life lived fully is going to have some regrets, because every risk is not worth taking, but you don't always see that in time. Or if you do, you convince yourself that you'll be the one to beat the odds. Jenny and Sean had gambled, and it wasn't that they'd lost exactly. The dealer had simply swept all the chips off the table and placed them in the hands of an unborn child.

The tyranny of love. Love demands all, everything. Jenny was up to the challenge. Sean, it seemed, was not. I wasn't angry with him. I didn't think any of us were. We were just disappointed. I figured that in his own life, no matter how he played it, when Sean looked back, Jenny and his child would be one of his regrets. And that made me sad, too.

I slept off and on. Every time I woke, the pattern of moonlight on the floor of my room had shifted. I looked at the clock on the stand next to my bed. Three A.M. I got up, used the toilet, and went to check on Meloux. His room was empty. I slipped my pants on and went downstairs. The house was dark, except for a light under the door of the study where, earlier that day, Wellington had greeted us and Meloux had told his story. I listened at the door and heard the rustle of a page being turned. I considered knocking, but decided against it. I didn't think Meloux would be reading.

I had another idea. I went out onto the rear deck where I could see the lake, a great pool of silver poured out from the moon. I also saw what I thought I might see: the silhouette of Meloux standing alone on the dock. I walked across the yard, carefully because I was barefoot. The ground was cool against the soles of my feet. I coughed as I approached so that I wouldn't startle the old man. His head half-turned, but he didn't speak.

"Mind if I join you, Henry?"

"Your company is always welcome, Corcoran O'Connor."

"Get some rest?"

"Yes. I was tired."

"No wonder. Long, hard day. Hungry?"

"The morning will come soon enough. I will eat then."

I put my hands in my pockets and stared up at the stars the moonlight hadn't swallowed. "I'm sorry, Henry."

"Why?"

"I hoped, I don't know, that Wellington would be the son you wanted."

"How do you know he is not?"

"He hasn't been what I would call enthusiastic about seeing you."

"He has also not turned me away."

"Forgive me for saying so, Henry, but you set your sights awfully low."

Meloux didn't reply.

"What do you want to do now?" I said.

"I want you to smoke with me," he said.

He took a pouch from his shirt pocket and sprinkled a bit to the four points of the compass, acknowledging the spirits that governed each, then he sprinkled some in the center. We sat down on the dock. He took papers and, in the moonlight that bleached his old hands white, he expertly rolled a cigarette. He lit it with a wood match that he struck to flame on his thumbnail. For the next few minutes, we smoked in silence. On the lake, two loons called back and forth, but I couldn't see them. In the woods on either side, tree frogs and crickets chirred. The surface of the water was so still and shiny that it could have been made of polished steel. All this felt little different from any lake I'd ever sat beside on a Minnesota night, and I was aware that the vast wilderness, which began near the border of Canada, still ran relatively unbroken to the other side of the Arctic Circle. We were in the middle of a great, enduring beauty, and despite the danger and confusion involved in our being there, I couldn't help but feel a profound sense of gratitude. Probably, that was exactly what the old Mide had hoped I might feel when he asked me to share the tobacco and the moment.

I heard the deck door open and close. I saw Meloux cock his head slightly, as if he'd heard, too, but he didn't turn. Half a minute later, I felt the dock shiver under an added weight.

"I have seen you," Wellington said at our backs. "In visions. I've had them all my life. I never understood them or understood why they came to me."

Meloux spoke toward the lake. "You are my son. You have a gift."

"I isolated myself here years ago to try finally to understand that gift. It's been lonely and difficult. I was about to give up."

"Perhaps that is why I'm here."

"Mother never told me about you. She believed you were dead."

"Why?"

"She came back with Leonard the next spring and went to Maurice's cabin. She found the remains of two bodies, which the scavengers had cleaned to mostly bone. She thought one was Maurice and the other was you."

"She married Leonard Wellington."

"That was part of the bargain she struck with him. When her father died, she agreed to marry Leonard and give him access to her father's money. In return, he promised not to tell the police about your part in the death. She had no idea he'd already been here or what he'd done."

"How do you know these things? Did she tell you?"

"She wrote them in her journals."

Wellington walked to where we sat. He held out a book bound in soft leather. Meloux took it and opened it. Glancing, I saw that it was written in thin, precise script that would be difficult to read by moonlight.

"There are more than a dozen like it," Wellington said. "She left them to me, in the care of her attorney, not to be read until I turned twenty-one. I was a fighter pilot in Korea when I turned twenty-one and had no interest in reading them. I didn't get around to it until after Leonard died."

"He was a good father?" Meloux asked.

"We fought all the time. I could never please him. He was a man too absorbed in his own affairs. Finally I gave up trying. Poor Rupert, though, he worked so hard to be noticed. The man treated him badly, but Rupert just kept coming back for more. When I read the journals and finally understood that Rupert was his real son, it made me sad. Me, I just came with the contract, but my brother was truly his son, and Leonard still treated him like a dog."

In front of us, a small fish jumped, creating a circle of ripples that widened until they captured the reflection of the moon.

"I used to come here with her, just the two of us, and she would tell me stories about an Ojibwe hunter, very brave and handsome and noble. She called him Niibaa-waabii. She said it meant Sees At Night. She died when I was ten. After that, whenever I felt alone, whenever I felt that Leonard was a dense, unfathomable fog, I would imagine that the hunter was my father and that he was pleased with me."

Meloux said, "I am pleased."

He sat beside the old Mide. "After all these years, why did you come looking for me now?"

"My heart told me it was time." The old man laughed. "It gave me a good kick in the ass." He went quiet again, then asked a question that must have been heavy on his mind for seventy years. "Leonard Wellington said it was your mother who told him about Maurice and the gold. I never wanted to believe it." He turned his head and looked to his son. "Do you know the truth?"

"No," Wellington said. "I'm sorry."

I stood up. "I think I'll call it a night."

I left them on the dock. Inside, I looked back through the clear glass of the sliding deck door, toward the lake. Against the reflection of moonlight off the water, the two men stood talking. It had taken seven decades for this to happen. For a lot of people, that was more than a lifetime. I had the feeling that for Meloux and his son, a new and remarkable kind of life had just begun.

I went up to bed and lay there thinking that sometimes stories did have happy endings.

The problem was that this story wasn't over.

FORTY-EIGHT

I woke to Schanno pounding at my door. The sun was up, already high. A cool breeze lifted the curtains on the window. I figured I'd opened my eyes to a good day.

"We're waiting for you downstairs," Schanno said when I swung the door wide. He was dressed in clean khakis and a white short-sleeved shirt with a button-down collar. He looked very Ivy League and refreshed.

"We? Meloux's up, too?"

"He says he never went back to sleep after you left him alone with Wellington. He spent the night talking with his son, then reading Maria's journals." Schanno's face held a look of warm affection. "He's something, that guy. Wellington's brother is here, by the way."

"Rupert?"

"Does he have another I don't know about? Yeah, Rupert. And Benning's fixing us up some breakfast, so get your ass down there, son. Time's a wasting."

I splashed my face with cold water, ran a toothbrush across my teeth, threw on the clothes I'd worn the night before, and joined the others downstairs. They were gathered in the shade of the umbrella table on the rear deck, drinking coffee that smelled like it came from caffeine heaven.

"Mr. Wellington," I greeted Rupert, who accepted the hand I offered. "This is a surprise."

"Mr. O'Connor," he responded cordially. He wore jeans, a light blue polo shirt, and expensive Gore-Tex hiking boots. He appeared tired, especially around the eyes.

Meloux sat next to his son. I thought he'd look happy, but in the Ojibwe way, his face betrayed no emotion.

"Sit down, Cork." Henry Wellington indicated the empty chair. "Would you like some coffee?" He poured me a cup from the white ceramic pot on the table. "Breakfast should be ready soon."

"You flew up?" I asked Rupert. I used my cup hand to wave toward the floatplane tethered to the dock.

"I did."

Henry Wellington flicked a deerfly from the table. "In his younger days, Rupert was quite a bush pilot."

Rupert shrugged off the compliment. "It didn't compare with being an honest-to-god war hero like Hank, but it had its moments."

"When are you going to let go of that, Rupert? How many times do I have to tell you I don't feel any glory in what I did."

"Right," Rupert said. He gave his brother a little smile, tight-lipped and unpleasant.

"Let's not get into any of that sibling stuff in front of guests, all right?"

"Sibling?" Rupert's tone was one of mock surprise. "We have different mothers. And according to your mother's journals, we have different fathers as well."

"Come on, Rupert, we're brothers. We were raised that way."

Rupert shot him an obviously angry look. "You knew, what, forty years ago that my father wasn't your father? When exactly did you plan on telling me? A deathbed confession?"

Wellington took a deep breath. "I didn't see any reason to tell you. What difference would it have made?"

"You always made decisions without talking to me."

"I'm ten years older than you. Sometimes decisions had to be made, and you simply didn't know enough to be able to contribute."

"Do you think I know enough now?"

"I would never have turned the reins of Northern Mining over to you if I didn't think so."

"Northern Mining," Rupert snarled. "Do you ever read the correspondence I send? Do you even care?"

"I'm finished with that part of my life."

"Right. You live the pure life of the ascetic now. How utterly noble. So tell me, since you've stepped back from any responsibility for the company, do I get to make the decision about what to do with the information Mr. Meloux has offered us about Dad?"

"I think what we do is obvious, don't you?"

"Enlighten me."

"I think, at the very least, there's a lot of restitution to be made."

"Restitution?" Rupert seemed genuinely surprised. "To whom?"

"For starters, the families of the two men who died up there at the ruins of the old cabin. And we need to check the documentation on mineral rights to be certain Leonard didn't actually jump a claim."

"Ancient crimes, Hank. It's like giving the descendants of African slaves restitution for what was done to their ancestors. It solves nothing. It absolves no one. But, hell, it's easy for you to propose, I suppose, considering that Leonard Wellington wasn't *your* father. Think of me for just a moment, Hank. For once, think of someone besides yourself."

"You're proposing what? That we ignore the truth and go on as if nothing ever happened?"

"Hank, how do you know that what he's said is true? You told me not half an hour ago that there's nothing in your mother's journals that corroborates what he accuses Dad of doing."

"I didn't tell you everything, Rupert. Yesterday, he showed me irrefutable, fourteen-carat proof. Look, I understand that this is going to be hard, especially for you, but we don't have a choice. I mean, these men here, they all know the truth. Even if I agreed with you, what would you propose to do about them?"

Rupert swung his eyes slyly across Schanno and me. "It's my firm belief, gentlemen, that everyone has a price. Am I correct?"

It was Schanno who broke the embarrassed silence that followed. "You may know business, Mr. Wellington, but you're no judge of men."

Rupert settled his gaze on me. "He speaks for you?"

"He took the words right out of my mouth," I said.

"Very well." He offered that unpleasant smile again. "I think you're about to find I'm not such a terrible judge of men after all, Mr. Schanno." He lifted his hand and gave a little wave toward the house.

Benning stepped out, and he wasn't alone. Dougherty was with him. They didn't bring us breakfast. They carried a couple of high-caliber automatics.

"Dougherty?" Wellington said.

"He flew up with me," Rupert said. "I dropped him off on the other side of the point before I taxied here. He hiked in."

Wellington addressed Benning and Dougherty. "What's the idea with the weapons?"

"You'll have to ask the other Mr. Wellington," Benning replied.

"I'm asking you."

"As their employer?" Rupert laughed. "I told you everyone has a price, Hank. I bought these men from you a long time ago. Morrissey, too. In fact, they haven't really worked for you since almost the beginning."

Wellington again addressed the two men from Manitou Island. "Is that true?"

Benning shrugged. "He says shoot, we shoot. Nothing personal."

Wellington faced his brother. "And are you going to say 'Shoot'?"

Rupert drummed his fingers on the table, as if considering. "Maybe not. We'll see."

I was trying to figure out a move, some way of distracting Benning and Dougherty. Without obviously turning my head, I checked the field of fire from the deck. If one of us was able to make it to the ground and run for cover, could he reach the woods without being cut down by the automatics?

Rupert laughed.

"What's so funny?" Wellington asked.

"You thought all those years that you were protecting me from the truth. Hell, Hank, I learned the same time you did that we had different fathers. You told me you didn't read your mother's journals until after my father died. Well, your mother wasn't the only one who kept a journal. My father started his as a way of recording his prospecting expeditions, but he ended up including just about everything in his life. After he died, I found them in his personal safe. All these years, I've actually known more than you because not only did I know he wasn't your father, I also knew about what happened at that cabin in the hills. Those journals your mother wrote? My father read them, or at least one of them. When Carlos Lima was in the hospital dying, Maria left the journal out and open. Leonard took a look, read about the Negro, and went back north where he did what he had to do to get what he wanted."

I saw a look of relief cross Meloux's face. An important question had finally been answered. From his hospital bed, he'd told me Maria's beauty was a knife. Now he knew the truth.

"And so you sent Morrissey to take care of Meloux," I said to Rupert Wellington.

"You can understand it's not a story I'd like people to know. It's not just that there are legal ramifications that could shake Northern Mining, but the entire legacy of my father would be rather horribly sullied." He drilled his brother with a sudden, angry look. "You never cared for him, Hank. You made that clear. Me, I loved my old man."

Henry Wellington shook his head sadly. "Enough to kill for him?"

"Love and money, Hank. What else is there of importance?"

I thought it was time for a desperation punch here. "Other people know Meloux's story," I said.

He dismissed it with a quick wave. "The ramblings of an old man who had no proof. And who, by the way, won't be around to defend his claims."

"How do you intend to work that?" Schanno asked in a rather disinterested tone.

"You, O'Connor, and the Indian will just disappear. There are so many lakes up here, nobody'll find your vehicle or your bodies. As for Hank, well, everyone knows how bizarre his behavior has become. His suicide, when it's discovered, won't be a great surprise."

"My children know the truth about me, Rupert."

The younger Wellington grinned coyly. "The perception of family is unreliably altered by love."

"The police will look at you very hard," I pointed out.

"At this very moment," Rupert replied, "I'm being seen at the wheel of my sailboat as I glide out of the marina in Thunder Bay for a day on the lake. I took a lesson from you, Hank, and found myself a man who impersonates me quite well. I've used him successfully on several occasions."

"A lot of risk," I said.

He gave a philosophical shrug. " 'A man's reach should exceed his grasp; else what's a heaven for,' right?"

"I thought I knew you, Rupert," Wellington said.

"You've always been too wrapped up in yourself to see anyone else clearly, Hank. All the headlines, all that glory. When I was a kid and you came home from Korea, I wished some MiG had shot you down in flames."

His older brother looked amazed and disturbed. "I didn't realize."

"And then you handed the business over to me. Do you have any idea how often I've heard 'Henry didn't do it that way'? I could live in your shadow, Hank. I've done it all my life. But I won't let you destroy my father."

I'd calculated that I might be able to jump the deck rail and zigzag my way to the trees. If Benning and Dougherty were good with their weapons, they'd nail me before I was halfway there, but I figured if I didn't try something, we were all dead anyway.

Schanno beat me to it. He wrapped his enormous hands around the table and heaved it in the direction of Benning and Dougherty so that the big umbrella blocked their view for an instant. He vaulted the rail and hit the ground running. He cut one way, then another, and the automatics opened up, sewing a jagged stitch across the yard. I saw Schanno falter, and I knew he'd been hit.

Just as I tensed to launch myself at the two men, the pop of a rifle came from the woods beyond Schanno. The glass of the sliding deck door exploded. Benning and Dougherty dove through the empty door frame toward safety, inside the house. Rupert Wellington was right behind them.

The shots kept coming, chunking into the logs, shattering glass inside the house. For a man of ninety-plus years, Henry Meloux moved remarkably fast. He was down the steps and hightailing it for the woods in the opposite direction Schanno had gone. It was a good move because it would divide the attention and the fire of the men with the automatics. Henry Wellington was at his heels. Me, I went after Schanno, who was crawling toward the cover of the pines.

Benning and Dougherty returned fire into the woods. Their bullets clipped branches and sent splintery sprays of bark flying as they raked the area where the shots seemed to have originated. That gave me the chance to grab Schanno, help him to his feet, and both of us reached the cover of the woods, where we flattened ourselves in the underbrush.

"Keep moving, Wally," I said.

He tried but couldn't go far.

"Where are you hit?"

"Leg," he said, clutching his right thigh.

Blood wormed between his fingers, and I took a look. The bullet had gone cleanly through his leg, leaving two holes, entrance and exit. He was bleeding badly, but it wasn't pulsing, so I didn't think an artery had been clipped. I took my shirt off, tore it in half, and made two compresses, one for each hole. I still had on the drab green T-shirt I'd put on underneath that morning.

"Hold those in place," I told him.

I slipped my belt off and wrapped it around his leg so that it covered the compresses. I pulled the belt as tight as I could and looped it in a knot to hold it.

"Don't move," I said.

"Where are you going?"

"To find out who saved our asses."

"We're saved?" Somehow, Schanno managed a smile.

I kept close to the ground and worked my way north, away from the lake. The shots from Benning and Dougherty had become intermittent. The shots from the woods had ceased altogether. I wondered about that. I also wondered about Meloux and Henry Wellington.

In the undergrowth, thirty yards from where Schanno and I had taken cover, I spotted a booted foot sticking out from behind a fallen log. I approached carefully. What I found nearly broke my heart.

Trinky Pollard lay on a bed of brown pine needles, staring up at the canopy of branches high above us. Next to her was a carbine. The rifle butt was splashed with blood. The blood had come from a bullet hole torn through Trinky's fine, slender throat. I knelt and felt for a pulse, but I knew in my heart it was hopeless. A round from the house chunked into the trunk of the nearest pine and I flinched in reflex.

How she had managed to get there, I couldn't begin to guess. Somehow, she'd found a way to cover our backs and had paid an awful price for saving our lives.

Two more rounds popped from the house and snipped off branches far to my right. They were firing wildly. That one of their rounds had found Trinky Pollard was pure blind luck on their part.

I grabbed Trinky's carbine and dug in her pockets, where I found two extra clips. I aimed at the doorway of the deck and pulled off three rounds in rapid succession. I loped to Schanno and handed him the weapon and the clips. He frowned at the blood, still wet on the stock.

"Where'd you get this?" he asked.

"I'll tell you later. I want you to use it to keep them occupied."

"What about you?"

"I'm going to get my rifle from the Bronco. If these guys are bright, they're going to divide up and go hunting pretty soon. We need to even the odds."

"Whatever you say." Schanno propped himself against the trunk of a pine, laid his cheek against the carbine stock, aimed through the underbrush, and fired.

I took off and circled toward the front of the big house. At the edge of the yard, I paused, eyeing the couple hundred feet of open ground that lay between me and my old Bronco. I didn't want to get caught out there, but I didn't have a lot of choices. I finally committed to a mad dash, keeping the Bronco between me and the front porch. I pressed myself against the passenger side. The metal was heating up in the morning sun, and I felt it, warm, through the back of my T-shirt. I reached around to grasp the handle of the rear door.

That's when I heard the front door of the house open. I ducked, but not before I saw Benning and Rupert Wellington step onto the porch. Wellington held a weapon, a scoped rifle. I dropped to the ground and flattened myself on the gravel of the drive. I could see the bottom of the porch steps. I watched the feet of the two men descend and saw them separate. Benning dashed for the woods that hid Schanno. Wellington headed in the direction his brother and Meloux had gone.

After they left, I slipped into my Bronco and pulled my Winchester from its zippered bag. I grabbed a box of cartridges from the toolbox where I'd stored them. Quickly, I fed several rounds into the rifle and put a handful in my pocket. I started for the woods, after Benning. At the back of the house, Dougherty and Schanno were still exchanging fire. Schanno thought he was keeping them busy.

Dougherty knew the score better, knew that Schanno was about to be hit from the flank. I had to get to Benning fast.

I caught a glimpse of him creeping his way toward the lake. The deep layer of pine needles under our feet deadened the sound of our movement. I saw Benning pause and study the ground. I realized he'd found Trinky's body. It confused him, delayed him in his mission, and gave me an opportunity to get myself set. It wasn't a difficult shot, and I didn't hesitate to take it. My rifle cracked; the recoil kicked my shoulder; Benning dropped like a boneless man. I ran to the spot. He'd fallen a few feet from Trinky, where he lay facedown while tendrils of bright red blood crawled into the brown needles. I took his automatic, which turned out to be a 9 millimeter SIG-Sauer with a full clip. I returned to the front of the house. Leaving my rifle at the door, I slipped inside with the SIG. From the back came the pop of Dougherty's automatic. I worked my way through the rooms and peered around a corner at the sliding deck door. Dougherty stood with his back to the wall. A couple of seconds later, he swung through the glassless opening and pulled off a round in Schanno's direction. Before he could turn back, I put myself in a firing stance with the SIG and aimed at his torso.

"Drop your weapon, Dougherty!" I shouted.

His head swiveled. He stood frozen, caught in a moment of indecision. Then he spun, bringing his own weapon around to fire.

He bucked forward before either of us got off a shot and he fell to the floor. A dark red stain bloomed low on the back of his shirt. Schanno, I thought. Dougherty, in the moment he stood wavering, had presented a fine target for the carbine, and Schanno hadn't wasted the opportunity.

Dougherty groaned. I crossed the room and took his weapon. If I'd had time, I would have tried to do something for him, but Rupert Wellington was outside, bent on killing his brother and Meloux.

I stuffed the SIG into my belt and retrieved my rifle from the front porch.

Then I went hunting.

FORTY-NINE

I entered the woods where I'd seen Meloux and Henry Wellington disappear. Their trail was easy to follow, unsettlingly easy. Obviously, they'd been more intent on speed than secrecy. They'd headed west and very quickly joined the trail that led to the ruins of the cabin in the hills. There was a lot of evidence of their recent passage: footprints where the soil was soft, trampled weeds, brush along the edges of the trail with visible broken branches. Meloux and his son were blundering along like elephants.

I found the place where Rupert Wellington had picked up their tracks. His own were just as easy to follow.

They were many minutes ahead of me. Meloux, spry as he was, was still quite old, and I didn't believe he could hold very long to the kind of pace that would be necessary to keep them ahead of Rupert. I wondered why he hadn't just taken to the woods and used all he knew, his vast knowledge of hunting and tracking, to hide himself. Probably it was because he had his son with him and that made a difference in his thinking.

I padded along as quickly and quietly as I could, knowing it would do no good to give myself away and get shot in the bargain.

I'd gone a quarter of a mile when I came to a little creek I remembered from the day before. Beyond it was the meadow where Meloux had paused to take in the mint scent of the wild bergamot. On the far side of the clearing, just slipping into the trees, was a flash of light blue. Rupert Wellington's polo shirt. He wasn't far ahead.

I leaped the creek but waited before entering the meadow. I didn't want to risk becoming a clear target for Wellington, should he look back. From my right came a low, birdlike whistle. There was Meloux, twenty yards away, with his son beside him, both of them eyeing me over a fallen, rotting log. I wove toward them through the underbrush at the edge of the clearing.

"Henry, you were too easy to follow," I whispered. "Rupert knows you came this way."

The old man actually gave me a sly wink. "A trick the Ojibwe learned from the bear. Give the hunter an easy trail, then circle behind." He stood up. "We can go back now. Or" —he looked to his son for the decision—"we can become the hunters."

Wellington turned to me. "What's the situation back at the house?"

"Benning and Dougherty have been taken care of. Wally's hit. He needs medical attention. And, Henry," I said to Meloux, "Trinky Pollard's dead. They killed her."

Meloux's face was stone. His eyes were dark ice. In the quiet at the edge of the clearing, his breath became fast and angry. I couldn't ever remember seeing him upset, but I could see it now.

"If we go after Rupert," Wellington said, "we risk ourselves and your friend Schanno. What's the point? We should go back."

I thought Meloux probably felt differently. Hunting Rupert Wellington, the black heart behind so much recent misery and the son of a heart even blacker, would have been his choice. Meloux was Mide, concerned with the wholeness and balance of being. Hunting an enemy was not alien to his understanding of the forces that kept that balance. But he'd given the decision to his son, and the decision had been made.

He nodded and we all turned back together.

From his house, Wellington called the provincial police station in the town of Flame Lake. Then he turned his attention to Dougherty, who'd lost a lot of blood but was still conscious.

Henry and I went to see about Schanno. He wasn't where I'd left him. We found him sitting propped against a pine tree next to the body of Trinky Pollard. He looked empty, his face pale, his eyes blank.

"You need to lie down, Wally," I told him gently. "You're going into shock. The wound," I said, though I suspected it was more than that.

"I don't get it, Cork." He stared, uncomprehending, at Trinky's body.

"She must have followed us, been watching our backs, Wally."

Later, the police found her green SUV, the one that had tailed us from Thunder Bay, parked in the woods, not far away.

He shook his head slowly. "I was the one who was supposed to watch our backs."

Meloux had seated himself between Trinky Pollard and Benning. He began to sing softly. Singing, I knew, to help guide them onto the Path of Souls.

"Lie down, Wally." I took his shoulders and urged him into a prone position. I lifted his feet and propped them on Benning's body to keep them elevated and keep blood flowing to his brain. I didn't think about the irony of that situation. I did it because it made sense.

Schanno stared up at the sky, which was broken into blue fragments by the green weave of pine boughs above us. "I'm too old for this," he said.

I put a hand on his shoulder. "Is anybody ever young enough?"

From far away came the cry of a siren, a sound as out of place in that quiet morning as all the death that had come before it.

Schanno and Dougherty were airlifted by helicopter to the community medical center in Ignace. Dougherty, devastated by Benning's death, talked to investigators and told them what he knew, plenty to corroborate the story the rest of us had given.

Trinky Pollard's body was taken to Thunder Bay. A stepbrother arranged for her memorial service, which was held a week later. Schanno and I drove up from Minnesota for it. Most of the people at the service were former RCMP colleagues. She didn't have much family. The memorial was brief, and afterward her stepbrother, in accordance with her wishes, went out on a boat he'd chartered and spread her ashes across the water of Lake Superior.

A couple of days after the shootings, Rupert Wellington walked into the police station in Flame Lake and turned himself in. The press had arrived by then, and the papers and television news were full of images of him, dirty and tired and hungry, trying to use his hand-cuffed hands to block his face from the cameras. Later, we would all learn that the sounds of the sirens had alerted him to the danger of returning to his brother's place, and he'd kept to the woods, hoping to figure a way out of the mess he'd gotten himself into. There wasn't any.

Meloux stayed in Canada. He spent ten days with his son and his grandchildren, who came from British Columbia and Toronto to be with him and their father. I had no doubt Meloux's heart was as light and healthy as it had ever been.

Immediately after the shootings, I spent a night in Ignace making sure Schanno was okay in the hospital there. The doctors wanted to keep him a couple of days for observation. The provincial police had given me permission to return to Minnesota, with the understanding that they could call me back if I was needed. The next morning, I took off for home.

At a gas station in Grand Portage, just south of the border, I called Jo. I tried her office first, but Fran, her secretary, told me she wasn't going to be in all day. She wouldn't tell me why, and I didn't like the reservation in her voice. I called home. Jo picked up. I could tell something was wrong.

"It can wait until you get home. You've been through enough the last couple of days," she said.

"Jo, what is it?"

She was quiet, considering whether to put me off or let me in.

"It's Jenny, Cork. She started bleeding last night. I took her to the hospital. She lost the baby."

"Ah, Jesus." I leaned my forehead against the wall above the pay phone. "How is she?"

"A mess."

"I'll be home as soon as I can. No more than three hours."

"Don't push it, Cork. It's over. Just get home safely."

I spent the rest of the drive feeling shitty, railing at God, beating myself for not being there for my daughter when she needed me.

I pulled into the drive in the late afternoon and parked in the shade of our elm. Stevie came running from the backyard with Walleye not far behind. My son was all bounce. Walleye ambled along with a kind of patient obedience. His tongue was hanging out, and I felt sorry for the old boy. Stevie had clearly worn him out. Walleye was probably hoping Meloux was with me, a sign that they could both return to their quiet lives as over-the-hill bachelors.

"Dad!" Stevie cried. "Watch this!" He turned to the dog. "Come on, Walleye. Come on, boy."

Walleye took his time but eventually joined us under the canopy of the elm.

"Okay, boy, sit."

Walleye sat, blinking tolerantly.

"Now roll over, boy."

Stevie used his arms in an exaggerated rollover gesture, but Walleye didn't get off his butt.

"Here, like this."

Stevie eased the dog's front legs forward so that Walleye's whole body settled on the ground. With his small, eager hands, my son urged the dog onto his side, then his back, and finally onto his belly once again.

"We're still practicing that one," Stevie explained.

"Good work," I said. "Your mom inside?"

"Yeah." Stevie's face clouded and his dark young eyes got painfully serious. "She's with Jenny."

"Don't work him too hard." I nodded toward Walleye, who'd lowered his head onto his paws and was relaxing in the grass. "There's a saying about old dogs and new tricks."

"I know that one," Stevie said. "But Walleye is extra smart. Come on, boy. I'll show you how to catch a Frisbee."

Walleye's placid brown eyes gave me a brief, pleading look.

"Come on," Stevie said. He nuzzled the dog's nose against his own.

What could Walleye do? What could any good heart do in the face of such uncompromising affection? The old dog staggered to his feet and lumbered after Stevie.

Jo met me at the door. She kissed me warmly and gave me a long, heartfelt hug. She whispered against my neck, "I'm glad you're back. I've been watching the news reports of what happened up there. It sounds awful."

"I imagine what's happened here hasn't been easy either. Jenny upstairs?"

Jo nodded. "She hasn't been out of her room since we came back from the hospital."

"Does Sean know?"

"I called this morning. He wanted to come over right away, but I told him that wasn't a good idea. She needs some time."

"Okay if I go up and talk to her, you think?"

"She could use you right now."

Jo went to the kitchen to make some coffee. I started up the stairs. My legs felt heavy.

I was thinking about all the things we leave behind us, or lose, or whose value we don't recognize until it's too late. Sean had been a part of something that could have been beautiful for him, if he'd let it be. The chance was gone. No matter how much he loved her, Jenny was beyond him now.

A part of Jenny had been lost. Not just her baby, but also who she'd been. And the truth was that she'd lost it even before the blood began to spill from her womb, taking the tiny life with it.

I was thinking about me as well. Two days before, I'd killed a man, the greatest of sins, but it mattered so little to me compared with the question of what comfort I could be to Jenny. Somewhere along the way I'd left behind whatever it is in a human being that grieves when violence becomes the answer. If Benning stood before me again, I'd shoot him again.

I knocked, opened Jenny's door, and offered my precious daughter the only comfort I had: my arms to hold her as she wept against my chest.

EPILOGUE

On a Sunday morning near the end of August, after we'd all returned home from Mass, we stood outside the house, gathered around Jo's Camry, which was packed with boxes and suitcases containing all the things Jenny was taking with her to Iowa City. She and Jo were driving down together, a mother-daughter road trip. I was staying back to tend the home fires.

Anne and Jenny had already said their good-byes. They'd been up most of the night talking in Jenny's room. Stevie suffered his big sister's parting hug. I kissed my daughter and told her how proud I was of her and that I knew she was going to set the world on fire.

"I'll just be happy if I don't flunk out, Dad." She smiled. Like all her smiles those days, it seemed like a bird struggling to fly.

"There'll always be an apron for you at Sam's Place," I said.

She got in the car quickly and stared straight ahead, waiting for her mother.

"Let me know you've arrived safely, okay?" I told Jo.

"You know I will."

We waved good-bye as the Camry shot off down Gooseberry Lane, taking Jenny to a different life, one that we would know about in letters and emails and in the stories she would tell at Thanksgiving or Christmas. We would know only what she wanted us to know of the life that was all her own now. And even for that we would be grateful.

Anne and Stevie stood looking at the empty street.

"Wish Walleye was still here," Stevie said sadly.

"Let's take a drive, too," I said.

Ten minutes later, we pulled up to Schanno's house. He was standing in the front yard with Trixie yanking on a long leash and investigating every bush that the length of her tether would allow. There was a FOR SALE sign stuck in the ground near the street.

Stevie had been quiet on the drive over, but when he saw the dog, he brightened and ran toward it. Trixie jumped all over him. Annie joined them while I spoke with Schanno.

"You're sure about this, Wally?"

"I'm sure. Hell, an old man shouldn't have a young dog. Besides, every time I call her name I think of Trinky." He walked to a little redwood bench in his yard. He had to use a cane. He looked old beyond his years. I'd thought—hoped—that in asking him to back me up in Canada, I was offering a way for his spirit to rebound from the loss of his wife. Instead, something in him had died, died out there with Trinky Pollard, died for good, I was afraid. He sat down and stared ahead. "Realtor says the house'll move fast. My daughter's looking for something for me near her in Maryland. Condo, town house, something like that."

"Mind's made up, huh?"

"I'm tired, Cork. I'm just so damn tired." He nodded toward the kids. "Have you told 'em?"

"Not yet."

"Don't you think it's time?"

"Hey, guys," I called. "I've got a surprise. Trixie's coming home with us."

"We're taking care of her for Mr. Schanno?" Stevie said eagerly.

"We're taking care of her for good. She's ours now."

"Really? I love her, Dad. I love you, Trixie." Stevie put his face to hers, and she licked him like a lollipop.

The biggest word in the human vocabulary has only four letters and no definition that's ever been adequate. We love our dogs. We love our children. We love God and chocolate cake. We fall in love and fall out of love. We die for love and we kill for love. We can't spend it. We can't eat it when we're starving or drink it when we're dying of thirst. It's no good against the bitter cold of winter, and even a cheap electric fan will do more for you on a hot summer day. But ask most human beings what they value above all else in this life and, five'll get you ten, it's love.

We're a screwy species, I thought, as I watched my son and daughter roll in the grass with the puppy slobbering all over them.

"Dad," they squealed happily, "help us!"

And I did my best.

ATRIA BOOKS

PROUDLY PRESENTS

TAMARACK COUNTY

WILLIAM KENT KRUEGER

Coming soon in hardcover from Atria Books

Turn the page for a preview of
Tamarack County. . . .

CHAPTER 1

Like many men and women who've worn a badge for a good part of their lives, Corcoran Liam O'Connor was cursed. Twice cursed, in reality. Cursed with memory and cursed with imagination.

In his early years, Cork had worked for the Chicago PD, the South Side. Then he'd spent a couple of decades in the khaki uniform of the Tamarack County Sheriff's Department, first as a deputy and finally as sheriff. He'd seen the aftermath of head-on collisions, of carelessness or drunkenness around farm or lumbering equipment, of bar fights with broken bottles and long-bladed knives, of suicide and murder in every manner. And so the first curse: he remembered much, and much of his memory was colored in blood.

The second curse came mostly from the first. Whenever he heard about a violent incident, he inevitably imagined the details.

And so, when he finally understood the truth of what happened to Evelyn Carter, he couldn't keep himself from envisioning how her final moments must have gone. This is what, in his mind's eye, he saw:

It was seven o'clock in the evening, ten days before Christmas. The streets of Aurora, Minnesota, were little valleys between walls of plowed snow. It was snowing again, lightly at that moment, a soft covering that promised to give a clean face to everything. The shops were lit with holiday lights and Christmas trees and Santa figures and angels. There were people on the sidewalks, carrying bags and bundles, gifts for under the trees. They knew one another, most of them, and their greetings were sincere good wishes for the season.

Evelyn Carter was among them. She was small, not quite seventy. All her life she'd been a good-looking woman and had taken good care of herself, so she was attractive still. She wore an expensive coat trimmed with fox fur, purchased when she'd visited her daughter in New York City in October. On her head was a warm gray bucket hat made of rabbit's fur. In her left hand, she gripped a shopping bag filled with little gifts, stocking stuffers. A cell phone was cradled in the gloved palm of her right hand, and she stood on the sidewalk, looking at a photo of her grandson dressed as a shepherd for the church pageant this coming Sunday. When the door of Lilah Buell's Sweet Shoppe opened at her back, the smell of cinnamon and cider ghosted around her, and she smiled in the wash of the good spirits that seemed to her a beacon of hope in an otherwise dark winter season.

Her big black Buick was parked on Oak Street, and by the time she reached it and set her shopping bag in the passenger seat, she was tired. Evelyn had a good but troubled heart. She carried nitroglycerin pills in a tiny bottle in her purse. She was feeling some uncomfortable pressure in her chest, and when she'd finally seated herself behind the wheel, she sat for a moment, letting a nitro pill dissolve under her tongue. She hadn't yet started the engine, and as she sat, the windows gradually fogged from her slow, heavy breathing.

She didn't see the figure approaching her door.

She was thinking, maybe, about her grandson in Albuquerque, or her daughter in New York City, saddened that all her family had fled Tamarack County and moved so far away. She knew the reason. He was at home, probably staring at the clock, complaining aloud to the empty room that she'd been gone too long and had spent too much. And if it was, in fact, her husband she was thinking of, she probably wasn't smiling and perhaps her chest hurt a little more. The windows were heavy with condensation, and maybe she felt suddenly isolated and alone, parked a block from the bustle of Center Street and the welcoming lights of the shops. So she finally reached out and turned on the engine. She was undoubtedly startled when the shadow loomed against the window glass near the left side of her face. And that damaged thumper of hers probably started hammering a little harder.

Then she heard the familiar voice. "Hey, Evelyn, you okay in there?"

She pressed the button, and the window glided down.

"Hello, Father Ted."

It was the priest from St. Agnes, Father Ted Green, bending toward the window and blowing foggy puffs from where he stood on the curb.

"I saw you get in and then nothing," he explained with a smile that conveyed both reassurance and concern. "I was afraid maybe you were having some difficulty."

He was young and wore a black leather jacket, which looked good on him. To Evelyn Carter, there'd always been something a little James Dean about him (she was fond of saying so over coffee with her friends), and although that unsettled her a bit during Mass, she didn't find it at all unpleasant.

"Just tired, Father," she replied.

His gaze slid to the shopping bag in the passenger seat. "Busy afternoon, looks like. I hope you're planning on going straight home and getting a little rest."

"A little rest would be good," she agreed.

"All right, then. See you Sunday. And please give my best to the Judge." He straightened and stood erect, smiling a kind of benediction, and he watched as she pulled carefully into the street and drove slowly away. Later, when he reported this conversation, he would say how wan she looked, and that he continued to worry.

She headed past the high school and the gravel pit and took County 6 into the low, wooded hills west of town. The snow was coming down more heavily then, and maybe she was concerned that if it began to fall in earnest, the way it had so often that December, she'd be trapped, alone with her husband until the plows cleared the rural roads. If this was what she was thinking, there was a good chance she was frowning.

Two miles out of Aurora, she approached what everyone in Tamarack County called the Orly cutoff. It was washboard dirt and gravel, but it was the quickest way to get to the tiny crossroads known as Orly, if you were in a hurry. Evelyn Carter and her husband, Ralph, whom everyone except Evelyn called the Judge, lived on the cutoff, whose official name was 127th Street. Through a thick stand of birch and aspen long ago blown bare of leaves, Evelyn could see the lights of her home, which had been built a good hundred yards back from the road at the end of a narrow tongue of asphalt. Their nearest neighbor was a full quarter of a mile farther north, and to Evelyn, the lights of her home looked cold and isolated and uninviting. When the Judge finally passed away, she was planning to sell the house and move to New York City, to live where she had family and where there were people all around her instead of trees and emptiness.

As she approached her driveway, she slowed. It was a difficult angle, and the Buick was enormous and felt awkward in its maneuvering. She always took the turn with great care. When the Judge was with her, he usually complained that she drove like an old woman.

Once she'd negotiated the turn, she stopped abruptly. Someone was kneeling in the middle of the drive. In the headlights, the snow was like a gauzy curtain, and what lay behind it was vague and uncertain. She couldn't quite make out who it was on his knees on the snow-packed asphalt, head bowed as if in prayer. But then she recognized the red wool cap she'd knitted for her husband the Christmas before, and although she couldn't make sense of the whole scene, she relaxed and rolled down her window and called out, "What are you doing there, Ralph?"

The figure didn't move or speak.

"For heaven's sake, are you all right?" Evelyn was suddenly afraid. Not for her own safety, but for the well-being of her husband. The truth was that, as his faculties had declined and his reliance on her had increased, she'd often imagined his passing, imagined it as if it were the pardon of a long prison sentence. But faced with the actuality of some crisis, her natural response was concern. She unsnapped her seat belt, opened the door, and slid from the car, leaving the engine running as she hurried toward the kneeling figure.

Too late, she saw, in the glare of the headlights, the flash of the knife arcing upward to meet her. The blade, large and sharp and made for gutting deer, sliced easily through her fox-fur-trimmed coat and lodged deep in her belly, where the ice-cold steel quickly warmed. And although she was probably too stunned to speak, maybe with a final bewilderment in a life that she'd never really understood anyway, she looked into the face she knew well and asked herself the unanswerable question: *Why?*

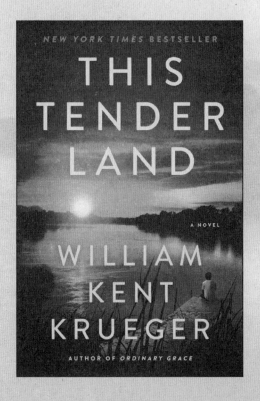